BEYOND GOSPEL PASS

Beyond Gospel Pass

JESSICA MEREDITH

HAY
PRESS

First published 2005 by Hay Press Ltd
Gwynfe House, Cross Keys,
Herefordshire HR1 3NP

Copyright © Peter Burden

All rights reserved. No part of this publication may be Reproduced, stored in or introduced into a retrieval system, or transmitted, in any form, or by any means (electronic, mechanical, photocopying, recording or otherwise) without the prior written permission of the publisher. Any person who does any unauthorized act in relation to this publication may be liable to criminal prosecution and civil claims for damages.

A CIP catalogue record for this book is available from the British Library.

ISBN 0-9550050-0-0

Typeset by Stephanie Slade, Hereford

Printed and bound in Great Britain by
Antony Rowe Ltd., Chippenham, Wiltshire

This book is sold subject to the condition that it shall not by way of trade or otherwise, be lent, re-sold, hired out, or otherwise circulated without the publisher's prior consent in any form of binding or cover other than that in which it is published and without a similar condition including This condition being imposed on the subsequent purchaser.

Thanks to everyone who has helped in the writing of this novel......

Damian Russell, Malcolm Williams, Lucy Philips, Catherine Mansel Lewis, Al Cotterell, Sara Maitland, Anne Harbour and Sophie Sutherland.

One

MAY

Mark glanced over his shoulder at a languorous tabby cat, draped across the back seat of the car like a large fur croissant. He broke a short silence as he turned back to his driving.

'I hope Grimond enjoys a few days in the hills.'

'He will.' Elizabeth Powell smiled and stretched an arm behind her to stroke the animal. 'He loves to tease those Welsh farm cats. Don't you, boy?' Although she'd been living in London for fifteen years, her voice still had strong traces of a childhood spent in New England.

She sat beside Mark, looking out at London's ragged fringe beyond the crash barriers of the fly-over as their silver-green Saab sailed westwards, high over unremarkable suburbs. She gazed with sleepy hazel eyes at the cars below, crawling along crowded avenues, pouring into the car-park of a giant Do-it-Yourself warehouse.

Mark saw it too, and laughed. 'My God, Beth, look at that lot! Behold, the Cathedral Superstore of St Joseph, patron saint of wood-butchery, lagging and screwing!'

Beth half raised an eyebrow with a faint smile and groaned softly. For ten years she had been married to Mark, loyally acknowledging his laboured puns until the reaction had become almost automatic. Although he didn't seem to notice, she knew that as long as she loved him, she'd carry on groaning.

Besides, she didn't really mind; Mark was in the word business – a publisher, for whom chronic wordplay was an occupational affliction, like a traumatised elbow he wrapped in a neoprene tube every time he used a keyboard.

She looked at his profile, deceptively strong in his dogged search for a gap where he could use the car's discreet power. She sighed, because he still liked to find gaps and because he looked as good at thirty-eight as he had when she'd first caught a glimpse of him through the shelves of the library at University College in London.

Or maybe, she thought, his physical deterioration had simply been slower than hers. It wasn't fair, she thought. Her lips, as smooth on the surface as they had ever been, tightened in a sharp wince, and she knew without looking that they made a row of tiny but visible vertical wrinkles around her mouth, until it turned up in a smile of reproach at her own vanity.

She was conscious that she ought to have been able to rationalise her fear of ageing, but as usual, her thoughts skirted around the core of the problem before she would admit it. After seven years of trying, and, more recently, trying almost anything, she still hadn't been able to conceive a child. And the failure was beginning to hurt, a lot.

It was more than guilt that she felt; it was the denial of an overwhelming, sensual urge to procreate; a craving as primeval as a tribal maiden's. Although she had friends who liked to argue that it was absurd and irrelevant at the start of the twenty-first century, she found it impossible to ignore.

As Beth's mind set off down this familiar path, Mark found his gap when two lanes became three. He booted the throttle, jerking his wife from her melancholy as the car surged past the string of taxis that had been blocking their escape.

They left Brentford for the sham rurality of Osterley Park. Mark gave a triumphant shout. 'Free at last! Thank God! And onwards to the Land of Llewellyn and glorious Glyndower!'

Beth laughed. 'You don't have to start being Welsh just for me. You're not doing a bit on the local radio - and there's not a voter in sight!'

'But I *feel* it!' Mark snatched a quick sideways glance, seeking her approval. 'Every time we get out there I feel my Welshness; I empathise with the people.'

'But you never talked about being Welsh before you'd heard of the East Brecknock constituency.'

'Because I wasn't really conscious of it before,' Mark justified. 'Of course, I always knew there was Welsh blood in me with a name like mine. But we never traced back far enough to know when our ap Hywel ancestors fled the Pays de Galles for England's lusher pastures.'

Beyond Gospel Pass

'It must have been quite a few centuries back. Your Celtic genes seem pretty diluted to me.'

'Even so, I know I belong up there among those mountains.'

Beth smiled and shook her head. She turned once more to check the condition of Grimond, whose sleek body now heaved in untroubled sleep. She settled back in her seat and looked out of the window but found no inspiration from the ugly grey blocks of flats that lined the motorway near Slough. She switched on *Radio Four* and let the chattering voices wash over her. It seemed as if no time had passed before the car was flying across the khaki waters and mud banks of the Severn, between the twin towers of the northern bridge.

Mark turned to his wife and smiled confidently as he inserted a new Arvo Påart CD into the player, which perfectly reproduced the wistful, eerie notes of the Estonian plainchant.

Beth lifted her brow a few millimetres. She would have preferred Jeff Buckley. Instead of saying so, she offered to take over the driving when they left the motorway at Newport.

A short burst up the Usk valley carried them past the flat-topped Sugarloaf and beyond, where the southern fingers of the Black Mountains reached down from the high ridge that stretched twelve miles to the north – an old sandstone spine which for centuries had marked the boundary between the meagre-soiled, wind-blown uplands of the Celts and the lush, warm meadows of the Saxons.

Beth turned the car off to the left, into a lane that snaked up the Llanthony Valley, towards the elegant skeleton of an ancient priory.

'Look!' Mark said, animated, with one eye closed, his right hand stretched in front of him, index finger erect. 'Alfred Watkins was right! There's a dead straight line through the Priory tower, along the track, up to the cairn above Capel-y-ffin!'

Beth glanced at him, indulgently. 'Is this another of your ley lines?'

'Not mine. It was the first one that Albert Watkins identified. Extraordinary really – he was a corn merchant and inventor from Hereford in the nineteen hundreds, though I don't suppose he had any idea what he was starting.' Mark gave a short laugh. 'There's still a hell of a lot of mileage in earth mysteries.'

Jessica Meredith

Archimedes Press, Mark's small publishing company, was about to launch a book called *The Leys of the Land,* produced recently – with a little too much haste – by one of his more opportunistic authors. Beth was unconvinced by the concept of ley lines and the array of other woolly theories they had spawned, but she was open-minded, and had an American admiration for Mark's capacity to enthuse over any new book he was publishing or, for that matter, over any other new project he'd taken on – like his recent foray into national politics.

Beth thought of the eight people, the East Brecknock constituency Liberal Party selection committee, who would be gathering the next evening, a few miles to the north in Hay-on-Wye where, below the brown-green shoulder of its distinctive Bluff, the river town nestled between small round hills.

The committee would be meeting to discuss their choice of candidate for parliamentary election a year away, and in choosing, would decide her husband's future.

Her husband's future; not hers.

She took her left hand off the wheel and reached across to squeeze his thigh. 'I really hope it goes OK tomorrow.'
The Saab was creeping along behind a small blue and rusty Fordson tractor, where the lane had narrowed and sunk between banks overhung with alder, sycamore and hornbeam. Despite its low-key image in London, the car gleamed incongruously beside the lush growth and run-down buildings of the valley.

'God, it's so great to be here in summer at last,' Beth said, easily putting aside her earlier gloom, and accelerating as the tractor turned in at a field gate.

'I rather liked it in winter,' Mark answered. 'I thought you did too.'

'I did, but everywhere's better in the sun.'

Mark laughed. 'I never thought I'd hear you admit it.'

As he spoke and she made a face at his gentle jibe, a sheep barged through a straggling hedge and ambled up the road in front of them. Daglocks dangled from its dirty rear and chunks of ragged fleece trailed off its back. After a few yards, it stopped and turned to stare warily at them.

'Oh, get on!' Mark grumbled.

Beyond Gospel Pass

'Chill out,' Beth said lightly, but braking hard. 'Try and wind yourself down to rural speed.'

Mark grinned. 'You could hardly call me uptight, but it's no wonder there's been nil development round here in the last three thousand years.'

'But, Mark – that's its charm, isn't it?'

'Yes. Of course it is, but the causes aren't very laudable. The charm's a sort of benign by-product of the congenital doziness of the locals. Who is that, anyway?'

A tall, well-made man – in his late twenties, Beth guessed – had pushed his way through a gap in the hedge. A sheepdog – black with a white muzzle and bib – followed as he scrambled down the bank fifteen feet ahead of them.

His legs were in faded jeans that clung to narrow hips. The leather jerkin and black cotton singlet he wore revealed hard, tanned muscles and his dark chestnut hair fell in unruly waves to his shoulders. He saw the Saab, and Beth driving it, and stopped. He stood with his legs slightly apart, leaning on a long crook. With his mouth poised in what could have been a scornful sneer or a secret smile, his dark-peat eyes held her gaze.

For the brief seconds the contact was there, she suddenly found herself feeling inexplicably queasy. Her hands were trembling on the steering wheel; she looked down at them and took a long, quiet breath, which Mark wouldn't hear; she wondered what the hell was happening.

She forced herself to lift her eyes again, but the shepherd wasn't looking at her now. He nodded with faint indifference at Mark before he turned and, with the dog's help, drove the wayward ewe up the bank, following her through the hedge.

'Hmm,' Beth murmured, nodding her bob of russet-brown hair, trying to sound normal. 'That must be Michael Rhys's brother – Owen, I think he's called, the one we've not met.' Her voice raced on. 'Isn't this the Rhyses' land here?'

'I dare say,' Mark said with a cynical grunt.

Beth gave him a puzzled glance 'Have the Rhyses done something to upset you? They own the land, sure, but you haven't made any Liberal pledge to nationalise it.'

'Okay,' Mark said, trying to give an easy grin. 'But you've got to admit, they're bloody mercenary; it's rather disillusioning. Look how unhelpful Michael was about bringing the electricity in.'

Beth lifted one side of her mouth and looked at him. 'He wasn't so unhelpful; in fact he seemed pretty happy to let you do it. He just wanted three hundred pounds.' She laughed, to help him laugh at himself. 'C'mon – you'd be pissed off if someone tried to put a bloody great pole in the middle of your precious field.'

She was relieved when Mark grinned again and nodded. 'Yes, I suppose I would.'

Beth put the car in gear and drove on. 'But I wonder if that was Owen?' she mused.

'Is that the man who was supposed to have found water for Ruth by dowsing with a pendulum?'

'I don't know about the dowsing,' Beth shrugged sceptically. 'But I think it must have been.'

'He didn't look much like a mystical New Ager to me.'

'No, but you know what Ruth's like, always ready to dig deep. Maybe we ought to get him to find a new well for us.'

'Maybe,' Mark chuckled. 'But all that dangling chains and things - it's all just magic and fairy stuff - utterly unscientific.'

'A lot of things are...' Beth said, '...like ley lines,' she added with a grin.

After another two hundred yards, they reached the entrance to a short drive up to a neat, stone house – unusually tidy in this remote valley.

Mark climbed out and opened the new wooden five-bar gate he'd hung the month before. Beth nosed the car into a three-sided courtyard in front of the house and turned off the engine.

For a few moments, she was content to sit in the car and gaze at the ancient landscape, listening to a thrush proclaiming his territory in the still air. She watched with affection as Mark walked up through the yard. He sat down on the edge of a well-scrubbed stone drinking trough fed by a spring gushing straight from a crack in the rocky hillside. He cupped his hands and drank a mouthful from it. It was always the first thing he wanted to do when he arrived.

'Do you know,' he said quietly, in his reasonable voice, which she'd always liked. 'I don't think I'll ever get used to this total lack of noise pollution.'

Beyond Gospel Pass

'Marco, sweetie – you'd go barking mad after a few weeks,' Beth said cheerfully as she stepped from the car. 'But okay, I agree; it sounds pretty good right now.' She opened the rear door and lifted the cat from the seat. 'Come on, Grimond, time for a bit of exercise.' She fondly stroked the animal's soft head before putting it down on the ground where it extended its front legs in a feline stretch. 'Off you go, boy!' she urged as the cat shook itself before stalking haughtily across the yard.

The Powells' new country home, Pant-y-Groes, had been a Welsh longhouse, half dwelling, half barn, with more cattle sheds and other buildings projecting from the corners. Now the drinking troughs were filled with flowers and in the yard, the builders had found cobbles beneath a mat of manure at least a hundred years old. To the right of the house, a large patch of gently sloping ground had been seeded with fine fescue in early March and was beginning to look like a lawn of implausibly green whiskers, around which Mark was keen to plant exotic shrubs.

The farm had been built at the foot of a steep hillside, facing west across a deep-banked brook, to the far side of the valley. As Beth helped Mark to unload the car, the sun still poured over the ridge, splashing onto the slate roof of the house and the fields above. Beth was looking around slowly, in simple gratitude for the untainted view when she saw Ruth Calloway further up the hill.

Ruth was feeling the underbelly of a pregnant llama, but she'd spotted them too. She stopped what she was doing to wave.

Beth could almost see the winsome smile on Ruth's face, and waved back.

She walked across the cobbles and stretched. Despite being folded and wrapped in a car for three hours, she felt fresh in the loose, white cotton dress and flat shoes she was wearing.

Mark stood up. At six feet, he was a few inches taller than her. He was dressed in beige cords and a dark green cotton drill shirt. His soft, light brown hair eddied in a gentle breeze, which rippled up the valley. He grinned at Beth with shining eyes. 'God, it's good to be back at Pant-y-Hose!'

'I wish you wouldn't call it that,' Beth said, putting an arm around his waist and pinching it.

'Sorr-ee,' he said, and made a remorseful face. He looked up at the empty blue sky between the high ridges and took a long, noisy breath. 'Selection time,' he announced confidently. 'I must ring round the committee – find out what's happening; get a line on the current mood. D'you know, I really feel I belong already, and I know I can do so much for these people.'

'Mark, listen,' Beth said quickly – to protect him from his own optimism. 'You're not the only guy on offer. It's not in the bag – not by a long way, and even when you've been selected to stand, you've still got to win the bloody election.'

She saw at once a screen drop over his eyes.

'Beth, I'm going to win it; you know that. Just let me do it my way.'

'You mean, let you talk yourself into believing it? Think positive? All that American-style sales pitch?'

'But Beth, angel, unfortunately politics is mostly about selling – like almost every other aspect of human existence.'

Mark walked back to the car and opened the boot. Beth saw him glance up the hill at Ruth as he cautiously heaved a case of his favourite burgundy up to the broad-panelled blue front door of the house. He put down the wine and hunted for the key in his trouser pockets.

When he had unlocked the door, he swung it open like a small boy entering his secret den in the woods. He went in and dumped the wine on a scrub-top table in the middle of the room. Beth followed with a box of food – half finished cheeses, organic fennel and celeriac, a loaf of Italian bread and bags of fresh pasta from a shop in Upper Street, which they passed on the way from Hackney out of London. She put it beside the wine and flexed her shoulders while she sniffed the familiar, pleasing mustiness beneath the newer scents of pot pourri and polished pine in the low-beamed kitchen.

Grimond came in behind them and scampered straight upstairs, Beth assumed, to harass any careless mice that had failed to take cover.

'Oh, I forgot to tell you,' she said. 'I called Ruth before we left London and asked her down for dinner.'

Mark turned to her, surprised but pleased. 'Great, but what are we going to give her to eat?'

Beyond Gospel Pass

'I bought a mountain of fresh tagliorini and some home-made pesto from Luigi's.'

'Why did you ask her?'

Beth shrugged a shoulder. 'Just trying to be neighbourly, I suppose. Anyway, I thought you fancied her, just a little,' she added with a grin.

'Only in an academic way,' Mark huffed as he transferred the wine bottles to a rack of rough terracotta cylinders in a bay beside the range.

Beth emptied the contents of her box onto the table. 'I'd guess Ruth was really beautiful once, before the vegan pallor took over; and she's let herself get much too scrawny.'

'She's just very fit,' Mark defended. 'You'd be scrawny if you were running up and down a mountain, chasing llamas all day. Anyway, she's not a vegan - she drinks sheep's milk; it's just that she doesn't like eating red meat.'

'That's fine — just so long as she doesn't try to eat yours....'

Mark gave a quick laugh. 'I won't encourage her. Now,' he said, putting on a practical manner, 'I've got things to do.'

Beth watched him stride from the room to get on with some nonessential but presumably therapeutic act of property maintenance. Mark always liked to be doing something; it was this, Beth thought, that made people who didn't know him well comment on his energy and capacity for work; they didn't understand his frustrating brand of laziness. Mark was energetic, she acknowledged, and would work avidly all day, but only at the tasks he enjoyed. Any chore, duty or essential function of his business or domestic life that bored him, he either ignored altogether or simply put off until it had run out of currency.

Beth pushed aside the thought with a pang of guilt, conscious that as she grew older, it had become easier to see the flaws in the people close to her than to see their strengths.

An hour later the sunlight in the valley had withdrawn to the upper slopes of the eastern ridge of the mountain, high above Pant-y-Groes.

The tranquillity of the evening slowly stole over Beth until she had slipped into the gentler pace of the ancient landscape. She was satisfied that her kitchen was in order and, with Grimond back outside hunting and Mark absorbed by some project in the old barn, she sat at the table, enjoying the orderly composition of a shopping list. She happily consigned to her subconscious her current professional preoccupation over a claim for political asylum, and her shoulders felt as if they'd been physically relieved of the yoke of her work.

She looked up from her list to find a recipe for rabbit terrine from a Roux Brothers book which Mark had given her ten years before and which she'd never used. She was flipping over the pages when, through the small panes of the window, she saw two shyly smiling children walk into the courtyard, each carrying a small wicker basket.

Her heart gave a reflexive lurch before she could pull herself up with a rebuke at her own weakness.

She got to her feet and hurried to open the door. 'Hello, Dai!' she called. 'Hello, Abby. It's wonderful to see you! Have you got our eggs?'

They were the children of Michael Rhys, whose family had farmed at the head of the valley for generations. Dai, nine and competent, nodded. 'Yeh, we got 'em. Abby's marans laid 'em.'

'We got the milk, too,' his seven-year-old sister squawked, like a Welsh Donald Duck.

Beth saw a dozen big, speckled eggs and two screw-top bottles in the baskets. She smiled at the children and tousled their hair. 'Thanks a lot. Would you like a drink and a piece of cake?'

The children nodded briskly.

Beth beckoned them into the house and sat them at the table. She poured them each a glass of lemonade, and put two slices of carrot cake on a plate in front of them.

'Got any sweets?' Dai asked hopefully.

She shook her head. 'Sorry.'

She should have come prepared; she knew from her limited dealings with her senior colleague's boys – very close in age to these children – that an appreciation of what food they liked was fundamental to any relationship with them.

Seeing their disappointment, she tried to shift the despondency, which contact with children always seemed to cause her. 'So, how *are* you? I haven't seen you for ages,' she said, rather as if they were neighbours in London. Before they could answer, she tried again. 'Have you been at school today?'

'No,' Dai said. 'We went up the tump to fetch the ewes back down with Uncle Owen, for shearin'.'

'Shouldn't you have been in school?' Beth asked.

'Mum don't mind,' Dai said. 'Not if there's work to do.'

'Is Owen your father's brother?'

Abby and Dai nodded.

'I think I saw him this afternoon with some sheep, down the lane,' Beth went on. 'Quite tall, with a sort of leathery waistcoat?'

'Yeh, that's him. The sheep got out while we was comin' down the 'ill.'

'Has he got children too?'

'No; he's not married.'

The door from the inner part of the house swung open and Mark came in wearing dirty jeans and a Notting Hill Carnival T-shirt. 'Hello, kids,' he said heartily. 'Brought the eggs then? Great!'

'That *was* Michael's brother we saw in the lane, by the way — their Uncle Owen,' Beth said.

'Uncle Owen, eh? What's he like, then?' Mark asked.

Dai looked surprised by the enquiry. 'Owen? He's okay,' he said, non-committal. 'He's clever, mind. Mam says he's got the old powers.'

Mark smiled, as if the boy were suggesting he should believe in magic. 'What "powers" are those, then?'

'Don't you know?' Dai asked as if the world knew about his uncle's gifts. 'He can find water, and metal, and things wrong with people.'

Mark was about to laugh when Beth asked with genuine interest, 'You mean, he's a kind of a healer?'

'That's what they say. He sorted out Lord Brecon's back,' the boy added proudly.

'Lord Brecon's back, eh?' Mark repeated with an indulgent smile. Lord Brecon, once Martin Evans-Finch, had been Tory MP for the neighbouring constituency until the last election, when he'd been easily lured away with a peerage to make room for a thrusting, thirty-something investment banker.

'That's fascinating,' Beth declared. 'I'd love to talk to him about it some time.'

'He don't talk about it much,' Dai muttered, discouragingly. 'They came from the telly once, from Cardiff, to talk to him, but he wouldn't come down.'

'That says something for him, I suppose.' Mark nodded in grudging approval of this reticence to submit to the seductiveness of television fame. Beth refilled the glasses of lemonade. 'Well, I think we should ask him to come and see us. Ruth told us how he found her well, and we think we need one here - the spring's already almost dry; we were warned it would totally dry up by midsummer's day.'

'Okay - and he could have a look at my elbow while he's at it,' Mark said.

Neither child responded.

'Can you ask him to come and see us about a well?' Beth pressed.

'Okay,' Dai said uncertainly, and looked at Abby. 'We gotta go.'

They both drained their glasses, and left the carrot cake untouched. Beth walked around the table to let them out. She lingered a moment on the door-step as they walked away across the yard and out of the gate without looking back.

'I wonder,' she said slowly as she closed the door and turned back into the room, 'if all kids are so enigmatic.'

'Beth, of course they're not,' Mark said gently. 'These people live in comparative isolation, don't forget. They've intermarried for generations; looking at some of them I wouldn't be surprised if there was still a bit of Neolithic blood lurking in this valley. There are a few pockets further up the valleys and beyond Plynlimmon, you know,' he added.

'What? Stone Age folk?'

'Well, they didn't just disappear off the face of the earth when the Celts arrived.'

'So those Celtic genes you're so proud of may not be enough to open every door up here. Perhaps these Rhyses are Stone Age men, and you'll never get along with them!' Beth chuckled.

'Perhaps they are. Anyway,' Mark said with a change of tone. 'I've nearly finished hanging the pictures in the study. I think I'll take a walk and flush the foul London air from my lungs.'

He let himself out of the kitchen into the yard. Beth watched him as he climbed the new post and rail fence into their small paddock and set off with a determined stride towards the head of the valley.

Beth knew his head would be churning with extravagant ideas and plans to stem the torrent of problems drowning his business.

Beyond Gospel Pass

Then, with a mental flick of the wrist, he would bounce his thoughts away to embrace a new future – a future where Mark Powell, popular, reasonable yet radical, had become the cherished Liberal Democrat Member of Parliament for East Brecknock.

She watched him go with a protectiveness that was almost maternal, until his head and shoulders sank below the surface of the bracken sea, and, trying to subdue her concern for him, she returned to her tasks in the kitchen.

In the country, where her legal work didn't dominate as it did in London, Beth liked to lose herself in domestic activity, preparing meals and cleaning. But soon after Mark had left, she was interrupted by the phone trilling on the dresser.

'Hello?'

'Oh, hello, Beth. It's Trish here.' Trish was Mark's secretary. 'I was wondering if I could talk to Mark?'

'He's out, communing with nature. Can I take a message?'

'Well, I'm not sure...'

'Is it important?'

'Yes; it's rather bad news, actually.'

'You'd better tell me, then, and I'll try to break it to him gently.'

Beth could almost hear the woman trying to weigh up the consequences of either talking or not talking to her boss's wife. Trish, it seemed, was quickly swayed by the prospect of not having to give him the bad news herself. 'Marcel Gehring's agent rang just as I was going home. She said he's accepted a bid from another publisher for *The Time Pirates*.'

Beth couldn't suppress an anxious shudder on Mark's behalf. Marcel Gehring was one of two small jewels in the lacklustre crown of Archimedes Press. 'I see.' She tried to speak calmly. 'How nice of his agent to ring as soon as we've got to the country.'

'Yes,' Trish agreed. 'I expect it'll rather spoil your weekend.'

'I expect it will, ' Beth said. 'Anyway, it'll probably be easier if I tell him about it. But I expect he'll ring you when I have.'

'I'm afraid I'm just about to drive to Sussex. I'm having a day off tomorrow.'

'Don't worry about it then. Have a good weekend.'

'Thanks, Mrs Powell.'

Jessica Meredith

Beth put the phone down, thinking about the way the English tended to revert to formality as a kind if protective device. Even after ten years, she still couldn't completely relate to 'Mrs Powell'. In her work, she'd always been Ms Elizabeth Langthorne.

As if to compound the gloom after Trish's call, the cat swaggered in from the fields to present her with an offering – a mutilated shrew. 'Ugh, Grimond,' she sighed. 'I suppose I'm meant to be grateful you're such a good hunter.' She picked up the gruesome trophy from where he had deposited it on the floor, wrapped it in a page of the *Evening Standard* and dropped it in the bin.

In the flattering light of three candles in terracotta pots, Beth looked at Mark across the scrubbed pine boards of their kitchen table. His profile, square-jawed like the hero in a boy's picture book, puckered in sympathy as he talked earnestly to Ruth, who was sitting beside him. She was wearing a skimpy T-shirt in faded purple and a skirt sewn from a length of hand-dyed maroon Indian seersucker. A faded shawl she had been wearing now covered the back of her chair.

The pasta bowls from which they'd eaten had been stacked on the wooden draining board and replaced by plates of Cambrian goat's cheese and a basket of Italian bread. Up until now, conversation over dinner had been easy – a little local gossip, which encouraged the feeling that Beth and Mark were already a part of their wild valley; some broad, congenial agreement on local politics, and harmless dissent over the Turner Prize. Mark was slightly drunk, but in a mood – always easier to handle – where his desire to be liked outweighed his need to be right.

Beth hadn't told him about Marcel Gehring. She felt guilty about putting it off, but she didn't want to see the pain and panic in Mark's face; or the blustering excuses and sleight of logic that would somehow turn the disaster into a benefit.

Convincing herself it would be more constructive to tell him in the morning, she poured herself another glass of wine. Mark picked up the bottle and refilled Ruth's glass.

Ruth took it in a slender hand, hampered by a bulky plaster around one finger. The glass fell from her awkward grasp and shattered on the stone floor, splashing red wine on her skirt and Mark's cords. Ruth looked at him with dismay. 'I'm so sorry, Mark. Was it valuable?'

Beyond Gospel Pass

'Of course not,' Mark laughed generously as he leaned down to pick up the fragments of glass. 'It couldn't matter less; and fortunately, the wine blends in rather well on that skirt of yours. What happened to your finger, by the way?'

Ruth heaved her narrow shoulders in a rueful shrug. 'I caught it in the rotovator and now it's gone septic. It's a bit of a nuisance just at the moment.'

Mark nodded with eager sympathy. 'I can imagine; poor you.'

There was a moment's silence. Ruth smiled at him. The smell of her patchouli oil hung in the atmosphere, discernible among the strong aromas of garlic and basil. Her big dark eyes, set in a pale fine-boned face, made her look a little as if she'd been using stage make-up. She turned to Beth, anxious to include her in the conversation.

'It's so kind of you both to let me use your field. I'm afraid I put the tup in terribly late and I've still got two more ewes to lamb, and the llamas did brilliantly there. I've had to put Pedro up in the top paddock. I don't want him pestering the girls, now they're all pregnant.'

'I'm so glad to hear all your ewes and llamas are expecting...' Beth took a mouthful of wine, '... unlike us.' She had meant to say it lightly, but the alcohol had blunted her usually precise command of inflection; she was embarrassed by the edge of bitterness that had crept into her words.

Grimond, who had been purring on her lap, roused himself and jumped onto the floor.

Mark looked sharply at his wife with a worried frown.

Ruth's eyes were shining compassionately beneath her kohl and purple lids. 'Oh, no! Aren't you having any luck then?'

Beth hesitated a moment before abandoning her reticence. 'Luck? My God, if I became pregnant, it wouldn't have anything to do with luck. If you knew what we'd been through!'

Mark laid a hand on her arm. 'Beth, love; I shouldn't think Ruth wants to hear about our fertility problems...'

'...All the samples we've produced and sent for tests,' Beth persisted. 'My pee, Mark's sperm. We've discussed everything – intrauterine insemination, IVF, intracytoplasmic sperm injection, even traditional Chinese herbal tea. You wouldn't believe the hours we've spent with thoughtful, gentle gynaes telling us our "personal chemistry" just isn't right and there's nothing wrong with us, apparently, except our lives are far too stressful.'

Mark winced and gave Ruth an apologetic glance. 'Come on, Beth, angel...'

'No, Mark,' Ruth extended her unbandaged hand towards him with dramatic calmness. 'It's fascinating. I'd love to have a baby too, but I couldn't bear all those hospitals and chemicals. And anyway, I've never met anyone who could remotely share my life with my work and my llamas.'

'He wouldn't have to share your life to get you pregnant, if that was all you wanted.' Mark was more drunk than Beth had thought. 'You could put an ad in the *Hereford Times* for a surrogate father. I'm sure there'd be a few takers.'

'Actually, Mark, I was being serious,' Ruth said with a quick tightening of her small mouth. 'Besides, I have thought of asking someone simply to father a child for me – without any of the responsibility of bringing it up, but I wouldn't like the idea of anyone using my body just for a quick orgasm.' Ruth turned her sympathetic eyes on Beth. 'But why hasn't it worked for you two? I suppose you were on the pill for years?'

'It's not my fault, Ruth, if that's what you mean. None of the clinics have come up with any reason why I shouldn't get pregnant.'

'Beth, angel, it isn't me either,' Mark said.

Beth reached out and touched his hand. 'Yes, sweetie, I know.' She turned to Ruth. 'There's actually nothing wrong with either of us. Apparently we just don't happen to click – the luck of the genetic draw, so to speak. They say *in vitro* might work, but neither of us can stand the thought of such a mechanical way of doing it – it wouldn't really seem like conception at all...'

'Anyway, Mark,' Ruth said, still smarting at his suggestion, 'if you think it's such a good idea, why not let Beth put an ad in the *Hereford Times*?'

'I'm not stopping her,' Mark laughed. 'But she'd probably only get a few randy young farmers applying.'

'Hmm,' Beth smirked. 'What's wrong with a randy young farmer?' She glanced at him. 'But being real for a moment, a surrogate father might be an idea, don't you think, Mark?'

Beyond Gospel Pass

Mark looked at her, to see if she meant it. He tried to deflect the idea, by pretending he didn't mind. 'Why not – if your gynaecologist wasn't kidding and you're really functioning properly.'

'I suppose it would depend on the man,' Beth said, and almost let out a gasp as a completely unbidden image of Owen Rhys suddenly appeared in her head.

'It would obviously have to be someone with a Mensa IQ,' Mark said, anxious to keep the idea a joke, 'otherwise people would know the baby wasn't mine.'

'And he'd have to be reasonably good-looking for me to go through with it.'

'Gosh,' Ruth said. 'Can you two really be so dispassionate about it?'

'I'm not sure, if it came to it,' Beth conceded. 'After all, Mark, it may not be a question of just once.' She saw a sudden alarm in his eyes and laughed. 'Don't worry; I'm not really being serious; just talking through one of the options. Obviously we'll have to go down all the medical routes.'

'Oh, Beth,' Ruth said, disappointed. 'I thought you meant it!'

Mark sighed, and topped up his glass. 'I must admit to being conventional enough not to particularly relish ...'

He was interrupted by a hammering on the door. He got to his feet, but before he'd taken a step, the door was flung open and the small boy who'd brought the eggs a few hours earlier burst into the room.

'Ruth,' Dai blurted breathlessly. 'You better come. Dad says one of your ewes is lambing and she's not happy. He couldn't stop though.'

'Oh God!' Ruth groaned. 'I bet it's Claerwen; I knew she'd have problems; she's so small.' She pushed back her chair noisily on the uneven flags and stood up. As she hurried towards the door, the chenille shawl she had draped across her shoulders swept another wine glass to the floor.

They all ignored it this time. Mark got up to follow Ruth, but hesitated when he realised he knew nothing about this sort of crisis. Ruth turned to him with big, pleading eyes. 'Mark, come on! You'll have to help me. I can't put my hands inside her with this nasty infection on my finger – it's just too dangerous! Have you got a torch?'

He stopped and clutched the back of his chair. 'Christ, Ruth!' he spluttered. 'I don't know anything about lambing!'

'You don't have to. I just need your hands.'

'Couldn't you use rubber gloves?' Mark pleaded.

'Surgical ones – if you've got some?'

Beth got up from her chair. 'No, of course we haven't.' She walked across the kitchen to grab a torch from a hook by the door. Mark looked at Ruth, who stood rigid, waiting for his co-operation. He reached across the table, topped up his glass and drained it in one long swallow. 'Okay,' he muttered.

Ruth turned and walked quickly into the crisp night air behind Dai; Beth followed, lighting their way.

Ruth turned to her. 'Let me have the lamp,' she said. 'I know where I'm going.'

Mark climbed over the style into the paddock after them.

From the darkness of the field, a ewe was bleating repeatedly. Ruth cast a shaft of light along the hedge on the far side until she spotted the sheep crouched below it. She ran across to it, revealing as she'd predicted, a small grey ewe bloated with lamb, still standing but obviously in severe discomfort.

Dai, Beth and Mark ran behind her. When they reached her, Ruth was already on her knees behind the animal. She dropped the torch on the ground where most of its beam was absorbed by the long spring grass. Beth picked it up and shone it on the scene. Ruth lifted the sheep's tail and gazed in distress at its dilated vagina. 'Mark, come on! I'm sure the lamb's breached; there's no sign of it. Poor Claerwen! She must be in agony! You'll have to roll up your sleeve... and be very gentle.'

Beth turned to Mark, who was swaying and panting a little from their run across the field. He made no move to get down and join Ruth behind the straining ewe.

'For God's sake, Mark, Ruth needs help!'

'B...but I don't know what the hell do to.'

'I'll tell you,' Ruth gasped and squatted back to make way for him. 'Now put your hand in.'

Mark stared at her. 'I can't do that.'

'It'll be fine! It's her womb, for heaven's sake! It just feels soft and silky and it's very clean.'

'Please, Mark!' Beth begged.

Beyond Gospel Pass

He staggered forward and dropped to his knees beside Ruth. Hesitantly, looking nauseous, he unbuttoned his shirt sleeve and rolled it up. Warily he inserted his hand in the sheep, up to his wrist, where it stopped.

'You'll have to reach right inside her,' Ruth said urgently. 'Find the lamb's head and shoulders and try to pull them round. It's got to come out with its front feet first!'

Mark clenched his jaw and forced his hand, then his forearm, further into the small ewe's interior, until the sleeve of his crisp, dark green shirt was rucked up to his shoulder. He started trying to do what Ruth had asked, but his face showed that his repugnance was beating him. The ewe shifted in her severe discomfort, and twisted Mark's arm. He grunted with pain and sweat broke out across his contorted red face. 'I can't do this,' he panted, and stopped grappling with the unborn lamb.

'Thank God!' Ruth said from the darkness behind him.

Beth turned and was strangely surprised to see Owen Rhys looming out of the night into the small illuminated circle around the sheep.

Owen said nothing. He stepped forward and knelt down beside Mark, who hurriedly extracted his arm from the sheep with a grateful sigh and staggered backwards as he stood up.

Beth's gaze returned to Owen.

Without any preamble, he inserted his hand, then his forearm and blindly manoeuvred the small new sheep until a tiny, pale cloven hoof appeared, and then another, which he gently tugged until a head and body followed, then the hind legs, and the lamb was free, still shrouded in its ruptured birth sac.

Behind Owen, Mark laughed nervously. 'Congratulations, Ruth. What are you gong to call it?'

Owen took a quick look over his right shoulder, unimpressed, and turned back to the lamb, already tottering up onto its slender, quivering legs. Whatever thoughts occurred to him at that moment, he gave no hint of them and cast a last approving nod at the lamb before striding off into the night with young Dai hurrying behind him.

Two

Beth put the phone down, glad that she'd made the effort to ring Father Aidan. The priest had sounded pleased that she'd asked him to dinner. She wondered how often he was invited out, and how much of an impact it made on the strict routine of his monastic life.

She was standing in the kitchen, gazing at an untidy arrangement of yellow and purple wild flowers she'd picked earlier as she tried to make sense of the numbing depression brought on by the small drama on the hillside the night before; not the drama itself, so much as the comparative performances of the players, and she wished she'd been able to say something to make Mark feel better about it.

It was a relief to hear a car drive into the courtyard; she looked up and watched Ruth park her Land Rover. She went out to meet her.

'How's the new lamb?'

'He's fine, thanks. Eating his head off.'

'That's good,' Beth said, pleased for her friend. 'Can I get you a cup of something?'

'Yes please.'

Beth led Ruth back through the blue door and walked across the kitchen to slide a heavy iron kettle onto a hot plate on the spotless range.

'So,' Ruth asked, 'how's Mark?'

'Feeling a little sheepish.'

They both laughed. 'Beth, that's not kind. Poor man, and he was quite drunk.'

'He was pissed as a rat; if he hadn't been, he wouldn't have got his hand an inch inside that poor sheep. But I have to say, your friend Owen was quite masterly.'

'And gentle,' Ruth added.

Beyond Gospel Pass

Neither woman spoke for a moment. Beth reached up to a shelf beside the range for a Clarice Cliff teapot that she thought Ruth would appreciate.

'Do you know him well?' she asked, spooning some fine China tea into the pot.

Ruth sat down on a smoke-blackened elm chair. 'I shouldn't think anyone knows Owen well. He's very sort of... self-contained.'

'But do you see much of him?'

Ruth's pale lips briefly shaped themselves into a private smile. 'I've seen all of him.'

Beth was surprised that she should feel shocked, until she realised with a ridiculous, racing pulse that she was as jealous as a schoolgirl in first bud.

She grasped the handle of the kettle and slid it off the hob. 'You've... slept with him?'

Ruth smiled with a shrug that Beth wished she could interpret.

'Aren't there any other options around here?' Beth asked, overfilling the small art deco pot. 'What about all the book freaks who flock into Hay? Or all those over-sexed authors lurking in decrepit cottages round here?'

'Well, there are a few of those,' Ruth admitted. 'But they're not into commitment of any sort.'

'And is the enigmatic Owen – your gentle, caring shepherd?'

Ruth looked at Beth with wide, mocha brown eyes, puzzled by her sarcasm. She shook her head. 'Oh, no. Not Owen.'

'Just another rural chauvinist, you mean?' Beth suggested, wanting it not to be true.

'I wouldn't say that,' Ruth murmured. 'There's certainly a thoughtful side to him, which isn't something you find much around these hill farms; it's hard enough just keeping alive up here. Abstract ideas aren't a luxury they can afford.'

'But he can?'

Ruth shrugged her shoulders. 'He does what he has to do; and he knows what he's doing. I guess he's supremely competent - not because he would have chosen to be a farmer, but because his people always have been. And he's one of those people who'd be competent whatever they were doing.'

'Unless, maybe, it involved a little imagination; a little creativity.'

'Beth, what's got into you this morning?' Ruth's voice rose peevishly. 'There are lots of other things he could do - if he wanted.'

'Like what?' Beth asked.

'Oh, I don't know,' Ruth said with a flick of the wrist, 'but definitely something creative.'

'Hah,' Beth retorted. 'The poetic shepherd... It's a bit of a cliché.'

'How can you know he's not creative? You've hardly even met him.' Ruth's thin, earnest voice had become more nasal in her defence of Owen. 'Just because he's not some trendy metrotype doesn't mean he doesn't have a line on eternal truths.'

'Oh, shit!' Beth gasped with a sudden pang of guilt, putting her hand over Ruth's long, skinny fingers. 'I don't know what I'm saying. It's just Henry talking.'

'Henry?' Ruth asked, not knowing the man to blame for Beth's sudden aggressiveness, but relieved and ready to believe that the moment was over.

'You know; Henry – the curse? Sad old schoolgirl talk – sorry.' Beth was by now full of remorse for attacking a man she'd never spoken to and for hurting a woman she was inclined to like very much. After all, she thought, despite some of her flaky ideas, Ruth was a very kind and thoughtful person.

Ruth was smiling her humourful, compassionate smile. 'Beth, you should have said.'

Beth winced away the sympathy. 'Doesn't matter; and it's not just that. I've been worried about Mark, too.'

'Where is he?'

'Doing one of his favourite country chores – buying stuff from the whole-food shop in Hay.'

'It's a lovely place,' Ruth nodded. 'The smell of paprika and pimento... It's a bit expensive for me, though. But why are you worried about him?'

'I know I sound like a mother grumbling about a student son, but I just wish he'd get a grip on reality. I think he looks on this whole business of being adopted by the local Lib Dems as if he were auditioning for a role in the Uni drama society, and naturally, being him, he hasn't got any doubts that he'll get the part; he always used to – with justification as it happened; he was a bloody good actor.'

'Yeh, I can imagine,' Ruth nodded, sipping her tea.

Beth looked at her; and saw her naked with Owen.

Angry with herself, she tried to block out the image. She felt as if she was heaving a boulder into the crack of a bursting dam. She stood up, and turned away from Ruth to clatter some clean plates by the sink while she tried to deal with her thoughts.

It took only a few seconds for her to decide to tell the truth. 'Bloody hell!' she said. 'Do you ever suffer from irrational sexual fantasies?'

'Yes,' Ruth chuckled unexpectedly. 'As often as possible. They're so much less hassle than the real thing.'

'No need for a shower after, either,' Beth laughed.

'What fantasy have you been having, then?'

Abruptly, Beth didn't want to tell, but she was committed. 'It sounds silly,' she tried to belittle the massive, insane emotion which raged out of control inside her, 'but I dreamt that I met Owen, up on the hills. I don't know what I was doing; just walking, I suppose, but there he was, out of the blue, shooing a few ewes around. We didn't speak; we just looked at each other, and next moment we were...' Beth's shoulders dropped and she sat in the nearest chair.

Ruth was leaning forward, her eyes bright with the bawdy secret. 'You were making love?'

'I wouldn't call it that,' Beth said evenly. 'We were just fucking.'

Ruth sat back, involuntarily shocked by Beth's bluntness. 'What was it like?' she almost whispered.

'For God's sake, Ruth, you know.... don't you?' Beth asked, and could see at once that she didn't. 'You said you'd seen him... naked, and you'd slept with him?'

Ruth shook her head slowly. 'I said I'd seen him; I didn't say I'd slept with him.'

'But how did you see him naked if you weren't.... doing anything with him?' Beth was embarrassed by the peevish note in her own voice.

Ruth didn't seem to notice it. She was looking at Beth's arrangement of wild flowers with an embarrassed grin. 'It was a couple of years ago - a really hot day in May. I was up at the head of the valley, near where the brook rises in a big pool by a rock called the Wergin stone. I was coming down the hill; I heard a man singing; I didn't want whoever it was to stop, I was so thrilled to actually hear anyone singing like that up there, and I crept up as quiet as I could, keeping behind the rock, and when I looked round it, I saw a pile of clothes; I recognised that jerkin of Owen's.' She tittered. 'So I stopped and just poked my head a bit further round until I could see him, swimming in the pool. I suppose he was sluicing himself down after a hot day. But the longer he was in and I watched him, the more difficult it was going to be for me to show myself, and I just couldn't tear my eyes away. At first I could only see his top half, but then he heaved himself out and stood naked on the edge of the pool and shook himself like a dog.' She stopped and looked at Beth. 'He's got a body as beautiful as anything you've ever seen, in Florence or anywhere.'

Beth shut her eyes. 'What... what was he singing?'

'What?' Ruth stared at her. 'I can't remember. Why on earth do you want to know?'

'I'm just more interested in that than... than his personal dimensions.'

'I think it was some old Beatles song - or was it? I don't know. Anyway, I didn't sit around gawping at him, I disappeared as soon as he was out.'

'Do you suppose he does it often.'

'Beth! You want to go and see for yourself, don't you - to see if he measures up to your dream.'

Beth forced herself to smile. 'I don't think that's possible. I doubt there's a man in the world who could live up to a woman's fantasies about him.'

'Still,' Ruth said, 'at least you've got Mark. He's good-looking, gentle too, I should think, and I bet he's quite a romantic.'

'Yah,' Beth said with a loyal grin. 'He's romantic. I just hope he's not expecting too much romance in politics.'

Ruth stood up with a sudden decisiveness that had surprised Beth before. 'Look, I've got to go down to Hay now. Why don't you come with me? We can have a good talk, then you can meet up with Mark and come back with him.'

'You know,' Beth said, 'that's a very good idea.' On that sultry morning the valley seemed suddenly too quiet to distract her.

Beyond Gospel Pass

Beth watched Ruth's face as she drove, and thought that she treated her ancient Land Rover with the same consideration she might have shown an elderly pack animal. She made encouraging noises and chatted to it while she drove, though she barely interrupted the rapid flow of her conversation with Beth.

Beth was fascinated by an anomaly in Ruth's character that, in spite of her declared love of solitude, she seemed to treat conversation as a rare and precious commodity, and it was plain that she didn't want to lose a morsel of it while it was on offer.

'You know the Lit Fest starts at the end of next week? One of the stars is coming to stay with me.'

'One of the stars?' Beth wondered how Ruth categorised literary stars.

'Yes. Laura Chichester - she's walking up the Offa's Dyke Path from Chepstow, arriving in time to give a talk about her book on Ecuador.'

'Gosh!' Beth was impressed. She'd never taken any serious notice of Laura Chichester's brand of gushing, self-assertive but cosy post-feminism, although she acknowledged that she had successfully carved herself a niche in the iconography of English media women. She seemed, on the face of it, a strange companion for Ruth, unless Ruth was fundamentally shallower than she'd always believed; or Laura Chichester had greater depths than were apparent on television. 'How do you know her?'

'It sounds really bourgeois, I know, but I was at school with her; we were pretty good friends, and we always stayed in touch. I spent a bit of time with her when she was in Ecuador two years ago.'

'Was that the trip she based this new book on?'

Ruth turned to Beth with a lopsided smile. 'Up to a point.' She paused for a moment before being disloyal. 'To tell you the truth, I think she makes a lot of it up - at least, she pinches it, then sort of makes it fit.'

Beth was surprised to feel a little shocked and disappointed. 'Good Lord! I never really liked that treacly style of hers, but I always gave her credit for writing about real experiences, even if they were rather bizarre.'

'Of course, she does go on a hell of a lot of trips, but when you think about it, it would be amazing if *all* those things had happened to her. I mean, it would mean her feet never touched the ground, but she really is walking up the Offa's Dyke path the fifty or so miles from Chepstow to here.'

'With her luck, she'll walk straight into your friend Owen stripping off up in the hills.'

'She certainly would, if I told her about it,' Ruth tittered.

'Well, don't,' Beth said firmly.

'Actually, I was going to ask you and Mark if you could come up for supper that night?'

'I'd guess Mark would love that. He's anxious to practise being a public figure.'

'Why do you make fun of him, Beth? He's so clever - and I'm sure he must be a good husband.'

Beth looked at Ruth's face, screwed up in concentration as she navigated the narrow sunken lane.

'*Good*?' Beth sighed. 'That's one of the most ambiguous words in the lexicon. When I was an innocent little girl at St Agnes' Catholic school in Boston, it seemed utterly obvious to me what "goodness" was. Then I began to realise that what I'd thought was goodness in other people was often just well-presented charm, or enlightened self-interest, or a simple yearning for the approval of others. But yes, of course Mark's good in some of its senses.'

Ruth didn't pursue that line. 'But wouldn't you like to come too? I thought you'd get on with her rather well. I mean, you're both "can do" sort of women.'

' "Can pretend" in her case, apparently,' Beth observed. 'But yes, I'd love to meet her.'

Beth and Ruth left the Land Rover in the car-park below Hay castle and walked down by the softly worn stone pillars of the Buttermarket to the whole-food shop which for a lot of people represented the essence of a town in which for years no supermarket had been allowed to open its doors.

They found Mark in the depths of a shop more spicily aromatic than the traditional English grocer it partially mimicked. He looked faintly anachronistic himself, dressed in a jacket of dull tweed, loose cords and brogues as he stood gazing closely at the label on a packet of pulses.

'Hi Mark,' Ruth greeted him with a light touch on his forearm.

Beyond Gospel Pass

'Hello.' He smiled self-consciously. 'I'm sorry I was so useless last night.' He made another face at the accidental innuendo, glancing around for reactions from any of the half-dozen people cluttered in the shop. He saw Beth coming in behind Ruth. 'I'm going to have to be more careful what I say once I start showing my political face round here.'

'Yes, you will,' Beth agreed, as he kissed her on one cheek.

'But don't worry about last night,' Ruth shrugged her narrow shoulders sympathetically. 'It takes a bit of getting used to.' She turned to Beth with a warm smile. 'Let's hope it's not the last birth he's present at for too long.'

'Thanks, Ruth,' Beth said, ashamed to find herself also glancing around, not wanting anyone else to hear.

If they had, they weren't showing it and by now Mark was creating a distraction, questioning the nutritional qualities of the mud-coloured Mexican beans he'd found. He wasn't listening to what the girl behind the counter was telling him, but he bought the beans anyway, and some home-made pesto, a tub of olives and some Welsh goats' cheese.

Beth bought bread and ham, and in a loose trio, they wandered from the shop onto a narrow pavement where country people from the local hills and bibliophiles from everywhere thronged and spilled over into the path of muddy Japanese four-by fours, well-used Citroens, Volvo Estates and old bicycles with no gears, but plenty of character.

Mark suggested they go for coffee, or a glass of something in a small bar squashed into a V between two of the narrow streets. But as they passed the next bookshop, they were sucked through the door with the inevitability and reverence, Beth thought, of Catholics genuflecting in church.

She made a stand. 'No, I don't want to look at old books,' she said loudly, stopping in the doorway behind the others. Mark glanced back at her with a frown, then grinned.

'Well, of course, now we live here,' he offered as explanation to the handful of earnest browsers who had glanced up with Bateman-like surprise.

'Actually, I could do with coffee,' Ruth backed up Beth.

Mark held the door for her and smiled around at anyone who was looking and they walked to the wine bar.

Jessica Meredith

In the semi-basement gloom, two tables were already taken. One held a group of half a dozen men and women who looked to Beth like archetypal book hunters. The other table was occupied by two men and three women - thirtyish, fashionably dishevelled and attractive. They gave Ruth a friendly smile. One of the women, the best-looking, smiled at Mark.

Beth saw he was pleased, and thought - Why shouldn't he be?

Mark returned a faintly knowing smile as he steered his party to a table on the other side of the room, ostensibly just out of earshot. He even held a chair for Ruth and tucked it under her bottom as if they were at a grand dinner party.

'What would you like? I was going to get a bottle of Chilean Chardonnay.' His voice echoed around the room and a female face turned briefly in his direction.

'Fine,' said Ruth.

Beth nodded. 'Suits me.'

Mark walked over to banter with the barman while Beth spoke quietly to Ruth. 'Who are that lot over there?' She leaned her head towards the interesting looking group.

'The man with his back to the wall runs the Festival.'

Beth inspected the man with more interest. 'He doesn't look very English. What's his name?'

'Paul Ricardo. I'm not sure where he comes from. I don't really know him very well.'

Mark came back with a bottle in an ice bucket, sat down and filled three wine glasses. Like Beth, he nodded towards the group opposite. 'Who are those people?'

'Ruth was just saying the dark, good-looking guy is Paul Ricardo.'

'The man who runs the Lit Fest?'

'Yes,' said Ruth. 'And the blonde girl - the very blonde one - is his lover.'

The girl who had smiled at Mark.

Mark, reluctant to show too much interest, turned back to Beth. 'You haven't told me why you've come in to Hay.'

Beth lifted a shoulder. 'Ruth was coming here. She's got to go on somewhere but I thought I could come back with you.'

'Well, now you're here, we may as well stay and have lunch. Did you forget that I've got my meeting with the selection committee at four? It seems pretty pointless for me to flog back to Panty-hose, then turn round and come straight back.'

Beth didn't bother to pick up on 'Panty-hose' like she usually did. In fact, she found she didn't at all mind the idea of spending the next five hours in Hay; she was beginning to recognise places and people she liked; she was enjoying getting to know the town, as she might have a cousin, perhaps, often heard about but never previously met, with whom she was finding more in common than she'd imagined.

'Okay, fine,' she said, 'and I can keep an eye on what you drink before this meeting. Do you suppose the Chapel influence is still strong enough here to affect attitudes to that sort of thing?' she asked Ruth.

'No,' Ruth shook her head. 'I think they've all rather given up chapel since the telly arrived and the pubs started opening on Sundays.'

'Come on, Ruth.' Mark admonished. 'Don't be so cynical; it's not like you.'

There was a note of defensiveness for his soon-to-be constituents in Mark's voice. Abruptly, it occurred to Beth that Owen Rhys would be one of his constituents; Mark's selection suddenly seemed more important.

It had been important to her before; but, up until now, Hay, the mountains and the valley had merely been places of intermittent escape from the powerhouse of London and the intensity of her work. Now, without warning, the priority was not so much to escape from London as to be here.

She saw that she'd drunk all her wine, although she was barely conscious of having taken a sip.

'Mmm,' she grinned appreciatively, waving her empty glass. 'Crushed elder flower, a hint of almond and an aftertaste of wild sorrel.'

'Does that mean you want some more?' Mark laughed, and refilled her glass. 'I'm glad you're not in front of the committee today.'

'What do you mean - "today"? Why should I ever be?'

'I did warn you,' Mark frowned. 'They'll want to see you, too – I mean the candidate's wife is an important part of the package.'

'Oh God.' Beth wrinkled her nose in a rare display of nervousness that she had learned normally to keep well hidden. 'An important part of his baggage, you mean? You never told me they'd want to inspect me too.'

'Well, I thought that was obvious; anyway, I'm sorry, but they do - and not just as some kind of decorative chattel; I'm not applying for the Tories.'

Beth sighed; she didn't want to let Mark down. 'When are they going to want to see me, and in what circumstances?'

'I don't know,' Mark confessed. 'I'll find out.'

'What are they like – your Liberal selectors?' Ruth asked.

Mark opened his mouth to answer, but closed it again abruptly. He was looking towards the door with a cautious smile.

Beth followed his eyes. In the doorway, blocking out the daylight, was a woman in her late fifties, tall, large-framed but not obese, with the healthy remnants of young beauty enhanced by the skilful colouring of her wavy blonde hair.

'Boo!' Mark greeted her as he got to his feet. 'How are you? Come and have a drink.'

Beth guessed how the woman would sound before she'd opened her mouth.

'Hello, Mark,' she said in a husky, old-fashioned voice that was accustomed to shouting at dogs. 'Thanks, I could do with one.'

Trailing two bulging plastic bags from the whole-food shop, she steered herself across the cluttered bar. She nodded a greeting at the barman and the proprietor, who had just come down, as well as taking in the group at the Lit Fest table.

'This is my wife, Beth,' Mark was saying. 'This is Boo Llewellyn; you've probably heard me being hugely complimentary about her husband, Henry - chairman of the local party.'

Boo nodded. 'Excellent bullshit. I must tell him.' She turned and gave Beth an approving smile. 'Hello. Henry's looking forward to meeting you, too.'

Beth couldn't help returning the smile. 'Mark's only just told me I'm up for a grilling.'

'Smart American lawyer like you could run rings around that gang of humourless hicks,' she said loudly. The people at the Lit Fest table heard, and laughed.

'I'm sure they're not that naive,' Mark said. 'I heard someone on the radio the other day saying, "If you want a fool in the country, you'd better bring one with you".'

Beyond Gospel Pass

'That's about as true as saying everyone has a book in them, or fifteen minutes of fame in their lives,' Boo Llewellyn chortled as she settled into the chair Mark had drawn up for her. 'In my experience, ninety-nine percent of people achieve neither. If you want a fool in the country, just throw a stick in the air on market day and you won't miss.'

'But surely... ' Beth started.

'Yes, yes of course there are a lot of very canny old countrymen; some of them surprisingly intelligent, but you have to bear in mind the rhythm of rural life doesn't adjust easily to change, so people don't know how to deal with new ideas.'

'Do you live here all the time?' Beth asked.

'Yes, most of it. I'm a local girl too, so it's always been home. Funny thing is, I longed to get away when I was an innocent virgin. I went to London yearning for the fulfilment of my womanhood, and met Henry; I hadn't seen him since I was five at some children's tea party up at The Neuadd. A year later, I was back here, marrying him and moving into the place.'

'I wonder if it was shared genes that inevitably attracted you to each other,' Ruth said.

'I doubt it. Henry's Welsh and I'm as Anglo as they come. But what about you two?' she said looking at Mark and Beth together. 'Where did you meet?'

'Very boring,' Mark said. 'In the library at UCL.'

'Thanks to the vagaries of Dewey classification,' Beth said. 'I was looking for a book on Jung in the psychology section, and on the other side of the rack, Mark was looking for something on cricket in the sports section. We ended up gazing at each other through a gap in the shelves.'

'But that sounds very romantic - Jung and Wisden,' Boo laughed. 'What did you do when you realised the vast discrepancy in your reading habits?'

'I went for his body,' Beth grinned.

'And I lusted after her mind.'

'That sounds so ideal, I don't think I believe it.'

'Sort of yin/yang,' Ruth offered.

They all looked at her. 'Sort of,' Mark nodded.

'That reminds me, Ruth,' Boo said. 'I meant to ask you about your lecture. When is it? Is it part of the Festival?'

'Sort of,' Ruth said, anxious not to be overheard by the festival people. 'But don't call it a lecture; that sounds so boring. It's more of a workshop really.'

'About your Peruvian book?' Beth asked.

Ruth nodded earnestly. 'Yeh; the relevance of Andean Indian culture to our own life goals. I mean, they've learned the art of attaining inner tranquillity in the harshest physical conditions, so they have a lot to teach us.'

'Maybe we should all live sixteen thousand feet up the Andes,' Boo suggested. 'That'd make us all bloody stoical.'

Mark was reluctant to contradict the wife of the local party chairman so early in their relationship. Nevertheless, he wanted to support Ruth. 'Well, I think it's great they're giving you the chance to publicise your book. Are they paying you as well?'

'Sort of. They said I could have a case of Observer Wine Club burgundy.'

'How are ticket sales going?' Beth asked, praying that some had been sold.

'I should think most people will buy them on the night; that's what Paul said, anyway.'

'We'll get ours today,' Beth said.

'I'm afraid it clashes with Martin Amis,' Boo lamented. 'I've got him staying in the house, so I suppose I ought to go and listen to him, in case he expects an opinion from me.'

'I'm sure Ruth's talk - sorry, workshop - will be much more interesting,' Beth said.

'Actually, I think you *will* find it quite interesting.' Ruth looked grateful. 'It's great that you're coming.' She glanced at the clock on the wall and gathered up her bag and coat. 'But I'd better be going. I've got some things to collect, and Owen's coming to look at the ewe and lamb later.'

'Oh, is he?' Beth heard herself say. 'In that case, perhaps I will come back with you and see what he says about them. After last night's drama I feel rather involved in their future.'

'I thought you were going to stick around while I had my grilling,' Mark said, a little testily.

'Well.... I was thinking. It means me hanging out for another three or four hours, and I've got a lot of stuff to get on with.' She stood and turned to Boo Llewellyn. 'I'm sorry we have to go, but I'm very glad to have met you. Maybe we'll see you again soon?'

'I'm sure you will. In fact, after Martin's show we're having a party up at The Neaudd. I'll send you an invite, and Ruth, too, of course,' she added.

'Great!' Mark said. Implicit in the single word was the certainty that they'd need a party after an hour and a half of Ruth's workshop. 'Thanks. That would be wonderful.'

'Half Lit-Fest people and half locals. Hard to say which lot are worse, but they make a good mix.'

'I can imagine,' Beth smiled. 'Well, I'd better not hold Ruth up.'

With a wave and an awkward grin, Beth and Ruth extricated themselves from the cluttered bar which had been filling up with lunchers while they'd been talking to Boo.

Outside, Ruth said, 'You didn't need to come.'

'No problem.'

'But didn't you want to be around to support Mark?'

'To tell the truth, he doesn't really need my support. He's a firm believer in himself.'

Ruth glanced at her. 'You don't think he sometimes appears overconfident to compensate for being married to a woman as strong as you?'

Beth laughed. 'Strong?' she asked. 'I'll admit to clever; quite tough, maybe; but "strong" suggests a kind of emotional muscularity that I wouldn't want to own up to, even if I had it. Besides, a lot of my so-called strength is down to professional training – courtroom stuff.'

'Maybe; but I'd love to be strong.'

'Good God, Ruth! You're not exactly feeble, running around with your sheep and llamas and chopping your wood.'

'Now you're talking about *physical* strength when we were talking about *emotional* strength. Why do you think I lavish so much love on my llamas? Because they accept it at its face value and don't fling it back at me.'

The image of a llama reciprocating Ruth's affection diverted Beth's flow of thought. 'But surely, llamas aren't exactly demonstrative,' she ventured.

'They can be,' Ruth protested. 'Subtly... and at least they're more consistent than man.'

At this, Beth had to laugh. 'Do you mean man, or men?'
Ruth laughed too. 'Men, of course.'

As she watched Owen stride away up the valley, Beth felt like a little girl who'd waited hours by the roadside to watch the Prince ride by, to be rewarded only with a fleeting glimpse.

Although she'd had more than a fleeting glimpse of Owen, she'd had barely a fleeting moment of communication. There had been eye contact between them for just a second before he'd turned to concentrate on Ruth and her ewe, running his strong hands over the beast's limbs to assess its health and, like an oracle, pronouncing it good.

He had spoken less than a dozen words before he placed a hand softly on Ruth's shoulder. 'Keep well yourself, Rhiannon,' he said, and was gone.

Beth turned away, trying to understand her disappointment while Ruth was occupied for a moment, helping the eager lamb in its quest for mother's milk. Beth took a deep breath. 'Who's Rhiannon?'

Ruth looked up and laughed. 'Some Druidic goddess, I think.'

'Is Owen interested in that sort of thing, then?' Beth asked.

'I don't know. But he's an interesting mixture of the mystical and the man of action. You saw last night how practical he can be, and how much he knows about animal care; he's supposed to have healing in his hands, too.'

'So little Dai told me. Have you ever seen him do it?'

'No. I once asked him but he wouldn't even talk about it.'

'He doesn't really talk much at all.'

'But when he does, it means something,' Ruth defended.

'Oh,' Beth said, dismayed. 'I'm sorry; I wasn't criticising him. I think it's pretty impressive to be so taciturn and, sort of... self-contained.'

'Good. I'd hate you to laugh at him.'

Alone in her kitchen, Beth forced herself to think of other things – of Mark, alert and confident in front of his panel of selectors, and she soon found herself praying. She had always prayed for anything that was outside her immediate control, and she would sometimes admit to people – to her mother, to her Catholic aunts, though not to the pragmatic humanists in her chambers – that her prayers brought results; at least, the things she prayed for often happened. But she felt a flush of guilt at the irony of praying for Mark's selection and eventual election, principally because it would provide her with what the nuns who taught at St Agnes' school used to call an 'occasion of sin'.

'If it please you, God,' she pleaded, as if God were one of the older Chancery judges in the High Court. 'Please, I understand that I will expose myself to temptation, but I can handle that. I'm asking you to help because Mark will be a very good Member of Parliament for these people. His motives are absolutely sincere.' She ignored the less than perfect truth. 'And also, he's tried so hard in his career' – more lies – 'and he's having such a terrible time with it now, he needs this chance.' That, at least, was true.

It was this truth that brought her up short in her plea. Abruptly Mark's true financial position seemed more important to her than it had. She knew without his having to tell her that he was in trouble, but she didn't know how deeply – because she had her own professional problems to deal with, because she had always taken the position that it was Mark's choice to tell her however much he needed to; and because, frankly, there wasn't much she could do about it anyway.

That was the downside of independence; her husband's career was a matter only of academic or, at most, emotional interest. Beth was economically self-sufficient; if there was one advantage in not being a mother, that was it. There were no offspring to be dependent on her, and she in turn was in no way dependent on her husband. His presence or absence had little bearing on her material well-being.

She walked through to the small back room that Mark had made his office. She found his briefcase, clicked it open and started to leaf through the papers, letters and unopened envelopes inside.

She read them in no particular order, but the more she read, the more obvious it became that Archimedes Press was in far worse shape than she'd realised. When she'd seen everything in the briefcase, she turned to the two small cupboards where Mark kept paperwork that he planned to deal with while he was up here.

The files and folders of untidily stowed letters, reports and professional advice contained further evidence that the business hadn't been viable – or even solvent – for over a year at least.

The reasons for this were clear enough. Only the previous year Mark had insisted that their recent higher profile merited a move from Fulham to Kensington and twice as much office space. Beth read for the first time that the company's accountants and Mark's co-directors were strongly against the move until they'd achieved a couple more sound, consolidating years.

But Archimedes had been flying high, at least in the best-seller lists, that spring; Mark easily overlooked the tiresome truth that only two of their twenty-eight titles were selling; and that was partly due to competitive pricing and extra big discounts claimed by the book chains that were shifting the largest quantities.

Looking at a profit and loss sheet, Mark tended to become bored as soon as he'd read the sales figures, and if they were up, that was good enough for him. Beth focussed her thoughts and reckoned he must have found it easy to convince the bank, who had been so keen to lend him money for his expansion and who were now, it seemed, even keener to have it back.

Reading on, she deduced that besides taking on borrowings out of all proportion to his company's turnover, for the last year Mark had also had to pay three times more rent for his new offices. And, presumably anticipating a growth in turnover to follow the higher profile of the firm and its list of titles, he'd taken on more staff, too – graduates mainly, at high salaries – who had yet to justify their existence.

Now he'd lost Marcel Gehring.

Beth thought it likely, even inevitable, that Marcel had gone to Jonathan Mundy, a former partner in the business who, in response to Mark's suggestion, had left the kitchen when things had got too hot, taking two key members of staff with him.

Going through the scraps of correspondence from the agent and the author herself, Beth deduced that Mark was even in imminent danger of losing Vanessa de Selincourt, his second most bankable author.

Beth stood up and took a deep breath. She gazed for a few moments at the untidy stacks of damning text before tidying it all away in the drawers and the briefcase where she'd found them. When she was satisfied that her actions would not be detectable she walked from the room through the hall and out into the cobbled courtyard. She sat on the edge of the stone trough and gazed at the crystal spring water trickling in.

Her tidy, legal mind wouldn't let her overlook the evidence and she found herself more upset than she might have expected by the

Beyond Gospel Pass

discovery that Mark seemed to be scurrying like a lemming towards the cliff top. But while she would have preferred him to retain his self-esteem by persevering with his first career, she knew intuitively he'd already convinced himself that the voters of East Brecknock would provide him with the safety net of an alternative one.

Three

As the sun dropped out of sight behind the ridge, Beth watched Mark drive through the gate.

He climbed out of the car, stretching himself until he saw her walking down through their field towards the house.

She clambered over the new post and rail fence and he put on a broad smile for her.

'Hi,' she said brightly. 'How did it go?'

Mark nodded. 'Fine. No trouble. Henry Llewellyn's asked us to dinner tomorrow night. He's definitely on my side,' he added, with a confident chuckle, strolling towards the house.

'What about the rest?' With her eyes, Beth pleaded that Mark would drop the pretence that everything was fine.

He saw the plea. 'Let me get a drink, first.' He pushed open the kitchen door.

Beth felt a rush of relief that she'd taken the trouble to put all his papers back as she'd found them. She followed him inside and frowned at the eagerness with which he tore the foil off the bottle he'd taken from the fridge.

He pulled the cork and filled two glasses. Beth sat down with him at the table.

'So, tell me all about them,' she asked. 'How many of them were there?'

'Eight, plus Henry. I must say, I'm very glad I've got him on my side.' He picked at a wicker bread basket in front of him.

'You said; but have you got any of the others?'

'Well, not all of them.' He took a quick gulp of wine and looked up. 'Not yet. Ah,' he added, looking out of the window. 'Here's Ruth.' He stood up and walked to open the door. 'Hi there, come on in. We were just having a drink and a post-mortem.'

Beyond Gospel Pass

'Oh, well, don't let me get in the way,' Ruth murmured. 'I only came to see if I could borrow your chainsaw.'

'Good God! What are you going to attack with it?'

'Just a sally tree that's come down by the brook; it's half flattened the fence there.'

'The saw's quite a hefty tool.' Mark grimaced doubtfully. 'It's got an eighteen inch blade.'

'He had to buy the biggest he could find,' Beth grinned over his shoulder.

'Anyway,' Mark said. 'Come on in and have a drink, then we'll go and find it.'

'Okay,' Ruth gave a grateful shrug of her skinny shoulders.

Inside, they sat down around the table again.

'Mark was just telling me about the committee that's been interviewing him,' Beth said, still wanting to hear herself.

'They're a strange mixture,' Mark said. 'But then I suppose one's got to expect that with the Liberals. There's one really right-on, chippy woman called Maggie Watkins; she thought I wouldn't be able to relate to an unmarried mum in one of the villages, or to a retired farm worker up in the hills.'

'D'you think you could? ' Beth asked.

'I don't see why not; it wouldn't take a degree in psychology. Then of course, she had a dig at the fact that not only was I not a single mum, I wasn't even a dad.' Mark laughed. 'One of the others, a solicitor, I think, called Richard Thomas groaned so loudly he stopped her mid-sentence.'

'It sounds as if you've got a bit more work to do on her, then,'

'Yes,' Mark agreed. 'And there's another dopey old geezer called Doctor Williams who wondered how I justified publishing *The Number One Gene*. He said the ideas in it were contrary to the fundamental dignity of mankind.'

'Was that the last Marcel Gehring book?' Ruth asked.

Mark nodded.

'It had some brilliant reviews,' Ruth gushed.

'And a few spectacularly vicious ones,' Mark said, 'which helped the publicity a lot. Anyway, I told Dr Williams, however much I deplore some of the views of the genetic determinists, I believe in open debate on major moral issues. That shut him up.'

'I'm sure it did,' Beth said. 'Did you see your rival?'

'Geraint Pugh? Yes,' Mark laughed. 'I bumped into him outside as I was leaving. He was getting out of a battered old Volvo stuffed full of snotty-nosed kids and his harassed little wife was straightening his tie.'

Beth looked at Mark's knitted silk tie. She remembered her father wearing one like it, back in the Sixties. And abruptly, she found herself comparing Mark's tweed jacket with Owen's leather jerkin.

'They've asked me back next week,' Mark went on, 'with you this time. That should clinch it.' He gave her a confident nod and lifted his glass to take another drink.

'That's great,' Ruth said. 'But do you think we could find the chainsaw now? I want to get on with it this evening while there's not much water in the brook.'

Mark stood up and led her away to one of the barns where all the expensive outdoor equipment he'd bought was stored, and seldom disturbed.

Ruth waved at Beth through the window. Beth didn't want her to go; she wanted to talk to her all evening, in case the subject of Owen cropped up again.

Mark came back into the kitchen. 'So, what's on the agenda? Maybe we should try having a quiet evening in, just the two of us, listening to music, chatting over a bottle of this delicious wine.'

'I'm so sorry, love,' Beth replied. 'I haven't had a chance to tell you. Father Aidan's having dinner with us. I asked him to come at eight.'

'Father Aidan?'

'One of the monks from the Abbey. He's a lovely man; very holy, with a great sense of humour.'

'That sounds somehow impossible,' Mark observed. 'Humour, laughter, these are enjoyable things.'

'Being holy doesn't mean he can't enjoy himself.'

Father Aidan arrived in a small car, exactly at eight. A tall Irishman from Munster, he was surprisingly handsome, with thick brown hair and bright, impenetrable grey eyes. He'd told Beth that he had entered the Benedictine monastery in Hereford when he was twenty and she guessed he was in his late thirties now. He'd been sent to one of the Abbey's offshoots, a mission in South America, for several years, and worked away in some of the far-flung English parishes for which his

Beyond Gospel Pass

monastery was responsible. Soft-spoken, smiling, he possessed a serenity which Beth thought must puzzle people unfamiliar with the Rule of Saint Benedict and the object of celibacy.

Aidan knew Mark only by sight, but he was evidently an admirer of Beth's, and not unaware of her attractiveness.

'Beth, it's lovely to see you.' He greeted her with a kiss on both cheeks, and shook Mark's hand warmly, accepting his offer of a glass of wine.

Grimond sidled up to the monk, rubbing his back against the back habit that covered his legs, intuitively understanding, it seemed, that this was a man who meant him no harm. Aidan picked up the cat and scratched his chin, and sat down with it where Mark waved him.

'I have cousins in Ireland, you know,' he said, still stroking the happy Grimond, 'black protestants, strangely, but close friends and lovely people who live in an enormous, fierce and castellated dwelling. You'd expect beatings and torture to be going on, but the place is filled from top to bottom with cats, so I'm pretty used to them.' He made them laugh with his easy telling of stories, the cadence of his speech and his obvious love of words, all influenced by a profound compassion for everything around him, without a trace of the cynicism that prevailed in almost every corner of the world Beth usually inhabited.

Beth had cooked a deliberately simple lamb casserole for dinner. She was careful not to drink too much. She noticed during dinner that Aidan made two glasses of wine with water from the spring last all evening.

The Benedictine was, as Beth had told Mark, an erudite and witty man. He was observant and wise where others might have been merely cynical; he accepted that there were nearly always reasons, if not excuses, for odd or antisocial behaviour. Aidan also had a firm, traditional belief in the accountability of individuals for their own actions, and failings.

Beth guessed that he was used to people asking him into their homes when some particular crisis in their lives provoked awkward questions. She tried to lead round to her own dilemma without too obviously sign-posting the way to Mark.

'We had a bizarre conversation here a couple of nights ago, Father,' she said casually, when they had finished the lamb. 'The Church says that the primary purpose of sex is to procreate, right?'

Aidan nodded, faintly.

'And that enjoying sex is something God sort of tolerates, provided it's performed with procreation in mind.'

Here the priest put his head to one side.

'What we were trying to establish,' Beth went on, examining an academic point, 'was the moral position of two people, not married, having sex for no other reason than the creation of a child who would be brought up by the mother and her husband.'

'It would be adultery,' Aidan said simply.

'But surely, there's a difference to the simple sin of adultery. I mean, it wouldn't be done for pleasure, like having an affair or in any mental or emotional sense being unfaithful to a spouse. I'm thinking of a situation where a married couple simply couldn't reproduce, but where the female is theoretically fully functioning.' She glanced at Mark and saw his face tighten, ready to join the conversation. She went on quickly. 'And the wife seeks another partner with her husband's consent, solely to provide them with a child?'

'If a couple can't have children, they must accept that this is God's will.'

'What about *in vitro*?'

'That usually involves both parents in the creation of the child, and would be acceptable.'

'But if that option wasn't there?'

Aidan shrugged. 'I've often told you, the church isn't concerned with telling you what you might get away with. Its function is to tell you what you need to do to be a saint. We say: "If you want to be truly holy; if you aspire to absolute saintliness, this is how high you must jump".'

Mark leaned forward and looked at the priest with a bland, slightly drunken smile. 'But hardly anyone jumps that high, or reaches that level of holiness, do they?'

'No,' Aidan agreed. 'Saints are very rare.'

'So you really don't expect your followers to come up to the mark?'

'I have no followers; and we expect nothing; we hope and pray, and encourage people to jump as high as they can.' As he spoke, he rewarded the patient Grimond with a sliver of lamb.

Beyond Gospel Pass

In bed, later, Beth lay awake listening to a tawny owl in the *cwm*. She listened to Mark's breathing, too, and knew he wasn't asleep.

She knew he'd drunk enough to be stimulated, but not enough to preclude performance. She sensed that he wanted to make his way across their big bed and coax some response from her.

She also guessed that his instincts, or possibly just experience, were telling him that her response would not be wholehearted.

It wasn't that she didn't still love him, she told herself – if only he would stop pretending there were no crises in his life.

After a while, from the dark warmth of the night, his muffled voice reached her.

'Angel, I know how desperate you are for a baby; me too. But I wish you wouldn't discuss it with all and sundry. I'm sure that poor priest must have been really embarrassed.'

'Aidan embarrassed? I doubt it. There's very little he hasn't heard over the years. He must be one of the most receptive listeners I've ever come across.'

'But why did you have to tell him about our situation?'

'I didn't, Mark,' Beth protested gently. 'I was just rather fascinated by the hypothetical morals of it.'

'I didn't think you'd taken Ruth's idea seriously.'

'I hadn't, but it's an interesting moral dilemma.'

'I don't think so. The Catholic Church is all arse over tit if it can't accept the priority most married couples give to having children.'

'Of course it does, but anyway, do you really give it that much priority? I sometimes think you just say you do to support me.'

'No, I want children as much as you.'

'So, if there was a real possibility of doing the surrogate father thing, you wouldn't object?'

For a few moments he didn't speak.

Beth heard him swallow hard and his breathing became a little heavier as he moved across the bed. She felt herself tighten as he approached and his hand touched her, gently enough, on the arm.

'I'm afraid there's no point trying tonight,' she said, grateful to be telling the truth.

'Oh.' The disappointment was palpable, the blow to his self-esteem discernible in the single syllable. He rolled back to his side of the bed and muttered, 'To be absolutely honest, there's no way I could handle you going off to make love with someone else, even if there was a cast-iron guarantee of a baby.'

'Stop worrying about it,' Beth murmured. 'Anyway, that's exactly the point I was making to Aidan - it wouldn't be "making love". Besides Marco love, it's not for real, you know; I was only being hypothetical.' She stretched out a hand to squeeze his before turning over to sleep.

Beth was up early next morning. She quickly pulled on jeans, T-shirt and Timberlands. Before Mark had woken, she had eaten a grapefruit, fed the cat and begun walking up the valley towards Blaen Fawr, the original Rhys family farm.

She followed the lane towards Gospel Pass for a mile, until the valley divided below the peak of Yr Twmpa. She branched left and tramped up a punishing half mile of stony track to the farm.

Ruth had told her that Rhyses had lived in the ancient stone farmstead as long as anyone knew. They still farmed several flat meadows beside the young river below, and a few hundred acres of thin sloping pasture. They also enjoyed traditional graziers' rights over the tan and purple mountain ridge behind.

It took Beth half an hour to reach the copse of stunted oaks – the highest in the valley – that clustered around the southern end of the farm. A scrawny hedgerow petered out at a pair of large, upright flat stones, which looked as if they'd been pilfered from a graveyard and had once supported a gate, long since removed. Beth walked on up and through the open end of a three-sided range of buildings. Facing her was the house itself.

The whole place was bent and warped and seemed ready to collapse. Relentlessly spreading ivy had taken vigorous hold wherever it could; young ash and sycamore sprouted from fissures in the stones and mortarless gaps between them. The roof ridge sagged and at Beth's feet, the ragged cobbles of the yard looked just as they'd been laid, two or more hundred years before.

Apart from a power line stretching loosely from the last of the poles that straggled beside the track up from the valley, there were few signs of twenty-first century living. Beth looked at it all with an enervating mix of shock and fascination.

All around was evidence of livestock – droppings, heaps of sodden straw, ragged tufts of grimy wool, scattered scraps of hay.

Beyond Gospel Pass

One of the buildings was open-fronted to the yard and housed a collection of mouldering farm equipment – a battered two-furrow plough, which might once have cultivated the meadows on the valley floor, an ancient Fordson tractor, an old tedder and a baler, along with rolls of rusting barbed wire and stacks of half peeled softwood posts.

Beth walked across the desolate quadrangle as if she were intruding on a past time. She rapped her knuckles on the flaking brown paint of a door set under a stone-tiled canopy.

While she waited for something to happen, she took a step back and looked around. Beyond the first appearance of desertion there were some signs of human activity. A pair of clean wellington boots stood beside the muddy doorstep. She saw a brand new car battery in a corner, under a small lean-to. Above, a television aerial was just visible, loosely fixed to the angle of a crumbling stone chimney.

The house itself was surprisingly large – five bays wide, three storeys high into a deep, gable-windowed roof of broad stone tiles. Much of the fabric of the building was coated in grey-green lichens that thrived in the unpolluted air.

Beth was struck by a sense of timelessness about the place, a feeling that if she had come to knock on the door a hundred years before, little would have been different. Even the sounds – the light wind whining through the ancient barns, a distant buzzard keening over its nest, the raucous bark of a crow among the mossy oaks – seemed like echoes from another age.

And she thought of Owen, born and growing up here, for whom this strange displacement must be normality.

Beth took a startled pace back when the door suddenly creaked open. In front of her stood a small woman with wispy grey hair.

The woman, perhaps seventy, was wrapped in a pinafore made from pre-war curtain material. Sharp brown eyes swept up and down Beth, taking in and appraising every detail.

'Mrs Rhys?' Beth asked nervously.

The woman nodded.

'I'm Beth Powell... from Pant-y-Groes.'

Mrs Rhys nodded again, inviting an explanation with her eyes.

'I hadn't been up this way before; I hope you don't mind.'

'There's nothing up here.' The woman's gaze swept the empty hilltops opposite.

'Oh, I wouldn't say so,' Beth protested. 'It's very beautiful, and peaceful.'

Mrs Rhys didn't react, as if Beth hadn't spoken. 'What do you want?'

'Nothing. Your grandchildren, Dai and Abby – they are your grandchildren?'

The woman nodded.

'They bring me eggs and milk.' Beth tried a smile. 'But they don't live here, do they?'

'There's just me as lives here.' The old woman paused and added, as a careful afterthought, 'Me and my son.'

'Is your son here now?' Beth asked, and felt suddenly absurd, like a stuttering teenager.

For just a second, there was a flash of fear in the old woman's eyes, until the moment passed and she was looking at Beth as if she were mad. 'He's working,' she grunted and gave the hills another sweeping gaze to indicate that her son could have been anywhere out there. As she spoke, she retreated a little into the darkness of the ancient house, and the gap between door and jamb diminished.

'Tell him I came,' Beth said, regretting a slightly desperate edge in her voice. 'Please,' she added as the door closed with a soft thud.

She stood and stared at it for a few moments, wondering why the tough little woman should have been frightened of her.

Did she think, perhaps, that Beth had come as a predator, to take her son from her?

If that were so, she told herself, even as she condemned the fantasy, then Owen must have talked about her, at least mentioned her in a way that showed his interest.

Beth sighed and dismissed the thought. She turned and walked across the farmyard, out onto the hillside with a sense of release. She felt as if she'd been temporarily caught in a time warp within the purlieus of the ancient farm.

The sun was warming the air as she walked back down the valley towards Pant-y-Groes. The going was easy on the grass verge and she looked around her, thinking that she might get a glimpse of Owen somewhere on the hillside.

Beyond Gospel Pass

There was no sign of him, but the walking seemed to subdue her fantasies and she arrived back at the house with her thoughts in better perspective. There was nothing particularly odd about a childless woman of her age becoming obsessive to the point of grasping at anything that might give her a baby. It was an understandably powerful instinct. But in the end, she told herself, it was just that, and needed to be handled with dispassionate logic.

Mark was out in the yard, dressed in old jeans and a T-shirt. He greeted her enthusiastically, crowing at the arrival of another brilliant day. 'I'm just going over to Ruth's to get my chainsaw back,' he added prosaically.

Beth watched him stride out of the gate and drop down the bank to cross the brook. She thought about how she would have felt if Mark and Ruth became lovers. Ruth, she guessed, wouldn't mind. And if Mark began to feel a need to assert his manhood, he might not find it easy to resist any temptations Ruth laid in his path.

For the rest of the morning, Beth settled for decorating what was going to be the main spare bedroom. The colours and the fabrics had all come from a visit to St Remy de Provence, where she and Mark had been on a gastronomic pilgrimage earlier in the year, so the room now had a brightness that seemed to place it outside the deep Welsh valley.

Mark brought Ruth back with him later, and they all sat down to eat pasta salad with a bottle of wine at a small wooden table in the yard.

During lunch, Beth was restless. As soon as she'd cleared the plates, she announced that she was going for another walk.

'Anyone coming?' she asked, correctly guessing there'd be no takers. 'If I go to sleep now, I'll wake up feeling like hell, and I suppose I ought to be on best form for your dinner this evening.'

'Not *my* dinner,' Mark said. 'Henry rang this morning to stress that the invitation has nothing to do with the selection process.'

'Whatever,' Beth said. 'I'm going for a walk. I'll see you later.'

Shortly after, Beth left by the back of the house and headed up across the field that separated it from the open hill, where the only paths were narrow winding sheep tracks between the bracken and bilberry bushes.

Jessica Meredith

A deep peace hung over the valley. It was too hot for most living creatures to be moving or vocal. Only the occasional bleat of a lamb echoed across the valley.

With an easy stride, in spite of the wine she'd drunk, Beth zigzagged up the hillside. In view of the heat, she had changed into a pale yellow tank-top and a flimsy white cotton skirt. The gentle breeze eddied between her legs while the sun warmed her naked shoulders. She felt a rare, unexpected burst of simple happiness and felt glad to be alive.

Every so often she stopped to look down at the diminishing farmhouse. The table where they'd eaten their lunch was hidden by the building, but after she'd been walking for twenty minutes, she saw Mark walk across the yard with Ruth. They stopped at the gate. After a moment, Ruth carried on alone, across the road, down towards the crossing point over the brook that led to her own small farmhouse.

Beth called down in the still air; Mark turned and waved as he walked towards the house, and was soon out of sight. She took a few lung-filling breaths of the heather-scented air that drifted down from the top of the ridge and was inspired to climb higher. She found the dry gully of a winter brook and followed it up, using the shade of the twisted thorn bushes that straggled beside it.

Unexpectedly, the ground levelled into a small, half-circular shelf, set into the hillside, giving shelter to a grove of stubby oaks.

From a cleft in the bare rock in the gloom at the back of a small natural amphitheatre, a spring burst and tinkled into a pool. It was from here that the brook she'd followed up would normally have flowed, but now, with so little rain, the stream dived almost at once underground, to reappear further down the hill.

With a sudden shock, Beth noticed that there was someone crouched down in front of the spring. From behind, she could see at least that it was a man, taking a drink, while beside him a black and white sheepdog lapped quietly.

Beth instinctively stepped back to take cover behind the bushes that fringed the coppice.

The man straightened his back. Before he'd turned, she knew it was Owen.

In the first moment she saw his face, all the sane self-analysis and sober rationalising of the morning deserted her. She stepped further down into the gully, shrinking back behind the bushes as, feverishly she tried to decide what to do.

Owen was evidently in no hurry after his drink. He walked to the edge of the grove and lowered himself, as lithe as a cat, onto a grassy bank in the shade of the largest tree. He lay back and closed his eyes.

The dog dropped down beside him, aware, apparently, of Beth's presence but sensing no need to draw his master's attention to her.

Beth smiled at the dog and looked at Owen.

At rest, uninfluenced either by physical effort or by the natural reserve she'd already observed in him, his smooth, sun-browned features had the beauty of a sculpture by Michelangelo.

It was the face of an artist and thinker, not the heir to a hundred small-minded, xenophobic farmers; nor a man whose sole destiny was to keep sheep in the hills for the rest of his life and who might, one day, consider finding himself a wife to provide him with sex, meals and an heir of his own.

Beth found herself trembling at this insight. Her breath came faster; she cleared her throat and scrambled up from the gully.

'Hi, there.' She made a face at the triteness of the greeting.

Owen opened his eyes and turned his head.

'Hello,' he said simply, unsurprised, in his soft Marches' lilt.

He turned his torso towards her and propped himself up on one elbow. He looked at her directly and, this time, allowed his dark chocolate eyes to linger. Nothing specific in his face expressed approval at what he saw, or pleasure at her sudden intrusion on his privacy, but nor did he make her feel excluded or unwelcome.

He nodded at the dog, still prostrate beside him. 'Mack knew there was someone here.'

Beth looked around for the right opening to their conversation. 'I think I'll have a drink from the spring,' she said. 'Is that all right?'

Owen lifted a shoulder slightly. 'It's free; you've a right to it same as anyone.'

Beth nodded and smiled. She walked ten paces to the source of bubbling water, leaned down and put her lips to it. The water was pure and sublimely refreshing. She gulped and gasped a few times, wiped her mouth with the hem of her skirt. She turned to look across the copse. Owen had swivelled round to watch with a faint upturn at the corner of his mouth.

'Beautiful water,' she said, strolling back towards him.

He nodded. 'It tastes of nothing, but it tastes good, doesn't it?'

Beth thought of a dozen themes she could have developed from that simple but succinct idea, but she knew she mustn't gush into them or allow all the hundred thoughts in her head to tumble out, all muddled for once. 'Mmm, it does,' she nodded.

She noticed his clothes – the dusty singlet and jeans stained green with bracken juice, the rich darkness of his loose long hair, his eyes which moved, then stopped dead still. The muscles of his upper arms, like a ship's hawsers, gleamed as he reached up strong hands to wipe away drops of water still glistening on his tawny cheeks.

'Is it okay if I sit down here for a moment?' she asked. 'I've just walked up from the house.'

Owen nodded with a faint smile. 'I saw you starting out.'

Beth was pleased by the idea that the empty hills held such observant eyes. She sat down with the dog between them. She leaned back and gazed across the valley, laid out opposite them on a right angle plane.

In the fields below the hedge that marked the upper limit of enclosure on the far side, a dozen llamas – Ruth's pregnant girls – stood and stared with camel-like disdain at the docile sheep beyond. Alone in a post-and-rail paddock below, a single male llama fretted. Beside this was Ruth's white farmhouse, protected by two mighty ash trees. In a lower field, her flock of small grey Herdwick ewes cropped the wiry grass among their lambs.

Beth turned and looked at Owen.

Through half-closed eyes he was watching a pair of buzzards as they banked and soared with gentle *peeows* to disguise their plans for a lazy strike.

Unconsciously, it seemed, he pulled from the pocket of his loose-fitting jeans a heavy gold ring on a worn chain and passed them lightly through his fingers in the same way Beth had seen old Cretan shepherds fiddle with their worry beads.

Beth took a deep breath. 'What's that?' she asked.

Owen's eyes opened as they turned to her. He gave no sign of resenting the question. He looked down at the ring. 'My grandfather gave it to me, when he was dying. It was the pendulum he used to find water; I was the only one who learned from him.'

'I'd heard that you could dowse; didn't you find Ruth's well for her?'

He nodded, but offered no more. His attention had been taken by something on the far hillside. Beth followed his eyes to a faint track that headed up behind Blaen Fawr. Two walkers' packs moved along it like alien bugs, hard pink and turquoise against the fresh green fern.

'Do a lot of people come walking up the valley?' she asked, for something to say.

'Quite a few.'

'I expect you think it's pretty strange - people coming all this way from the cities just to tramp up and down the hills where you work'

'I don't think it's strange. If I lived in a big city, I'd come here looking for the truth.'

Beth realised more with each answer he gave that she must adjust her earlier assumptions about him.

'How do you mean?'

'Out here,' he waved a complacent hand at the valley, 'there's no lies. There's only what you see.'

Owen stretched out his legs, lay back and closed his eyes with the ghost of a smile lingering on his lips.

This time Beth did feel excluded but not rejected. She lay back too, closed her eyes and tried to let her mind drift free among the soft sounds and fragrant breeze.

It may only have been a minute or two before the rattle of an old diesel engine across the quiet valley drowned the buzzards' mewing.

Beth raised her eyelids and leaned forward. Ruth's Land Rover was creeping up the track from her barn with a bale of hay on the open back. The vehicle came to a halt, the engine was turned off and the small sounds of nature could be heard again.

Ruth climbed out and walked to a low stone cairn. Four hundred yards was too far to see details, but Beth could almost smell the tang of fresh hay and patchouli that always hung around Ruth.

She wondered if Owen knew that smell too.

'That's the water hole I found for her.' His voice took her by surprise. She hadn't thought he was watching too.

Jessica Meredith

She turned to him. 'I suppose you know her pretty well?'

A suggestion of movement in the muscle of his cheek was Owen's only answer, for a moment.

'In some ways I do, but she's changeful, like; that's how she protects herself.'

This view surprised Beth, but she didn't challenge it.

'Don't get me wrong – she's a real person and she loves her stock. I can guess what she's saying now,' he said with a quiet voice that seemed to hang in the air, 'talking all soft and airy. "Here you are, Pedro. This'll keep your mind off the girls for a bit".' He smiled lazily as the distant figure hefted the bale from her vehicle into a timber hay-rack by the lower hedge. 'I could do that for her,' he said, shaking his head with soft grunt of censure. 'She always struggles, don't matter how hard she pretends not to.'

Beth knew what he meant. She could imagine Ruth's arms, tight-sinewed with the strain and trembling as she made the final heave of hay over the high side of the V-shaped rack.

Beth shivered and she thought of Owen gazing hungrily at Ruth's eager, skinny body draped across her iron bed, loosened by wine and cannabis, as anxious to provide pleasure as to receive it.

Although Ruth had denied it, Beth felt certain she and Owen had been lovers, and she was almost sick with an absurd jealousy that surged through her. She pushed herself to her feet, avoiding Owen's eye as she brushed grass and bracken from her skirt.

'Goodbye, Mack,' she said to the dog. 'Goodbye,' she said to Owen without looking at him. 'I've got to get back home... things to do.' She tried to speak brightly. 'Maybe I'll see you around here again soon. I'm staying up for a couple of weeks, you know – working at home.'

'I expect I'll see you then – Mrs Powell.'

She looked at him now, prayed he wouldn't see the panic in her eyes. 'Beth,' she said. 'Please call me Beth. And I'll look forward to that.'

Four

Beth and Mark drove through Hay on their way to dinner at the Llewellyns'. The town was more full than usual of incongruous urbanites, arriving for the imminent festival and making the whole place seem to her as bogus as a badly painted film set.

Once they had crossed the river, the landscape around the broadening flood plain of the meandering Wye was soft and gentle, in sharp contrast to the shadowy clefts of the Black Mountain valleys they'd left behind.

Henry Llewellyn's house, The Neuadd was set on a woody slope of the hills to the north, where the topography turned from Welsh to English.

On the site of a medieval manor and *ad hoc* court, the house had been built in the mid-nineteenth century with money flowing from the early industrialisation of South Wales, rather than the earlier spoils of high office.

At eight o'clock, the sun was still high over the Brecon Beacons, illuminating the house which was framed by lofty, alien sequoias planted by a Victorian Llewellyn. Beth looked at Mark's smile of satisfaction as they drove through a pair of high white gates. They followed a long drive that curved between wrought iron fencing, across an upward sweep of parkland pasture, where a herd of small black cattle grazed.

She took a deep breath and made herself focus on his concerns. 'Your local chairman seems to have done well for himself.'

'Ah,' Mark turned to her, relieved. 'You've decided to rejoin the world, then?'

'Yes, thank you. I'm okay now,' Beth said with what she hoped was convincing brightness.

'Henry inherited all this. I'm sure he runs the estate well, but I wouldn't have thought he was a particularly entrepreneurial farmer.'

'I hope not,' Beth said, 'given the agri-policies in the Liberal manifesto.'

Mark stopped the car on a large gravel circle between the house and an elegantly terraced garden below it. They both climbed out and stood for a moment, taking in the serene beauty of it and the valley beyond.

'By the way,' Mark said quietly. 'Boo Llewellyn isn't really a political animal, so there's no point in spending much time talking politics to her.'

Beth heard, but didn't answer. They walked towards the wide stone porch. The front door opened before they reached it and Henry Llewellyn came out to greet them.

He was a kind-looking man, a few inches shorter than Mark, with thick, grey-black hair, like a rough-coated terrier's, and bushy, untrimmed black brows. In the loose tanned flesh of his round face, his gray-brown eyes displayed an eagerness to please in an intelligent, thoughtful way. Beth wondered how good a chairman that made him.

'Hello, Mark. Mrs Powell, I'm delighted to meet you at last; I've heard so much about you.'

Beth gave him a self-deprecating smile. 'Beth, please.' She shook his hand and thought it had just the right amount of firmness. 'It's kind of you to ask us, especially while the selection's still going on.'

'Oh, for heaven's sake; this is *not* a political occasion, I can assure you.' Henry spoke with a deep voice and the intonation of an old-fashioned army officer. 'Quite apart from anything else, my wife Boo gets very twitchy if people talk too much politics at dinner, and that suits me very well.' He laughed and led them to a small sitting room in a corner of the house, with windows on the south and west walls.

'What a wonderful room,' Beth said.

'Stunning views.' Mark nodded.

'Yes,' Henry agreed. 'Now, drinks?'

He poured strong gin and tonics for them before going out to tell his wife they had arrived.

Mark walked to the window and looked out, sipping his drink. 'I bet old Geraint Pugh doesn't get asked to dinner here,' he said in an undertone.

Beyond Gospel Pass

'Maybe not,' Beth said, 'but don't get too excited. It's the rest of the committee that has to want you.' She joined him at the open window. A collared dove purred from somewhere in the trees behind the house. Beth looked across the golden tops of the mountains and thought of the Rhyses' farm on its craggy perch up the valley side, and Owen, returning there each night to a supper cooked by the grey, ghostly little woman.

'Hello,' Boo Llewellyn boomed as she came into the room. 'How kind of you to come at such short notice. I hope you won't find everyone too boring.'

'Boo, darling,' Henry said, behind her. 'Hang on; let them make up their own minds.'

'Talking of making up minds,' Boo said, 'has your committee adopted Mark as the next candidate yet?'

Boo's bluntness amused Beth.

Henry looked surprised. 'Not yet. It'd be a rare committee that showed signs of unanimity at this stage in the proceedings.' He turned to Mark. 'Personally, I'm not that keen on Geraint Pugh. He thinks he's a leading member of the community, where in fact he's just a self-important busybody, and most of us know it.'

'Sounds like ideal parliamentary material to me,' Boo laughed.

Henry screwed up his mouth. 'In many ways, he is ideal for the job - at least viewed from ground level in Hay - but I don't think we'd do ourselves any favours putting him up; besides, he's got a dodgy ticker. If we go to all the trouble of getting him elected, and then he pegs out, the voters might feel cheated.'

Boo put up her hand. 'Now, that's enough. I see more guests arriving.' Beth followed her gaze through the window, to a gleaming new Range Rover which had just pulled up outside. 'One of our local celebrities,' she said.

Beth watched a tall, lean man and a short pretty woman climb down from the vehicle.

'By the way,' Boo went on, as if there were a connection. 'How's Ruth?'

'Fine. She's a really useful friend to have in the valley.'

'So, do you see much of her?'

Beth nodded. 'We had her to supper the night before last. She's taken some grazing from us. In fact one of her ewes started having a breached birth just after we'd finished eating.' Beth wanted to go on and describe how Owen had appeared like an angel of the night and quietly dealt with the problem.

'She's wonderfully loopy, isn't she?' Boo said, making sure with one eye that her husband had gone out to greet the new arrivals. 'But watch her; she gets a bit lonely up there; I don't know what she does for sex.'

'Perhaps she doesn't do anything...'

Boo glanced at her quizzically. 'That would surprise me.' She turned to greet the tall man and the woman who had just come into the room. 'Charley, Deborah, how are you?'

Beth and Mark were introduced. Charles Winter was a novelist, well respected although not as famous as his manner suggested. Beth knew that Mark had once tried and failed to buy the rights to one of his books. She watched her husband turn on the knowing charm that he reserved for authors. He would soon be making overtures about the next book, she guessed.

Beth talked to Deborah. She was a painter who owned up to a precarious life with the author, until she'd persuaded him to move from the temptations of London to a farm in the Radnor hills. 'When people ask him what sort of farmer he is,' Deborah giggled, 'he says, "organic – acres of organic words – born out of shit and devoured by pests".'

Two more men with their wives arrived soon after - a member of the family who controlled a famous drinks maker in Hereford, and the colonel commanding the local Special Forces regiment.

Beth did her best with the men and their wives. Conscious that most of her women friends in London had significant jobs of their own, she tried to suppress her misgivings about women prepared to play supporting roles to their husbands'.

Still feeling detached from the party, she heard herself talking and laughing as if she were on the other side of the room. Out of habit, she was sympathetic towards the wives, witty with the men. She knew that the soldier and the novelist both fancied her, though this gave her none of the usual frisson.

It was a relaxed, even noisy dinner, but Beth was glad when it was over and Mark was saying goodbye to their hosts with extravagant gratitude and promises to have them back to Pant-y-Groes.

Beyond Gospel Pass

When they were leaving, on the doorstep, Boo said goodbye to Beth. 'And by the way, I feel rather bad that I haven't sent Ruth an invitation to the party here after her talk. Do bring her along with her current lover.'

'Has she got a current lover?' Beth asked doubtfully.

Boo shrugged. 'I saw her in Hay the other week with a very hunky chap – a real, live Seth.'

'I don't know who on earth that could have been,' Beth said, though a quaking in her guts told her otherwise.

During the night, clouds had invaded from the west and in the morning lay soggy and grey over the tops of the mountains.

It wasn't raining, but the leaves and the grass dripped with moisture, and the droplets suspended in the air were evident in every lungful Beth took as she walked across the courtyard to the car.

It was a little after seven, and Mark had complained when she'd accidentally woken him.

'You're going to do *what*?' he'd grumbled hoarsely.

'I want to go to Mass at the Abbey; there's one at eight o'clock.'

'What on earth for?'

'Mark, I've told you hundreds of times why I go to Mass.'

'All right, but why all the way to Hereford? Why not go to Hay?'

'I'd like to see Father Aidan.'

'But, for God's sake...' Mark, thinking perhaps that he'd answered his own question, gave up protesting and turned over in bed.

Beth drove carefully down the deep, narrow lane to the southern end of the valley. As she passed the ruins of Llanthony Priory the serene beauty of its ancient stones seemed to comfort her.

Leaving the looming mountain ridge behind her, she relished the silence of her own company as she tried to understand what was happening to her. The conflict between her guilt at what she knew she wanted, and her elation at the thought that it might happen, was almost intoxicating – like nothing she'd known since adolescence.

She was nevertheless appalled that she had abandoned her principles so easily, before she'd committed even a single physical sin with Owen. And she was deeply ashamed that she had so easily reduced her husband to no more than a minor obstacle.

Later, in the sheltered peace of the Abbey church, she prayed to God to help her avoid a course of action that would lead to inevitable self-recrimination. Deep within her, though, she knew that not only would she succumb when the temptation was presented, but also, if it wasn't offered, she would go out and look for it.

After Mass she lingered in the church to inhale the nostalgic aroma of incense and freshly snuffed candles while she considered whether she should light a new candle in front of a statue of the Virgin Mary toting her chubby infant Jesus – a plaster Madonna whose features, complexion and robes were more like those of the nuns who'd dominated her juvenile years than of a young teenage Israeli girl who had lived two millennia ago.

In the end, she dug a coin out of a purse in her bag, lit a candle and slipped out of the church, relieved not to have seen Father Aidan. She drove away from the Abbey, disappointed that God was not making it easy for her to justify her intention to make love with Owen with her commendable, and inescapable longing for a child.

With the image of the Madonna and her child lingering in her head, Beth found herself thinking of her own mother, wondering how she would have dealt with a dilemma like hers. She was grateful for the balanced detachment she had been taught by her, though she smiled at what her snobbish Bostonian grandmother might have said if she'd heard she was considering an affair with a Welsh hill farmer.

Back at the farmhouse, Mark didn't notice any change in her. They talked about the small jobs he said he would do around the farm, about how bright his political prospects now were, after the previous night's dinner, and how there was a good chance he would get Charles Winter's next novel for Archimedes.

At midday, he announced that he was going to get to know some of his future constituents by drinking a few pints of bitter with them in the pub at Llanthony. 'Why don't you come?'

'No thanks. I don't fancy swilling beer with a lot of anal hill farmers. But you go; you've got to be seen around the place if you want to get elected. And Mark, try not to lecture them too much,' she added, with a laugh to soften the advice.

Beyond Gospel Pass

He was obviously relieved that she wasn't coming with him. She watched him drive away like a man going on safari to spot rare animals at their drinking hole.

Beth spent an hour looking though a fat file of papers concerning her asylum case before she took a break, found some rosemary and shallots and cooked a small leg of Welsh lamb. Mark came back from the pub, pleased about new openings he'd made with the valley people. Lunch was harmonious and constructive. Beth was pleased with herself.

'Thanks,' Mark said when he'd finished his second plateful. 'That was the most delicious piece of lamb I've ever eaten. It's such a pity these poor farmers are getting paid bugger all for them.'

'That's a local problem you'll be able to deal with, if you get in.'

'If?' Mark laughed.

Beth didn't contradict him. 'You should make a special study of hill farming – BSE, the risks of foot and mouth from imports, all that sort of thing? There's a lot of public sympathy for the farmers up here - not like the fat cats down in the plains.'

Mark nodded. 'I've been working out my ideas and I think a fresh, outside view would make a lot of difference.'

'By the way,' Beth said casually. 'When are you going back up to London?'

'Tomorrow morning at sparrow fart, if you don't mind leaving then.'

'I don't have to go back; I've got a lot of work I can do at home, and it's so lovely, I thought I might just as well stay and do it up here.'

Mark nodded again, careful not to crow at Beth's apparent conversion to the special qualities of life in the Marches. He looked at her fondly. 'I wish I could stay with you, but I've got to get back and wrap up the Marcel Gehring deal.'

Beth quickly got to her feet and started gathering up plates. She felt suddenly very guilty that she still hadn't told him about Marcel Gehring, since Trish had rung with the news on Thursday evening. But Beth knew that if she told him now, he'd want to stay in Wales for a few more days before dealing with the crisis which the news would inevitably precipitate. It would be better for everyone, she thought, if Mark went back to London and faced it there.

'That's a shame,' she said. 'By the way, Trish rang to say Marcel's agent had been on.'

'What! When?' There was a frightened look in Mark's eyes. Beth realised that he was already half expecting a problem.

'Thursday evening, I suppose. She was off for an early weekend. But Ruth came round and I forgot all about it.'

'For God's sake Beth, you should tell me if people ring!'

'Why are you so upset? If he's going to do the deal, he's not going to change his mind just because you haven't rung back within twenty-four hours.'

'No, you're right,' Mark said, trying to sound unconcerned. 'It'll keep till tomorrow; I'm sure it will.'

In the morning, Beth came down at six and drank a mug of coffee while Mark made himself breakfast. Grimond, it seemed, was already out. It had rained during the night, but now it had stopped; the air outside was rich with the scent of damp lichen and heather. Though the sun had not yet appeared over the ridge behind them, the sky glowed over Yr Twmpa, limpid blue with a hint of pale tangerine.

The earthy scents, the smell of coffee and toast, the first sounds of early day – warblers in the sallies by the brook, collared doves crooning in the ash trees – seemed there especially to mark the watershed in Beth's life – so clearly that she was feeling almost nostalgic about the person she'd once been, while she bubbled with suppressed excitement at what she was to become.

As she drove Mark to Hereford to catch the seven o'clock train, she couldn't disguise her animation.

'If I get enough work done this morning,' she said brightly, 'I'm going to see if I can take those kids up the hill for a picnic this afternoon.'

'Which kids?' Mark asked.

'Dai and Abby, of course.'

'It'll be rather damp up there after all the rain last night.'

'I thought we'd walk up through the woods by Glynfach. I love the smell of woodland after rain.'

'I don't suppose it'll be much of a novelty to the kids,' Mark said.

'I'm not so sure. As far as I can tell, their parents never do anything with them, never take them anywhere or give them treats.'

Beyond Gospel Pass

'They're lucky enough to have been born into a rural idyll. What more could they want?'

'Stimulation?'

Mark shook his head with an understanding smile. 'All right, angel, as long as you're not just using them to fulfil your own maternal instincts.'

'Maybe I am,' Beth admitted. 'But I never seem to get the chance to spend time with children. Even when I'm in Cape Cod, Jemma always finds some excuse why I shouldn't take the boys out for a treat.'

'Your brother's kids would be hard to have fun with anyway, they're so over-regulated. Even Mary Poppins would find them a couple of little stuffed shirts.'

Beth was grateful for Mark's obvious desire to protect her from outside pressure to conceive and her own sense of inadequacy, though only up to a point. 'It's okay, sweetie, Jemma's got her own agenda, which I sort of understand. But why shouldn't I take Dai and Abby out, if I'm helping them too?'

At the station, she watched the train out of sight. She felt like a mother sending her son off to boarding school for the first time, knowing that life would never be the same.

She drove back dreamily, past the Abbey, towards the rugged border, lit now by the risen sun, and thought it would be a perfect day for a picnic.

Megan Rhys's eldest son, Michael, and his wife Susie lived with their two children in a small stone house. It had been freshly whitewashed, with the timberwork picked out in pale blue. It was closer to Pant-y-Groes than it was to the Rhys farm at Blaen-Fawr and, apart from Ruth, Michael and Susie were Mark and Beth's nearest neighbours in the valley.

Beth had been to their house a few times to arrange deliveries of milk and eggs but she felt guilty that, until now, she hadn't made any real effort to get to know the family.

She pulled up in the Saab by the farm gate. Michael was outside the cottage, repairing the engine of a small tractor. He stopped and looked up, wiping his oily hands on his overalls. Beth studied him more closely than before. He was, she thought, a coarser version of Owen, older and squatter.

He regarded her warily from beneath brows that met in a thick black line beneath his shallow forehead.

'Morning, missus,' he grunted.

'Hi. I wondered if Abby and Dai were here?'

'They'll be at school.'

'I thought they might like to come up the hill with me later,' Beth suggested nervously, 'and have a picnic?'

'You wants to ask their mother about that.' Michael picked up a grimy spanner and waved it to indicate that he had more important things to do.

Beth nodded with a smile. 'Okay. Is she inside?'

'Aye.' He jerked his head at the door of the cottage.

Beth walked across the stony forecourt and knocked on the broad planks of the door.

Susan opened it. She looked more up-to-date than the family she'd married into. Beth guessed she was still in her twenties; the influences of the world of magazines and television were evident in the way her hair was done and the combat trousers she wore. She was, Beth thought, too pretty to be a farmer's wife in this lonely valley but, unlike Ruth, she looked at least sturdy enough for the job.

When she saw Beth, she glanced nervously at her husband to see if he had a view on whatever was going on, then, reassured, gave a quick smile of welcome.

'Hello, Mrs Powell. Is everything all right with the eggs and that?'

'Oh yes, thanks, Susie. They're lovely eggs; it's one of the things we look forward to most when we come up here.'

Susie looked doubtful at this extravagant claim but invited Beth in with a small gesture.

'The reason I came over was to ask if I could take the children up the hill for a picnic,' Beth said.

'Oh?'

'Well, I thought they might be able to show me around a bit. You know how kids always know about places that grown-ups haven't found,' she smiled. 'Somebody said there was a nice place to bathe up there too.'

'Well, there's the pool up past the Wergin stone.'

Beyond Gospel Pass

'What's the Wergin?'

'It's just a big stone, really, you know, sort of sticking up out of the ground. Owen says it means something, but I forget what.'

Beth had seen the stone marked on Mark's large-scale map of local ley lines and mystical places. She had already identified it as the site of Owen's naked swim.

'Would that be a good place for a picnic?'

Susie looked at her blankly. 'I dunno. I suppose so.'

'Well, would it be all right if the children came?'

Susie's doubts showed only for a moment. 'Yes,' she said. 'Maybe they'd like that.'

'I could pick them up from school.'

'No need for that. The bus comes right up the valley.'

'All right. So shall I call for them here, about four?'

Susie glanced at her husband again, then nodded.

Beth drove the few hundred yards back down the lane, wondering if she'd made a fool of herself by suggesting something so apparently unusual as a walk and a picnic.

Too bad, she thought. Why shouldn't the children be shown another view of the world around them? Why should their upbringing be confined by the blinkered attitudes of the hills, if she was willing to provide another perspective?

She had vivid, warm memories of her parents taking her, at seven or eight, with her younger brother, Edward, up into the Green Mountains of Vermont, above their uncle's summer cottage outside Rutland. In the late spring, amid the sprawling forests of spruce, hemlock, birch and maple that draped the long rocky spine of the New England state, they'd played never-ending games of hide-and-seek. They'd brought their nature books and ran around, marking off raccoon's nests and chipmunk dens, squirrels, deer and toadstools, before settling down on rugs for mouth-watering picnics where their father would tease them, telling them to rattle their tin mugs to scare away the black bears. And then he would ask them to recite their favourite poems, which she always loved to do.

How wonderful it would be, Beth thought, to provide memories like that for these lonely children.

Inside the house, she washed up and tidied the kitchen a little before going into the study to work.

She knew how to make herself focus on a job; she had the ability to clear her mind of everything except the case that currently occupied her. Despite the emotions that had been sizzling continuously inside her, she worked solidly for three hours before she leaned back and pushed the papers away, satisfied that she'd made useful progress.

Looking at her watch, she was struck by a sense of dread at having three hours to fill before Dai and Abby came home.

She stood up, stretched and walked to the kitchen. Through the open door, a broad shaft of sunlight fell across the flagstones and seagrass matting. She now barely registered the faint sounds of the hills, drifting in with the breeze, which had pleased her so much when she and Mark had first visited the valley a year before. The calls of sheep and buzzards, the shrill fluting of what she'd identified as stonechats, and the creaking of overgrown, unsound willows down by the brook now provided a constant soundtrack to her life, and often it was only when they ceased that they impinged on her consciousness.

But she heard Ruth's voice echo across the valley, calling plaintively to one of her llamas, and then, further up the hill, the distant buzz of a chainsaw. She was sure it was Owen; she could imagine him, hot, muscular and competent, handling the unwieldy, lethal tool, and she absolved him of the offensive sound.

She felt hot, too, almost dizzy, and looked down at her hands; they seemed to be shaking just at the thought of him. She breathed in sharply and smoothed her shirt over her breasts; she tried to steady herself and make sense of a woman of her age and intelligence being so totally overwhelmed by the mere thought of a man she'd seen briefly – only four times – and whom she barely knew.

And how could she seriously be hoping for another encounter that afternoon, when the chances of it happening were so slim?

It had to be like that, though. For she knew, despite the flawed reasoning, that she would feel less guilt if the meeting came about by chance, and not by arrangement.

Dai and Abby sidled from their house with no obvious enthusiasm. Beth thought they looked subdued and submissive. Disappointed, she guessed Susie had had to badger them into coming. But like a conjuror, she produced two big ice lollies from behind her back and for the first time approval shone in their eyes.

She wasn't proud of the tactic, but she'd spent hours organising the picnic, including a six-mile trip down to the garage on the main road to buy all the shamefully indulgent sweet things they liked. She was taking no risks. No carrot cake or sour home-made lemonade was going to mar their feast.

'I'll have them back before dark,' she said gaily to Susie who'd appeared in the doorway.

'It's ever so kind of you to take them.' Their mother smiled at the children happily sucking on lollies she hadn't had to pay for. 'Where you going?'

'Up by the Wergin stone, I thought.'

'You might see Owen up there. He's been taking some ewes up the mountain.'

Beth couldn't believe that the woman didn't see the red flush in her face or the sudden agitation in her eyes, but Susie carried on. 'If they swim, they can go in their pants,' she said.

'Okay,' Beth said quickly, to conceal the quaver in her voice.

Beth ignored her eco-conscience as she drove the children a few hundred yards along the road; she was eager to get up the hill. She parked the car by a gateway where a well-defined bridle path, used mainly by the Rhyses' tractors, began a switchback course up the side of the hill.

She took a big rucksack out of the boot and heaved it on to her shoulders. She was wearing a light cotton shirt, loose chinos tucked into her Timberlands and a baseball cap; she felt prepared for anything.

They set off up the hill. The children, delighted by the ice lollies and the promise of more, plodded up easily. Beth envied them as her rucksack became annoyingly heavy, and she began to wonder if they would eat a quarter of the food she'd packed. But she put on a cheerful face, and probed the children about their interests.

She learned that Abby was besotted with all types of animals, except those, like foxes and the raptors roaming the skies above them, that tended to molest her own pet animals.

'The fox has got to eat, though,' Beth said, thinking as she did that a debate about foxes with this seven year old could become impossibly complex.

'Yes, but he takes more'n he needs, like. Uncle Owen says the fox have taken three lambs already.'

'What does Uncle Owen do about that, then?' Beth asked, slightly dreading the answer.

Abby didn't understand the question. Dai answered. 'The hunt never gets much - not up here - but Uncle Owen don't like shootin' 'em; our dad does, though.'

'Why doesn't Owen like shooting them?'

'I dunno,' Dai said with a mystified shrug of his shoulders. 'He just don't like shooting; he's weird like that.'

Beth, walking behind them now, raised an eyebrow but didn't say anything. She was still thinking of what Susie had said, that she might see Owen coming down. She knew it wasn't likely; the hillside was wide, and there must have been half a dozen other routes down. But she clung onto the prospect, with the occasional quaking of her limbs as they climbed towards the next horizon.

'Now, are you hungry?' she asked the children when they reached a band of woodland that draped the dingle halfway up the hillside.

'Yeh,' they nodded.

'All right,' Beth said, a little too brightly – like Mary Poppins, she thought. 'We'll stop and have our picnic here.'

They were in a clearing. Above the tops of the small oaks and hornbeams, the sky was deep blue. The sun slanted through the trees, splashing light across the leafy ground. A small stone barn, with most of its roof intact and covered in ivy, stood at the edge of the glade. Inside it were a few hay bales and a haphazard pile of oak logs.

Beth lowered her rucksack and unpacked a plaid picnic rug which she spread on the ground between two broad tree stumps. Dai perched on one of the stumps and screwed up his dark, tight little face as he waited to see what food Beth had brought. Abby sat prettily on the rug with her legs neatly crossed.

Beth opened two large polythene containers and took out fresh, squashy rolls filled with peanut butter, chocolate spread and thick slabs of cheddar with pickle. There were bags of crisps and

Beyond Gospel Pass

tortilla chips, mini-rolls, jam tarts, little apple pies and, in a cool bag, some toffee ice cream.

She'd brought Coca-Cola, and Irn-Bru for Dai.

'They called it boys' beer in the shop,' she said, pouring some for him.

Dai took his glass gratefully, and for the first time smiled at her. It surprised Beth that the simple provision of food that they really liked should make such a difference to a child's perception of an adult. And yet, she remembered clearly the rush of gratitude she'd felt as a seven year old, being sent by her uncle to the shop in the mountian village with a dollar to spend on any sweets she liked.

Both children were absorbed with eating until they'd finished most of the feast Beth had brought for them. She had joined them with a cheese roll and a bottle of spring water.

For her, it was a sudden glimpse of family life and the apparently effortless enjoyment children could provide. Content and grateful, now able to relate to someone who so obviously appreciated their needs, the children began to answer her questions.

They chattered spontaneously about what they liked doing, and where they dreamed about going. The cinema in Abergavenny, Dai said, and Barry Island Amusement Park, which their school friends had all visited and they hadn't, and the May Fair in Hereford, to which their mother had promised, then failed to take them.

'It's the biggest fair in the world,' Dai said, his eyes big in his thin, pointed face. 'My friend went on Death Wall, and the Rotormator. He said it was wicked.'

'When does that come then?'

'It's gone two weeks ago.'

'Well, there'll be a lot going on in Hay for the next week or two. There's a children's book fair as well, you know.'

'What's a book fair?' Dai asked, liking 'fair', but not sure about 'book'.

'It's about stories and things. I tell you what,' Beth said, seeing that she had their attention and goodwill. 'I've brought a book with me today. I'll read you something from it, if you like?'

She pulled a small volume from the bottom of her rucksack and started to flip through it. 'Have you ever seen one of those big red kites up here?' she asked them.

Dai nodded uncertainly.

Jessica Meredith

'Ruth says she's seen some,' Beth said. 'They live over in the west, past Rhayader, by the dams. They're lovely big birds. Now I haven't got a poem about a kite, but I've got one about an even bigger bird - an eagle, written by a man called Lord Tennyson.'

'Is he like Lord Brecon?' Abby asked. 'He came to see Uncle Owen, Mum said.'

'I don't know Lord Brecon, so I don't know, but I doubt it. Anyway, this poem's very short. Maybe you can learn it by heart.' She settled herself, cleared her throat and started to read. '"*The Eagle*."' She glanced at the children to make sure they were listening. '"*He clasps the crag with hooked hands....*"'

'Eagles don't have hands,' Abby said. 'They got claws.'

'Talons, you mean,' Dai corrected her.

'You could say either,' Beth said laughing. 'Look at my hands now!' She made cat's claws of them. '"Hooked hands" is just Tennyson's way of describing them. Now just listen to this:

"*He clasps the crag with hooked hands;*
Close to the sun in lonely lands,
Ringed with the azure world, he stands.
The wrinkled sea beneath him crawls;
He watches from his mountain walls,
And like a thunderbolt he falls.".'

Beth looked at each of the children in turn. 'Well? Did you like that?'

'Yeh, it was good,' Abby nodded. 'The sea is sort of wrinkled, like.'

'Do you know any other poems?' Beth asked her.

'I know the Stingaling.'

'Who's that by?'

'Roald Dahl. It's about a scorpion.'

'Uncle Owen says poetry sometimes,' Dai said. 'But he's strange.'

'So you've said,' remarked Beth. 'But I didn't know he liked poetry.'

'He's just weird,' Dai muttered.

After tea, they walked on up the hillside. The children knew the way to the Wergin stone and the pool beside it.

Beyond Gospel Pass

The Wergin was an unequivocally phallic shaft of red sandstone. Thinking of all the fanciful theories in Mark's book about its origins, Beth had to admit that it certainly didn't look as if it had occurred naturally. The notion that a Celtic god had dropped it from the sky, or that it was the erect and petrified penis of some long-buried giant who'd fallen asleep after drinking from the pool, was almost more plausible than it being created from the action of glacier, wind and rain over twenty thousand years.

Beth guessed that the pool beside it was filled by a small spring below its surface and topped up by rain. It lay in a small corrie, the legacy of the retreating glacier that had formed the valley itself.

The water in the pool was icy, and clear enough to drink, if it could be believed that no sheep had died or fouled around its margins. The sun was still high and warm; the children were keen to swim. They said they'd swum up here before with Owen. With happy squeals, they pranced across the sheep-grazed turf in their pants and plunged in with a confidence she couldn't imagine in her American nephews.

Beth watched, delighted by the fun they were getting from such a simple thing as a mountain pool. She sat down and tried not to be consumed by the image that kept leaping into her mind of Ruth crouched behind the Wergin stone, peering round at Owen as he sluiced the sweat off his hot naked body. For a second, she had a reckless urge to strip off and plunge into the water herself, but was restrained by the thought that these children weren't hers. Soon they were running around shrieking as they dried off, until Beth felt it was time to gather everything up and go back down to the farm.

For the next two days Beth set aside a few hours each morning to work. She was surprised that she could still think usefully about the complicated and controversial asylum application she was handling.

But every time she stopped and let her mind free, her thoughts focused automatically on Owen.

His name ricocheted around her head in the same way that the name of the first boy she had loved once had. He'd been called Tony. He could hardly have been more different from Owen, Beth thought with a laugh, and how angry she'd been with her father for not appreciating him.

Tony – blond and pretty; fey and dim; good at tennis, bad at kissing; utterly vacuous. She'd met him again in London, a year before, at Wimbledon, as it happened; he had laughed a lot, in a boisterous, American way, at nothing in particular; Beth couldn't help questioning the point of his existence.

Tony; Owen. Fifty per cent of the letters in common; nothing else. Except that, many years apart, both names had filled her head, and heart; arteries and lungs. It seemed hardly possible that now she was the same person she'd been at sixteen, who had aspired to such a different sort of man.

When she finished working, she would get out her paint pots and decorate more of the house, or stroll across the hillside, stopping every few minutes to survey the valley for signs of human presence, fighting an urge to walk up again to the farmstead brooding at the head of the valley.

Five

By Wednesday evening, with only the secretive Grimond for company, Beth felt she needed to get out of Pant-y-Groes. It didn't matter where.

She went outside, opened the door of the Saab and sat in the driver's seat. For a while she considered which direction to take before she drove through the gates and turned north.

When she reached the track that forked up to Blaen Fawr, she slowed, but made herself carry on to the head of the valley and Gospel Pass. She emerged from the narrow gloom of the col into the brightness of the sun still hanging in the north-west above the Radnor Hills, painting the breadth of the Wye Valley a soft gold.

She pondered, as she often had, the strong contrast between the two landscapes - the narrow, challenging place she had just left, where, for the time being, she lived, and the broad, open bountifulness of the meadows and corn-fields spread out below her.

The sun glittering on the Wye led her eye to Hay and its castle, clustered on a small knap above the river.

On the edge of the town, white oblongs of great marquees marked the imminent arrival of the literary circus that would subsume the place for the next fortnight. As the Saab cruised down an unfenced road across the sheep-grazed slopes at the foot of the Bluff, she sighed with happy recognition, like a pony whinnying at the sight of a stable mate, although she had no idea what she wanted to do or whom she would see in Hay.

Beth drove into the big car park on the edge of the town and walked towards the centre, where she thought some of the shops might still be open.

She was looking at the display in the window of an unexpectedly sophisticated shop that sold domestic arts and crafts, when someone spoke behind her.

'Beth?' A strong, contralto voice.

She turned. Boo Llewellyn was looking at her with evident pleasure.

'How lovely to see you. Are you here for anything exciting?'

Beth shook her head. 'Mark's in London; I've been working like hell at Pant-y-Groes for the last few days, and I suddenly felt I had to get out.'

'Perfect!' Boo exclaimed. 'I know exactly what you must do.' She made a face and cautiously lowered her voice. 'I'm on my way to a private view of a one-woman show - a "Welsh" artist. Bulgarian wine and iffy cheese, but there'll be a decent crowd. Come with me; it's the only thing going on here tonight.'

'Thanks,' Beth said. 'I'd love to.'

Boo was not her notion of an ideal companion, but a private view party was just what she felt like.

Boo led her through the old stone pillars of the Buttermarket and down a narrow street towards the clock tower.

'You should have let me know you were on your own up here,' Boo chided. 'There's nearly always a shortage of attractive girls.' Beth wondered if she minded being thought of as an attractive girl. 'And even fewer who are intelligent as well,' Boo redeemed herself. 'Mind you, there'll be hundreds of smart-arse publishing women milling around for the next ten days, and all the literary groupies.' She lowered her voice again. 'I should think more sex goes on at the Hay Festival than at the average rock festival.'

'I'd never noticed that publishing was a particularly sexy business,' Beth observed.

'And you married to a publisher!' Boo exclaimed.

By the clock tower they passed a large gathering of walkers and book-fanciers sitting at tables outside an organic cafe, and carried on down the hill until they reached a large, ecclesiastical building. Above the door was a sign: 'Marches Gallery'. In the only visible window, a single, small abstract canvas had been hung, slightly off-centre. Boo ushered Beth through the open door into a large, airy space.

More pictures like the one in the window were hanging on the walls. Beth thought the people inside - middle-aged, middle-class - must have been much the same as those at any provincial gallery party. A few of them were gazing intently and uncomprehendingly at the pictures, while the place echoed fiercely with loud talk and laughter.

Boo took Beth's arm and led her across the room.

'What did I tell you?' she said with a laugh. 'You'd have to be bloody morbid to want any of these daubs.' She nodded greetings at several people as she passed. 'I'd better introduce you to the artist first, then you'll understand the paintings.' They had reached a larger knot of people. Boo raised her voice. 'Eleanor, what a marvellous turn-out!'

The group around the artist opened up for Boo. Beth looked at Eleanor; she was in her mid-forties. She looked as if she'd led a life filled with trauma. She was wearing a voluminous dress made from ethnic Indian embroidered cotton and stone earrings. Her long, straight, grey-brown hair framed a face that looked as if it had been shaped by chronic pessimism.

'Oh, Boo. I'm really glad you could come.' Eleanor's quiet, earnest voice was slightly nasal, like Ruth's.

'I've brought a friend, too,' Boo said. 'I hope you don't mind.' She beckoned at Beth. 'This is Beth Powell. Her husband's hoping to stand for the Liberals here next time.'

The other people in the crowd seemed to have heard and focused on her while Boo asked Eleanor, 'Many red spots up yet?'

Beth didn't hear the artist's reply as she tried to answer the questions of a thin, serious man, about the same age as Mark, who wanted to know about his stance on rural education.

Someone touched her bottom and gave it a light squeeze. She turned to register feminist outrage, and found herself facing Charles Winter, the novelist she and Mark had met at the Llewellyn's at the weekend.

He was grinning slyly at her through opaque grey eyes, daring her to make a fuss; placing himself, it seemed, as a creative writer, in some special category exempt from accusations of minor sexual assault.

'Hello, Charles,' she said, trying to hide her distaste. 'Catching up on the local culture?' she asked, and wished she'd thought of a smarter opening.

Beth had the impression that Charles Winter was one of those men who liked to challenge anyone he met, without provocation, in order to establish whether or not they were worth talking to. Beth knew that in her case at least, it produced the opposite result. She wished she had the strength of mind to tell him to get stuffed.

'Even the water of a fouled oasis will quench a man's thirst in the desert,' he said.

'A woman's too?' Beth challenged.

'I dare say; I have no direct experience.'

'Have you never written from a woman's perspective, though?'

The author shook his handsome head with an indulgent smile. 'Writers should know their limitations,' he said. 'And being male is one of mine,' he smirked.

Beth thought of Boo's observation on sexual activity in the literary world and thought that this vain man looked a likely participant. She felt sorry for his wife; sorry, too, for his lovers. She reflected, though, that there was a time when she'd have found his particular brand of clever arrogance irritatingly attractive.

'It certainly is,' she said lightly, and turned away.

Later, she was wandering through the crowd with an empty wine glass when she met up with Boo again.

'Had enough?' Boo asked.

'I think I ought to be getting back,' Beth didn't really want to go anywhere else, but Charles Winter had made eye contact with her again, more than once; he was undoubtedly working up to a pounce.

'Fine. Let's go then.' Boo took a couple of steps towards her artist friend. 'Bye, Eleanor. I'll come and pick up my picture when the show's over, shall I?'

Eleanor nodded vigorously and looked pleased. 'Yes, do.'

Boo and Beth made their way to the door through the still noisy crowd. 'At least I've made someone happy today,' Boo said. 'Poor Eleanor, she's one of those people who always has a disaster of some sort on the go; I had to buy one of her dreary daubs. God knows where I'll put it. I suppose I could give it to someone as a wedding present; or do you think that would be rather unkind?' Outside, she said, 'Let's have a quick drink in Dino's.'

Both a little drunk by now, they ordered a bottle of Chardonnay in the crowded wine bar.

'My treat,' Beth said, 'and thanks for rescuing me from our distinguished local author.'

Beyond Gospel Pass

'Ah yes, but I must say, I always look forward to the Lit Fest,' Boo said. 'Though I'd hate it if it went on for longer than it does.'

'We only came to a couple of things last year,' Beth said, 'But we thought we'd see as much as possible this time. Mark has an author appearing, and Ruth's having Laura Chichester to stay when she comes to give her talk, so we'll have to come and see her.'

'Good heavens! Does Ruth know that tart?'

'Do you mean Laura Chichester?' Beth asked, surprised by Boo's enmity.

'Yes, I do. Laura Chichester screwed her way on to television.'

'How do you know that?' Beth asked.

'Hugh, my brother, was her first producer, and as soon as she'd got the first series out of the way, and wrecked poor Hugh's marriage, she dumped him.'

'She gives the impression of being rather prim and correct.'

'I'm amazed at a sophisticated Londoner like you being taken in. As a general rule, the most unpopular English public figures are the most charming in private - like Ken Livingtsone, and Tony Benn - and the most popular are the trickiest, like Laura Chichester.' Boo took a large swig of her wine. 'Do you always tread the straight and narrow?'

Beth took the unexpected question straight between the eyes, and blinked. Her first instinct was to shake her head vigorously, and yet, she'd always felt there was no point in discussing anything if she wasn't prepared to do it truthfully. 'Not exactly.'

Boo cocked her mass of blonde hair to one side and looked quizzical. 'That's a bit of a non-answer.'

'Boo, it's true,' Beth said, 'and it's the only one you're going to get tonight,' she added with a laugh.

In the morning an early sun was soon obscured by rain that drizzled steadily from a sky the colour and texture of cold porridge, and the top edges of the valley became barely visible.

Cradling her cat, Beth looked out of her kitchen window, and thought of all the planning and arrangements that were going on down in Hay, and how the rain could be devastating for the Literary Festival. These thoughts were enough to induce a mild depression, not lifted by the vacuous prattle of a presenter on Classic FM.

She made strong coffee and a slice of toast before settling down to enter some notes on her lap-top and e-mail a couple of queries. But today she couldn't make herself concentrate. She found to her horror that she simply didn't care if her clients – apparently honest, deserving and persecuted Slovak gypsies - were kicked out of England tomorrow. The grey, soggy lid over the valley was too oppressive; she knew, weakly, that she had to flee again.

She felt disloyal as she left the protection of the valley and sped over the pass, to be met this time by a panorama as dank, grey and dispiriting as the golden glow of the previous evening had been uplifting.

She didn't know why she was driving to Hay. She had no need to go, no one in particular to see, and wasn't in the mood to browse through bookshops or market stalls. But she had to go somewhere.

Angry at her own lack of purpose, she stopped below the Bluff, turned the engine off and wound her window down. She took a few deep breaths of the damp, gusting air and tried to talk herself into going back to Pant-y-Groes, to get on with her work. But the valley would only depress her with claustrophobia. It could even frighten her; certainly it would force her to confront herself in a way she didn't want.

She let off the handbrake and the car began to roll down the gentle slope while she started the engine. The road switch-backed down to the town and she felt like a discarded autumn leaf floating down to the river.

In Hay, the rain had stopped and a pale sun showed through a thin gauze of high cloud. Beth walked through the town and allowed herself to be carried along, until the smells of spices and fresh coffee beans caught her attention. She found she was outside the whole-food shop.

With no specific object, she went in and wandered around, looking at labels, picking up packets and sniffing them; reaching up to higher shelves for more obscure spices. But she couldn't generate any enthusiasm for shopping and after a few minutes, she turned to leave.

With a shock, she saw his back, knowing it was him at once, just as she had when he stood up after drinking from the spring. But – she didn't know why – this shop was one of the last places she would have expected to see him.

She was aware of her cheeks twitching nervously as she approached him and composed herself to speak. 'Hello, Owen,' she said quietly, so that only he could hear.

Beyond Gospel Pass

He turned unhurriedly. His eyes locked on to hers and, for a moment, she felt paralysed, unable to back away if she'd wanted. She could only stare at his uncompromising, unshaven features.

'Hello.' He spoke with the faint suggestion of a smile on his lips. Without any sign of awkwardness, he offered nothing more.

'What brings you in here, then?' Beth tried to ask brightly.

'Yeast.' He held up the bag he was holding.

Beth was perplexed. She'd known for a long time that she was a good reader of body language and facial subtext; it was useful in a barrister. But she could make nothing of Owen's reaction to her. There was nothing hostile about him, but no invitation either.

She realised that she was seeing him as an alien, an obscure inhabitant of a parallel world beyond Gospel Pass, to which she didn't belong. With a jolt, she saw clearly that communication between them was just not possible; their cultures were too diverse, their terms of reference too disparate.

Then she remembered her conversation with the children by the spring, when Dai had said Owen was weird, because he sometimes recited poems.

She took a deep breath as if she were about to dive from a high board into a pool of unknown temperature and depth.

'Have you got time for a coffee - a drink or something like that?' The words gushed out. 'There was something I wanted to ask you - I need your advice about.'

'What's that?'

She couldn't make herself say she wanted to talk about poetry, or she wanted to be near him, to smell him, to feel his stubbly cheek on hers. 'We need a new bore hole.' Why had she said "we"? 'I wanted to ask you about dowsing - you know - to find the water?'

He didn't answer for a moment, but his eyes didn't leave hers. 'Okay,' he nodded.

The organic cafe was warm. It smelled of coffee and coq au vin. The big main room was furnished with naive chintzes, small, dark bentwood chairs and pitch-pine pews from a redundant church. Shapeless slabs of oat and honey cake, wheatgerm crisp and wholemeal scones were displayed unpretentiously on glass shelves.

The place was already bustling with an eclectic mix of local Welsh, incomers from the book trade, outdoor tourists and visitors who'd arrived for the Literary Festival, which opened at the weekend.

Owen wanted just a mug of tea; Beth had a coffee.

They found a table in a corner. She took off her damp waxed coat and sat down opposite him. She shook a few drops of rain from her auburn hair and smiled. 'I hope you don't mind my dragging you in here?'

'No. I sometimes come here when I'm in town. I sell them a lamb now and again.'

Beth nodded at his bag. 'What do you need the yeast for?'

'That's for my mam. She makes elderflower wine.'

'How lovely. Is it good?'

'Not too bad.'

'Are you into all that sort of thing, too?'

Owen nodded. 'Oh, yes. All the country pursuits.' He gave a quick, sardonic smile. 'The ones worth doing, anyway.'

It was strange, Beth thought, he must have been ten years younger than her, yet he seemed much wiser and self-contained.

'Hunting, shooting and fishing?' she asked, and immediately thought how stupid that sounded.

'No,' he said with a faint laugh. 'Of course I have to shoot things now and again; I don't like to do it, but a fox might be taking the lambs and if I waited for the hunt to come....' he raised an eyebrow.

Beth was fascinated by his speech. There was no mistaking the Welsh cadence to what was otherwise a soft west-country burr. But his use of words and his construction made sense of his reported interest in poetry.

'I might take a trout from the brook sometimes,' he went on. 'It's one of the best things - to cast a small fly across the lower pools on a summer's evening.'

'I love just walking,' Beth said. 'I find it helps me think. It's something to do with generating endorphins and releasing them into the bloodstream and the brain.'

'And the rhythm,' Owen nodded with a quick grin. 'You know, there was a man - a composer - used to walk all across the Malvern Hills to write his music.' Owen nodded over his shoulder to the east. 'They say he wrote it at his own walking pace, seventy-two beats a minute.'

Beyond Gospel Pass

'Elgar, you mean? You're right!' Beth gushed excitedly. 'And that same rhythm seems to evoke ideas and stimulate the imagination. I find it a great way to work through a problem.'

'Do you have many problems to work through?' His eyes focused on hers, and didn't move.

Beth was conscious that this was the first direct question he'd asked about her. 'My work is totally about problems – legal conflict, dissent, disagreement, opposing views of justice. And the problems of presenting difficult but nonetheless valid view-points to courts and tribunals. So, yes, you might say I've a lot of problems to work through.'

'I heard you were a lawyer.' He lifted his arm and swept a hand through the strands of hair that had fallen over his forehead – perhaps, Beth thought, to distract her from the admission that he'd talked about her to other people.

'What else had you heard?' she asked, leaning forward eagerly with a mischievous grin.

Owen sat back slowly and settled himself on the pew. 'I don't take much notice of second-hand information; usually gets twisted in the telling. I'm only concerned with what I see and hear for myself.'

'I bet Ruth told you all about us – ' she faltered at "us" '– when we arrived here.'

'She told me a bit. She likes to talk.'

'You can't blame her - up in that valley, all by herself.'

Owen very faintly lifted a shoulder. 'It's her choice.'

'You and she must be good friends,' Beth said tightly.

'She relies on me, I suppose. I wouldn't like to let her down.'

'Why's that?'

There was faint reproach in Owen's eyes. 'She's a neighbour.'

'Of course,' Beth conceded meekly. 'She's been a very good neighbour to us - helped us a lot when we first arrived. As a matter of fact, she suggested that you might be able to help us with our water.'

'You said.' Owen gave another faint smile. 'I could have a look for you.'

'That would be great. Though we've got the spring, we were told that it dries up in summer. Last year just after we'd bought the house, it was barely a trickle, and that was in quite a wet summer; we're just waiting for it to peter out.'

'That spring always dries in the summer. Old Tom Gwillam used to bring a pipe in from another one along the hill, but he wouldn't have used half so much as you'll want, with baths and dishwashers and all.'

Beth drew herself back. 'We're not that wasteful...' she protested.

'It's all right,' Owen raised a mollifying hand. 'I didn't say there was any reason why you shouldn't want to be clean. Any road, Tom was a smelly old bugger.'

Beth felt foolish for having tried to defend herself. 'Oh, well,' she said, dismissing the topic. 'How exactly do you find water?'

'I use my ring – as a pendulum.' He pulled from his pocket the ring and chain she'd seen when they'd met up on the hill the Sunday before.

'But what does it do?'

Beth watched Owen's beautiful mouth twitch into a momentary smile. 'It isn't the pendulum or hazel fork or anything else you might use – they only show up your own response, so you can see for certain when you're onto something.'

'Something?'

He shrugged a shoulder. 'Water, most likely; sometimes minerals.'

'But what on earth makes your hands do that?'

'They say it's a change in the magnetic field.'

'But... why can't more people do it?'

'I don't know.'

Beth had slowly leaned forward again as they talked. 'Dai told me that you could cure people with your hands, too.' She looked at them resting on the table in front of her.

Owen shook his head. 'Just sometimes, certain kinds of injury.'

'Do you use your ring for that too?'

'I can usually find where the trouble is with it,' Owen nodded.

'Then how do you cure it?'

'People have told me different reasons.' He didn't seem keen to talk about it. 'All I know is if I lay my hand a few inches above the damage for a while every few days, it helps it to mend.'

'But do you have no idea how that happens?'

Beyond Gospel Pass

'I've got a sort of idea, but it's not important.' He stood up abruptly.

Beth looked at him in sudden panic. Had she said something to offend him? Had she asked too much?

'I have to go,' he was saying, mildly enough. 'Thanks for the drink.'

'Oh, that's okay – but will you come and look for the water?'

'Yes, I'll come.'

Beth wanted to press him – when would he come? Would it be soon?

Tomorrow – before Mark got back?

But she'd already overexposed herself. 'Great!' she said, thinking she sounded like a Radio One DJ. 'That would be a real help,' she went on more soberly, standing to say goodbye.

He nodded without speaking again and turned to weave his way between the crowded tables.

Outside, the weather hadn't improved. Ragged wet clouds were still stretched across the sky and an uncomfortable wind funnelled down the narrow streets.

Beth knew that she must take firm, two-handed control of events in her life. She had to get this crazy fantasising about Owen into perspective.

For a start, she had to accept that a Welsh hill farmer in his late twenties wasn't going to be interested in a thirty-nine year old London barrister.

Okay - she thought - she wasn't in bad shape for her age; she was entirely confident that for a broad category of men she was still a desirable woman.

But Owen wasn't in that category; and on other levels - culturally, socially in the broadest sense - there could be very little common ground.

Yes – Beth answered herself wearily – he liked poetry, and had a few half-formed ideas about Elgar's composition habits. But that didn't necessarily mean much.

Besides, what on earth did she understand about the land where he lived, on which she and Mark perched from time to time when it suited them, like a couple of butterflies? Or the mysterious energies in the earth, which Owen could unlock with his ring and chain?

This gift in itself was a clear manifestation that his relationship with nature was entirely different from her own; she just about understood the structure of the seasons and the cycle of the moon, but knew very little of the Earth's other rhythms and resonances.

She also acknowledged, with some shame, that one of the most marked differences between him and other people she knew and respected lay in the obvious absence of any need to impress or to impose his personality on her or, as far as she knew, on anyone else.

She barely noticed the growing crowd of excited bibliophiles who were filling the streets of the small grey town as she hurried up below the castle to her car and drove out of Hay on the narrow lane that led to Gospel Pass.

Over the next twenty-four hours, Beth worked at her computer. When she stopped to eat or to have a bath, she tried to keep Owen out of her mind by playing the radio loudly enough to keep her distracted.

The night time, though, wasn't so easy.

She'd been planning to stay at Pant-y-Groes for another week; in the morning she made up her mind that she would go back to London with Mark after the weekend.

The claustrophobia of the steep-sided valley was getting to her, narrowing her world along with it and skewing her judgement. She thought a week away from it in London would quickly adjust her focus.

When Mark phoned after breakfast, she was surprised how relieved she was.

'Hi, angel,' he greeted her effusively. He always refused to believe she disliked the endearment. 'I'll be at Hereford at three. Can you pick me up from the station? We're due in Hay at four-thirty for our grilling, so we can talk about it on the way over.'

'I'll certainly pick you up, but what do we have to talk about?'

'Oh, you know - it's important the way you come across. I've been thinking about it and I'm sure you can sway a couple of the waverers.'

Beyond Gospel Pass

'I'm not so sure, but anyway, I'll see you at three. By the way, how did it go with Marcel's agent?'

She just heard the faint hesitation before he replied. 'Oh, fine. He's pushing for a bit more dough, of course. He tried to tell me he was going to go to Jonathan Mundy, but I managed to speak to Marcel directly, and now they're reconsidering our offer. Actually, I've asked him to come and stay up at Pantihose. I know he'd enjoy that, and I think I could clinch it then.'

Beth sighed to herself. Mark's ability to sell his own optimism was probably his most dangerous talent. 'Great,' she said flatly. 'Let's hope that does it.'

He heard her doubt. 'I'm sure it will. Anyway, Marcel's not the only bloody gene guru on the beach. So, I'll see you later.'

He rang off. Beth put the phone down slowly.

So many words – she thought – so much language.

She'd learned from Mark long ago that the strength of a statement was frequently in inverse proportion to the number of words used to make it. Now she found herself thinking of the spare, unembellished conversations she'd had with Owen.

She turned back to her work and spent an hour on the phone talking to her instructing solicitor on the asylum case. When she'd finished, she felt unexpectedly boosted by the reflection that although she might be an ignorant ingenue within the shadows of this primitive valley, in her own wider world she was a woman to be reckoned with.

As she worked, the wind dropped and the sun warmed the slopes like an open hearth. At midday, she made herself a salad and took it out to the table in the yard to sit in the shade of a big green parasol. The sun here was as hot as spring in Provence, and the crickets were performing a pianissimo version of the sounds of the maquis, which she and Mark had listened to only a few months before. When she had eaten, she leaned back in her deck chair and started to doze.

'Beth?' A woman's voice.

She jerked her eyes open and saw Ruth walking across the yard with her particular small steps.

'Hi. Have some wine,' Beth offered.

'Yes, please, that'd be lovely.' Ruth sat down at the table.

Beth went into the house to collect another glass and came back to sit opposite Ruth. She looked at her appraisingly.

Ruth was looking more attractive than normal, Beth thought, though at first she couldn't identify why, until she realised that her hair had been cut and slightly styled.

'Hey, Ruth, I never thought you'd succumb to the tyranny of the beauty business!' she teased.

'Why not? I always wear make-up and things.'

'But somehow, the stuff you usually use isn't part of the industry, is it?'

'No, I suppose not, but I saw Paul Ricardo in Hay yesterday and he said why didn't I have my hair done for the crowds of people who are coming to my talk. He said the more they liked looking at me, the more they'd listen.'

'I'm glad he's got his academic priorities right,' Beth laughed. 'I suppose that's why he's booked your friend Laura.'

'Don't you think Laura's work has value, simply as a writer?'

'I'm not sure, especially since you told me how much she embroiders her stories. Though I suppose you could say that was more creative than just telling the truth. But I don't think I like the way she writes, really.' Seeing Ruth hurt by criticism of her celebrated friend, Beth corrected herself. 'Well, that can't be strictly true; I've read three of her books, and enjoyed them all.'

They talked for a while about Laura Chichester. Beth was by now quite looking forward to meeting this infamous creation of television and self-promotion.

When she spoke again, Ruth caught Beth unprepared. 'Owen says he'll be coming tomorrow afternoon to see about your water.'

Beth gulped inwardly. She hoped Ruth hadn't seen her reaction.

Hell - she thought - *Mark would be here!* She tried to crush the thought at once, to erase it from her mind. She had absolutely resolved that she was not going to let any wild dreams take control of her life.

'Oh, great! I saw him in Hay, funnily enough. We had a drink, and I asked him then.'

Ruth nodded. Beth strained, despite herself, to spot any subtext in her body language.

'Yes,' Ruth said. 'He told me last night. He dropped in to see if all the ewes were okay.'

'Is that all?' said Beth, regretting the words before they were out of her mouth.

Ruth sighed. 'Why are you so certain Owen and I are having a scene? And anyway, why on earth shouldn't we? I thought you agreed, he's a bloody good-looking man.'

'Sorry, Ruth and of course you're right – he's an attractive man; perhaps I'm rather jealous.' She laughed a little too loudly.

'You, jealous? ' Ruth grinned in disbelief. 'With so much talent and a really sexy husband of your own?'

'D'you think Mark's sexy?' Beth asked, genuinely intrigued.

'Of course. He takes the trouble to really engage when he's talking to someone.'

'Oh, that,' Beth nodded. 'It's one of his little tricks. Someone told him years ago what an attractive trait it was in a man. Apparently, you don't have to listen to any of the dreary stuff people are saying to you as long as you look them straight in the eye and nod now and again.'

Ruth laughed. 'That's just the sort of nice, self-effacing thing he would say about himself, isn't it?'

Beth realised that Ruth had missed the point, but she laughed too. 'Talking of Mark,' she said, looking at her watch, 'I've got to go and pick him up from Hereford station at three. I'd better get these things in and go.'

'I've spoken to Henry.' Mark said.

He was driving. They were ten minutes out of Hereford, heading west between blossoming orchards on a straight, uncluttered road. On their right, a handsome stone mansion was set in its park on the slopes of a wooded knap. In the misty distance, the Black Mountains and the steep Bluff seemed to beckon them away from the soft, easy country of the river plain.

'He says some of the committee are grumbling about having to see me tonight,' Mark went on. 'It's the first night of the Festival, so Geraint God-help-us Pugh made himself available for them yesterday. I'd have come up too if they'd asked me, sod it!' Mark thumped the wheel with his hand. 'I can't believe the tricks people get up to.'

'Come on, Marco. Don't be naive; this is politics. Anyway, it can't be too critical. If they want you and you're obviously so much better than Pugh, they can't really hold it against you that you didn't change your date with them, especially if they didn't even ask.'

'No, but you know what some people are like; they don't make decisions based on obvious logic. Sentimentality or whatever they had for lunch are probably more important.'

'In the end, it'll be a question of whether or not they think you stand a better chance of winning. It's meant to be a very winnable seat, after all.'

'Oh, it's winnable all right. It's been Liberal for twenty-seven of the last fifty years.' With conscious display, he took a deep breath; he was 'adjusting his attitude', as he called it - something he'd learned to do on some extravagant American leadership course he'd been on a few years before.

Beth was inclined to admire him for his ability to bulldoze negative thoughts from his head when they were getting in the way. She guessed that the crisis at Archimedes had deepened. If the truth was that Marcel Gehring had been irrevocably lost to them – which wouldn't surprise her– she wasn't going to upset Mark by raising the subject, especially now he had adjusted his attitude so resolutely.

The selection committee of the East Brecknock Liberals met in a distinguished eighteenth-century stone building in one of the quieter streets of the town. It looked like a large private house, apart from a couple of discreet lawyers' name-plates beside the entrance.

The meeting was being held in a room on the first floor. Mark pushed open the front door and, as was his habit, stood aside for Beth to go up the stairs first. She walked into the room in front of him, in the high heeled shoes and trim, olive-green suit she'd chosen for the meeting.

It was, she thought, a handsome enough chamber, and not at all 'Liberal'. Oak panelled and furnished with what looked like good Georgian mahogany, it could not have changed much since it had been built by a prosperous corn merchant two hundred years before.

The eight members of the committee and the chairman were loosely gathered around three sides of a large, twin-pedestal table. They all looked up when Beth walked in.

Beyond Gospel Pass

Mark was in a buoyant, though almost submissive mood for the rest of the evening.

'You did brilliantly,' he conceded as they drove up the winding wooded lane towards the brown-green bluff. 'They fell for you hook, line and sinker.'

'Even Maggie Watkins?' Beth laughed.

'She thoroughly approved of your more feminist opinions. And a couple of the men - that awful old farmer - were absolutely drooling. Perhaps you should be putting yourself forward instead of me,' Mark admitted with rare humility.

'No thanks – not my scene,' Beth said. 'I don't think I could sustain the dishonesty.'

Mark glanced at her. 'What do you mean? What did you say at that meeting that was dishonest?'

'For a start, while I suppose I have a kind of general regard for the well-being of all my fellow members of the human race, I can't truthfully say I care deeply about every individual constituent of East Brecknock.'

'I will, if I'm elected,' Mark said emphatically.

'Funnily enough, I believe you will, but anyway, I have no plans to put myself forward, so you won't suffer any indignity on my account.'

Mark grinned. 'But you were amazing. Do you know, I'd forgotten just how good you are in court. Thanks.' He reached out his left hand and put it on her thigh. Tentatively, he squeezed as he slid his hand up her leg, rucking up her green linen skirt. 'God, I missed you this week.'

'Did the Gehring business really get you down, then?' she asked, a little to divert his attention.

'It was a bit touch and go,' he admitted cautiously, offering a little truth. 'But I sorted it out.'

'Really?' Beth pressed.

'Yeah.' Mark looked away, and fixed his eyes on the road snaking across the hillside beneath the ridge that loomed above them. 'Pretty much.'

She knew Mark wanted to make love to her that night. She couldn't plead her period again, and she let him, though, afterwards, she couldn't dispel a sense of guilt over her deception.

Six

Beth opened her eyes. Her radio clock told her it was just after seven. She watched Mark sleeping. He looked, she thought, surprisingly content, considering the pressure he must have been under. But his lovemaking had been unexpectedly protracted the night before and she guessed he felt quite pleased with himself; she was sure he hadn't noticed anything unusual in her.

She slipped out of bed without waking him, dressed and went downstairs. She fed Grimond, but didn't feel like eating any breakfast herself. In her stomach, a rumbling nausea made even the thought of coffee repellent. She unlocked the door and walked out into the yard, to drink straight from the spring.

But the scant rainfall of the last few weeks had reduced it to a slither on the shiny rock wall. There wasn't even enough flow to catch a cupped handful – just as Owen had warned. She hoped the spring-fed holding tank, buried in the ground above the house would hold out until they could pipe in water from elsewhere. At least, she thought, they really did need Owen now to find a new source of water.

The sun was already up over the ridge behind the house. Beth decided to walk up and see how much water there was in the higher spring.

Carrying a plastic flagon, she set off up the hill, through the bracken-clad open land beyond their field, and up beside the gully.

When she reached the small oak spinney, she found the spring still welling up and babbling into the pool, though noticeably slower than it had been a week before. She scooped up several long drafts; the water tasted like champagne after the warm climb up from the house.

When her thirst was well quenched and she had filled her flagon, she walked to the front of the copse and lowered herself onto the mound of soft grazed turf where Owen had lain when they talked.

Beyond Gospel Pass

She tried to clear her head of all the images and doubts, guilt and excitement that the place evoked. She leaned forward and for a few minutes pushed her face into V-cupped hands, as she had when she was a small girl praying in church and, also like then, she found her mind wandering inevitably into taboo corners of her mind where dangerous thoughts lurked.

But slowly the bracken and soft heather smells, the chatter of the wheatears, the melancholy calls of the buzzards brought her head up until she was gazing through misty eyes across the valley. Opposite lay Ruth's untidy collection of small stone buildings beside their tall ash sentinels; a few hundred yards to the right, the sun splashed down on the white front of Michael Rhys's house.

Inexorably, her eyes travelled on until they rested a mile away on the stand of trees that hid the mossy stone face of Blaen Fawr. She shivered in the warm air, and knew, however hard she tried to deny it, that she longed to see Owen again.

Later, with dwindling resolve and a growing sense of guilt, she tried to listen to Mark as they drove out of the valley and over the pass. It was no help to remind herself that she hadn't done anything wrong yet because she knew, beyond any doubt, that she would do it as soon as the occasion was offered.

When she asked herself how she could be so sure that Owen would reciprocate, she brushed the doubt aside, but her preoccupation made it hard to pay much attention to her husband. She wondered why she had agreed to go shopping with him on a Saturday morning. Perhaps she just couldn't trust herself alone at Pant-y-Groes.

Mark was talking ebulliently about the strategy he planned to use with each member of the selection committee, relying, Beth gathered, on the strength of his personal gifts.

'You haven't arranged to meet any of the committee this morning, though, have you?' Beth asked flatly.

'No, I told you – I want to look at lawnmowers and timber shuttering for my raised beds.'

Beth had a sketchy recollection of Mark telling her the night before about some medieval technique he'd read about for producing vegetables, by sowing them so densely that no weeds would grow. She tentatively suggested that he'd never have time even for this trouble-free horticulture if he expected to be elected.

'And wouldn't it be easier just to get someone in to mow the lawn?' she added.

Mark turned to her with a indulgent grin. 'Who?'

'I don't know - Ruth maybe?'

'You're joking!' Mark chortled. 'She's got more to do than she can manage anyway.'

'Or Michael Rhys?'

'No, there's something about him I don't really trust.'

'Mark, you'll have the CRE after you! Just because he's a bit Welsh and shy...'

'Well, you must admit he looks like one of Owain Glyndower's more eager rape-and-pillagers.'

'I'm sure he's just a normal, hard-working hill farmer – like thousands of the people you're so eager to represent.'

'Anyway, he'd be far too busy as well, and I shouldn't think he's even got a mower. He certainly hasn't got any lawn.'

Mark turned into the main road that ran through the middle of Hay. When they reached it, the big car park on the edge of the town was already full.

'Oh shit!' Mark groaned. 'Why's there never anywhere to park in this fucking place?'

'Easy, Marco.' His wife drew her head back with a warning grin. 'That's no way to talk about the hub of your new political career.'

'No, all right,' he conceded, 'but this bloody festival screws the whole town up.'

'Only for ten days, and it puts a few million quid into the local economy. I expect most of your future constituents think it's worth the aggravation.'

'Okay, okay!' Mark shook his head, exasperated as he drove around the few acres of tarmac twice more before finding a space.

Beth laughed and shrugged off the inconvenience, although she refused to look at lawn-mowers. She wanted to buy some bedding plants to brighten their bare and tidy garden, so she arranged to meet Mark later in a small timber yard at the bottom of the town, between the river and the remains of the old railway track.

The timber merchant's was run by a small, weasel-faced man who introduced himself as Ishy Price. He gave Beth an odd look of recognition as she walked into the yard with Mark, but he didn't refer to it, and she couldn't recall seeing him anywhere before.

Mark missed it, and adopting his most genial manner, explained in great detail what he needed.

Beth noticed Ishy Price's lack of interest in raised vegetable beds as he scribbled details of what was wanted on a scrap of paper. It was only when Mark gave him their address for delivery that the little man's eyes sparked up and he looked again at Beth. 'You live up by Owen Rhys, do you?' he asked.

Beth nodded, not trusting her voice.

'That's where I seen you,' Ishy Price went on, glad to confirm he hadn't been wrong. 'Outside the cafe with him, Thursday morning.'

Beth felt her throat go dry. She couldn't look at Mark.

'Oh?' said Mark, mildly, without a trace of cynicism. 'You didn't tell me you'd seen Owen in town.'

'Oh, yes, I did,' Beth said quickly, as if she'd just remembered, still focusing blindly on Ishy Price's knowing face. 'We had a cup of coffee; I meant to tell you,' she added in a rush. 'I asked him if he'd come round soon to see about the water, now that our spring's nearly dry.'

'Oh, good,' Mark said. 'Anyway,' he returned his attention to Ishy. 'Does that mean you know where to find us?'

'Yes, it do. I'll drop the timber off there one day next week.'

'Before the weekend?'

'I should think so.'

'Fine. I'll pay you when you deliver.'

Watching Owen jump down from his battered green Daihatsu in the still warmth that filled the valley, Beth could hardly believe that he had really arrived – had come here to Pant-y-Groes at last – because he'd chosen to.

By the time she and Mark had come back from Hay after lunch at Dino's, the post had arrived with a pile of background documents relating to a new case she'd taken on. She had tried to work on them, but had soon given up and admitted she would have to go back to London the following week and get to grips with it.

Now she was in one of the small upper bedrooms, where she'd been painting the walls and windows, wearing shorts and a loose T-shirt. Radio 4 chattered in the background, helping to fill the long, hot afternoon.

It was after five, but the sun was still strong and seemed to spotlight Owen as he walked from the shade of the lane where he'd left his truck. He opened the gate and walked into the yard with the long, lazy stride Beth had already admired.

She held her breath and clenched her fists lightly. She waited for Mark to go out and greet him first.

Owen passed out of her sight and she heard him tap on the door - a moment later, the sound of the door being opened, and Mark's voice.

'Oh, hi,' he said affably. 'My wife said you might be up today. Kind of you to come in this heat.'

'No problem,' Owen replied softly. 'I won't be able to do anything today. I was passing so I came to find what it was you wanted.'

'Oh, fine.'

Beth heard the disappointment in Mark's voice. Despite the doubts he'd already expressed, she knew he'd been looking forward to watching Owen's dowsing technique. She'd noticed that he'd brought back some books about the art from London and had now placed it firmly in the same category as ley lines and the other earth mysteries dealt with in the new book he was publishing. 'Come on in, then,' Mark was saying. 'I've got all the maps here.'

Beth doubted that Owen would need maps.

She managed to wait a few minutes more before she went downstairs, knowing that Mark would take some time to explain his view of their water needs and the potential problems in finding it.

They were in the study. She walked in quietly, barefoot.

Owen glanced up from the map, which Mark was still studying. His hair was dishevelled, slightly wavy from earlier exertions and lightly coated with coarse sawdust, which also lingered in the creases of his jeans.

He pushed away a curl of hair from his brown forehead and looked at her. In an instant, something invisible but infrangible had joined their eyes. She tried not to redden or betray the sudden frailty in her joints and leaned back against the door frame. 'Hello, Owen,' she said.

Beyond Gospel Pass

He nodded. 'Your husband's been telling me where he thinks I'll find water.'

She was sure this time that she saw a faint smile. She silently applauded the complete lack of irony in his voice.

'Oh, good,' she said. 'He's been reading up on the subject; did he tell you?'

Now Owen really did smile.

Mark looked up, not seeing it. 'I'm not claiming any expertise, of course, but it seemed to make sense to look at the geological analyses of the area, too.'

'So, what have you decided?'

'I think, in the end,' Mark conceded generously, 'it's probably best to leave it to Owen. He'll find what he can as near as possible to the house. It's a question of whether or not there are any stable aquifers or underground watercourses within sensible pumping distance.'

'What do you think?' Beth looked at Owen.

He shrugged. Where the sun shone in through the small window, it caught the motes of sawdust shaken from his body and enveloped him in a glowing beam.

The thought jumped into Beth's head that perhaps that was how the angel had appeared to Mary; straight from Joseph's carpentry shop, covered in saw dust, and giving off a radiant glow of sunbeams.

'I'll find water for you all right,' he said simply.

'When will you come?' She hadn't wanted to ask.

'Sometime next week.'

She knew that she would have to stay.

'Tell me, Owen...' A thirst for arcane knowledge glowed in Mark's eyes. 'I've been reading up a bit about old Alfred Watkins - you know who I mean?'

Owen shook his head a few millimetres.

'The man who discovered ley lines; he was a corn merchant from Hereford, believe it or not. But he was a keen photographer as well and it was while he was snapping away out here that he noticed how often three or more landmarks seemed to be in alignment.' Now Owen nodded. Mark went on. 'The Priory is right at the intersection of several lines. There's a very marked one, look?' He ran his finger along a pencil line he'd drawn on the local large scale map. 'Through this notch above Capel-y-ffin, then the Wergin stone, straight down this track to the Priory.'

Owen nodded again. 'I've crossed the line with my ring when I've been looking for water.'

'What do you suppose it is?'

Owen shrugged. 'The earth's full of different energies. They all need a place to flow – like water in winter.'

Beth saw Mark's face crease in frustration. 'But if you've actually detected them, you must have some idea of what's coursing down these lines.'

Owen, too, frowned slightly. 'I only know they're there.'

Beth remained silent, unembarrassed by Mark's insistence on answers to these mysteries.

Mark was unbuttoning the right cuff of his shirt. 'By the way, your brother's kids told us you can find injuries with your ring, and cure them.'

'No,' Owen denied quietly. 'Sometimes I do find trouble by dowsing; sometimes I can cure it with my hands.'

'I'd be fascinated to see what you'd make of this elbow.' Mark had bared the joint and now presented it to Owen.

Owen looked at it and almost imperceptibly raised an eyebrow. 'I have to go now,' he said with no discernible sign of regret.

Mark quickly hid any affront he felt at this rejection of his ailment. 'But I hope you'll be able to come and dowse for our water soon? My wife loves her bath.'

'I will,' Owen said, already turning to walk from the room. His arm brushed Beth's as he passed.

She wanted to reach out and touch him; instead she put a hand up to smooth her hair, and stepped back as Mark saw Owen out.

'Well, it was very good of you to come.'

Owen stopped in the kitchen door and looked back at Mark then, more deliberately but only for a second, at Beth. He inclined his head slightly. 'I'll come in the week.'

He walked out of the door. Beth listened as he strode across the yard, the gate banged shut and the Daihatsu clanked into motion.

'He's an awkward bugger,' Mark said watching the muddy green vehicle disappear up the lane. 'Of course, these people still live such isolated lives, I suppose you can't expect them to be too skilled in the art of conversation.'

Beyond Gospel Pass

'Unlike you,' Beth smiled impishly.

Mark turned and looked at her with surprise. 'Well, I may not be the most charming man in the world - I hope not anyway - but at least I've got a few social skills.'

'Mmm – is that what they are? Poking your elbow at him as if he were the village witchdoctor?'

'That's no different than I'd do with my regular GP,' Mark protested.

Beth was quick to relent. 'I suppose not. But it just seemed a bit clumsy; after all, you hardly know him.'

'He doesn't strike me as the sort of person anyone ever gets to know.'

'No,' Beth conceded, 'but that's not surprising, really; living up in a place like Blaen Fawr can't be easy.'

Mark nodded. 'I was talking to one of the Jenkins in the pub last week - you know, the family who farm Pont-y-Wern below Ruth - and he said they practically never see old Megan Rhys, ever since she buried her husband getting on for thirty years ago.'

'Wasn't there some sort of tragedy – an accident or something?'

'That seems to be a source of endless speculation,' Mark said, fascinated as he always was by unresolved history. 'Apparently he fell off the rocks on the hill above Blaen Fawr and nobody knows if he was trying to save a sheep or if he did it on purpose. Either way, he fell two hundred feet and smashed his head open.'

'Why should he do it on purpose?'

Mark shook his head with a laugh. 'God knows what murky doings go on up those dark cwms. But anyway, since then, Megan only appears once a year at the sheep sale in Llanthony; and occasionally in that little Baptist Chapel at Capel-y-ffin. She never leaves the house otherwise; Owen does all the shopping.'

'He was buying yeast for her when I bumped into him on Thursday,' Beth said, feeling absurd to be jealous of the few scraps of information about Owen's family that Mark had already gleaned.

Seven

London publishers, literary stars, agents and commentators stood out in the crowd that gathered on Sunday morning for the Festival sponsors' official party.

Beth had driven into Hay earlier, to go to Mass, where she had engaged in a short skirmish with her conscience over taking communion, given what she intended would happen the following week. Her legal mind argued that contemplating a sin had the moral equivalence of conspiring to commit a crime – which often carried a higher penalty than the crime itself. In a state of resentful confusion, she walked slowly across the town to the Festival site.

She waved her invitation card at an anxious steward and was ushered into a crowded marquee, which hummed with quiet, considered voices. What struck her most immediately, after ten days of being away from London amidst the aroma of bracken and heather, was the distinct redolence of fashionable scent.

She looked around for Mark; he'd said he would come to Hay in the Land Rover with Ruth, who was also invited to the party. There was no sign of them yet. She pretended to look at the exhibition of pictures that hung on the walls of the marquee while she looked out for other faces she knew.

'Hello. It's good to see you.'

She turned and found Paul Ricardo's chocolate eyes smiling at her from beneath a mop of shiny black hair.

Although she had seen the festival director when she'd been in the restaurant with Mark the previous week, they hadn't been introduced. She smiled back.

'It was kind of you to ask us.'

'A distinguished London publisher and his beautiful wife? We're lucky to have you here.'

Beyond Gospel Pass

Beth forgave him for casting her as an appendage and smiled at the compliment. 'We haven't actually met, have we?'

'No, I'm sorry. But I saw you with your husband in Dino's the other day – didn't I?' he added with inoffensive vagueness.

She knew that he knew perfectly well they had seen each other. She nodded with a grin.

'Let me get you a drink,' he said, 'and introduce you to a few people.' He swept an arm towards a girl carrying a tray of champagne glasses and scooped one off for Beth, turning in the same movement to a tall, dark-haired and well-groomed man of sixty or so who had been standing beside them.

'Martin, have you met Beth Powell? This is Lord Brecon, one of our patrons.'

Beth shook hands with the Tory ex-MP and wondered how Paul Ricardo would explain who she was.

'Mrs Powell's married to Mark Powell who publishes Archimedes; he's also hoping to be adopted by the local Liberals.'

Martin Brecon's eyebrows rose a few millimetres and a ghost of a smile crossed his face. 'That should be fun for him.'

Beth took up the challenge on Mark's behalf. 'Oh, why do you say that?'

'I'm told they find it very hard to agree in the local party. I have to say, it's always worked to our advantage.'

He had assumed, Beth noticed, that she would know who he was, and probably at least the outlines of his political career.

'I should have thought there was always quite a lot of dissent in most local parties of any persuasion.'

'Well, yes, of course, but this lot are notoriously unaccommodating. I can't think why poor old Henry goes on with it. Still, best of luck.'

'Thanks,' Beth said, without emphasis. 'But forgetting politics for a moment, I seem to remember your name coming up the other day in rather strange circumstances.' Beth was entertained to see Lord Brecon suddenly stiffen while an anxious shadow passed over his eyes. 'Apparently you did something to your back and a local healer cured it for you.'

Lord Brecon looked relieved but puzzled. 'Who on earth told you about that?'

'We've bought a house in the valley the other side of Gospel Pass.'

'Ah, you've come across the mystical Owen Rhys, then?'

'It wasn't he who told me, it was his nephew – he brings up our milk and eggs.'

'They're a bizarre family, as far as I can remember. They wouldn't let me into the house, you know. Rhys would only work his magic outside. I had to sit on a bale of smelly old hay!' He gave a professional charmer's laugh.

'Why do you suppose they wouldn't let you in?"

'I've no idea. A lot of these families still live a hundred years in the past, even now. It's in the nature of hill farming that change is treated with great suspicion, and outside influences are very much spurned. I had a lot of that when I was member here. Mind you, in the case of old Mrs Rhys, I think there are some exceptional circumstances. Her husband committed suicide, you know.'

'Did he? I thought there was some doubt.'

'In as much as the coroner couldn't categorically state it, but I don't think the locals were in any doubt at all. Not that they'd talk about it to incomers like you.' He stopped and looked faintly embarrassed. 'Sorry, that wasn't meant to sound derogatory; after all, there's no crime in not having lived out here all your life, but it is considered an almost insurmountable short-coming by those who have.'

Beth nodded. 'I've sort of sensed that. I'm not sure that Mark has yet.'

'He'd do well to,' the ex-MP advised.

Paul Ricardo grinned. 'I knew he'd have a few tips for you.' He moved away smoothly, Beth assumed, to lubricate relationships between sponsors and their literary lions.

Lord Brecon was already looking over Beth's shoulder at someone behind her.

'Tell me,' she said at her most assertive, anxious to know. 'Did Owen really cure you?'

Lord Brecon's eyes were drawn back to her by the urgency in her voice. 'Why? Are you relying on him for a cure yourself?'

Beyond Gospel Pass

'God, no!' Beth tried to laugh. 'It's just that Mark's asked him to look at his elbow.'

'Computer elbow?'

Beth nodded.

'There would be a pleasing irony,' Lord Brecon murmured, 'in the cure of a hi-tech injury by swinging a pendulum and laying on hands.'

'Yes,' she agreed wholeheartedly, 'but does it work?'

'As a matter of fact it did for me – very well, though I've been careful not to publicise the fact, or the great unwashed will all be wanting it on the National Health. But the fact is the London Clinic charged me a fortune and couldn't do anything about the chronic pain in my back; Rhys cleared it up completely and wouldn't take a penny, which disproved a few of my prejudices about our hill farmers.' He chuckled in a way that Beth interpretted as – *Don't you think I'm rather amusing, but excuse me, I'm rather important too, so I'll have to move on.* 'I expect we'll meet again,' he said smoothly.

Beth didn't impede him; she stepped aside to allow the next candidate for audience to approach.

By that time, several familiar faces had drifted into view; some Beth was glad to see; others not. She delivered an unambiguous rebuff when she met Charles Winter's lascivious eye, before turning away to talk to Paul Ricardo, still conveniently close and, it seemed, happy to talk.

When Boo Llewellyn made an unmissable entrance to the marquee a few minutes later, Beth was surprised how glad she was to see her. Quickly analysing her reaction as she approached, she came to the conclusion that Boo's spontaneous honesty more than outweighed what Mark, with his penchant for hyperbole, called her "Falangist leanings".

Ten minutes with Boo produced a rich harvest of potted biographies for half a dozen other people in the tent, and by the time she moved on, Beth felt she was finding the measure of this gathering. She had temporarily forgotten that Mark was supposed to be at the party too. It was only when she was thinking that she should go and make some kind of arrangements for lunch that she registered he still hadn't arrived; and nor had Ruth.

She saw them both in the car park.

They hadn't seen her. They seemed to be arguing about something.

Mark must be slipping, Beth thought, if he didn't realise that a public row in the town, especially with a woman who wasn't his wife, would be noticed and widely broadcast within a few hours.

And she began to wonder what they were arguing about, and why they were late. What had they been doing, for God's sake?

An absurd suspicion leaped abruptly into her head. She tried at once to crush it. It was crazy to think, just because they were late, that they'd been having sex or working up to it. But if they had - she thought of Ruth looking tenderly at Mark and putting her slim, pale hand on his at supper - and she found it so hurtful, how would Mark feel about what she herself had been contemplating almost ceaselessly for the last few days?

When she reached them, announcing herself in plenty of time, there was more colour than normal in Ruth's face. Mark looked irritable. He was holding out hands covered in oil, looking around vaguely for somewhere to wash them. Beth told him where to find the men's lavatories in the Festival's tented compound and he hurried off, muttering that he still intended to get a look-in at the opening party.

'Oh God,' Ruth said watching him go. 'I'm so sorry, Beth. I'm afraid Mark's in rather a rage. The bloody Land Rover conked out just before we got to the pass. Mark tried to mend it but he couldn't, then he managed to push it to the top, and we came the whole way down without the engine.'

'Good Lord,' Beth was impressed. 'It must be at least eight miles down from the top.'

'Yes, it is, but it's nearly all downhill. And then, just before we reached the bottom, Mark put it into gear and bump-started it.' Ruth shrugged slightly embarrassed. 'It was okay after that, but now it won't start again.'

They walked back towards the marquee and the party, talking about Ruth's Peruvian workshop. 'The two musicians are supposed to get here this afternoon. They're coming in a taxi from Hereford station. I feel really bad about it; they haven't got much money; I know I ought to go and meet them myself.'

'I'll pick them up if you like, as long as you promise to keep Mark busy,' Beth offered.

Beyond Gospel Pass

'God, would you? That would be amazing. I'd feel so much better, and maybe Mark could help to get things ready for my talk.'

'I'll make sure I'm back by then, or you won't have any music.'

Ruth ate a little pasta with them in Dino's before Beth set off in the Saab to drive twenty miles down the Wye valley to Hereford.

She was glad of the distraction, and to be alone. She was almost scared to think about the week ahead; and she wasn't particularly looking forward to sitting through a rambling account of Ruth's travels in the Andes and the homespun, mystical New Age theories she promised to reveal; or the party afterwards at the Llewellyns'.

She identified the Peruvians as soon as they stepped off the train. They had nut-brown, aquiline faces and wore incongruous, brightly striped llama wool mountain ponchos over skin-tight jeans. She led them out to the car, chatting to them in bad Spanish.

As they drove back to Hay, she was delighted by their innocence and honesty and amazed how much they managed to communicate. She felt again the excitement she'd known as a student when she'd first learned to appreciate the great value of some primitive cultures.

Beth gathered that Luis and Ramon were very fond of Ruth. They spoke of her with obvious affection, and Beth suspected that Ramon, at least ten years younger, had been nursing physical longings for Ruth. He was sitting in the passenger seat next to her. She glanced at the straight lines of his passionate brown profile and his long black lashes. Thick ebony hair fell in shiny waves to his shoulder, his smooth narrow hands rested on sinewy denimed thighs; and Beth envied Ruth.

The walls of the small Baptist Church hall where Ruth was holding her workshop were washed pale green. The floral curtains looked like somebody's thirty year-old cast-offs, and Beth didn't think she'd sat on a canvas and iron-tube cantilever stacking chair since she'd been at her first school in Boston. About fifty of the chairs had been lined up in front of a plain table on a low dais.

A map of Peru and posters of the Andes and of the massive, man-made striations on the high plateau were pinned on the wall behind the table.

Jessica Meredith

A carousel slide projector was set in the middle of the room with its lens pointing at a screen beside the table. There were two hand drums, a small Andean harp and a few flutes and pan pipes on a side table, next to a pair of shiny beech stools.

Several bright, coarse wool blankets were hanging from a skimpy picture rail. A strong whiff of cannabis hung in the air, drifting from a group of defiantly dreadlocked New Agers in the back row. In addition to them, there were twenty other people sitting with an air of tolerant expectation beneath the deadening white light of six neon tubes. Beth was relieved to see that a few spotlights had been installed which would illuminate the table and anyone standing by it.

Mark wriggled in his chair. Beth looked at him. He was glancing around, tight-lipped, making no effort to disguise his expectation of boredom. 'Poor Ruth,' he said out of the side of his mouth. 'Not exactly a sell-out. Still, maybe some of the people who can't get into Martin Amis will show up.' He turned round and looked at the door at the back of the hall, which was the only entrance. 'I wonder when she's getting here.'

'When did you last see her?' Beth asked.

'Just before you arrived with the Peruvians; she's obviously met up with them because their instruments are here.'

There was a clatter as the door swung open. Ruth walked in, flanked by her two musicians. She had changed since Beth had seen her at lunch. Now she was wearing a long embroidered Peruvian linen dress and the same dramatic make-up as she had the night she'd come to dinner when the lamb had breached.

She swept up the aisle between the chairs and the wall, giving Mark and Beth a quick, grateful smile as she passed. One of the Festival's minor volunteer functionaries stood up from a chair in the front row to introduce the evening's event.

Beth guessed that only those who knew Ruth well would notice the quaver in her voice as she settled down to her talk, undoubtedly bolstered by the infatuation in Ramon's beautiful eyes and the earnest commitment with which he sucked and blew into his pipes.

For more than an hour Ruth spoke with passion and obvious affection for her subject. She dealt with the geography, culture and spiritual beliefs of the descendants of Atahualpa's Inca people.

Beyond Gospel Pass

She outlined the complex relationship between the Inca and the invading Spaniard, and touched on the economic and physical effects of conquest. There were a few murmurs of sympathetic horror from her audience when she showed some of Caillot's appalling images of Spanish atrocity. She spoke, Beth thought, with conviction and authority, making good use of her musicians and slides to transport her audience back in time, across the world to the snow-clad *cordilleras*.

As her talk came to an end, over a whisper of pipes and a spectacular shot of the Andean peaks, Ruth lowered her voice.

'So, I hope I've been able to put across some of the many spiritual secrets I learned from the Andean people. The wonderful thing is that there's nothing complicated about their attitude; they simply glory in the hardships that confront them and turn them into inspiration and a source of inner contentment.' Ruth paused and gazed passionately at her audience. 'And this must have some relevance to all of us now, in a world which seems to crave instant, transient fulfilment, which in the end is found to be no fulfilment at all.' She looked around the room with a serene smile. 'I can't tell you how grateful I am that so many of you...' she gazed at her audience as if she were sharing a secret with each of them '... have taken the trouble to come and hear what I've learned from these wonderful people. I only hope I haven't gone on too long.'

There was loud murmur of denial, especially from the back of the room. Ruth nodded her thanks. 'Then, at this point, I'd like to open the discussion up to all of you. This is meant to be a workshop, not a lecture,' she smiled. 'Does anyone feel they have any further input?'

Beth held her breath, in the guilty hope that no one would respond, but a few rows in front of her, a man in his mid-forties, with long grey hair and a chunky third world sweater, held up his hand and leaned back in his chair with a knowing smile.

'Ruth,' he said in a lazy Oxbridge voice, 'what worries me is that the attitude you're propagating sounds pretty like what the medieval church preached to the working classes to stop them feeling acquisitive and rebellious. I mean, maybe what you encountered up in the Andes was simply a legacy of the priests who followed in the wake of de las Casas and the conquistadors...'

Ruth shook her head with a tolerant smile. 'You'll find their culture is far older than that.' She dealt with the query, and a few more abstract observations, before thanking them all for coming and inviting them to pursue the discussion any time they happened to be passing her farm, a thousand feet up the side of the Black Mountains.

When it was over, there was no doubt that the talk had gone well; there had been willing laughter at Ruth's unsophisticated humour and the final applause was generous. Mark clapped enthusiastically too, though Beth suspected he hadn't heard much of it. As he clapped, he turned to her. 'The crusties at the back liked it all right, didn't they?' he grinned.

The New Agers were whistling their approval, and Ruth was blushing with exhilaration. She invited the beaming Ramon and Luis to play a last tune, which was greeted with more applause. It was only when this was dying down, that Beth turned to see what sort of a crowd had turned up in the end.

She spotted Owen at once. He was leaning against the wall at the back of the hall. He looked, she thought, peculiarly out of place at this event and yet there was no reason why what Ruth had to say shouldn't have had more direct relevance to his hard, lonely hillside life than to the rest of the audience.

Mark followed her gaze. 'She must have asked him to come - her source of inner contentment, eh?' He gave a quick, smutty grin.

'I've told you,' Beth said quickly, 'I'm sure she's not sleeping with him.'

'Why on earth shouldn't she be? Oh, hello Ruth... well done!'

Ruth was standing by them now, looking pleased with herself. 'Thanks. Was it all right?'

'Brilliant,' Mark enthused. 'I can't wait to read the book. By the way,' he added as he turned to leave, 'I see your boyfriend's turned up. I wonder if he followed much of what you said.'

Ruth looked blank until she realised Mark was talking about Owen. Beth turned away to hide her embarrassment. Then she was struck that perhaps he was jealous.

'Owen?' Ruth was saying. 'Oh, he knows all about the Andeans.'

Mark looked doubtful, but didn't pursue it. He turned to Beth. 'Didn't Boo say we should take Ruth up to this party?'

'She more or less issued a command,' Beth grinned.

Beyond Gospel Pass

'I don't know,' Ruth shook her head. 'I've got to go and sign copies of my book at the Festival shop, and then Owen said he'd take me back. The Land Rover wouldn't start again when I was getting the stuff down here so I'm leaving it for the garage to have a look at on Monday.'

'Well, if you change your mind and come up to the Llewellyns', you could always come home with us,' Mark offered expansively.

Mark drove them out of Hay through the last of the dusk towards The Neuadd.

Beth leaned back in her seat and looked at her husband. 'I suppose the reason you're rather patronising to Ruth is that you fancy her. Am I right, or am I right?'

He smiled at her. 'I wouldn't go as far as that, but to give her her due, she looked bloody good tonight, even if she was talking a lot of New Age balls.

'She'd slapped a bit of colour on her face – that makes a difference; but I've always thought she's a good-looking woman; she's got amazing bone structure.'

'But Boo's right, ' Mark said, 'she's loopy.'

'There's no point in telling her, though.'

Mark didn't reply for a moment. Beth could see signs of an erratic mood swing, the sort which could cause uncomfortable twists and turns in his reasoning.

'So,' he said, 'were you just playing along with her the other night when she started talking about surrogate fathers?'

Beth felt a sudden guilty tension in her stomach, but she laughed. 'I told you then - it was just a joke. I was wondering when you'd bring it up again. Of course I wasn't being serious.'

Mark turned his head to look at the road ahead. 'Listen angel, once we've got this selection in the bag, we can justify spending a lot more time up here...' he laid a hand on her thigh and adopted a Neil Kinnock accent, '...maybe these old Welsh hills will work their magic and babies'll start popping out right, left and centre.'

'There's lovely.' Beth managed to smile with him.

Eight

In the bright moonlight that had replaced the dusk, Mark drove the Saab across the stretch of level parkland that had been set aside for car parking at the Llewellyn's party. Boo, with an instinctive understanding of what was required for such an eclectic gathering, had borrowed an army marquee for their party and booked a Cajun band to play. The marquee was glowing through its khaki skin and the music billowed invitingly across the open ground.

They got out and Mark started to stride up towards the house, where the rest of the party was in progress, though in a lower key. Beth kept up with him until they reached a gate where they had to decide between going into the house or the marquee.

'The music sounds great,' Beth said. 'Let's go and have a look there first.'

The band were in full swing on a small stage at the end of the tent. They looked wild. A heavily sweating drummer hammered with his sticks behind a frenzied girl in a tiny leather skirt who played the violin with furious vigour. Beside her, a stout woman in a bowler hat was squeezing a massive accordion and a dark-eyed gypsy man played the guitar and sang.

The guests, a hundred or more of them between sixteen and sixty, were loving it, dancing vigorously, whooping and leaping about. At first Beth was almost overwhelmed by the contrast between the soporific air of Ruth's talk and the riotous bedlam aroused by the Cajun band. She and Mark were given a glass of punch on the way in. Beth made her way closer to the stage to see the band and the people on the dance floor. Mark followed. 'Let's dance,' he said, his eyes glowing.

Beyond Gospel Pass

Beth nodded and submitted to the music, glad to let her mind float free; she found that she'd forgotten how liberating dancing could be.

After three dances, Mark was sweating. 'Right, I've had enough of this,' he grinned ruefully. 'Let's join the old farts in the house.'

Beth shrugged, and went out with him. But she was still buzzing from the physical excitement of the music, the heat and the drink. Behind them, the gypsy man sang in raucous patois, "*Jolie blon', ma jolie blon*". The sound diminished as they walked by the light of sporadic torches at the side the path to the terrace in front of the house. Through an open French window, they entered a large room – the dining-room, Beth recognised – filled with people, the familiar buzz of ardent talkers and the smells of wine, scent and warm bodies.

Mark was hailed by several people who already knew who he was and why he was there. Beth was relieved that she could leave him with a small group of supporters, and wandered through into the main hall.

As soon as she walked in, with a shock, she saw Owen - taller than everyone and, anyway, owning a presence that made him impossible to miss.

Beth tore her eyes from him and tried to find someone else to talk to until she'd collected her thoughts.

There were no immediate openings into which she could jump; she settled for studying a large and grandly framed painting of what looked like a local eighteenth century landscape.

'Hello.' He was standing right behind her. 'Do you like that?'

Beth turned.

Owen was looking at the picture.

'It... it's okay. It's a bit sort of obvious,' she muttered, wondering what she meant.

Owen looked as though he'd heard, but he said nothing.

'Did you come with Ruth, then?'

'Yes. She said you wanted her to come.' He shrugged. 'I brought her up.'

'Are you staying for a while?'

'I might.' He looked around at the press of people in the room, some of whom Beth recognised as being important or, at least, well-known literary figures. 'Are these all people who write books?' he asked.

'Some,' Beth said. 'Some are publishers; some are journalists who write about books.'

'And those girls? They don't look much like writers.' He nodded at a group of three attractive, self-confident women in their early twenties.

As Beth turned to look, Charles Winter appeared at her side. The oiled-teak flesh of his face wrinkled up into a randy grin, before he cast his eyes up and down Owen's tall, muscular figure, deciding how rude he could be.

'Have you met our guest of honour?' he asked.

Beth shook her head. 'No and I didn't go to his talk either.'

'I did,' the author said dismissively.

Beth couldn't resist the urge to provoke. 'What do you think of him?' Charles Winter shrugged. 'If you like writing that's strutting, self-conscious and full of swear words, he's your man.'

Beth had to laugh at his arrogance. She also knew she had to get away from him, though she didn't know how. 'Owen was just asking me who those girls are,' she said.

Charles Winter looked at the women and smiled. 'One of them works in the PR office of my publisher. I expect the others do the same - Sloane Rangers with rich daddies, who don't need to earn anything serious - it's a great old publishing tradition.'

'What do they do?' Owen asked.

Charles looked at him and raised his eyebrows. 'As far as I can tell, they're employed to fuck the authors when they take them off on publicity tours. I expect it saves a lot of expense and embarrassment having in-house girls for the job.'

If he'd thought he was going to shock Owen, he was disappointed. Owen nodded slowly at what seemed a rational explanation.

Beth wildly thought of what she could do to get rid of Winter before he did anything that got rid of Owen.

'Nice to see you, Charles,' she said with abrupt decisiveness. 'But Owen and I were just going down to dance to this Cajun band.' She started to walk towards the door where she'd come in and prayed that Owen would follow. She didn't look back until she reached the French windows.

Beyond Gospel Pass

Owen was right behind.

Outside, on the broad stone terrace with the music wafting up from the marquee, she stopped.

'Thanks,' she said. 'That awful man seems to hound me wherever I go.'

Owen nodded and, in the moonlight, she thought she saw a smile on his lips. 'He obviously thinks he's more than he is,' Owen said simply. 'Is he a writer, too?'

'Yes, I suppose one has to grant him that. He's quite successful - not in sales so much as in attracting long-winded reviews. It's ages since I read anything of his.'

'And you didn't want to talk to him. Did you really want to go and dance, too?'

'Mm, no, it's okay.'

'That's a pity,' he said. 'Maybe later, then.'

Before she could do anything, Owen had stepped back into the house. She stood there, fuming at herself for blowing the opportunity.

After a few moments, she followed him back in. She couldn't see him anywhere in the first room, and carried on back to the hall, where she'd been talking to him before, hoping that Charles Winter had moved on. There was no sign of the novelist; she was just looking around again, conscious of having been there, doing the same only ten minutes earlier, when Boo Llewellyn sailed across the room in front of her, carrying a bottle of champagne.

Boo's eyes lit up. 'Beth! I'm so glad you've come. Everyone's on very good form.'

'It's a wonderful party - the first real party I've been to here.'

Boo leaned forward confidentially. 'I just spotted those two lovely young creatures coming out of the loo - I suppose they're with one of the publishers. I'm sure they've been sniffing beastly substances, and the Chief Constable's here! Let's hope Henry doesn't get arrested.'

Beth laughed and followed Boo's eyes to a pair of the PR girls she'd seen earlier. They were giggling with obvious excitement, talking to a tall man. It was Owen. While Beth was looking at him, he turned.

'Oh, look!' Boo said. 'That's that horny ram you were talking to earlier - you lucky girl!'

'Who?' Beth asked, as if Boo were talking nonsense.

'Oh, come on, I saw the way you were looking at him. Don't pretend you don't fancy that rustic Romeo. I wouldn't blame you. They don't often make 'em that good round here, I can tell you. Mind you, it looks like that pair of Camillas have got their teeth into him already,' she laughed. 'Anyway, I've got to get on.' She waved her bottle. 'There's a ton of food left, if you haven't had any and if you want another drink later, it's in the library. I've just got to dash off and tank up our star guest. Enjoy yourself!'

She cruised on, to be replaced almost at once by Ruth who grasped her wrist and spoke breathlessly. 'Beth, those stupid girls have been trying to persuade Owen he should become a writer.'

'Why?' Beth laughed in disbelief.

'They were saying he's got just the right face and image for a 21st Century novelist.'

'What a load of crap!' Beth blustered. 'What do they know? It makes me feel old just looking at them. Do you know, if Mark and I had got our act together, we'd probably have children nearly that age.'

'No, you wouldn't! You've only been married twelve years, haven't you? Oh God! Owen looks rather pissed off. I bet he wants to leave – this party, those girls, they're not his scene at all. Sorry, Beth, I'd better go and check if he's okay.'

'I'd have thought he could look after himself, frankly.'

'Yeh, okay, but if he's going, I ought to go with him - I mean - he did bring me here. If I don't come back, I'll see you tomorrow, okay?'

Beth felt suddenly desolate as Ruth walked away. Why hadn't she taken her chance when Owen was there and, as far as she could tell, perfectly ready to go down to the marquee with her?

With an effort, she forced herself not to look and check if Ruth really was dragging Owen away. She was relieved to spot Henry Llewellyn through the door of the study; without looking back she walked across and into the room.

Henry greeted her with obvious regard for her merits both as a woman and as a professional person.

'I suppose this is all rather a rough sort of bun-fight for trendy metropolitans like you?'

'Not at all. I love the band.'

Beyond Gospel Pass

'You've been down and had a look have you? That was Boo's idea, egged on by Ellie - our daughter; she's come up for the week with a gang of dope-smoking oafs.'

'What does she do?' Beth asked, thinking that a cross between Henry and Boo could be interesting.

'Don't ask.' Henry shook his head with a wry grin. 'She's a painter - rough stuff; makes Jackson Pollock look like a Dutch old master. I wanted her to do law, like you. I told her it can be a springboard for anything else you want to do, including art. Still, she's no fool; she may come right. But you, you're a different proposition,' he went on approvingly.

'I'm a different generation, too,' Beth laughed.

'Not to me. You know, you were bloody impressive the other day, in front of that gang of dead-beats in our selection committee. You really should think about standing yourself.'

'Me? I don't think so. That's not an immediate aspiration. Besides, one MP in the family would be enough.'

'If there's ever an MP in your family, I'd say it's more likely to be you.'

Beth felt a quick cold clamminess. 'Does that... do you mean Mark's not going to get selected?'

Henry closed his eyes, and shook his head. 'No, I'm not saying that, and as far as I'm concerned, he's the best bet we have.'

'But....?'

'You might say that this is a very unpredictable constituency. These farmers don't like to feel anyone's making up their mind for them. But don't worry; if it matters to you, he's got a good chance - at least of getting to stand.'

'Henry, of course it matters to me,' Beth bridled.

He held up a hand, gently, to stem any discord. 'That's fine, then. But not all wives really want their husbands to do it, you know. They think they'll be starved of attention.'

'Well,' Beth said, making a conscious effort to calm herself. 'Right now, that isn't a prospect that worries me.'

The blue and white taxi that had come to Pant-y-Groes from Hereford to take Mark to the station swung out of the gate. Beth watched it thread its way down the lane until it was hidden by the overhanging hornbeams, and she felt a load fall from her shoulders.

Although he wouldn't admit it to her, Mark had been too absorbed with his business hassles to query her decision to stay in the mountains for another week. Besides, that was what he'd been trying to get her to do since they'd bought the house. Beth knew that Mark had arranged another meeting with Marcel Gehring's agent; she knew that he knew he'd lost the author, but couldn't let himself accept it with dignity, and he would go on clutching at the slightest possibility long after there was any hope of salvaging the deal.

Although he hadn't asked her why she wanted to stay, she'd told him that she had a lot more work that she could do up here. Now they were on line, she could call down all the information she needed to carry on preparing her case.

'And all this walking is beginning to make me feel so much fitter,' she'd told him when she jumped out of bed that morning.

She saw him admiring her soft, lean contours; desiring her half-naked body. She had dressed quickly.

Once the taxi was out of sight, Beth quashed a murmur of guilt evoked by her relief at Mark's going as she walked up the hill behind the house, from where she could see Ruth's farm across the valley.

She'd been intensely relieved that Owen's vehicle hadn't been there when she went out to look first thing that morning, and now she saw the two Peruvians walking around outside, inspecting the llamas and drawing water from Ruth's well.

Beth wondered if Ruth had slept with Ramon, or Luis, or both - any combination, she didn't mind, as long as it hadn't involved Owen.

She was confident, anyway, that last night it hadn't. She was sure that her brief liaison with Owen the evening before and their short, tacit conspiracy to escape Charles Winter had brought them closer together.

For the next few hours she managed to work, although at midday she thought about asking Ruth to come and eat with her but decided she wouldn't enjoy hearing all about whatever had happened with Ramon, or Luis, or both.

She ate alone and, afterwards, went up to her bedroom to change.

Beyond Gospel Pass

She stripped off her cotton blouse, unzipped her denim shorts and let them fall to the ground around her ankles. As she peeled off her skimpy pants, she looked at the curve of her hips, and the smooth lines of her thighs where they merged in a neatly trimmed, dark brown bush. On a sudden whim, without stopping to think why, she didn't replace her underwear when she pulled on a short calico skirt and a cropped jersey top that just covered her breasts.

It wasn't subtle, but thinking of Owen didn't make her feel subtle. She lay on the bed and let her hand, like a stranger's, stroke her thighs until it crept up and reached the warm opening and her tiny clitoris beneath a mound of springy curls. She lay with only the slightest stirring beneath her skirt, and a vision of Owen filling her head until her crotch was damp and she was gently delirious.

Beth looked at her watch. She thought it must have been for the hundredth time that afternoon. It was six thirty and Pant-y-Groes would soon lose the sunlight. But the day's warmth lingered in the air and she was outside, filling the flowerbeds below the windows with the plants she had bought at the weekend.

She was still wearing the short top and mini-skirt with a pair of canvas flip-flops. There was soil on her hands and a gloss of sweat on her face. From time to time she reached up a hand to push aside a falling wisp of auburn hair and her forehead was streaked with earth. She carried on with her gardening and thought how pitiful she was to want this man so badly.

She heard the soft footfalls – leather soles on old, round cobbles.

When she turned, his face was half hidden in shadow, but she could just see him, looking down at her with motionless, enigmatic eyes.

'Oh, hello,' she said lightly, standing up quickly and brushing down her skirt with muddy hands, acutely conscious of her lack of underwear.

He looked at the streaks of earth on her face and clothes. He smiled faintly. 'You've been working hard, then?'

She glanced down at the chaos of purple and red Busy Lizzies she'd planted. 'I wanted to brighten the place up a bit, now we're going to be up here more.'

'You will be, will you?'

Beth nodded. 'That's why we wanted to be sure of our water. There'll probably be quite a few people coming to stay, and... you know, and they'll want baths and all that sort of thing.' She wondered why she was talking like someone in a Jilly Cooper novel

'Hm,' Owen nodded, with no apparent sympathy for her problem. 'Whatever, I've found a watercourse for you - on your own ground.'

'What? You've already done it?' Beth cried. 'But I wanted to watch.'

To her surprise, Owen seemed embarrassed. 'I've just done it, but I could do it again,' he shrugged.

'Would you? Please?'

He nodded and started to walk towards the field gate, pulling from his jeans the ring and chain Beth had seen him fiddling with, up by the high spring.

When they reached a slight depression that ran for fifteen yards down the hillside Owen told her to wait while he carried on to a point twenty feet further on, where he stopped and turned. He wrapped the loose end of the fine gold chain around his thumb, leaving the ring dangling on the other end, twelve inches below his hand.

With total absorption, he became completely inert until there was no movement in the ring, despite the gentle breeze that had started to caress the hillside. Then, slowly and deliberately, he walked back towards her, stopping after each pace, while the ring still hung, motionless on the end of his chain until he reached the centre point of the dip in the field. The ring began slowly but distinctly to rotate. Beth looked with disbelief at Owen's hand; there wasn't so much as a tremor in it. She glanced up at his eyes; they were focused intently on the ring, as he gradually extended his arm towards her, until it was a foot in front of him and almost abruptly, the ring stopped spinning. By the time he reached her, it was entirely still once more.

'Did you see it?' he asked.

'Yes, of course,' she said, a little breathless. 'It was very obvious; and you're sure that's where we'll find water?'

'Yes. I looked down the valley too, anyway, and it comes out just below the lane and runs on down to the river above ground.'

'So we could just pipe from here?'

'Yes. Simple.'

'And it won't dry up?'

'I couldn't promise that, but I doubt it.' As he spoke he leaned down and gathered up a dozen or so small, loose stones scattered across the surface of the pasture. He walked back to the point where the ring had spun and piled the stones into a small cairn. 'I'll come back and put a rod there, so's you know where to find it again.'

'Thanks, Owen,' Beth said, thinking that was the first time she'd called him by his name, and how strange it sounded. 'Now you must come in and let me settle up with you.'

'There's no need. I don't charge for that.'

'Well, at least come back and have a drink.'

He hesitated, only for a moment, but to Beth it felt a full agonising minute.

'All right,' he agreed.

She went first and almost had to stop herself from running and skipping back through the gate and into the house.

Owen followed her in. She pulled out a chair for him; he ignored it but put his ring and chain on the table in front of him.

'Wine?'

'Okay.'

'Red or white?'

'I don't mind.'

She turned and leaned down to get a bottle. She knew his eyes were on her; she wondered if he'd see there was nothing under her skirt; she leaned a little further. As she felt the loose cotton ride up her naked legs, she could hardly believe that Elizabeth Langthorne QC, leading civil and women's rights lawyer, was capable of such primitive tactics.

Without looking, she grasped a bottle from the bottom of the rack, not caring what it was, and stood up. She turned; he had stepped closer to her so that he was right in front of her, and her breasts pushed lightly against his ribs. She didn't look up at first, but breathed in the warm smell of fresh sweat and meadow hay that hung in the air around him.

When she felt his hand on her waist, it seemed so hot that she flinched; she glanced up quickly to show she hadn't meant to.

Jessica Meredith

The pupils of his dark eyes grew bigger, as if he were on some hallucinogen, and every life-creating organ in Beth's body was filled with a surge of hot blood.

He didn't speak; his lips opened into a broad, gentle smile as they closed on hers.

His mouth was soft beside his coarse-grained cheeks. Beth tasted heather, fern, the sweet water of the springs, the soft red rock of the hills, and in her ears rang the sound of buzzards, the hill top wind, wheatears and lambs. When she wrapped her arms around him she felt as if she were holding to herself every pulsing, vital force in the natural world.

His mouth left hers and lingered on her cheeks, her chin and neck. She was suddenly conscious that she was still clutching the bottle of wine and she drew her arm from behind his back.

'Shall we take this into the sitting room?' she asked, reddening at the hoarse nervousness in her voice.

He smiled. 'I'll open it first.'

Beth looked around, trying to focus, and found a corkscrew on the dresser. She handed it to Owen with the bottle. He extracted the cork. Beth picked up two glasses and led him into the small room.

Until Beth and Mark had bought the house, the room had been a byre and they had left some of the old mangers on the wall. The uneven floor was covered in natural coir, and the log fire she'd lit earlier was glowing strongly. A cluster of six fat candles which she'd bought from the shop at Belmont Abbey stood on a low elm table. She put the glasses beside them and lit them all. The pictures, the polished oak and wrought iron fittings gleamed in the soft light. In front of the fire was spread a big soft alpaca skin that Ruth had given them. Beth knelt on it and piled more logs on to the fire. Owen filled the glasses and joined her.

He put his arm around her and she turned to him. This time, when their lips came together, she sucked his tongue greedily and drove hers deep into the fleshy depths of his mouth, occupying it; colonising it.

As they kissed, they stretched themselves across the soft, deep fleece until they were lying face to face, interlocked with his leg between hers. She grasped his thigh, hard and muscled as a python, and kneaded it with her fingers while his hands played up and down her naked legs, never quite reaching the place where she wanted him to touch her.

The outline of a full erection showed through his jeans. She moved her hand up to feel it. As she did, her eye was caught by the flicker of the fat candles and she thought of the mighty paschal candle that used to burn in the chapel at school for Easter; she was reminded, too, that this was the first time since she had been married to Mark that she'd ever wanted to touch another man's flesh. A hot surge of guilt made her tremble as she decided that if this were to be done, it should be properly done. 'Let's go upstairs,' she whispered.

There was something surreal in the way he lifted her off the alpaca skin, but nothing imaginary about the strength of his arms, the firmness with which he carried her and mounted the stairs while she guided him along the corridor to the freshly painted spare bedroom.

He dropped her lightly on a Provencale bed cover, which, abruptly, she remembered choosing with Mark in Tarascon. She forced the thought from her head as he lowered himself onto the bed and lay beside her; they kissed and wrapped themselves around each other again until she felt the sweat in her armpits and between her legs. 'Owen,' she whispered. 'Are you going to take your clothes off?'

'Mmmm,' he murmured and swung his legs off the bed.

Beth turned and propped herself with one elbow on a pillow to look at him, black against the light from the window behind him as he tugged his T-shirt over the back of his head and bent down to unlace his boots before unbuckling a wide leather belt and shaking his jeans to his ankles, so she was able, in a way, to possess him first with her eyes – the muscular torso, the long, hard thighs, the firm, gleaming flesh jutting from his groin.

As he leaned towards her, she lay back. He put a hand behind her shoulders to draw the cotton top gently over her head so her breasts were freed and stood proud-nippled on her chest.

She shook her hair and smiled at him while he reached behind her back to unclip the waistband of her skirt; she raised her hips as he slipped the garment beneath her naked buttocks.

Owen let his hands linger on their way down her smooth limbs to her ankles, and slowly they returned until his strong fingers, sensitive to suckling lambs and hidden water, touched the tingling lips of the warm niche between her open legs. He lay beside her, twining his feet with hers and kissing her while she fondled his bulky sac.

He turned and lay on his back. Slowly he lifted her on to him; she tried to quell the trembling as she lowered herself, until he filled her with his pulse and she squealed and almost choked with pleasure.

When she climaxed on a tide of orgasm she'd never allowed herself before, she heard her own voice calling his name. Even as it happened, she knew that she'd needed it more than anything she'd ever wanted.

Then, at some drifting moment, cut loose from time, his whole body stiffened in a palpitating spasm beneath her while he filled her, and she wanted to laugh as his sperm flowed and tears of joy trickled down her cheeks and splashed onto his chest and face and settled in a pool below his Adam's apple.

He was very soft with her and understood; he drew her to him so her head nestled on his chest and his arms held her secure while she murmured and wept, laughed and stroked every bit of him that had given her so much.

Owen was gone when she woke, but the sheets were still warm where he'd lain. She wasn't hurt. He had his work, and he hadn't wanted to spoil her sleep.

Reluctantly, she showered away the physical vestiges of the night's lovemaking, but still found she was floating as she went downstairs and made breakfast of coffee, boiled eggs and toast. Afterwards she wandered dreamily around the house in bare feet and a short cotton dress. When she found Grimond, she picked him up and held him to her, looking out at the valley from each window in turn. The land glowed in sporadic sunlight; she strained to see the cluster of trees that marked Blaen Fawr and wondered if Owen were there, or on the hills.

She was in no doubt that their first kiss, in her kitchen the evening before, marked a critical watershed of her life and she didn't question a powerful intuition that it had profoundly altered the course of her life.

It didn't surprise her to find how much easier it was to work, with the certainty that she would see Owen again, perhaps later that day.

Beyond Gospel Pass

When she rang her office to speak to her junior, he commented on her cheerfulness. Then, full of energy, she rang her mother, Moira in Cape Cod. Without being specific, she hinted that it was possible that Moira might, one day, be a grandmother.

Dealing with Mark was not going to be so easy. However much she told herself what she had done was justified by the potential creation of the child they both wanted, she knew at the heart of it had lain a deep yearning to experience the physical love of an alien and unreachable man.

Even if she had confessed the sin there and then to Father Aidan, it would have be invalid; she knew that the firm purpose of amendment the sacrament required was entirely absent, as she could not for a moment deny a longing for Owen to make love to her again.

Clumsily assuming a warm cheeriness that was so out of character she couldn't understand why he didn't challenge it, she spoke to Mark magnanimously, to bolster him against the tide of bad news that she guessed must be overwhelming his business. He sounded pleased, if a little surprised by her concern, and amplified her guilt by thanking her warmly and telling her not to worry.

She put the phone down limply and gazed blearily through the study window at hills, seeing them, in her turmoil, as Van Gogh might have painted them.

When Beth had asked the children, they'd told her that Owen often went to eat in the middle of the day with Michael's family. As she was making a salad for her lunch, she rang Susie.

'Is Owen coming to your house today?'

'Yes,' Susie answered guardedly. 'Him and Michael's coming back for dinner soon.'

'He was kind enough to come over yesterday to help us find more water but there was something else I wanted to ask him about it. Do you think you could ask him to give me a ring me when he gets to you?'

'All right.'

Every ten minutes or so, Beth went out and walked a few yards up the hill from where she could see Michael's lime-washed house, hoping to see the Daihatsu parked outside.

She was coming in for the fourth time, with her confidence depleted, when she heard the phone. She waited for a few more rings before she picked it up and said calmly, 'Hello?'

'Susie says you rang me.'

'Oh, yes,' Beth laughed sheepishly. 'I wondered if you could meet me, by the upper spring where we met the other day - about six?'

There was a moment's pause, long enough for a dozen rejections to leap into Beth's head, before he answered. 'All right. I'll see you then.'

The sun would still be shining up by the top of the ridge at six, Beth thought, looking up at it. She opened the fridge and took out a bottle of cold wine like the one they'd drunk and Owen had said he liked the night before. She put it into a cold bag, which she stuffed into her rucksack with two glasses, a corkscrew and a Peruvian blanket Ruth had given her.

She set off up the hill with an airy spring to her stride, still quivering at the memory of the previous night, certain of what was going to happen this evening. During the long day, she had tried to convince herself that it couldn't be so wrong to do what she had done and planned to do again, when her purpose in the act, the primary purpose prescribed by the Catholic Church, was to conceive. The raw bliss that had filled her, she argued with herself, were mere supplements to this.

Her innate honesty, though, still wouldn't allow it. Only with a great effort of will was she able to quieten the rumblings of guilt inside her to a muffled murmur – a sense of faint nostalgia for the morally defined person she had once been.

Lying stretched out in the sun, she saw his dog first at the edge of the oak copse. It came sniffing and busy through the trees to check her out. She stretched out a hand, to show friendship, at the same time felt a faint, ridiculous pang of jealousy that the collie had spent all day with Owen.

The dog sniffed her hand sociably and Owen appeared behind it.

Beth looked up at him from where she lay, propped on one elbow on the Peruvian rug, squinting into the sun.

'Thanks for coming.'

Beyond Gospel Pass

He smiled and sat down beside her. He made no move to kiss her, which she longed for, but he seemed completely at ease, a different person, almost, from the last time they'd lain side by side on this soft, grassy bank.

'I brought some wine,' Beth said, fumbling in her rucksack and pulling out the cold bottle. She opened it and filled the two glasses.

Owen took his and drank. 'Thanks,' he said, propping his drink against a tussock and lying back, as he had last time.

Beth knelt beside him, looking down at him hungrily. His hair gleamed in the sun, his tanned face looked soft in rest, with no a hint of the frustration or disappointment that seemd to affect the lives of nearly everyone else she knew.

He was wearing a white shirt, without the stiff collar which once would have been attached and over the shirt, a well-worn brown tweed waistcoat; both garments migh have belonged to his grandfather – perhaps from his Sunday chapel outfit. Beth couldn't help a quick smile at the Lawrentian references prompted by this garb, heightened when, with his eyes closed, he fumbled in one of the slit waistcoat pockets and pulled out a short length of hazel twig. Opening one eye, he handed it to Beth.

'I made it for you, in case you mean to get a dog of your own sometime.'

Examining the slender twig more closely, Beth recognised a precision crafted whistle, which she put straight to her lips and blew. The thin, almost inaudibly high note it produced had Mack immediately pricking up his ears, bracing himself for action. Beth grinned, impressed by the affect.

'Don't blow it again now,' Owen rumbled lazily. 'You'll get him all geed up.'

Thrilled at what may have lain behind the gift, Beth lay on her back beside Owen and stared up at the frothy white clouds suspended in the blue air.

'Do you sometimes feel guilty?' he asked, so suddenly that he startled her.

'Of course I do,' she answered, before she had time to think. 'At least, I feel accountable. Catholics have a reputation for feeling guilty,' she laughed, embarrassed, wondering how she'd let herself in for this. 'Quite wrongly, as it happens. Right now, for instance, I don't feel the slightest hint of guilt,' she lied, wishing she didn't have to, now she was really talking to him.

'I do,' he said softly.

Abruptly Beth's euphoria evaporated from fear of the admission he was about to make.

'You feel guilty? But why....?' Wildly, she wondered if, perhaps, there was a wife whom Ruth had never known about; or, more likely, some girl in the valley, simple, sturdy, coyly attractive.

He turned his head to her with dark chestnut eyes wide open. He knew what she was thinking; he reached out a hand and laid it softly on her thigh.

'I'm not talking about that sort of guilt,' he said. 'It's just sitting here, in the day, knowing that my family, my forefathers...' He looked up at a pale pink ripple of cloud in the clearing sky and spoke with unexpected harshness. 'Miserable, dried up little dung-balls, most of 'em - if they could see me, they'd despise me for lying here in the sun with a beautiful woman and dreaming, when there's work to do.'

Beth listened, fascinated by this unexpected flow of words, while Owen shrugged off his ancestors' reproof. 'Of course, there's always been work to do. But for my people, life on the hills has meant nothing more than that - work, or no life on the hills. It was such a basic truth for them that it's been sort of passed to me - like through my father's seed and my mother's egg.' He looked at Beth with a glint of humour in his eyes. 'What Ruth called a "gift-parcel of tribal knowledge", about her Andeans.' He smiled at the idea of Ruth purveying wisdom. 'I'd have always known the value of work, anyway, without being told every day for the first twenty years of my life.'

'But don't you like the work you do, then?' Beth asked, with a vague sense of disappointment.

'I don't mind it; matter of fact, I like it in some ways; I like a challenge. Nothing big, like - but things that would be too much for most of the people up here in the valley.'

'Do you often reach those targets?' Beth asked.

'Usually.' He shrugged indifferently. 'At least it gives me a reason for doing them,' he said, with no apparent desire for sympathy. He reached for his wine.

In the ten minutes they'd spent together up on the hillside lying on the rug, gazing across at the long shadows of the trees, like

Beyond Gospel Pass

dark green splashes down the far slope of the valley, Beth was seeing some of her preconceptions about Owen proved hopelessly wrong. She could see now that she wasn't, after all, talking to a semi-educated hill farmer, ten years younger than her, whose initial attraction for her had been overwhelmingly physical. She was beginning to realise that their relationship, such as it was, would from now on be dictated by other criteria.

Excited, a little frightened of the possibilities this offered, she looked across at his beautiful profile – the long lashes resting on a tanned cheek, subtly flawed by a slender scar; the generous lips and strong, dark-stubbled chin.

An eyelid flicked up; he turned his head to her and reached out a hand to touch her face. Instinctively, her body wriggled towards him as she looked into the velvet darkness of his eyes. She felt a flush of adrenalin and the strong drug of passion, until everything that mattered in the world was focused in the few inches that separated their lips and the only sound was their own breathing.

The pregnant tension between them was shattered by an uproar of barking from Mack, the dog, who'd been lying peacefully at Owen's feet. Now he stood with his neck hair in a black ruff, displaying angry resentment as he gazed beyond his master into the copse.

Beth sat up and turned with Owen to see two men in shorts, T-shirts and hiking boots, with army bergens on their backs, standing at the spring, where they were filling their water flasks.

The destruction of the moment had been stark and sudden. For Beth, the anticlimax was almost unbearable. Owen more prosaically got to his feet, brushing moss and bracken from his jeans. He ordered the dog to be quiet while he looked at the walkers without expression. They were evidently aware of their rights as well as the disruption they had caused; they turned and nodded, grinning transparently and carried on filling their bottles.

When they'd finished, they walked across the copse. They were both in their twenties and healthy-looking, though there was a peculiar defensiveness about them.

'Do you live up here?' the taller of them said in flat Yorkshire.

Owen nodded.

"Cause there's a sheep back down 'track there,' He pointed north along the valley, 'all caught up in some of that square wire at 'top of field.'

Owen was immediately alert. 'Was it in the field or on the hillside?'

'It were on the hill. But it's got one leg through 'wire, like it's been knitted in.'

'I'll have to see to it,' Owen said briskly. He gave Beth a quick glance; he didn't need to speak, although she raised her eyebrows in an agony of regret as she got to her feet, too. 'C'mon,' he said to Mack and strode away across the clearing.

Beth was left standing with the walkers. She didn't want to talk to them, but she felt she couldn't simply go away without saying anything.

'Where have you come from?' she asked, uncomfortably aware of their salacious scrutiny.

'We're staying at the YHA at Capel-y-ffin, walking out from there every day.'

'We're going up over t'other side of ridge today,' said the other, also broad Yorkshire, and nodded up the hillside. 'They told us this were a grand place to fill our bottles.'

'Yes,' Beth agreed. 'It's lovely water. But,' she glanced at her watch, 'I must get back. Enjoy your walk. Bye.'

She didn't wait for any extension of the conversation, and turned to scramble back down the hill, beside the gully.

Once she was sure she was out of their sight, she stopped and sat down. Confused and angry, she surveyed the valley while she tried to calm her thoughts; after her short but revealing conversation with Owen, she still felt as if she'd been exposed momentarily to some exotic drug that was going to transport her to a parallel world, only to see it disappear from under her nose.

Owen hadn't even kissed her, and she couldn't understand why he'd left so quickly. But then, she considered, if sheep were Owen's work, they must take priority. But – dammit! – the animal wouldn't die if it was stuck for another half an hour, and besides, it might not be one of his anyway.

Suddenly, looking north, she found that she could see his head in the distance, bobbing sporadically above the bracken as he walked down the hill and she sat watching until he had disappeared for good while she tried to expunge a sense of childish hurt.

Mark phoned the next morning.

Beyond Gospel Pass

Through the thin veil of bravado he put up, Beth could tell that his problems were increasing. He told her with a rueful chuckle that his printers were 'giving him a hard time'. She didn't need to be told that this was probably because they wanted large sums of money, which he owed but couldn't pay them.

She didn't ask him about Marcel Gehring; she didn't feel she was capable of dispensing adequate sympathy.

'So... when are you coming back to London?' Mark asked.

'I'm not due in court until the middle of next week and I'm getting so much work done up here, it'd be disruptive to leave now.'

'But I rather miss you; and isn't your mother coming over at the end of the month?'

'I told her I couldn't see her until after the festival, so she put it back a week. And you'll be all right, sweetie,' she said, wanting to be kind and concerned for him.

He sighed. 'I suppose if you're working well up there, there's no point in spoiling it; that's one of the reasons we bought the place, after all. I'll be up on Friday anyway, in time for George Arbuthnott's talk. But if you see Henry or Boo, perhaps you could sound them out – you know, check how things are going and let me know?'

'Yes, of course I will.'

A few minutes after she'd finished speaking to Mark, the clerk in her chambers rang; her clients wanted an urgent meeting - the next day, preferably.

'But I'll see them next week, before we go into court,' Beth said, trying to hide the panic which the thought of leaving the valley and Owen had suddenly produced. 'What do they want, anyway?'

'Don't worry, Miss Langthorne. I've spoken to their solicitor and I think it'll keep. I'll just tell 'em "no", 'til next Wednesday.'

'Thanks, Herbert. It really would suit me and their case very much better if I could get on with it undisturbed up here.' She wondered if the clerk knew she was lying.

Herbert, she reflected as she put the phone down, was an astute man. He had no legal training whatever, but he seemed able somehow, perhaps by osmosis, to read the state of every case that his chambers handled, and to evaluate finely the relationship between his barristers and their clients. She felt confident and only mildly guilty about putting off her Slovak women until the following week.

Outside, she heard the postman pull up in his Royal Mail Land Rover. Through the window, she saw him skilfully lob the rubber-banded bundle of mail across the yard so that it landed smartly on the doorstep.

When she opened the door to pick it up, she found beside it a small sheet of lined paper, weighted down with a stone. As soon as she saw the writing, even before she'd started to read it, she knew it was Owen's.

Nine

Owen's writing was neat and sloped forward with a faintly italic shape to it.

I'll be up at the Wergin Pool this evening at nine.

Beth stared at the simple statement. It was neither request nor exhortation, presuming without question that she would want to be there with him.

She walked back into the kitchen and put it on the table. She made herself a small cafetiere of coffee, and read the note a dozen more times.

It was, she thought, one of the most beguiling messages she'd ever received – seductive and utterly confident, though without a trace of arrogance.

The Wergin was just the spot she would have chosen to meet him, too.

She smiled at her complete lack of objectivity in judging his first letter to her; but she felt exhilarated and proud that she had not underestimated him.

With a contented sigh, she switched the phone to answer mode and walked to the study.

Beth settled down in front of her laptop on the desk. She inserted a disk containing details of a recent immigration judgement and scrolled through the words that appeared on her screen. She sedulously highlighted the sections she considered relevant to the present case and printed them off for closer study.

She managed to work satisfactorily until midday, when thoughts of Owen stole back into her consciousness and began to affect her concentration. She switched off her computer and went outside in bare feet. She walked fifteen yards up the hill until she was level with the roof of the house, where she could look across and see if there were any sign of Ruth on the other side of the valley. A cloud was still draped along the ridge like a grey, fleecy rug, but she could see Ruth's farm and her Land Rover, back from the garage in Hay, presumably repaired, parked outside a small stone barn.

Beth hurried back into the house, slipped her feet into a pair of flip-flops, ran across the road and stumbled down the bank to the river. She paddled through the shallow water and scrambled like a child up the other side.

She found Ruth in her kitchen - a room that occupied at least half the ground floor of the small farmhouse. It was more than a kitchen; it contained a large deal table, like Beth's, as well as a pair of big, old chesterfields draped with Andean blankets. From the low, smoked oak beams hung clusters of drying wild flowers, herbs and sweet, musky mushrooms. The few patches of flat wall held a bewildering display of primitive paintings of such crudeness and integrity, Beth thought, they could have come from anywhere in the Third World – from the plains of Patagonia to the Siberian tundra.

Ruth was sitting serenely at the table, listening to the news on the radio while she cleaned two small trout.

'Who are you doing those for?' Beth laughed. 'Aren't you supposed to be a veggie?'

Ruth smiled as she switched off her radio. 'Fish don't count. There's too much goodness in them. Anyway, one of my little admirers brought them up for me and he'd be very hurt if I didn't eat them.'

Beth was looking around as if she were expecting to see someone else in the house. 'So, what's happened to your Peruvians?'

'They've gone,' Ruth said. 'They were only here for two nights.'

'That must have been nice for you.'

Ruth looked up from the trout in her hand and smiled like a cat that was about to devour it. 'It was. Lovely.'

'Maybe you should do it more often.'

'It's more beautiful if you don't.'

Beth laughed; she couldn't see that making love to Owen every day for a year could diminish the beauty of the act in any way. 'Perhaps you're right,' she pretended to agree. 'Even oysters would pall if you ate them all the time.' She looked at Ruth, and imagined her naked with Ramon. 'What will you do if you get pregnant?'

Beyond Gospel Pass

Ruth wasn't fazed by the abrupt change in Beth's tone. 'I won't; I made sure of that.'

'Okay, but suppose you did?'

'God knows,' Ruth said truthfully. 'I find it takes all my time to look after myself.'

Beth nodded. Despite Ruth's close affinity with Mother Earth, there was nothing of the earth mother about her. She had, as Owen perhaps implied in calling her Rhiannon, too mystical and ethereal a relationship with life to be involved with the physical aspects of child-bearing. Beth felt a glow of warmth in her own womb and felt sorry for her.

Ruth had finished with the trout and stood up, as if to divert the conversation. 'Do you want to stay and have some lunch?'

'Thanks, I'd love to.'

'I would have asked you before, but I thought you were going back to London with Mark.'

'I changed my mind. My mother usually comes over at the end of May to see an old friend who lives in Surrey, but she's not arriving until next Monday and I've been getting on so well with my work up here, I thought I'd stay.'

'That's great. And I see you're still walking up to the ridge every day.'

Beth detected a faint subtext in Ruth's words.

'Yes, it's doing me so much good.'

Ruth was taking a bottle of wine from the fridge. She turned and put it on the table. She started to peel off the foil. 'It must be. You look...' she paused, searching for a word '...radiant.'

Beth had never known Ruth to give way to cynicism; she looked hard at her now to see any outward sign of it. But when Ruth looked up, there was only a sweet smile on her fragile lips. 'I saw you talking to Owen yesterday, up at the spring on Loxidge Tump.'

At that distance, Ruth must have been looking at them through the binoculars that hung on the back of the door, ostensibly for watching birds in the valley. Beth was both relieved and sorry that she had seen them doing no more than talk. 'Yes, I bumped into him up there, with his dog. We had quite a long chat, curiously enough. He came over to find some water for us last Monday.'

Ruth nodded as if she knew all about it. 'And what did you talk about...?'

Beth hesitated. She wasn't sure if she wanted to share her discovery; at the same time, she was conscious that Ruth had already insisted there were unexpected depths to Owen.

'His... sense of guilt.'

'Guilt? Why should he feel guilt?'

Relieved that Owen hadn't already had the same conversation with Ruth, Beth answered slowly. 'He said the work ethic is so deeply ingrained in the people here, because life has always been so hard, he expects to feel guilty every time he stops working, or does anything just for his own pleasure. But he doesn't seem to feel he belongs to the same race as the rest of them.'

'No, in a way, he doesn't.' Ruth busied herself with a goats' cheese salad. 'He's stronger, bigger and finer than any of them. Like, sometimes, you see a tup, bred the same as any of the others on the hill, but so different from the rest of the flock that there's no question of keeping such a special beast on the mountains, nor any argument about sending it up to the ram sale at Builth. These little hill sheep are like the humans up here - they haven't got much need for showy genes.'

Ruth put a wooden bowl on the table and rattled in the drawer for cutlery.

Beth sat down and spoke casually, as if she wasn't longing for every scrap of information there was to hear about Owen. 'But how would Owen be any different, in that sense? As far as I can tell, there's a pretty small gene pool up here.'

Ruth laughed and filled two glasses with wine. 'They're not that inbred, really. And when they were building the big dam at Grwnyre Fawr in the next valley back in the twenties, there were three hundred Irish navvies there for a few years, living in huts and scouring the countryside for somewhere to plant their seed. There may not be any Irish names in this valley, but there are plenty of Irish eyes.'

'And you think Owen's family might have a few of these stray genes?'

'They say his mother's mother liked to wander over the mountain... who knows, seventy five years on?'

Beth found she liked the idea of Owen being some kind of Hibernian throw-back - a misfit Celt in a Celtic world, unwilling to

Beyond Gospel Pass

conform to the traditional drudgery of his ancestors' life in the hills. She was fascinated that, despite his recognition of these differences and even with his special gifts, he still lived in the hills; she wondered why he stayed.

Later, the breeze blew the cloud off the ridge, scattering it like shreds of tattered wool and leaving only a few faint streaks across the sun.

Beth was walking up the hillside towards a deep notch in the horizon, to which the long straight path she was following seemed to lead directly. She stopped and looked back, remembering what Owen had told her, and found that the way she had come led, without question, straight back to the ruins of the ancient Priory. She turned and carried on, conscious that her feet were being directed by this primeval path, prospected and laid by some prehistoric dodman, like the Long Man of Wilmington with his surveyor's rods, if the New Age theories in George Arbuthnott's book were to be believed. Soon, inevitably, the path would meet the large, softly sculpted rock of the Wergin stone, where Owen would be waiting for her.

Her head was full of Owen; he had begun to assume mythical proportions for her. There were too many remarkable things about him to ignore, and the total man had become for her more than the sum of his individual gifts.

That he possessed such strength and tenderness in such an uncompromisingly masculine frame seemed nothing less than a miracle.

But she remembered what Ruth had said, that he was a special breed up here – like some rare species of lichen or moorland bird – a golden plover among the meadow pipits.

She saw him first. He was sitting on the ground with his back propped against the old red sandstone megalith. His legs were stretched out in front of him, towards the glittering corrie pool - where Ruth had secretly watched him bathe.

He had placed himself on the shady side of the stone, though the sun was just beginning to light the edges of his face. His eyes were closed. He looked serene, Beth thought, and part of the landscape.

Beside him was a small khaki webbing bag that could have come from any army surplus store. It was slightly grimy, Beth guessed, from years of carrying midday sandwiches up to the hills.

His eyes flicked open and he smiled at her. He patted the patch of grass beside him. It looked surprisingly free of sheep droppings and detritus; she wondered if he'd cleared it for them.

She sat down close beside him and leaned up to kiss his warm, rough cheek.

He turned his mouth towards hers and they came together like two hungry animals. After a minute or two, the intensity of it left her breathless. She leaned back to look at him, and couldn't stop smiling. 'Owen, that was delicious!' she laughed. 'And I mean delicious. What have you been eating?'

Owen gave her a slow smile and hooked up his bag. 'I brought you something. I was tasting it just now.' He pulled out a jar of clear, pale gold honey. He unscrewed the lid. It was so fluid that his finger had left no impression. 'Would you like to try it?'

'Later.'

He put the pot down beside him and brought his arm back to take her shoulder and draw her to him again.

This time, as they kissed, they undressed one another, deliberately and without haste.

Beth faltered for a moment as he opened her small cotton top, and she felt her nipples swell and harden in the warm breeze.

'Owen,' she murmured reluctantly. 'Some one might come. Aren't we on a footpath here?'

'Mmm,' he nodded as he kissed her neck. 'More than that; this is one of the most powerful leys in the valley, maybe in all the Black Mountains.'

'But anybody could coming walking up here.'

'Mack'll let me know long before they do.'

'But he didn't bark when I came up.'

'He knew not to,' Owen said, as if it were obvious.

Beth felt she could trust absolutely everything Owen told her about living in these mountains. She relaxed, and slowly unbuckled his belt, savouring the added frisson of risk, being where they were, nearly naked under a pink and blue evening sky, with the mountain birds trilling in the furze, and the buzzards keening overhead.

From where they lay, the lower hillside and the valley floor were hidden by a small wood, but they had a clear view of the opposite ridge, Yr Twmpa and the two and a half thousand foot peak of Waun Fach beyond.

Beyond Gospel Pass

Beth thought she wouldn't care if by some bizarre mischance someone on the other side, or on the ridge behind, was gazing at them through binoculars. It was as if it were the only natural place to be making love to this man of the hills, with the shadow of the great stone pointing east up the hillside.

'Why does the ley pass right by this stone?'

'There are always lines passing old stones like this, and this one is important.'

'Ruth said it was a magic stone; but she didn't say exactly what it was supposed to do.'

'Oh, she knows,' Owen said with a short laugh.

'Why? What does it do?'

'Until not so long ago, if the women from down the valley found they weren't having children, they'd come up here and rub their naked breasts against the stone.'

Beth gasped at the thought of the discomfort and the realisation of what she was about to do directly beneath this great stone totem of fertility.

She wondered with a ripple of private laughter if Owen had deliberately chosen the rock, aligned on a conspicuous conduit of Earth energy and renowned for its special powers, as the ideal site for their love-making. Perhaps he'd already divined the strength of her procreative urge.

He lay on his back, naked in the stone's long shadow. She draped herself across him, laying her breasts on his hard chest and running her fingers through the light mantle of dark hair over his pectorals.

With his strong fingers he caressed her legs, still tanned from Provence, and the contrasting paleness of her buttocks, until with tantalising rhythm, he started softly to probe the warm depths of her tingling vagina.

She felt him grow bigger against her thigh; she moved her leg and arched her neck to look down at his shining glans, like a crimson bloom on its own broad stem. She laughed, thinking of flowers and bees alighting on them to collect nectar for their honey. He followed her eyes and smiled up at her.

She giggled and propped herself up a little. He raised his brow as she leaned over him to pick up the honey jar.

She unscrewed the lid and held it up. The sun diffused through the golden fluid and she lowered the jar until the scattered rays fell on Owen's rigid flesh. 'Do you know,' she teased him with a grin she'd never produced before. 'I think I might try some of your honey.'

As she spoke, she twisted round and with the tip of her tongue protruding between her teeth, carefully tilted the jar so that the honey cascaded down, glittering in the lowered sun, and covered his erection with a golden film. Slowly she moved her hand down its length until honey seeped in among the black curls at its base and made them glisten.

He didn't speak, but showed his thoughts with a broad smile.

Beth put the jar on the ground, lowered her head, and with the point of her tongue, began slowly to lick the honey from him.

It was truly delicious, she thought, and smiled at the image of herself – a bee drinking nectar from a mountain flower. She licked the sweetness from her lips and opened her mouth to envelop a shiny acorn of firm flesh.

Owen murmured and squeezed the softness of her buttocks.

She tenderly licked the sweet stickiness from him while his hands deftly fondled her own small acorn tip so she thought she might explode.

She took her mouth away and turned her lips up to his. They kissed again; he lifted her and she closed her eyes with a gasp as she began to rock back and forth with him inside her, filling her so it felt like he'd reach her heart and she was losing the power of reason; if an earthquake had shook the valley just then, she would never have known; it seemed as if a star had burst in her when Owen at last released his flood of precious seed.

He reached up and drew her softening nipples against his chest and wrapped his arms like a boa around her while she whimpered with joy and felt his heart beating just like hers and a trickle of honey from his groin run down her thigh.

The intensity of orgasm ebbed and the sounds of the natural world began once more to reach Beth's consciousness. The buzzards still mewed, and the small birds twittered their evening territorial airs. Beth felt the breeze on her naked buttocks, and clenched them, laughing, and squeezing his dwindling flesh.

It was only then that Mack began to bark.

Beyond Gospel Pass

Owen lifted Beth's shoulders so that he could see her face, and smiled into her eyes with unambiguous passion. 'Time for a swim,' he muttered hoarsely. He raised himself and lifted her, still on him. He carried her five paces to the clear pool and waded in. Beth gasped as the icy water touched her hot skin, but he plunged on towards the middle of the pool until they were submerged to their necks, ten feet from the edge.

The intruders announced by Mack's barking arrived a few moments later. The two of them gave no sign of having seen Owen and Beth at first but stopped abruptly when they saw the scattered clothing by the rock. They turned and looked at the pool. They were the men who had appeared the day before, up by the spring.

The taller one stared at Beth with undisguised excitement, though surely, she thought with alarm, he could only see her head as she shivered in the cold water, vigorously stirring it into ripples to obscure his view.

She turned away, suddenly frightened by his vicious gaze and sought reassurance from Owen.

He sensed her need.

He looked at the two men. 'If I was you, I wouldn't hang around here,' he said in an uncompromising rumble. 'There's a lot of loose energy about – a strong ley crossing in a solstice moon. It can be a dangerous place,' he added more sternly.

Both men reacted as if they understood and, without a word, took two steps back to the path and carried on towards the notch at the head of the valley without looking back.

Owen looked at Beth with a faint smile.

'What was all that? ' she asked. 'And why did they take any goddam notice?'

'You get hundreds of ley hunters up here following Alfred Watkins' tracks. They come from all over the world; you can always tell 'em. They believe anything anyone says about what they call earth mysteries.'

'I think they just thought you were going to leap out of the water and hit them,' Beth said through chattering teeth.

Owen laughed now. 'That too.' And he started to wade through the chilly water towards the side of the pool.

'It's okay,' Beth said, wriggling from his arms. 'I'll walk.'

The bottom of the pool was soft with peaty mud that squelched up between her toes. She shivered and laughed and staggered to the edge, where she stood on the grass, shaking the drops from her body.

She felt his hands on her hips and started to tremble once more. She turned to him, overwhelmed with tenderness for his strength and gentleness, for the excitement and the child she was sure he could give her. He wrapped his arms around her again and she kissed him with more passion than she'd ever felt for any man, easily dismissing the picture of Father Aidan's censorious face that had crept into her mind, and the guilt that still murmured deep inside her.

Owen's phallus, shrunken by the icy waters, began to stir; Beth lowered a warming hand. 'Will Mack still be on duty?' she whispered between kisses.

'Mmm,' Owen nodded.

Beth sank to the ground and lay stretched out on the short mountain grass, which a millennium of grazing sheep had made into a soft bed on a base of springy peat.

Owen joined her, and this time their love was slower, deeper, longer, more serene. When finally he came and Beth felt she was melting into the ground beneath her, the sun was dropping behind the hills in the far west and had daubed the sky with streaks of turquoise, gold, salmon and scarlet.

For a while, neither of them spoke until he carefully rolled over and lay beside her. He put an arm under her neck so she could turn and lie against him.

'Do you suppose those two awful men were watching?' she asked.

'No. Mack would have sent them on.'

Beth nodded, confident that these moments of ecstasy had been privately theirs, in Owen's secluded kingdom up here on the hillside with the sacred stone and the magic pool to guard them. 'You said they'd believe anything they were told about earth mysteries; does that mean you think it's all rubbish?'

Owen didn't answer for a while.

Beth prompted him. 'I know you've cured people, just with your hands, and you can find water and energy and stuff using that old ring - so why are you cynical about these things?'

Beyond Gospel Pass

'They're not mysteries to me. When I heal, all I do is help to sort out the electro-magnetic pattern – the aura, you could call it – you find around every person. And there are leys that make the ring turn, though not half so many as people keep saying they've found, and these people get all excited about UFOs and crop circles and well dressing and other stuff which is just meaningless old superstition.'

Beth looked at him and tried to fathom how much he really knew and felt, how much was instinctive and flowed from his physical closeness to the earth. 'Why did you choose to meet me up here?' she asked, nodding at the stone, which loomed across the clearing, now black against the dusky sky.

He smiled as he rubbed her cooling arms and legs. 'I just knew it was the best place.'

Beth laughed. 'It was. I've never been anywhere so deeply beautiful,' she said, surprised to find that she really meant it, feeling that she would have been happy to be here, just like this for ever.

But a sudden sharp gust of evening breeze caught her naked skin. She shivered. 'I'd better put some clothes on.' She wriggled out of his arms and got to her feet. Picking up her skirt, she dried the last drops of water before wrapping it around her waist and slipping the little jersey top over her head.

Owen lay watching her before he stood up and unhurriedly pulled on his jeans and boots, finally slipping a T-shirt over his muscular chest. He leaned down and picked up the half-full pot of honey. 'Would you like some more?'

Beth laughed. 'I'll take it home and save it for another time.'

'There's lots more; there's twenty hives in the river meadow and only mother and the two of us to feed.'

'And the two of you?' Beth asked, puzzled.

'Mam and me,' Owen said quietly.

'Oh,' Beth said. 'I met her the other day.'

'Yes, she said.' He didn't need to add that he wasn't pleased that Beth had been up to Blaen Fawr. 'C'mon,' he said holding out a hand to her. 'I'll take you home.' He started to lead her along the path the same way that the two ley hunters had gone.

'Are we going back to your house?' Beth asked, surprised.

Owen shook his head. 'No.'

'But this is the wrong way.'

A smile flickered across his face. 'It'll still be quicker.'

Beth wondered why there suddenly seemed a distance between them, when only minutes before they'd felt like a single, indivisible entity.

After the track had passed through a narrow stone gully between two rocks, where they had to walk singly, it widened into a shelf on the hillside with a cluster of scrubby bushes on one side.

Owen turned off the path and walked behind the scrub. He came out wheeling a big red quad bike.

Beth was aghast. 'Why have you got that?'

He looked at her quizzically. 'Why not? I have to get around the hills.'

'But I thought you used ponies.'

'Some do; most use these.' He gave a long, eerie whistle and a moment later his collie appeared from the hill below and jumped up onto the rack on the back of the ATV.

With a flourish Owen invited Beth onto the rear seat of the vehicle before he fired it into life.

It was almost dark and the headlamps beamed up the rutted track in front of them. Owen steered skilfully, obviously with long experience and after a few hundred yards, took a turn off the track, doubling back down the hill towards the valley floor.

They bucked and flew through the blackening dusk and the wind whistled wildly through Beth's hair. She had never in her life been on a quad or a motorbike, but she recognised that the exhilaration, on the edge of terror, was something like a fairground ride, and only bearable as long as she kept total trust in Owen. She wrapped her arms around his waist in the absolute certainty that he wouldn't let her be harmed, conscious of an omnipotence about him, reflected in all he did.

When they lurched off the track and onto the metalled upper lane that served the high farms and ran parallel to the river below, Owen opened up the throttle.

The hedgerows hurtled by, a few inches from her cheek, and Beth felt she was being carried off to another world where other senses and new rules of physics applied.

But suddenly the four-wheeled bike stopped with a crunch; the motor and its lights were switched off, and Owen turned to her in the silent darkness.

'Here you are. Home.'

Beyond Gospel Pass

Beth realised only now that they were outside the gates at Pant-y-Groes. She felt foolish, having no idea how they'd got here so fast. While she dithered, Owen took her hand and helped her off the seat.

They stood for a while, face to face in the dark lane, slowly seeing more in the new starlight as their pupils grew.

He put his arms around her and squeezed her. She stretched up, seeking his lips and they kissed again.

When she drew back, he released her, with a soft, 'Good night.'

But she knew she didn't want him to go. Phrases from her clumsy past leaped into her head. *Aren't you coming in for coffee? ..... It's late, why don't you stay?*

'Goodnight,' she murmured. 'Will you come and have supper here tomorrow night?'

In the gloom, she saw him nod. He leaned down and gave her one last, brief kiss before turning to straddle his quad. The peace of the valley was shattered a second later when he turned the ignition key and manoeuvred the bike round to face the other way.

With a supple toe, he clicked the engine into gear. She discerned a faint nod of his dark head and he shot away up the lane.

She stood where she was, listening to the noise of the vehicle as it buzzed its way up the valley towards Blaen Fawr. When it was almost gone she ran in through the gates and up the hill behind the house and stood where she could just pick out the headlight flashing through the alders and oaks that lined the valley road until there was nothing left to see.

Woken by an inquisitive Grimond, Beth blinked her eyes open next morning and looked at the clock by her bed. She shook her head, astonished to see how long she'd slept. Until she had finally lost consciousness the night before, her head had been a battlefield of righteousness and remorse where neither peaceful resolution nor sleep were possible.

Now, more calm, there was no doubt in her mind. She'd experienced something with Owen which she'd never even imagined before; there could be no question that an experience so beautiful and fulfilling could, in itself, be anything other than good. For she was certain, with no justification beyond the calendar and a powerful intuition, that she was pregnant.

Jessica Meredith

At the same time, tempering her rapture was her awareness of the firm spiritual and emotional commitments she'd made to Mark a dozen, generally happy years before.

She had left the curtains open when she'd come up to bed in the dark; now a weak grey light seeped through the windows. She shuddered while the moral conflict rumbled on in her head; she was almost angry that her intellectual honesty wouldn't allow her simply to wallow in the remembered ecstasy of the previous sunset.

She looked morosely out at the damp valley; the worst thing about these Welsh hills, she thought, was the way the weather could turn around so completely. Sometimes she'd noticed that when the Herefordshire lowlands were soaking up sunshine, beyond the first ridge that marked the border a few miles to their west, the clouds would be crouched menacingly just above the bleak moorland, thick as the fleece of a dirty, unshorn sheep.

Only the certainty that Owen would be coming back to her that evening allowed her to tolerate the hours between.

Resigned to the reality of the day, she applied herself to her work. She was even grateful for a while to lose herself in long conferences with her instructing solicitor and her junior.

Towards the end of the morning, though, a battered grey pick-up rattled through the gates of the courtyard in front of the house and a small man jumped from the cab.

Beth knew she'd seen his weasel face before but she didn't remember where, until he dropped the sides and started to pull some long sawn planks from the back of his lorry, and she remembered Mark's raised vegetable beds.

She sighed over the fatuousness of the venture and its almost guaranteed failure in the face of other things going on in Mark's life.

She was tempted to send the man – what was he called? Ishy Price – back to Hay, but, perhaps alert to her intentions, by the time she opened the door and walked out to see him, he'd got all the boards unloaded.

"Ello, missus. I brought them planks, then, for your 'usband's garden.'

She sensed his contempt for the idea beneath his oily smile, which made her want to support Mark. Sending the boards back, as she'd first intended, was now out of the question.

Beyond Gospel Pass

'Thanks. Would you mind stacking them in that shed?' She nodded at an open fronted barn where they could lie undisturbed for years, if necessary.

He didn't voice his obvious resentment and moved them. Once he'd finished, as if to get his own back, he asked, 'How's that neighbour of yours, young Owen Rhys?"

Beth prayed that he didn't see her flinch. 'All right, so far as I know,' she said airily. 'He's not really a neighbour. His farm's right up at the top of the valley.'

'He's a boy, though, isn't he?'

Beth longed to ask why Owen was 'a boy', but she was damned if she was going to get her information from Ishy Price.

'Thanks so much for bringing the timber. My husband'll be delighted,' she said, making it clear that the conversation was at an end.

Ishy dragged a grubby sheet of paper from his pocket and thrust it at her. 'I'll want some money, now.'

'If you give me the bill, I'll pass it on to my husband,' Beth said, to repay him for raising the subject of Owen.

'Oh no. If I'm not paid, I'll have to take it back. I can't afford to give credit.'

'My husband won't pay for it without seeing it,' Beth shrugged.

'I can't leave it.'

'Then you'd better take it away.' She was enjoying his discomfort.

He stood and squirmed, knew he'd lost, aware that if he didn't get his money now, once the timber had been checked, the chances were he'd only ever see part of it.

He sighed, giving in philosophically with an unctuous grin and handing over the bill. 'Oh well, I could see he was a gentleman - not someone to let down a small, struggling businessman. Could he bring in the cash at the weekend?'

'I'll be sure to ask him,' Beth said with her best New England graciousness. 'Now, if you'll forgive me...'

Ishy Price backed away and slipped into the cab of his small truck, hastily started it, turned and drove out of the gate, displaying his resentment with spinning wheels on the loose surface of the lane.

Beth didn't feel any better for the encounter. Depressed, she walked back into the house. She wanted to talk to someone who would understand the intensity of her dilemma. She didn't want to tell them about it, only to know that they could give her sympathy if she invited it.

She looked up the Llewellyns' telephone number and dialled it.

To her relief, Boo answered.

'It's Elizabeth Langthorne – sorry, Beth Powell – here. I wondered if it was too late to invite you for lunch today?'

'Why not?' Boo came back heartily. 'Did you mean up at your house?'

'No, no, that's much too far for you to come. We'll meet at Dino's, if that's all right.'

'I tell you what,' Boo said. 'I've got a better idea, and we've just about got time. I've got a voucher for lunch for two at Llyswen Hall. I won it in some raffle last year and it runs out at the end of the month. Let's use that.'

Beth didn't argue. Boo was, she guessed, a formidable opponent and besides, she liked the idea of lunch at a place that promoted itself as the finest restaurant in mid-Wales, modest claim though that was.

Beth arrived before Boo at the large former manor house, which had been lavishly converted a few years before to a hotel of some pretension. She sat on her own on a small sofa in a spacious ante-room with a glass of champagne in front of her. The room was full of people who, Beth thought, would have looked more at home in the crowded Soho bar of the Groucho Club than in this rural grandeur, but she gained some pleasure from the views across the meadows by the Wye and the russet ridges of the hills that rose on the other side.

When she looked at the menu and the prices, she saw why even Boo wasn't prepared to forego the chance of a free lunch.

The waiters all sounded French and Beth suspected some of them probably were. She smiled to herself; she enjoyed the incongruity of a place like this in a remote corner of Britain.

She heard Boo arriving in the lobby of the hotel with a lot of commotion and loud instructions to take water out to her dogs in the car. When she came into the room, Beth stood up and greeted her warmly, surprised how glad she was to see her.

Beyond Gospel Pass

Boo looked around the room with a grin. 'My God, this is all a bit flash, especially for Wales. Believe it or not, this is the first time I've been here since it became an hotel - and that must have been ten years ago. I used to know it when it was a house, though.' She lowered her voice a few token decibels. 'In fact, I was subjected to my first session of heavy petting out there, somewhere on that terrace, at a pompous little dance the de Traffords held here. I wonder who on earth comes here now... Have you been before?'

Beth shook her head. 'No, but it's absolutely full of people from the festival. A lot of the bigger authors stay here.'

'With their publishers footing the bill, no doubt.'

Beth nodded. 'Mark had to put Marcel Gehring up here last year. We were supposed to come over and have dinner with him one night but never did.'

'It's lucky I didn't tell them we were on a freebie when I booked. They'd probably have turned us down for some paying customers.'

In the busy restaurant, they ordered carefully and extravagantly - seafood, for the most part, with some good white wine.

Beth had already found that she and Boo, despite differences in their politics and nationality, used similar terms of reference and they could talk in that short-hand which follows shared basic perceptions about society. She wanted to expose just enough of her dilemma to evoke a reaction - preferably sympathy, possibly advice and, perhaps, a little envy; but before she did that, she was conscious that she had to establish Mark's position.

'Have Henry's committee made a decision over their candidate?' she asked casually

Boo glanced at Beth, assessing her resilience. 'If you can call choosing a course of action by default making a decision.'

Beth knew at once what was coming and though, logically, she should have been prepared, it caught her unawares. She felt a sudden surge of nausea. 'Pugh gets it?' she asked throatily.

'It's not a hundred per cent confirmed yet, but Henry was grumbling about it last night. He's much keener on Mark, but he's afraid he can't quite swing it. Those stodgy old farmers carry a lot of clout round here.'

'Why's that?' Beth asked, resenting these people who were going to take away her public reason for being in Wales.

Boo shrugged. 'They represent solidity, a continuum of wisdom. It's all balls, of course; they're just reactionary old stick-in-the-muds; they're only liberal because their fathers and grandfathers were chapel, not church. When you're up against that sort of thing, well...' She didn't need to finish.

'Poor Mark,' Beth said quietly.

'Did he think it was in the bag?' Boo asked. 'I don't blame him; but there it is.'

'Hmm,' Beth grunted, feeling truly sorry for Mark. 'We only bought Pant-y-Groes because he was so sure of getting the nomination.'

'Unpredictable stuff, politics; not always at all logical. Still...' Boo leaned back and gave Beth a speculative look, '...you seem to have enjoyed it up here, so it can't have been a complete waste of time.'

'No.' Beth thought of Owen's naked, brown shoulders rising and falling as the sinking sun turned the sky into a golden halo above his dark head. 'It hasn't been entirely pointless.'

'Rather a change from the Groucho Club, I should think, these rustic men.'

Beth guessed that Boo's antennae, well schooled and regularly exercised, were adept at sensing subtle undercurrents. She smiled, conceding, just a little, that she'd been rumbled.

'Sometimes,' she admitted, 'in London, it's easy to forget that there are so many other codes of existence beyond the arrogant political correctness of the chattering folk.'

Boo laughed. 'Don't take this the wrong way, but whenever I've heard anyone use the term "chattering classes" - crass generalisation that it is - I've always thought of clever people like you - though not as attractive - sitting around in million pound houses in Hampstead and Notting Hill, voting for Tony Blair and sending their kids to public schools.'

'We're not that bad,' Beth grinned, half agreeing.

Boo became more serious. 'How will your husband take it?'

Beth drew in a long breath. 'Not well. To tell the truth, I think he's been banking on it to make up for the business problems he's been having.'

Beyond Gospel Pass

'But I thought Archimedes was doing so well... Isn't this chap George Arbuthnott coming up to talk at Hay tomorrow? I see he's written a book about ley lines and a lot of other New Age mumbo-jumbo; someone was telling me it's selling like hot cakes.'

'It is, but not enough to offset the losses on all the others that aren't. Mark gets so carried away when he gets a hit, he immediately expands just a bit more than he can handle. I'm afraid a lot of bad decisions are coming to a head.' She stopped, suddenly feeling very disloyal. 'But Boo, please; I'm telling you this in strict confidence. You won't tell Henry or anyone else, will you?'

'I understand,' Boo said, quietly, this time. 'It's funny that for some of us, loyalty is the last emotion to fade.'

Beth didn't answer her; it was obvious that Boo understood there was some kind of crisis in her relationship with Mark. Though perhaps, she thought, that wasn't so astute after all; there must have been few people whose marriages didn't move through radical changes of equilibrium after a dozen years or so, and Boo wouldn't have to be a mind-reader to know that most women of Beth's age who hadn't had children would have started feeling deeply resentful about it.

She grinned at Boo with a playful tilt of her eyebrow. 'I wouldn't want to let Mark down, but I admit, it's good to be noticed by the outside world too, now and again.'

She wondered if Boo could read the lie - at least the omission - in her words.

Boo looked steadily back at her. 'Even so, I bet you find these Welsh hill people hard to interpret.'

Beth found herself teetering for a moment between full confession and retreat from the brink. She looked at Boo, sighed as she dropped a screen across the back of her eyes. She knew as she did it that she'd cut off a possible source of consolation, by holding out the sweets of intimate revelation on the palm of her hand, only to close her fingers over them suddenly and take them back. But she realised that now she'd entered a new phase in her feelings for Owen, she couldn't share them with someone who was connected to Mark's ambitions.

After all, she couldn't simply abandon her role in Mark's life. She was his anchor, the bedrock on which he had built much of his life over the last fifteen years; and now, facing failure on two fronts, he would need her more than ever. The least she could do was to concentrate her best powers of persuasion on getting Boo more firmly into Mark's camp as far as his immediate political aims were concerned.

At the same time, Boo took Beth's somewhat abrupt withdrawal of intimacy in her stride. She lifted a shoulder slightly, looking at a well-known author who had just come into the room with two girls.

'Aren't those the girls who were chatting up that friend of yours last weekend?' she said, as if this were the first time they'd referred to Owen.

Beth felt herself redden with discomfort and a little jealousy at what Owen might have thought of the luscious young women at the peak of their sexuality. But, realistically, she acknowledged that it was to her, not to either of them, that Owen had made love on the hillside the evening before, and she found herself growing warm at the memory of it.

'Owen, you mean?' she asked. 'I don't suppose they got very far with him.'

For the rest of lunch, the rapport that at first had seemed so full of promise gave way to a slight awkwardness between the two women. Beth raised the topic of Mark's candidacy again, but she drove away from Llyswen Hall knowing that her rearguard campaign on his behalf was probably too late. Nevertheless, she guessed that Boo had a strong influence over her husband, possibly over other members of his committee, and she was hopeful that the case wasn't absolutely lost.

On the credit side, her efforts on Mark's behalf seemed to have made up a little for her adultery, though she didn't pretend to herself that she wasn't longing to see Owen again. On her way through Hay she stopped at the whole-food shop to buy ingredients for the dinner she planned to cook for him. She didn't stint herself; she was eager to show him that she had earthy skills of her own. These thoughts made her positive and light-hearted about what was happening to her. When, in the window of a gallery next to the deli, she saw a painting of a bright summer sun over Hay Bluff and Gospel Pass, as if it might help to cement her lingering euphoria, she walked straight in and bought it.

Ten

Beth didn't recognise the new Volvo estate car in front of Pant-y-Groes when she arrived back there. She parked the Saab beside it and saw with a sinking stomach that there was no one in the car.

The front door of the house was unlocked. She pushed it open. Mark was sitting at the kitchen table with a glass of wine in front of him and the grin he wore when he was half way drunk.

'Hello, angel. We decided to come up this morning and have lunch at the Yew Tree so George could get a decent night's sleep before his show. This is George, by the way.'

He waved across the table at a man with the bland composure of a regional television newscaster. Beth recognised him from the photograph on the back of his book as George Arbuthnott, author of *The Leys of the Land.*

He must have driven, she concluded. He wasn't as drunk as Mark. He was the first to his feet.

'George, this is my wife,' Mark said. He also stood up and walked a little erratically towards Beth to kiss her on both cheeks.

'Mrs Powell, what a pleasure to meet you,' the author said suavely.

This was a man, Beth perceived, whose books were published as much for his perceived personal magnetism as for his qualities as a writer. But she acknowledged that he used his charm efficiently. She smiled at him. 'Hi. Call me Beth, please. You're appearing in the main marquee tomorrow, aren't you?'

He nodded with a knowing grin. 'Describing some of the Great Enigmas of our Mother Earth to the eager seekers of enlightenment in the tented lyceum of Hay.'

Jessica Meredith

This sounded to Beth like a well-rehearsed line. Still, she thought, he was good-looking enough to carry it off. At least it might help to shift some of Archimedes' massive stock of books.

'I look forward to it.' She turned to Mark, who had also got to his feet and was taking down a glass for her. 'No thanks, Mark. I won't have a drink yet. I've only just had lunch with Boo Llewellyn.'

Mark looked pleased but apprehensive. 'Did she say anything?' He held up a hand. 'No. Tell me later.'

'All right. Where is your author staying?' She glanced expectantly at George Arbuthnott.

'Here, of course. I've promised him fine wines and a sumptuous dinner, so I hope you're on good form.'

Beth thought bleakly of her plans for an evening alone with Owen. She turned aside, biting her lip and screwed up her eyes with disappointment. She would have to tell him not to come; getting rid of Mark and his author wasn't feasible.

She quickly collected herself with a deep breath and turned back. 'I've got everything I need for a sublime dinner,' she declared and smiled supportively at her husband.

Later, she banished Mark and his guest from the kitchen; they wandered out onto the hillside where the rain had eased off and streaks of blue showed through the broken clouds.

As she prepared dinner, she thought bitterly of what she would miss with Owen. She was dreading his arrival here. She had tried to contact him but when she'd dialled the number Susie gave her, she'd let it ring a dozen or more times before it was picked up and answered by a man's voice which she didn't recognise.

'Who is it?'

'It's Beth Powell here,' she'd said.

After a few seconds silence, the phone was put down.

Distraught with frustration, she rang back at once, but this time, the line was engaged.

She had tried a few more times, with no reply.

As she cooked, she talked herself into a frame of mind where she could cope with Owen coming. After all, he still had to talk to Mark about the water. But she didn't know how she could bear to see him if he couldn't stay.

Beyond Gospel Pass

The men came back in and went through to the sitting room. Owen arrived half an hour later. He looked at Beth for a second as she let him in. He had obviously seen the other car outside and showed no surprise at seeing Mark come into the kitchen.

Mark greeted him cheerily. 'Owen, how are you? Come on in; have a drink.'

Owen shook his head. 'I won't stop.'

'But you must.' Mark turned to George who had followed him into the kitchen. 'Owen's a neighbour; he's found a buried water course for us out in the field - divining with a pendulum!'

The author eyed Owen sceptically. Beth wondered if he believed in the mysteries about which he wrote with such authority.

'Owen,' Mark said with the animation that he always displayed when making opportune introductions. 'This is George Arbuthnott. We've just published his new book on ley lines - *The Leys of the Land*.'

George played along, reluctantly, Beth thought. He shook hands with Owen. 'I'd be very interested to see you work,' he said with implausible deference.

Beth made a face as she glanced at Owen, who looked back at George, offering nothing. 'I don't do it often, and I like to do it on my own.'

Defensively, Beth wanted to tell them how she had watched him find the water, but she caught his eye and knew he didn't need her protection.

'But you'll show me the spot, won't you, Owen?' Mark asked.

'I already showed Mrs Powell.'

'Yes,' Beth said. 'It's okay, Mark; I know where it is and he's marked it for you. But Owen, I've got masses for dinner, why don't you stay?'

Owen looked at her. He didn't speak at once. She tried to read through his motionless black pupils, until he shook his head a few fractions of an inch. 'Thanks, Mrs Powell. Another time.'

A moment later she was staring at his back disappearing through the doorway, watching the door close behind him. She gripped the back of the chair in front of her, and wished he'd looked back, just once, before he'd gone.

'Beth? What's the matter?' Mark asked.

She shook her head and forced a short laugh. 'Nothing - at least - nothing much. I just remembered I haven't put the rice on.' She turned to hide her anguish, and busied herself with a big pan of water on the range.

Later, while they ate a beef stroganoff that had worked despite Beth's quivering hands, Mark seemed to have sobered up. Beth noticed that he was drinking two glasses of water to every glass of wine. She guessed he'd realised in time that he was getting more drunk than his author and he was taking precautions against possible indiscretions. One of Mark's more self-critical pronouncements was that every verbal gaffe he'd ever made – and there'd been many – had been uttered when he was drunk. It occurred to Beth that with Gehring off the list, this supercilious pseud was now, de facto, Archimedes' biggest star. She quelled her instinct to put George in his place – he didn't present a satisfactory challenge anyway – and asked him instead about his subject.

'Do you know,' he said, smiling with pleasure at the sound of his deep, mellifluous voice, 'this valley contains some of the best examples of leys in the country. That's why I persuaded Mark to come up today. I'm going out early tomorrow to check some of the alignments for myself - something fresh to take to my talk. For instance, there's a major line that runs from the northern end of the valley through that wonderful old priory at the bottom.'

Beth wanted to tell him that she knew, that she had walked it and fornicated on it, but she restrained herself; it would have done nothing more than interrupt his carefully constructed flow of words.

'It's been known since the Twenties,' George went on. 'It comes down the east side of the valley, starting on a slight notch in the sky line by Gospel Pass, past a megalith called the Virgin's stone.'

'*Wergin*,' Beth couldn't help correcting him. 'A W and a hard G.'

'Undoubtedly a local corruption. You know it?' George took the trouble to ask.

Beth thought of the long shifting shadow the stone had cast over her and Owen as they had made love. 'Yes, I've been up there.'

'And there's a well, too I believe?'

Beth nodded again. 'A spring-fed pool; I swam in it.'

'Did you?' Mark asked, indignantly. 'You never told me.'

'I haven't had a chance to tell you anything yet. But George, go on about the ley line.'

Beyond Gospel Pass

'*Ley*,' he corrected her. 'That was what Alfred Watkins called them. Anyway it follows an absolutely straight course from the notch, through the Virgin stone, along an ancient track which is still marked on the map, straight across the nave of the priory church and on to a holy well on the far side. Now, the extraordinary thing is,' he hurried on before Beth could modify any more of his observations, 'is that another line has recently been plotted that converges on the Priory, running down the other side of this valley. It starts from a natural outcrop above a farm called Blaen Fawr, through the site of an old chapel in another farm and over a small tumulus to the Priory.'

'Which farm?' Mark asked, trying to pay attention.

'The Hendre.'

'Good God, that's Ruth's!' Mark laughed. 'She never told me she was living on a ley. I wonder if she knows.'

'I'm sure she does,' Beth said, 'if it's true.'

'It's certainly true,' George huffed. 'In my book I cite it as a prime example.'

'Then we must introduce you to her and you can ask her about it,' Beth said lightly.

'I'll go over tomorrow morning,' the author said in a businesslike way. 'Perhaps you could let her know?'

George talked about other leys in the area, producing a copy of his book to illustrate them. Beth noticed how he used words and phrases that seemed specially chosen for their sonorous qualities. She listened, and compared the authority with which he delivered his information to Owen's.

She was beginning to think that Owen wasn't only a rare creature on the hills, as Ruth had expressed it, but a rarity in her world too - a man who talked only within the bounds of his personal experience; though these seemed, paradoxically, to encompass far more than the cosmopolitan world inhabited by people like George Arbuthnott.

The author, with his glib theorising and artful extrapolations of Alfred Watkins's original and simple observations, seemed to her like an old-time huckster, a man who knew how to exploit a market for alternative, ersatz religions and had recognised appropriate qualities in some of the faintly plausible, if unscientific phenomena described as "earth mysteries". It was likely that he'd decided he could produce half a dozen best-selling books on the subject, without much research, or, for that matter, much risk of being seriously troubled by critics, literary or scientific.

She didn't condemn Mark's enthusiasm for the author; he'd always said that, as a publisher, his primary function was to entertain, and promoting unprovable theories about the alignment of untappable energies on the earth's surface, even endowing of the Earth herself with deistic properties, was harmless enough and – Beth smiled to herself – they also made the Catholic redemptionist creed she struggled to sustain look sophisticated. More than that, beside the brazen opportunism and verbosity of the author, Owen's spare pronouncements had the solid trustiness of the mountain bedrock.

She wished again that he'd given her some small sign before he'd left that evening, some acknowledgement of the depths they'd shared over the past seventy-two hours. She felt ashamed to be associated with an ideological carpetbagger like George and found herself wondering how someone as inconsequential as herself could hold any interest for a man of such gravitas as Owen.

Mark prompted George with a few more questions until the conversation drifted back to publishing. Beth didn't join in, but while Mark was out of the room, looking in his wine store for another bottle of the expensive vintage he'd offered the author and, Beth guessed, urinating in the paddock, George gave her a sympathetic and slightly mournful look. 'You know, I hope this book does well – as much for Mark's sake as my own.'

'Oh?'

'Well, yes. This is my third book with Archimedes, and they've been very supportive, but frankly, they're going through a rocky patch, and that makes it harder for them to get the kind of coverage this type of book demands.'

'Why should going through a rocky patch make that harder?'

'Because Mark's eye is off the ball.' George took a deep breath through quivering nostrils. 'You know he's lost Marcel?'

Beth nodded. 'Do you know why?

'Didn't he tell you?'

'Not exactly.'

'Gehring's an arrogant little shit who thinks anyone who disagrees with him is a Luddite and an intellectual pigmy, but sadly, he can't write and he needs his editor, and I'm afraid when Jonathan Mundy left Archimedes, he took the only suitable editor with him;

Beyond Gospel Pass

Mark should have foreseen that would happen; fortunately, I don't rely heavily on any outside guidance for my own prose.'

'So there's no chance of getting him back?'

'Absolutely none,' George said, then put a finger to his lips as they heard Mark coming back across the yard.

When they were lying in bed in the dark with the quiet sounds of the night drifting in through the window, Beth blamed a fictional pain in her innards on lunch at Llyswen Hall, and wouldn't let Mark make love to her.

Mark, already subdued by the week's onslaught of commercial troubles, didn't fight but spoke peevishly into the dark. 'Why did you want Owen to stay to dinner?'

'Why on earth not?'

'Well, you haven't before.'

'But we didn't even know him until two weeks ago, for heaven's sake! And he's a neighbour, and he found our water.'

'I suppose so, but you might have consulted me; after all George is quite an important author...'

'And you thought Owen might show him up for the charlatan he is?' Beth said scratchily, regretting it at once.

'Precisely,' Mark said, surprising her, and sighed. 'It's not easy keeping these people happy - their egos are so bloody tender.'

'Is that why you've lost Marcel?'

'Yeah,' Mark grunted. 'Thank God I've got a new career in sight.'

This was the clearest admission of Archimedes' failure that Mark had yet allowed her. She felt numbed by guilt at her inability to give him comfort, although he had reached the position he was in entirely on his own. But she knew too that she must tell him the truth about his political prospects before he started relying on them.

'Marco, darling,' she said gently. 'I don't know that you have.'

He sat up and turned to her. She didn't move; she lay still with her back to him, looking at the curtains billowing gently in the night breeze.

'What are you talking about? What have you heard? I thought you said you'd seen Boo.'

Beth sighed.

Mark stiffened.

'I did,' she said. 'She told me that Henry's entirely on your side, and two or three of the others, but she thought he wasn't going to persuade enough of the rest to drop Pugh. They want Pugh because he's local - a known quantity. Of course, Henry knows it's irrational and unrealistic and all that, but they're independent minded people and they like to show it.'

'I just don't believe they're all against me,' Mark said with quiet defiance as his robust optimism reasserted itself. 'Boo wouldn't know all the ins and outs.'

'She knows what Henry's told her.'

'Even so. Henry might have deliberately understated my chances. He probably knew she'd be seeing you, and didn't want to be heard making definite predictions. I mean - he's in a sensitive position.'

'Maybe,' Beth said. 'I hope so, anyway, but perhaps it'd be better not to count on it.' She stretched her arm behind her, found his hand and squeezed it. He pulled it away, rolled over and put his back to her.

Beth gazed into the darkness. There wasn't anything more she could do for him that night.

Beth woke and looked at Mark; he was still sound asleep. She wondered when he had lost consciousness. He must have been tormented most of the night by the hovering prospect of inevitable failure in his business and, now, in his second career, before it had even started.

Although they'd spoken too often about the dangers of expanding Archimedes, debated too often the risks of entering politics with any sense of certainty, she still felt sympathy for him. In that sense, she'd done all that one adult could for another, she nevertheless found that she still felt compassion towards the man whom once she had vowed, wearing a white silk dress with a tulle veil and jasmine in her hair, to love and cherish forever. She was devastated that she could do no more for him.

She slipped out of bed, dressed without waking him, and went downstairs.

George Arbuthnott was already sitting at the table, hunched over a large-scale local map. He looked up and smiled. Beth guessed from a speculative look in his eye that he was weighing up the chances of engaging her physical interest; which only added to her annoyance that this author now represented the best card in Mark's hand.

'I'd very much like to follow up what we were talking about last night,' he said. 'This is a new ley we've identified, and I'm bound to be asked about it this afternoon, as it's local.'

'So you want to go and see if it might really exist?' Beth asked.

George didn't answer for a moment. He gave Beth a cold, admonishing look, then said, 'Frankly, yes.'

'I'm sure Ruth'll give you lots of encouragement. Let me get you some breakfast, then I'll take you over to meet her.'

Beth was glad of the distraction, and as she'd predicted, Ruth greeted the hypothesis that her house was plum in the middle of a ley with eager nods of comprehension. 'That makes real sense,' she said. 'I've noticed the dogs always like to lie the same way here in the kitchen, and it's one of the most serene places I know; that's why I've stayed, even though it's played hell with my love life,' she added, with a droopy-eyed simper at George.

Beth left them to egg each other on, at least in the matter of earth energies, and walked back home across the river.

The sun hadn't appeared yet that morning, and the clouds looked unfriendly. Beth wasn't looking forward to a wet afternoon in the tented enclave of the Literary Festival. She was anyway unconvinced by the idea that any writer worth reading could heighten the impact of his work by speaking about it. As far as she could see, the solitary nature of the occupation of writing left those who practised it with either an awkward, unprepossessing presence and delivery or a severe tendency to attacks of verbal diarrhoea.

George, who wasn't what she called a real writer, would undoubtedly have his performance polished to a satisfactory gleam. The more she saw of him, the more she resented Mark's current reliance on him, and the more she valued the simple honesty she found in Owen.

She hoped profoundly that she would see Owen that morning. She thought he might come to Pant-y-Groes on the pretext of talking to Mark about the water, though she knew, really, that he'd already said all he needed to.

Mark was in the kitchen when she arrived back at the house. She made an effort to consider his needs, reminding him that they had been invited to Ruth's that evening to meet Laura Chichester, and deflected any serious talk by describing Ishy Price's visit. This prompted Mark to go out and inspect the timber, which she was more sure than ever would never be used. There seemed to her a bleak inevitability about the stillbirth of the raised bed project and she found herself wanting to reach that point as soon as possible, even if it meant the abandonment of Pant-y-Groes.

Beth arrived in Hay with Mark and George after lunch. She wasn't surprised to find that George's talk was a sell-out. Mark rushed on ahead with the author while she wandered into the muddy Festival compound. Walking quietly into the tent which housed a large temporary bookshop, she heard Paul Ricardo talking to a strong-featured woman, in her fifties and still assertively attractive, who was busily stacking up piles of George's last three books on a trestle table. They had been consigned by Archimedes, like all other publishers, on sale-or-return, for the author to sign for fans who would come surging into the shop after his talk.

'He's asked for a bottle of chilled Chardonnay and some sparkling Welsh spring water to be on the table while he signs,' the woman sniffed.

'Well, I shouldn't grumble at the cost of a bottle. His show's sold out; you'll sell two or three hundred books.'

'I told you he'd do well when you were sceptical,' she answered smugly. ' I'm at the sharp end of the business – unlike the pompous farts who write the Sunday reviews. I know what people *will* buy, not what they *ought* to.'

'I don't mind people buying books about crop circles and magic stones, but George Arbuthnott would be writing about aerobic ballet or fish diets or self-hypnosis if he thought he'd sell more.'

'So what?'

Paul Ricardo was about to answer with a guarded smile, when he saw Beth and smiled at her instead. Beth wondered if he remembered who she was until he said smoothly, 'Hello, Mrs Powell.' He'd obviously forgotten her first name. 'This is Belinda Sharp, who sells the books here. She's the only person who makes any money out of the whole show.'

Belinda Sharp glanced at Beth and turned back to the festival director with a quick snort of laughter. 'It's all right, Paul, you don't have to convince me you do it all for love,'

Beyond Gospel Pass

He was still looking at Beth. 'None of us do much for love, do we?' he remarked. 'Are you coming to see George? Oh yes, of course, he's one of your authors.'

'I wouldn't say mine,' Beth replied. 'I'm not really part of Archimedes.'

'But you've come to see him anyway? Let me take you in, make sure you have a clear view of his twinkling eye and chiselled jaw.'

Before George had walked onto the stage, Beth spotted Owen fifty feet away, sitting on a side seat up at the back, under the eaves of the marquee. She flushed, feeling foolish, and hoped he couldn't see from that distance. But he wasn't looking in her direction. While the crowd rumbled quietly, waiting for the author to appear, she carried on snatching glances at Owen until, suddenly, he was looking straight at her and for a few seconds it was as if their eyes were joined by a solid conduit which nothing could break. She seemed to feel his strength pour down it into her, until, abruptly, he turned away, the power supply was snapped off and she was left trembling.

A sudden squall squeezed and billowed the fabric auditorium like a panting whale, while a drum roll of rain on the canvas roof announced George Arbuthnott's entrance. He was introduced by a literary critic from one of the Sunday broad-sheets who didn't look comfortable at being roped in by Paul Ricardo at the last minute.

While George delivered a short resume of *Leys of the Land* and answered mainly sympathetic questions with polished deftness and wit, Beth glanced at Owen from time to time. Only once was he looking back at her. She made up her mind to see him when George's talk had finished. Mark wouldn't notice; he would be hanging around the author's signing session.

She waited restlessly for George to finish, but he was enjoying himself. He cleverly laughed his way out of every tight corner. He made a case for the newly plotted ley in the Llanthony Valley, which seemed to satisfy the sceptics in the audience. Beth thought of Ruth, living on the hillside on her own, on the newly discovered ley, with her healthy libido and continual proximity to Owen.

She wished Ruth had asked Owen to dinner that night and thought perhaps she could persuade her to. After all, he knew as much about walking these hills as anyone. Beth laughed to herself - perhaps

Laura Chichester would end up weaving one of her fantasy encounters around him.

As the crowd was leaving the tent to fill the bars and to queue for copies of George Arbuthnott's books, Beth fought her way against the tide to the exit nearest to Owen's seat.

She hurried back and forth through the crowd, trying to hide her anxiety at missing him, but there was no sign of him.

'Shit, shit!' Beth hissed under her breath, as much at her own reaction as at not finding him.

'Whatever's the matter, Beth?' Ruth was gazing at her with large, compassionate eyes. 'What's gone wrong?'

'Nothing,' Beth snapped, then tried to moderate her voice. 'At least, nothing important. I ... I dropped my credit card somewhere. I was on my way to the book shop, and now it's completely disappeared.'

'Oh no, what a drag! Can I help you look?'

'No, it doesn't matter. I'll phone and cancel it. I've got several others.'

'You would,' Ruth chided with a smile. 'You urban high consumer.'

'Talking of high consumption, is dinner still on at your place this evening? I forgot to ask when I brought George Bullshit round this morning.'

'Why do you call him that?' Ruth asked. 'I really liked him.'

'Oh, Ruth,' Beth admonished, 'you *couldn't*.'

'Well, I did, and I asked him to dinner tonight.' She saw Beth's face fall. 'It's okay, he couldn't come. He's got to get straight back to London after this.'

'What a shame,' Beth said sarcastically. 'But I did think you might like to ask Owen.'

Ruth looked back sharply. 'Did you? Do you think he'd fit in? He's not really the dinner party type is he – I mean...'

'Why not ask him?'

'Yes, all right,' Ruth said with sudden decisiveness. 'It would be interesting to see how Laura reacted to him!'

By now Beth and Ruth had walked out from the awning that surrounded the tent, and the sight of blue sky, bright sunshine and clouds retreating in the east provoked a new mood; suddenly people

Beyond Gospel Pass

were laughing and the Welsh sheep's milk ice-cream stall was doing brisk business. 'Would you like one?' Beth asked.

'Do you want to drive?' Mark offered Beth his car keys.

Beth took them and sighed to herself; Mark must have been very depressed. She looked at him for a moment; his face sagged as if the muscles in it had collapsed. He turned away and gazed up at the hills to the south.

Beth unlocked the car. 'Are you sure you don't want to go to the party at the gallery?'

'Frankly, yes; I'm certain I don't. I've had enough of Hay for one day.' He opened the passenger door and got in.

Beth climbed in beside him and started the engine. 'How did sales of George's book go?' she asked.

Mark grunted. 'Amazing,' he said flatly. 'It's staggering how many punters there are for that stuff.'

'Is it so surprising? Since everyone started abandoning the churches, they've been searching everywhere for alternatives. I'd say there's a great future for neo-paganism; maybe Archimedes should specialise in it.'

'That'd mean getting rather a long way from the principles of our namesake.'

'I'm sure he'd understand.'

Mark didn't answer for a moment as Beth steered her way through the mass of people milling across the road on their way from the various shows, back into the town to buy books and to eat. 'It's probably too late anyway,' he said.

Beth glanced at him. She'd never heard him sound so defeated. 'Come on, my guy. You've just published a hit! Use the chance to make a few changes. Cut all the waste in the firm. Get rid of those offices, remainder all the dud stock, and chuck out those expensive new graduates.'

Beth had never been so explicit in her advice to Mark, and she'd never thought she would hear herself advocating wholesale sackings, but she sensed that this was one of the few opportunities she would have to say what she thought, with any hope of Mark listening.

He turned and stared at her. 'What are you talking about? What waste?'

'Mark, you can call it what you like, but whatever it is, there's something about your firm that means it never makes any money, even when it's selling a lot of books, and while I'm the last person to grovel exclusively at the throne of profit, you can't keep on making a loss.'

Mark opened his mouth to speak, but closed it again.

Beth didn't press her point. 'But that's not what's depressing you, is it?'

'No.' Mark took a long, quavering breath. 'I saw Henry.'

'Oh.... and he told you?'

'Yes. He was very sorry, but there's no chance of my being adopted.'

Beth could tell that he was still stunned, not only by disappointment, but by disbelief, too.

'Boo did say that politics up here were particularly irrational and unpredictable,' Beth said quietly.

'What the fuck would she know about it?' Mark exploded, cloaking his self-doubt with anger. 'How much time do you think she spends thinking about the great issues of the day?'

'Since you ask, a lot more than you probably give her credit for. I think she's quite perceptive.'

'Do you indeed? Well, that is a statement about you, as your late lamented father would have said.' Mark stared ahead.

Beth didn't rise. She turned into the lane marked 'Capel-y-ffin' and drove on towards Hay Bluff. She understood how Mark felt, but when he started lashing out at everyone around him, she could only say 'I told you so'. She certainly wasn't going to argue about Boo Llewellyn.

She found herself wondering how Mark in his present mood would cope with the formidable Laura Chichester at dinner. Ruth had told her while they were eating their ice creams that she'd also invited a man who wrote for *The Guardian* and lived with his wife in the next valley. Beth decided not to tell Mark before they got there; she prayed that the journalist hadn't heard about his failure to get the Liberal nomination.

Inevitably, she thought of Owen. She wondered if Ruth would find him and persuade him to come too. Now, seeing Mark's state of mind, she knew that he and Owen at the same table could form the basis of a disastrous evening; she wished she'd never suggested it.

Beyond Gospel Pass

When they arrived back at Pant-y-Groes, Beth dropped Mark, and made an excuse to drive on to Ruth's.

Ruth was in the kitchen cheerfully preparing two menus - one for herself, and another for all her meat-eating guests. 'It wouldn't be like me to proselytise,' she said with a grin when Beth remarked on it.

'What about Owen?' Beth asked.

'He can't come,' Ruth said briskly.

Beth winced with sudden pangs of rejection. 'Did you tell him I'd be here?'

Ruth stopped what she was doing and looked at her. 'Should that have made a difference?'

'No,' Beth said hurriedly. 'No, of course not; I just wondered.'

'I didn't speak to Owen. I got his mother. She told me he couldn't come.'

'Why?'

'I don't know; I didn't ask. You don't ask Megan Rhys things like that.'

'Do you know her?'

'Well, yes, a bit. She's a funny old thing.'

'But I thought she never saw anyone.'

'She's rather secretive; she doesn't come out much, in fact, she only comes down the valley a few times a year. But I've seen her quite often since I've been here.'

'But have you ever been in the house?'

'No,' Ruth admitted. 'I don't think anyone's ever allowed in.'

'Doesn't Owen ever have people in?'

'No,' Ruth laughed at the silliness of the idea. 'Owen's not a party-giver.'

'I didn't mean giving parties,' Beth said impatiently. 'But he must have friends.'

'Not really. I suppose he might go to the pub once in blue moon if he had to see the landlord about something, but that's what's so wonderful about him; he's an absolutely self-contained entity; he's one of those men who truly don't need anyone else.'

'Not even girlfriends?'

'Oh, I don't know about that.'

Beth was burning with frustration at this tantalising lack of knowledge but with an effort she restrained herself. 'How's everything else going for this evening, then?'

Ruth told her what she was cooking. 'The guest of honour should be here any time now. Do you know, I'm really looking forward to seeing her. She's been promising to come for years and whatever her faults, she's very stimulating to have around. I think even you'll agree.'

'*Even* me?'

'Beth, you know what I mean.'

Beth supposed she did. 'I hope Mark perks up a bit in the next couple of hours.'

'Why? What's wrong?'

'Don't for God's sake tell him I told you, but he's just heard that he hasn't been selected as Liberal candidate for the constituency.'

'Oh my God!' Ruth put down the knife she was holding and stared at Beth with her mouth open. 'But he told me he had it; he wasn't in any doubt. What on earth went wrong?'

'Nothing went wrong. The old farts who dominate the committee simply liked the other man more. Of course, Mark, being Mark, assumed all along that the whole process was a mere formality. If my dear husband has a fault, it's that he suffers from what you might call over-sanguinity.'

'Poor Mark,' Ruth said in a hushed voice. 'Nobody else will know, will they?'

'I doubt it; I hope not anyway, and just for tonight, I'd rather they didn't. With luck he'll drink enough to forget about it and try to sign your walking friend to Archimedes. But perhaps it's a good thing Owen isn't coming,' she murmured, half to herself.

'Why?' Ruth looked at her sharply.

'Oh, I don't know. I think he makes Mark rather nervous. Have you ever had him to a meal here?'

'Yes, quite a few times, but not to "dinner".' She scratched the quotation marks in the air with her fingers.

'You mean, just you and him?'

'Beth, why on earth not?'

'No reason at all,' Beth said quickly. 'But how come he was at George Arbuthnott's talk this afternoon?'

'He dropped in this morning, after you'd brought George over, and George gave him a ticket; I think he was rather impressed with Owen.'

'I should think he was – and nervous, too.'

Beyond Gospel Pass

Ruth looked at her, considering. 'Yes, perhaps you're right. I don't suppose people like George would have a clue how to deal with strong silent men.'

'Nor would most people in publishing.'

Ruth nodded. 'But Owen does take the ley lines seriously. He's told me he's seen his pendulum react strongly to them.'

'Yes,' Beth said jealously. 'He told me too, when I saw him dowse for our water.'

'Of course, he laughs at a lot of the nonsense he hears. All these ley hunters think they know more about them, but he can actually feel where they are.'

'We met a couple of weirdos when I was with him the other day.'

'Where was that?' Ruth asked.

Beth hesitated before editing the truth. 'It was when you saw us up by Black Darren. They were filling their bottles at the crack in the rock.'

'The water gushing out of that crack always reminds me of Moses.'

Beth murmured a laugh; but she was thinking of the other evening, when the men had disturbed them and the honey was still fresh in her mouth.

Eleven

'Where have you been?' Mark asked with a hint of peevishness when Beth came back from Ruth's.

'Just talking to Ruth while she was preparing dinner.'

'Has Laura What's-her-name turned up yet?'

'She hadn't when I left. Ruth's expecting her any minute; she's very excited by the whole thing. There's a journalist coming too, by the way.'

'Oh?' Mark's ears pricked up out of habit.

'Luke Green, from *The Guardian*.'

'I do know who Luke Green writes for,' Mark said sourly.

'Do you know him?'

'No, but he's one of those smart-arse hacks who wants a fight with everyone he meets.'

'Then you'd better be on best behaviour.'

'I'm not sure I want to go at all.'

'That'd a be a first,' Beth grinned

'Come on, Beth, don't be unfair. I'm feeling bloody pissed off about losing the seat.'

'The opportunity to fight the seat,' she corrected gently.

'I'd have won it.'

'Mark, we can't be sure of that. Anyway, you may as well come. You might be able to get Laura to write for you - do a walker's eye view of ley lines and associated earth mysteries.'

Mark lifted an eyebrow and nodded. 'That's not a bad idea.'

Beth's misgivings about Luke Green's presence were confirmed the minute she saw him. He was five foot seven, stout and blond, with a malevolent spark in his eyes.

Beyond Gospel Pass

His wife Margaret, by contrast, smiled faintly and shyly at everyone through enormous glasses; her long, straight hair was cut with a fringe and she wore a dress from Laura Ashley's floral period.

The Greens were standing in Ruth's kitchen clutching large glasses of pale champagne. Luke gazed challengingly at Mark and Beth, then held out a hand. 'Luke Green; this is Margaret.'

'Mark Powell, and Beth Langthorne,' Mark said.

Beth saw the journalist trying to work out the relationship between them. She guessed that Ruth had told him Mark had a wife. 'Mark's been kind enough to leave me with my own identity,' she explained.

'You're the publisher?' Luke said accusingly to Mark.

'Somebody's got to do it.'

'Still missing the NBA?' Luke asked.

Mark laughed. 'Forgotten all about it. I'm more worried about collecting internet rights now.' And the two of them settled down to a short discussion about the marketing of information.

Beth turned to the nervous Margaret. 'Where's Ruth?

'She's upstairs getting something for Laura Chichester.'

'Laura's arrived, then?'

'I think she got here some time ago, but she seems to have been in the bath ever since.'

'I don't blame her, after a hard day's trudging.'

'But she's only come from the White Castle. We sometimes walk there and back in a day,' Margaret said breathlessly.

This unexpected bragging amused Beth. 'Perhaps she was up late last night collecting material,' she suggested.

Margaret hesitated for a moment before she saw the joke and laughed. 'Have you seen her programmes?'

'Once or twice; I don't watch TV too much.'

'I do, when Luke's away. It gets quite lonely up here. God knows what the old people did before telly was invented. My neighbour's eighty-five and his whole social life centres round *Emmerdale*.'

Beth understood that she was being rebuked for her elitist dismissal of a popular medium, and was apologising for it when Laura Chichester made her entrance.

It was clear from Laura's comportment that she expected everyone to stop and look when she came into a room.

Mark smiled appreciatively at her beautiful, tanned face, her healthy blonde hair and conspicuous breasts. Beth and Margaret nodded guardedly at Ruth's introduction. Luke Green took no notice; Beth observed Laura marking him down to be dealt with later.

'Oh, you and Mark haven't got a drink!' Ruth exclaimed. 'You should have helped yourselves.' She picked up a bottle. 'The Hendre's own champagne – elderflower,' she announced as she filled more glasses with the lightly fizzing liquid. She saw that Luke had barely touched his, scowling at what was in his glass. 'I suppose you want some whisky?' she asked with forthrightness that surprised Beth.

Luke's face lightened and he nodded.

'Don't you like Ruth's champagne?' Laura challenged.

'For a start, it's not champagne, and anyway, I hate all fizzy wine. It makes me fart.'

'I don't suppose that takes a lot of doing,' Laura retorted, with a smile that took the edge off it.

As she spoke, Beth watched her, fascinated. Laura wasn't just a good-looking woman with a spectacular body; despite wearing very little make-up, jeans and a plain T-shirt, there was no doubt that she possessed a distinct presence – 'star quality', Beth supposed - that was even stronger in the flesh than it was on television. It was obvious that she liked to control as much as possible of what was going on around her and Beth couldn't help admiring the skill with which she was overcoming the sharp little journalist.

It was only later, when they were sitting around Ruth's impressively battered old table that Beth spoke to her.

The walker deferred – genuinely, as far as Beth could see – to the supposed superior intellect required to do Beth's job, though Beth tried to correct this view by talking about the sheer crassness of some of the men in her profession; she agreed, though, that there were no dim women at the bar. Ruth had produced a simple red wine to eat with the lamb cutlets she was serving, and smiled happily as she ate a trout with a fagiolini and fennel salad. She was enjoying the banter, and preening herself a little for having brought together such well-matched performers.

Towards the end of dinner the conversation had turned to the day's events at the festival, and George Arbuthnott's talk.

Ruth told everyone excitedly about the new ley George claimed to have found, how it ran from the tump, visible at the top of the valley, through the barn outside, which had been a fourteenth-century chapel – an outlyer of the Priory in the valley – and the very room they were sitting in, along a straight old drove road that led from the Hendre to the Priory itself, and on to a small mound half way up Hatteral Ridge on the far side of the valley.

Giny wasn't surprised that Luke Green took the cynics' view. 'If I looked hard enough, I should think I could find twenty ley lines running through my house.'

'No, you wouldn't,' Mark said – out of loyalty to his author, Beth guessed. 'You'd find that just aligning three likely spots is surprisingly hard, and a lot of the lines Watkins found round here showed a clear alignment of five or six sites. You get your map out and try it.'

'I will!' Luke said fierily and Beth sensed a scathing piece for his paper in the making. 'And why the hell didn't Watkins find this one, if he spent so much time up here?'

'He didn't spot them all, and it was only discovered since the war that the barn had once been a chapel and was probably on an earlier sacred site,' Mark said in Arbuthnott's defence. 'And I think it's interesting that there's been very little dissent from the public about this one since the book was published.'

'That's only because you're preaching to the converted,' Luke dismissed.

'Well, I think it sounds amazing, and I absolutely believe,' Laura said defiantly. 'How far is it down to the Priory from here?'

'About a mile,' Ruth answered.

Laura stood up and walked to the window. She looked out across the valley towards Pant-y-Groes, lit now by a full and risen moon. 'Look everyone, it's a beautiful night out there.' She turned and addressed them. 'I sometimes think that moonlight walking is the best there is. You get an entirely different perspective on the earth around you, different smells and sounds, different shades.'

'And more scope for a creative imagination,' Luke said.

Laura ignored him. 'When we've finished dinner, I'm going to walk down to the Priory,' she announced, 'and sit among the ancient holy stones. Can you show me the exact route on the map, Ruth?'

'Oh, yes.' Ruth looked delighted that her old friend, the famous television walker, was finding exciting fresh material at her humble dinner party.

When Margaret said that she and Luke had to go, Beth was surprised by the affability with which the evening broke up, and she took the opportunity to suggest to Mark that they should leave too.

Ruth waved to them all, framed by the light shining through her door, and Laura appeared behind her, wearing a light anorak and her jeans tucked into hefty walking boots.

'So the intrepid Laura Chichester is off seeking moonlight adventures,' Mark murmured, slightly drunk. 'I'd pity any poor man that strayed across her path.'

Beth, who had drunk less, backed the car in front of Ruth's house and followed the Greens into the lane. 'Come on, Mark, you must admit she's quite impressive, and very attractive.'

'Attractive? There's a nice old euphemism. You mean a lot of men would like to screw her?'

'They might want to talk to her first.'

'I love the way you're always prepared to see the best in your fellow man, especially men.'

'But surely there are men who are interested in the intellectual stimulation a woman can offer them, as well as the sexual gratification?'

'I suppose there are.'

'Well, why did you marry me?'

'Because you were and still are a very desirable woman.'

Beth sighed. She ought to have been pleased that Mark still fancied her; but she wondered if Owen saw her only as a receptacle for his sexual needs. She bit her lip and asked herself how much she saw him as more than that.

Out of compassion, Beth let Mark make love to her that night. She tried not to show how little she shared his ardour, and thought of Owen. Afterwards she lay awake for a long time, while Mark purred gently beside her, and her state of mind swung between elation at what she had discovered over the past week, and alarming uncertainty about the future.

Beyond Gospel Pass

She finally drifted off to sleep, but almost at once, it seemed, she was woken by a banging on the kitchen door below the bedroom window.

Mark was still flat on his back, breathing deeply, anaesthetised by Ruth's wine and making love.

Beth swung herself out of bed and went to look from the window into the golden gloom of a very early mid-summer dawn.

'Hello?' she called.

Ruth turned her face up. She looked as if she'd run straight from her bed; her hair was a mass of tangled curls, her make-up was smudged and she was wearing a cotton kaftan which Beth knew she used as a night-dress.

'What's happened? What's the matter?'

'Can you come down? Something horrible's happened.'

'Okay. I'll put some clothes on.'

Beth quickly pulled on a pair of jeans and a sweatshirt against the crisp morning air and went down in bare feet to let Ruth in.

'Thank God I woke you.'

'What's the time? I haven't even looked yet.'

'It's five thirty. Owen just came to the house,' Ruth gasped. 'He had Laura with him. He found her by the track down to the Priory.'

'Owen? *Found* Laura?' Beth gasped. 'She... she's not dead or anything is she?'

'No, no. But when she went off on her walk, I didn't think any more about it; I thought she could look after herself.' Ruth gazed wildly at Beth, seeking her support. 'After I'd tidied away dinner, I was absolutely knackered and I went to bed. When Owen woke me, I'd no idea she hadn't already come back.'

'But what happened, Ruth?' Beth said, holding her breath.

'She was attacked,' Ruth sobbed. 'Totally raped!'

A black mist fell across Beth's eyes. 'But, for God's sake!' she gasped. 'How come Owen found her?'

'He's often up early, doing things about the valley. He likes the dawn, and he said he was driving up the track when he saw her lying there. He worked out who she was and managed to get her onto the back of his quad-bike and brought her back to the Hendre.'

'Oh my God.' Beth shook her head in horror as every sort of possibility crossed her mind. 'Is she hurt?'

'Not badly,' Ruth shook her head. 'She said she didn't struggle, not after the man produced a knife.'

'Did she see him?'

'No. It was too dark; the moon had gone and it was in a stretch of the lane where the hedges are very high.'

'But how long had she been there when Owen found her?'

'She doesn't know; she says she lay down when the man ran off, then she managed to pull her clothes back on and just passed out. Thank God it's been such a warm night.'

'But I can't understand what on earth Owen was doing down there. He doesn't farm there, does he?'

'He's got sheep on the hill down here and though I don't think he'd admit it, he might have been checking out the ley that George has written about.'

'Do you really think that's what he was doing?'

'Why not?' Ruth stared at her. 'You don't think he had anything to do with what happened, do you?'

Beth didn't answer.

'Beth! For God's sake – don't be crazy. Owen is the gentlest man you could meet.'

Beth shook her head as if to clear the craziness from it. 'Yes, yes, I know. Of course, I don't think anything like that. I'm just seeing it from a lawyer's point of view. He's going to have to be very careful when the police question him. Has anyone phoned them yet?'

Ruth bit her lip and nodded. 'Yes, as soon as Laura told me what had happened, I rang them. They should be out from Abergavenny any minute now.'

Laura Chichester was propped up in bed drinking coffee. She looked at the two women who sat either side of her.

'So, why are you two so concerned about this man?"

'He lives here; he was born here; he has to live the rest of his life here. And even if there's the faintest suspicion that he was guilty of rape, it would tarnish him for the rest of his life. Do you want to be responsible for that?' Ruth pleaded. 'I mean, it was he who found you and brought you back - in return for that at least, you should protect him.'

Beyond Gospel Pass

'For all I know, he might have done it.' Laura raised an eyebrow.

'No!' Beth heard herself almost shriek. 'No, he's no rapist!'

Laura turned her canny blue eyes on Beth. 'You seem bloody sure.'

'I've seen enough of him to know that he couldn't have done it. And anyway...' Beth caught her breath and tried to marshal her responses. '...for God's sake, he wouldn't have brought you back if he'd just raped you.'

'Maybe not – and I must admit, he was quite a hunk.'

'Laura!' Ruth gasped. 'How can you think about things like that after what's just happened?'

'What happened was pretty unpleasant, and I can see why it upsets so many women. But quite frankly, I just thought to myself, there are tens of thousands of women all over Britain who have to take this every night – either from their husbands who'll beat them up if they don't, or from clients who are going to give them twenty quid for their trouble. If they can take it, so can I.'

'But Laura, you must feel so dirty and abused!' Ruth shook her head.

'Yes, of course I do. I loathe the idea of some nasty little wanker getting inside me, but I've never known any crisis in life that's helped by getting hysterical.'

'Are you actually hurt at all?' Beth asked.

'Yes, frankly, I'm a bit bruised around the fanny and on my arms where he held me.'

'We'll have to cancel your talk at the Festival.'

Laura considered. 'Yes, I suppose we will. Now the police are involved there's bound to be some publicity.'

'Oh my God,' Ruth gasped. 'I hadn't even thought of that.'

'Hadn't you?' Laura took another sip of her coffee. 'But don't worry, it's not a problem. The thing about publicity is to handle it, to make it work for you, not against you.'

'But exposing yourself to all that speculation?'

'I shan't let them speculate for long.'

Beth wondered how much of this impressive self-control was authentic. Perhaps it was that which made her so manifestly a star; the absolute certainty that she was in control of everything that happened to her.

They heard a motor outside. Beth went to the window. The sun was just rising above the ridge to the north and a police car, white and clean, crunched up the track towards the Hendre; a man and a woman, both uniformed, climbed out. Ruth went out to greet them and to warn them that they were dealing with a woman whom they would probably recognise.

Beth sat with Ruth and talked to the sergeant while the WPC spent an hour with Laura in her room, until an ambulance came to take Laura, protesting but in the end co-operative, to a private hospital in Abergavenny, where a police doctor would examine her and take the necessary samples and smears for forensic.

It was nearly nine when the police had gone, and Beth walked back to Pant-y-Groes. As she waded the stream, she looked up at the fresh green bracken and dark grey shale of the hillside behind their house. She found her eyes focusing on the spot where she and Owen had first talked, and suddenly she remembered the bland smile and rapacious gaze of the walker who had filled his bottle there.

Mark was dressed and in the kitchen eating toast and boiled eggs.

'You've been out bright and early,' he grinned. 'I woke an hour ago and you weren't there.'

'Ruth came and got me,' she said. 'Mark, something really horrible has happened.'

She sat down slowly at the table, opposite him and told him.

'Good God!' Mark said, impressed at so momentous an event in the valley. 'It's hard to imagine something like that happening to a woman like Laura. How's she taken it?'

'Extraordinarily – totally in her stride; coping brilliantly. I expect she's already planning a chapter about it in her next book. She's the sort of woman who simply won't allow herself to look pathetic or out of control.'

'How did she get back?"

Beth hesitated. 'Owen Rhys found her. He was up early – looking for something, apparently.' Beth added, aware of the doubt implicit in the last word and wishing she hadn't used it.

'Bloody hell!' He was going to say more – Beth could tell, but stopped himself. 'Did Laura get a good look at the man who did it, then?'

'No, not at all. It was too dark.'

Beyond Gospel Pass

'Oh. Has Ruth got any ideas?'

'No; she says she can't think of any obvious suspect in the valley.'

'What will the police do?"

'They didn't say, but I should think they'll be dead keen to get a result – Laura being so high-profile.'

Later, after Mark had been out on the hill, he came back in with a knowing grin on his face. 'It's already started,' he said. 'I wonder if Ruth wants a hand.'

'With what?'

'The press. There are two cars outside her house already and a guy taking pictures around the place.'

'You'd have thought they wanted Laura.'

'I expect there's a gang of them already besieging the hospital. I don't think Ruth should have told the police who Laura was.'

'Laura told her to, because she was sure someone would recognise her sooner or later, and it's far better to tell everyone, so no particular paper thinks it's got a scoop.'

Beth wanted desperately to see Owen, to ask him herself how he had found Laura, and why he had been in that part of the valley, at that time of the morning, but she couldn't think of a plausible reason to give Mark for going to find him. To quell her frustration, she suggested that they should drive down to Hay and see how the Festival was taking the news that its star turn that day had been so spectacularly wiped off the bill.

The town was fizzing with rumours and misinformation. A lot of Laura's fans were sitting around looking disconsolate, even grief-stricken. For want of anyone else, Paul Ricardo was holding a press conference in one of the smaller marquees.

'I've spoken to Laura Chichester on the phone. Obviously, she's pretty shaken but says she's determined not to let this horrible event taint her life. She will make a full statement herself in the next few days. She says the police have been superb and are doing everything that traditional and modern forensic methods allow; and she's very sorry indeed not to be able to appear here today. She promises that she'll give the Hay Festival of Literature absolute priority next year. The police have confirmed that they are making progress, and hope to have firm information shortly.'

'Balls,' Mark growled quietly to Beth. 'How could they possibly be making progress?'

She shuddered and said nothing.

Both subdued by the violence that had taken place in their peaceful valley, they ate lunch in a pub that buzzed with talk about the rape. Some unsympathetic visitors to the Festival were amusing themselves with cynical speculation. Thank God, Beth thought, the information that Laura had been found by Owen had not been released.

They had been planning to go to Laura's talk that evening and didn't have tickets for anything else.

'I don't feel like hanging around here,' Mark grunted, pushing away a plate of unfinished venison sausages.

Beth agreed. She wanted to know if the police had got anywhere.

When they got back to Pant-y-Groes at three, there was a message from Ruth on their answer-phone. Could they contact Detective Inspector Price-Watkins at the police station in Abergavenny?

'Why the hell does he want to talk to us?' Mark grumbled.

'Let's go and ask Ruth.'

They went out and got back into the car because it was quicker to drive two miles via the bridge than to walk the three hundred yards across the brook. They found two police vans parked in a gateway, below the track that led from the Hendre to the Priory. To Beth, their presence made the whole incident more real. She shivered to think that there was a man out there, perhaps still in the valley, who got his kicks by terrifying women into having sex with them.

Ruth was half expecting them.

'What's been happening?' Beth asked as they walked in.

'The police have been searching the place where she was attacked with a fine-tooth comb. I watched them, and they found a fresh boot-print, so they made a plaster cast of it.'

'Anything else?'

'They wouldn't tell me. But the Detective Inspector chap, Price-Watkins, who's leading the case, came up and saw me. He questioned me for ages, about Laura's love life and so on.'

'What's happened to her?' Mark asked.

'She came back at lunch time in a police car. She took her stuff and went back to London. But Price-Watkins wants to talk to everyone who was at dinner here last night.'

'Did he say why?' Mark asked.

'He'll want to build up a picture of everything that was going on that evening,' Beth answered. 'It's not unreasonable.' She turned back to Ruth. 'Did he say when?'

'He's coming out here tomorrow at ten to talk to the Greens. You could come over then if you want.'

Beth glanced at Mark. 'We're going back to London after lunch, so that'll suit us fine.'

As they drove away from Pant-y-Groes, Beth looked back with more attachment to the place than she'd ever felt before. She sensed that this departure marked the start of a new phase in her relationship with the house, with the valley itself; so much of significance had happened here now.

If people's personal identities were, at least in part, products of their life experience, she thought, it was inevitable that she should feel quite different from the woman she had been when she and Mark had arrived here for his selection meeting only fifteen days before. *Fifteen days that changed my life*, she thought. Or could she narrow down the moment of change to a small cluster of ecstatic moments when Owen had first touched her?

She glanced at Mark. He was squinting through the glasses he had recently acquired and driving too fast with signs of anxiety that could become dangerous. He was heading back to a quagmire of troubles, mostly of his own making, and the police enquiries seemed to have unsettled him.

DI Price-Watkins had arrived at Ruth's when they were all gathered there and had insisted on questioning each member of the dinner party in private, one by one. Green, the journalist had become truculent, and Mark had emerged from his interview looking angry and insulted. After that, he'd drunk too much with the quick salad lunch they'd eaten with Ruth, and now Beth wanted to insist that she should take over the driving. But she didn't, because she felt partly responsible for his current state of mind; if she'd been prepared to devote herself, as she had in the past, to helping him find a balanced solution to his business problems, he wouldn't be feeling that his world was spinning away from him, out of control.

As the Saab progressed in spurts and jams on the motorway heading back to London, she thought about her mother, who had asked her to come and see her where she was staying in Surrey. Beth wanted to feel she could talk to her about the current unavoidable crises in her life, but she couldn't be sure how sympathetic her mother would be to Mark's problems, and she was certain she wouldn't be to her own recent experiences.

When they arrived at their home near Victoria Park in Hackney after a sticky crawl through North London, the house felt to Beth like a stranger, and her own familiar things like the possessions of another person – a person she'd known well, for a long time, but with whom she'd allowed herself to fall out of touch.

She cooked pasta for their dinner in the pale indigo and terracotta kitchen in the basement of their tall Victorian house. She tried to concentrate on Mark but other demands, confusion and emotional chaos crowded in on her.

'I hope you don't mind – I've arranged to go down and see Mum tomorrow,' she said when they sat down to eat.

Mark looked disappointed, though he reacted stoically. 'But it's a bank holiday tomorrow, and she's bound to be coming to London sooner or later; she always does.'

'Maybe, but Angela who she's staying with, is going off somewhere and she'll be on her own, and I thought it would be good to spend a whole day with her before I get completely wound up in this case for the next couple of weeks.'

'You already seem totally absorbed in something.'

'I'm sorry darling, ' Beth said more softly. 'I've had this case on my mind most of the time, even at Pant-y-Groes; then of course, this terrible thing that's happened to Laura.'

Mark shrugged as he opened a bottle and filled two glasses. 'It sounds as if she's not having much trouble dealing with it.'

'She's got a lot of guts and a lot of front - that's all. You just can't imagine how something like that feels to a woman.'

'Now that's where you're wrong. I may not have first-hand experience, but of course a man with an imagination can imagine, and probably come quite close. Males and females aren't that different. In fact,' Mark was getting into his stride, 'I can think of very few emotions that are felt exclusively by one or the other.'

'And what are the few that you *can* think of?' Beth asked.

'Well — and this touches both of us — I can see that having babies is massively important to most women - even the really hard-nosed ones. It's rather curious; there's been so much written recently about female "laddism". As far as I can see, the women's mags are full of stuff about how younger females these days are behaving like young males. They're saying the sources of women's motivations are fundamentally the same as men's. It seems to me it's only in the overwhelming need to fill their wombs that women are essentially different from men.'

'Mark...' Beth raised a hand to the flow of words.

'No, let me finish. In every other respect — the need to influence, to manipulate, to be gratified, to lie, plot, enjoy triumph — women are at least as bad as men — though of course, Charles Darwin — and probably Richard Dawkins — would say that having babies was by far the most important anthropological reason for their existence.'

'Quite honestly, I don't give a damn what a few arrogant male scientists would say; you're right, though it isn't about "having babies"; it's about actually creating life!' Beth stood up to emphasise what she was saying, and to disguise a little the strength of her feelings. 'Think about it. We were given the equipment to do this incredible thing — to create a totally new life! Of course the drive to use it is overwhelming!'

'Fine,' Mark conceded. 'But I was just giving it as an example of a strong female emotion that men don't possess - at least with nothing like the same intensity.'

'But you want a baby, too, don't you?'

'Yes.' Mark reached up, took her hand and squeezed. 'Of course I do; very much.'

Winterbourne Cottage, set high on the wooded slopes of Surrey's North Downs, looked to Beth like the understudy of every thatched cottage in a jigsaw catalogue. Climbing roses clustered around the porch and alchemilla crowded the margins of the short gravel path that led from a wicket gate to the front door.

She drove slowly past the small house, which belonged to her mother's oldest friend, and stopped a short way beyond it. She had been here before, several times, and marvelled that her very Boston Irish mother should be staying in this archetypal piece of Old England.

Moira Langthorne was descended on both sides from Irish emigrés. Beth's maternal grandfather and great grandfather had been hard-working, entrepreneurial builders as Boston suburbs had grown after both world wars. This had left the family with several large properties in Greater Boston and on the fashionable shores of Cape Cod, a ferry ride across the bay.

The fine old house in Brookline where Beth had been brought up had been given by her mother's father, despite Moira's disloyal decision to marry the academic son of a deeply WASP father and an English mother. John Langthorne, always known as Jack, was well-connected but impecunious. Beth had never been told why her clever father, after a promising start to his career at Dartmouth, had ended up on a modest salary teaching in one of the city's private schools, preparing rich kids for Yale or Harvard, and it had always seemed impertinent to ask. Perhaps the question was answered in part when he died suddenly in his fifties from a congenitally weak heart, in a quiet, unfussy way that reflected his unassuming persona.

It was partly her father's death that prompted Beth, aged twenty, to take her junior year out from Mount Holyoke College in South Hadley and come to England to extend her knowledge of English Literature. The idea of getting out from under the constraints of her mother's old-fashioned Bostonian Catholic culture aided her decision.

From the moment she arrived, she fell in love with almost everything about England, including a thirty-year-old law lecturer she met on her first visit to the RSC in Stratford. He claimed to see in her the ingredients of a legal mind and persuaded her to switch her ambitions. She found the case for staying in London irresistible and on the strength of her English grandmother was allowed to take up a place at UCL to read law.

She took to the subject from the start and was determined to be called to the English bar and make her career in London, even when her mentor, frightened, she concluded with unhappy pragmatism, by his own arduour, had admitted he was married and went back to his wife. Back in the States, her mother tolerated her decision, unaware of the influence of the lecturer, while her brother Edward went, like his father, to Dartmouth.

Beyond Gospel Pass

Three years later, with her finals passed and a pupelage arranged at a set of chambers in the Inner Temple, she rang her mother to tell her she going to stay in London. Moira Langthorne, living alone now on Beacon Hill, and sometimes in the Green Mountains of Vermont, was disappointed – even more so when Beth told her she was going to marry her new boyfriend, a former student at UCL who planned to set up his own publishing company.

After a few years, though, Moira had become happily reconciled to Beth's marriage to Mark. It gave her an excuse to come to England once a year, when she could see her great childhood friend, Angela Hutton. Angela had also married an Englishman, a British Army officer who had subsequently died in the Falklands, when she had chosen to stay in England and take British citizenship.

Beth understood and liked her mother's friend but she was relieved when she heard that Angela would be away for twenty-four hours and Moira was on her own in the house.

Beth stopped the car and got out to open a solid five-bar gate before parking behind a screening hedge. She walked round to the rose-fringed front door and knocked.

Moira Langthorne opened the door with a warm, broad smile. 'Beth, darling, it's wonderful to see you looking so... I don't know – blooming!' She hugged her daughter.

Beth stepped back, more pleased than concerned that her altered internal condition was so manifestly good for her. 'So do you,' she said as her mother led her by the hand into the cottage.

At sixty-five, Moira was fit and no more aged than most fifty year olds. The beauty of her youth lingered still through an ingenuous eagerness in her bright blue eyes.

'I am, thanks. I took Angela's labrador for a five mile hike along the ridge this morning. Angela's getting him ready for a sponsored walk along the Pilgrims' Way, she says the dog's already drummed up twice as much sponsorship as her. He's called Woggy – can you believe it?' she laughed. 'Nothing un-PC – just to rhyme with doggy.'

Beth followed her mother into the kitchen where Moira had already started to put coffee beans into a grinder.

'So,' Moira asked with a quick sideways glance. 'Tell me how you really are?'

Beth guessed that her mother had picked up the oblique reference to grandchildren the week before. 'Let's just say the Welsh mountain air is doing me good. I haven't felt so relaxed in years.' She thought of herself lying beside Owen beneath the Wergin stone, while buzzards cruised the evening thermals above them. 'I *was* concerned we were too tense for anything to happen; but maybe it will now. I mean, it hasn't been proved that there's a direct connection between stress and the failure to conceive, but there's a lot of anecdotal evidence of women conceiving once they've got away from what the women's pages call high-pressure lifestyles.'

Moira sighed quietly, neither wishing her anxiety to show nor wanting to create any tension between them. 'Jemma came to stay with me in Boston last week, with Alfie and Liam,' she said with an apparent lack of continuity. 'My goodness, I wish she'd let them go out and get a bit muddy now and again. Do you remember how you and Edward used to race around the woods in Vermon? And you'd come home filthy and blissfully happy.'

Beth was aware that her mother, like Mark, was in the habit of downgrading her sister-in-law's comparative success as a child-producer in order to make her feel less bad about her own failure.

Usually, she found it irritating – although she didn't let it show. Now, it didn't matter, and anyway, Alfie and Liam *were* like little old men – Walter Mathau and Jack Lemon in the *Odd Couple*, Beth thought. 'Well, don't you worry, Mama. When I have kids, they'll be smeared in mud from head to toe – all day, just like those women who sit around in health farms with nothing better to do.'

Later, when Beth was about to sit down to lunch in the dining room, she looked at a photograph of her brother, Edward with his wife, Jemma, and two boys, a toddler and a babe in arms, in a silver frame which Angela, his godmother, had placed on a sideboard. Beside it was an earlier photo of Edward wearing a mortar board at a jaunty angle and a big self-confident American smile.

'How is he?' she asked her mother when she came into the room with a tray of salad and dressing.

'Who, darling?'

'Edward, of course.'

Beyond Gospel Pass

'Pompous as ever,' Moira laughed affectionately. 'But doing fine at the moment; he's been made head honcho of a new department at the bank, trading some kind of incomprehensible bonds.'

'Sounds useful.'

'He certainly knows how to make a buck. He'll earn more with one annual bonus than your father earned in his whole teaching career.'

Beth didn't comment while she considered this.

'How's Mark?' Moira asked with a shrewd, searching look.

'In a mess,' Beth shrugged, not needled. 'Poor Mark; he believes his own propaganda, I'm afraid and then makes his decisions based on it. Curiously enough, the only sensible thing he's done recently is to publish George Arbuthnott's book on ley lines.'

'Is that so? That's interesting!'

'Good heavens, Mother, what do you know about earth mysteries?'

'Oh, I know all about Alfred Watkins and *The Old Straight Track* – all the theories that have grown up in the last thirty years about the earth's field of life forces and ambient energy points. Your father got very keen on it all shortly before he died. He wanted to come to England, funnily enough, to see the originals for himself – though God knows, people keep finding them all over North America now – but he never made it.'

Beth was astounded. 'How extraordinary. He never mentioned it to me once.'

'Well, you know he had rather got out of the habit of discussing his work with you children. I think he felt you didn't appreciate what he was doing.'

'But you knew?"

'Of course. He talked to me all the time – to himself really; he certainly didn't expect me to contribute to the discussion. And I can tell you, ' Moira said, showing an uncharacteristic interest in the ephemeral, 'I started to believe it all.'

'I.... we know a man who lives near us in Wales who can feel the forces in ley lines and identify them using a ring on a chain.'

'A pendulum dowser? How amazing!'

Beth, warming to the topic, grew more animated. 'Yes. In fact he came and dowsed for our water. He let me watch him.' She thought of Owen undressing in the small bedroom at Pant-y-Groes. 'We're bringing a pipe in from an underground water course across the field.'

'How marvellous to have seen it. I wish I had.'

'I wish Papa had talked to me about it.' Beth was suddenly aware of an empathy with her father which hadn't been there when he was alive, and felt cheated of this common ground between them.

'Sweetie, if you'd asked me, I never would have thought you'd take these New Age ideas seriously. I'd have guessed you'd find them far too woolly and unscientific. What's George Arbuthnott like?'

'He came up to Hay to give a lecture about his new book. He sold piles of copies, though I'm afraid poor old Archimedes needs at least a dozen best-sellers to get it back in shape.'

'Did you talk to him at all?'

'Yes, we had dinner with him the night before. Frankly, he's a bit of a charlatan, but he's very professional about it. He's one of those writers who're always casting about for the flavour of the month, hoping to get it right from time to time.'

'So you didn't like him, did you?'

'Not much.'

'And what about your dowser?'

Beth felt herself blush. She was holding a glass of water; her hand shook just enough to spill a little down her front so she could occupy herself mopping it up while she gained some control over her complexion.

'He's rather interesting, actually,' she tried to say casually as she dabbed at her shirt. 'On the face of it, he's just another Welsh sheep farmer, but he seems to know all about these strange phenomena. He's a healer, too; he cured Lord Brecon's back.' Beth thought of Owen telling her about generations of barren woman who had walked up from the valley to knead their naked breasts against the giant menhir. 'And he knows all the ancient folklore of the hills.'

'How super to have found a chap like that. Your father would have loved it. It's funny the way he got so keen on all that kind of thing. Poor old Jack – I think it was because he never could get anyone interested in his new theories about Turner.'

Beth remembered those ideas – at least, she recalled a few disjointed conversations with her father about the psychology of colour, which he had started to expound in what seemed to her more desperation than scholarship.

At the time, as an eighteen year old whose own views were beginning to take solid form, she'd resented his propensity for making her and all other women with whom he came into contact feel stupid. Now she recognised it as a symptom of his own, low self-esteem, but she'd never been able to eradicate entirely the scars from those early, bruising sessions between them.

Twelve

Beth rang Mark to tell him that as her mother was on her own, she was going to stay and have supper with her. Although he didn't say he was, he sounded unhappier than earlier; Beth was remorseful that she couldn't do any more for him.

She didn't leave the cottage until ten, to avoid the earlier torrent of holiday traffic crawling back into the capital. As soon as she started to drive away, she experienced the usual let-down that came after saying goodbye to her consistently good-natured mother.

On the way into London, passing a school with an unmistakeably ecclesiastical look to it, she was reminded of the strait-laced St Agnes' school where she'd spent most of her teen years and whose gentle nuns had seemed so completely at odds with 1980s America. But she'd kept warm memories of the place, where religious dogma and the rules of English and French grammar had been imposed equally with an unusual blend of docility and firmness.

Beth was prepared to admit to herself, despite any intellectual objections, that she'd enjoyed an old-fashioned, American life-style of tennis, evenings at the theatre, ballet lessons and a traditional education that had formed the basis of all her subsequent attitudes – even her flirtation with British socialism; though it had been the vitriolic tirades of the university young socialists against gentle people like her mother which had finally turned her allegiance from Labour to Liberal and sustained her Catholicism – albeit tenuously – for several years.

As she penetrated the heart of London, an indelibly ugly orange glow smeared the underside of the clouds, and the insistent squealing of pedestrian crossings punctuated the loud grumbling of traffic on every main road. The ugliness and the crowds of unconnected individuals hurrying along the streets, oblivious to one another, made her long for the peace of the valley; until she remembered what had happened to Laura – the brutal imposition of the sexual demands of a stranger.

She thought of the few strangers who walked the valley, and abruptly, as if it had been waiting to ambush her, she was struck again, more violently this time, by a picture of the Yorkshire ley hunter - the man who had leered at her in the Wergin pool while she was submerged to her neck, naked against Owen's chest - and the sexual hunger that flared briefly in his eyes until Owen had sent him on his way.

The man and his companion, she remembered, had been staying up at the Youth Hostel to walk the leys for a few days.

Laura had been walking a ley that night.

The bastard! The interloping, scummy bastard - coming to their peaceful valley to cause distress and fear in the women who lived there!

Someone had to tell the police - right now before the man went back to Yorkshire or wherever he'd come from.

She reached into her bag on the passenger seat and cursed the fact that she'd forgotten to bring her mobile that morning.

She crossed Westminster Bridge, desperate to get home and make the call – even considered stopping at a phone box.

As soon as she was in the house, she rushed down to the kitchen and picked up the phone. When she'd been given the number of the police station in Abergavenny, she dialled it with nervous haste.

A few moments later she was talking to one of the detective constables assigned to the case.

'I'm Beth Powell. One of your colleagues, DI Price Watkins came and interviewed me and my husband on Sunday.'

'I remember, Mrs Powell; I was there too.'

Beth started to tell him about the two walkers from the hostel, until she heard herself and realised she was blurting out her theory like an hysterical teenager. She stopped abruptly and took a deep breath.

'I'm sorry. I'll start again.'

'That won't be necessary, Mrs Powell. We've identified the parties you're referring to and investigated their movements.'

'And?'

'As the victim in this particular case has a high celebrity profile and there's a great deal of media interest, my Super will be making a further statement shortly. I can tell you though, in view of the urgency surrounding the case, and to restrict the chances of the culprit absconding, we started immediate proceedings for blanket DNA testing in the area, starting yesterday morning. An intimate sample has now been taken from every appropriate male, including the individuals you've just referred to.'

Beth immediately thought of Owen, giving a sample that would remove the last vestiges of suspicion that might still be hanging over him, as the man who had found the victim. 'Oh, that's good,' she said. 'So you definitely know about the two Yorkshiremen at the hostel?'

'We do, madam, but thank you for drawing them to our attention anyway.'

'Do you think one of them might be... involved?"

'It's possible; but the test will confirm or refute their story.'

'When will you know?'

The policeman sighed. 'All the samples will have been despatched to the Home Office Path lab in Chepstow in the next couple of days. They've been instructed to expedite the process. We may well have some results next week, but we'll make a statement regarding our findings in due course.'

'But you're making progress?'

'We will be making a statement. I've already told you more than I'm authorised to. '

'I just hope those two men are still there when you need them.'

'Thank you for your help, Mrs Powell. Now perhaps you'd like to leave a contact number in case we need to talk to you again.'

Beth was suddenly aware of how unprofessional she must have sounded, how like an ordinary, ill-informed member of the public, instead of an experienced QC who was accustomed to appearing in front of the highest courts in the land. She should have known so much better.

Prickling with embarrassment, she gave her number and put the phone down, thinking it wouldn't be the first time the police had had to deal with a breathless woman convinced that she knew the culprit of the latest rape.

Beyond Gospel Pass

Her discomfort increased when she heard Mark clear his throat behind her.

'That was a little shrill,' he said lightly.

'Yes, I know. I don't know what came over me. While I was driving back from seeing Mum, I suddenly remembered a highly suspect pair of hikers I came across a couple of days before the rape, and I was sure it was one of them. One in particular looked very, very strange.'

'In what way?'

Beth hesitated a moment, thinking of the extraordinary circumstances in which the man had come across her with Owen. 'Oh, I don't know,' she said, making less of it. 'He just looked at me in a real creepy way when I met him up by the spring.'

'What did the police say, then?'

'I only spoke to a pompous little DC. I should have asked for the DI in charge, but I should think they're in a major sweat over it, with dozens of tacky tabloid reporters hanging around asking questions all day. They've evidently got some material to make a DNA match. To give them credit, they've really kick-started the process. They've already taken what they call "intimate samples" from every appropriate male in the valley. At least that'll save them a lot of time chasing up blind alleys.'

'What the hell's an intimate sample?' Mark asked.

'Don't worry, it's not as bad as it sounds – a smear of saliva from inside the cheek, usually. I'm surprised they haven't asked you for one.'

'As a matter of fact they did, when they interviewed me, though I wasn't clear what it was for. I sort of thought they'd want something more....' Mark laughed. ' Anyway, let's have a drink.'

Beth nodded; she felt she needed one. Then she remembered the baby. 'Actually, I think I'll just have camomile and honey,' she said, reaching for the kettle.

Mark shrugged in surprise and took a bottle of vodka from the fridge. He poured himself a thick measure and tipped in a little tonic. They sat at the kitchen table, and Beth watched Mark take a long slug. She tried to look at him fairly.

Up until now she'd always told herself that she hadn't had to make many compromises with Mark, although she'd been aware, very early in the marriage that some would be necessary. But as her thirties had passed, she'd become more acutely aware that she had other feminine objectives to fulfil.

When it had emerged that she and Mark showed no sign of achieving conception, she had blamed herself as much as Mark - in fact, more than him when she'd inspected his semen under a microscope and had seen the army of frantic little spermatozoa wriggling around in their eager search for an egg to fertilize.

But now she was convinced that it was going to happen without him, she didn't know whether she'd fallen in love with Owen as a result, or falling in love with him had played an essential part in the process. Whichever, all that mattered now was the intensity and sheer exuberance she felt when she was with Owen.

Nevertheless, she owed it to Mark for the sake of those dozen years they'd shared, to treat him gently. With a tight smile on her face, she reached over, picked up his glass and took a long slug of vodka.

For the next two days, Beth was in court on a small but lucrative commercial case, and when she wasn't in court, she worked on the asylum appeal due to be heard on the Wednesday. She had the ability to turn off her responses to anything but the case in hand when it reached a stage where she could not afford to miss a single twist in the proceedings, and she was up against a formidable opponent in this case. The Home Office always picked their counsel from the top drawer when they were fighting asylum appeals, taking the view that any deft legal exploitation that might open a loophole had to be vigorously fought, to discourage the expectations of others who'd been refused.

But Beth's clients, a group of five leather-faced women with shingled crow black hair, eyes the colour of bitter chocolate and three or four children apiece, were so obviously and helplessly grateful to her for championing their cause, she knew they were relying on her to an extent which she could never have refused. If ever there had been an altruistic purpose in her going to the bar, it was cases like this, of these haunted, hunted Slovakian *Roma* people that evoked it.

Despite the distractions of the valley, Beth had been thorough in her preparation of the case. She was coming to this hearing confident that her clients' bona fides could be established quite easily in the face of the objections of Home Office lawyers, who would contend that the women were nothing more than illiterate but wily

Beyond Gospel Pass

economic refugees with powerful instincts to provide for their children.

The case was scheduled for a full day and Beth worked late in her chambers the evening before, rehearsing her material and every significant detail of her clients' backgrounds, as well as the various immigration acts on which the Home Office case hinged.

She left the Inner Temple exhausted, declining without regret the offer of a drink from some of her colleagues, who said they'd been missing her sparky presence around the building, and caught the tube back to Hackney.

To her relief, Mark wasn't back and there was a breathy, urgent-sounding message from Ruth on the answerphone. After a day preoccupied with a complicated case in the legal heart of London, her mind was tugged back to the valley by an image of Ruth in her whitewashed house and Owen going about his work as usual – perhaps as if the sublime moments of the previous week had never existed. Before she returned Ruth's call, she made herself a mug of blackcurrant tea and took it up to the sitting room, which opened onto a small paved garden at the back of the house and, beyond, a cluster of urban trees, which supported a flock of melodious songbirds. She sat on the sofa and leaned back. If she could block out the ambient traffic sound that spilled over the garden wall, with the sun breaking through the clouds and a brisk north-easterly flapping the curtains, she could almost pretend that she was back at Pant-y-Groes.

She would have to tell Mark about Owen.

She couldn't force herself back to the life they'd shared, simply to protect him.

God knows - she thought - *it isn't as if there are children to be hurt if we go in different directions.*

She sat up abruptly.

How had she let her mind wander down this channel? She was a grown and, she presumed, mature woman. The whole purpose of her liaison with Owen was to produce a child for her and Mark.

Wasn't it?

No, not any more, she sighed.

She picked up the phone from the table beside her and dialled Ruth.

'Oh, hi, Beth! Thank God you rang,' Ruth fluted.

'Why? What's happened?'

Jessica Meredith

'Have you seen the papers?'

'No, not today; I've been working all day and I've only just got back. What about them?'

'The latest on the hunt for Laura's rapist.'

'What's that?'

'They've taken DNA samples from every man in the valley.'

Beth sighed with disappointment. 'I know. I spoke to a DC on the case. I suddenly remembered two walkers who were hanging about the valley for a few days. There was something very odd about one of them, and I know they were staying up at the YHA.'

'You told me about them, but they've done everyone who lives here, too – including Michael, and Owen.'

'I assumed they would,' Beth said lightly.

'But it's so degrading!'

'Of course it's not; they're simply helping the police to eliminate themselves and not waste time on red herrings.'

'But don't you think it's insulting to even consider that these people did it?'

'Not for the police,' Beth shrugged. 'They don't have the personal knowledge of these men that you have.'

'Yes,' Ruth agreed reluctantly. 'I suppose you're right. Anyway,' she tried to perk up, 'how's everything down there?'

'Hot, sticky, noisy, polluted, depressing.'

'Oh, poor you! Why on earth don't you come back?'

Beth could almost smell the meadows and the bracken. 'I've got a big case being heard tomorrow. There's a very slight chance it'll be over in a day. If it is, I'll drive up. Mark's got to stay here, of course, so it'll just be me and Grimond.'

'It'd be good to see you. I feel sort of... frightened; I'd love to have you near by.'

Beth just wanted to see Owen; in truth, she felt a constant, nagging longing to be near him. By the time she'd put the phone down, she'd made up her mind.

Until now, she hadn't realised how even the idea of risk could make the adrenaline flow. The very decision to abandon control was astonishingly liberating; and now she'd made up her mind she was going to do it, she didn't know how she would get through the next day. Suddenly, she could understand what turned people into gamblers and how they might become addicts to their own secretions.

Beyond Gospel Pass

She would have to tell Mark, and release herself from the excruciating dilemma; commit herself; follow her instincts; embrace the risk.

Beth pointed the Saab's gleaming prow towards the west and tried to push from her mind the humiliating failure she'd undergone that day.

The Home Office counsel, with little regard for procedure, had produced at the very last minute a report from agents in Bratislava that Beth's supplicants' families, far from being hounded by the people of their home village, were moderately successful market traders, and were undoubtedly sophisticated enough to see that there was a system to be played to their advantage in Britain among the broad and generous conditions that still allowed asylum status.

She hadn't let her clients down - they patently didn't deserve what they were demanding - but she'd been guilty of bad judgement when she'd always believed that one of her strengths was to see through the bullshit - to spot a phoney. These crafty women had fooled her utterly and played on her sympathy for the underdogs that gypsies seemed to be in every country where they settled. She almost caught herself thinking that maybe these travellers deserved the widespread abhorrence they attracted, with their apparently innate skills in deception.

Eschewing the tedium and ugliness of the motorways, she chose the longer but more rewarding route through the Cotswolds and over the dinosaur's back of the Malverns to Hereford, where she apologised to her cat and stopped at Sainsbury's on the edge of the small city to stock up on household essentials. She hurried her trolley through a crush of evening shoppers, eager to get on, and within twenty minutes she was heading west on the Brecon road, through the Wye valley, which she had already come to love for its special unfolding views of the hills beyond.

Once she had passed the pronounced dip in the road that still marked King Offa's early border between his Mercian Saxons and the Celts beyond, she switched off the radio. She sometimes worried that she had become addicted to the incessant chatter of Radio 4. In its absence, she found her field of vision was suddenly deepened and the panorama of rolling wooded ridges seemed to broaden and let her spirit free as she saw the ridge of the Black Mountains standing out clear against a rose-pink sky.

Jessica Meredith

On her right, serene parkland swept down to the road, where massive oaks thrust dead, naked limbs through fresh-leafed crowns – so much more venerable, Beth thought, than the stand of Victorian Wellingtonias which towered behind the stone mansion that overlooked the park.

Further west, huge apple orchards which supplied the cider factory in Hereford glowed with the last blossom, alternating pink and white, and rows of soft fruit bushes draped the gentle slopes between fields of luminous yellow rape flower.

Reaching the brow of a long rise, Beth was presented with an entirely new vista of the mid-Wye valley, and as the road followed a sweeping curve, the several heads of the Brecon Beacons, side lit by the lowered sun, swept away to the west towards the higher peak of Pen-y-Fan.

Mark always liked to remind her, in a reverential tone he used for references to the elite regiment, that on this small but unforgiving mountain, the soldiers of the SAS were trained and chosen; and thinking of Mark, she was abruptly assailed by a surge of guilt.

After the hearing had folded soon after lunch, she had phoned him at his office and told him that now her case had collapsed so quickly and so completely, after the massive amount of work she'd put in, she needed to get away again.

He had sounded puzzled and faintly irritated, though not suspicious about her new enthusiasm for the Welsh house. Beth guessed that now he was beginning, at least in private, to accept that the liberals of East Brecknock didn't want him, Pant-y-Groes had become suddenly irrelevant, an extra tie he could do without.

Beth hadn't even considered telling him over the phone about her intentions; she'd even been relieved when he'd said that he would come up to Wales on Friday evening, if she could meet him at Abergavenny station.

Beth turned the car off the main road at Clyro and dropped down into Hay. She didn't stop in the town. It looked deserted now, compared with the week before when the Festival had filled it. There was a wilted, worn out air to the place.

By the time she drove over Gospel Pass, the sun had already left the valley and when she reached the house, it was in deep dusk. She unloaded her luggage and shopping; the noise she made seemed strangely loud in the stillness after only four days in London. When she could sit, she was glad to be alone for an hour or so, in candlelight, with a glass of wine in her hand and the soft air breezing gently through an open window.

But she couldn't ignore the urge to pick up the phone and ring Owen. When it had almost won, she shook her head resolutely, and dialled Ruth instead.

A quarter of an hour later, Ruth pushed open the front door and gingerly poked her head round it.

'Hi! Are you okay?' Ruth wore an expression of soulful commiseration, evoked, Beth guessed, by her own worried face.

Beth brightened. 'Yes, of course I'm okay - just a little tired. I had a hard day in court, a long drive and a barging competition in Sainsburys.' She grinned. 'Here, have a drink.'

Ruth nodded and sat down.

'How are you keeping?' Beth asked. 'What's new?'

Ruth sighed. 'Nothing really. They think they'll have the results of this DNA profiling next week, but that's not going to be much use if it was some marauding man from away. I mean, if he'd come out here to rape someone, he wasn't going to hang around to be caught.'

'You don't think it might have been some kind of stalker, do you, who knew that Laura was staying with you?'

'I suppose it might have been. I hadn't thought of that. I wonder if the police have.'

'I'm sure they have. I certainly have the impression they want a result. They wouldn't normally have set up the DNA testing so soon. Do you know how Laura's taking all the publicity?'

'Huh.' Ruth grunted and nodded her head. 'As cool as ever.'

When Ruth left an hour or so later, Beth was glad she had overcome the urge to ask about Owen. Despite her original plan, she hadn't taken Ruth into her confidence, wary of her chronic lack of discretion and unsure about her private feelings for Owen.

On Thursday morning, Beth woke completely refreshed. She had a sense that it was going to be a good day. To compound this, she slipped on a pair of shorts and trainers and went outside to flex her legs in the sun. She had planned to do some work before lunch; a new brief for a potentially ground-breaking sexual discrimination case had come in. She was looking forward to getting her teeth into it, but before she sat down, she found she couldn't resist the lure of the open hills; it seemed an affront to nature to ignore it. She vaulted the fence and set off at a steady jog across the grain of the hill behind the house.

Soon she was high enough to see to the top of the valley and Blaen Fawr, grey beneath its umbrella of trees and somehow reluctant to be lit by the morning sun.

She wondered again what it was that kept Owen in that depressing place, though she knew he was constrained by filial ties to provide security for his mother in a way that was hard for an urban dweller to understand. As suddenly as she had felt so sure where their relationship would go, she was doubtful now that she could ever compete with that kind of commitment.

She slowed her pace to a walk, took a few more deep breaths through clenched teeth and came to a decision. She set off diagonally down the hill, glad to have a specific destination. She wasn't interested in the aesthetics of the run any more; speed was the only factor. When she reached the valley road, she stretched her legs and pounded over the tarmac without having to watch for rocks or ruts.

Cackling magpies flapped up from roadside carrion and flocks of pigeons feeding on the occasional field of young corn clapped away to the cover of the woods by the river. And above the thumping of her heart and feet, she heard a plover call and the plaintive bleating of a thousand lambs looking for their mother's milk.

A few cars and tractors slowed to pass her. Their male drivers looked at her grimly, as if they disapproved of such alien behaviour. She slowed to a walk for a few minutes to replenish the oxygen in her muscles. These people, Beth thought, were Owen's people – relations, some of them, neighbours, at least, for several generations – and she judged it a sign of Owen's specialness that he was capable of seeing beyond the deadening insularity of the valley, into the soul of an outsider like her.

After the valley road forked, she turned left between the ancient stone piers, two broad flat slabs like gravestones, and loped up the rutted track towards Blaen Fawr.

Her heart beat faster as she slowed to approach the tall, frowning house. She took in more than she had the last time, relating everything more intimately to Owen - the chickens that scratched

Beyond Gospel Pass

around outside the building, providing his daily egg; the beehives in the meadow below.

The house, though, looked no less sinister as she walked across the silent yard; she seemed to hear her breathing echo from the walls of the ancient buildings. She reminded herself that it was absurd to be so nervous about approaching the house of a man with whom she'd already shared so much intimacy.

She took another deep, fortifying breath. She raised her hand to rap the door, when it was opened from inside and suddenly Owen was there in front of her, a step higher, looking down.

Behind him, hovering like a shadowy familiar, his mother tightened her lips in agitation.

'Good morning,' Beth said brightly, stretching a smile across her face, focusing back to the old woman, to include her.

Owen nodded enigmatically. 'Hello.'

'I was running up the valley, past the bottom of your drive, so I thought I'd just come up and ask if you'd call by some time to put up the marker for our water,' she blurted, plucking a reason from the air as she stood on the doorstep, feeling faintly ridiculous in her running clothes.

Beth detected a very slight inclination of Owen's head towards his mother as he said, 'That's no problem. It'll have to be this evening, though.'

'That's fine,' Beth said, nodding with eyes wide open to let the mother see that she was merely being accommodating. 'I'll see you then.'

The mother pursed her small mouth, identifying herself as opposition. Beth guessed she didn't want Owen involved with any other woman – especially not a woman from away.

Beth walked and jogged back to Pant-y-Groes, berating herself all the way for her visit to Blaen Fawr.

She knew it hadn't done her any good, either in Owen's eyes, or by stirring up resentment in his mother.

At the same time, she justified to herself, a man like Owen wouldn't be prey to the usual prejudice against a woman who was not ashamed to show her feelings, nor would he be cowed by the selfish jealousy of a widowed mother.

Jessica Meredith

In the calm of the house while she changed sheets and dealt mechanically with domestic chores, her confidence seeped back, until she was able to look forward to seeing Owen with uncomplicated excitement.

In the early afternoon, the telephone rang for the first time that day.

'Hello, it's Boo Llewellyn here. I'm just on my way to see an old girl at the bottom of your valley; I thought I might drop in and have a cup of something with you later - if you'll be there...'

Beth thought of Owen coming that evening. 'So long as it's before six-thirty; I have to go out then.'

'Oh yes; ages before that. I'm just making a condolence call on the widow of one of Henry's old gamekeepers; it won't take long.'

'See you later then,' Beth said, pleased at the thought of Boo coming.

Later in the afternoon Boo drove a gleaming white Morris Traveller into the courtyard at Pant-y-Groes. Beth watched her step out of the car and walk up towards the house; she went to open the door.

'Hello Boo... what a great old car!'

'She's sweet, isn't she, my first car. I've had her since 1965 and she still goes like a bird. Brings back a lot of memories; d'you know, I had my first sex in her!' She chortled and raised an eyebrow – an invitation, Beth sensed, to reveal a few secrets of her own.

She smiled as she led Boo into the kitchen and switched the kettle on. 'Must have been pretty cramped!'

'Oh, I don't know. There's a bit of room with the back down, and of course, one was so much more supple then.'

Beth thought about Boo throwing her long limbs around in passionate abandon in the back of the small car and laughed.

'Coffee?' she asked

Boo nodded. 'Of course, I was already twenty by then, but even in the Sixties, I didn't *really* know what to expect. Most of us weren't half as liberated as everyone thought.'

'It wasn't much better in the Eighties,' Beth nodded, spooning ground coffee into a cafetiere, 'though it wasn't 'til I left school that I discovered nearly everyone was on the pill by the time they were eighteen.' She poured boiling water over the coffee and put the glass pot on the table with two mugs. She wondered what Boo was expecting

Beyond Gospel Pass

to hear. 'I had a few boyfriends before, but it was only when I got to London, one of the lecturers, the man who persuaded me to go in for law in the first place got me drunk and into bed. He knew what to do, and it was fun; but when he got round to telling me he was married, I discovered I really didn't like him and spent the next two years side-stepping him. Especially once Mark arrived on the scene.'

'Mark?' Boo asked, and Beth knew she was asking how Mark had performed.

Beth, offered the chance to be disloyal, was glad to find she couldn't be. 'He wasn't bad; a few times it was brilliant; I didn't really know how often it ought to be brilliant. In a way, I used to think if it always was, it would just become ordinary, and by definition, less amazing.'

'Used to...?'

Beth had recognised her slip as she made it, hoping Boo wouldn't pick it up.

'Still think,' she said, too quickly.

'Do you? Really?'

'Boo,' she smiled shrewdly, 'if you think you can drag details of my guilty past from me....'

'It's your guilty *present* I'm interested in.'

Beth looked at Boo; she didn't know her well enough to recognise her motives, whether they were benign or malicious. 'Why?'

Boo shrugged. 'A greed for gossip, I suppose. Don't you find it very enjoyable to own a particular piece of information exclusively, even for only a few days or a few hours. I've always felt there's absolutely no thrill in gossip that one's read in the papers, which everyone else has seen.' She flicked a hand dismissively. 'But really, I suppose it's because I'm rather envious.'

'There's nothing to be envious about, I can tell you. To be honest, Mark and I have been going through what you might call a flat spell.'

'I sensed that. And I sensed that this bid of his for the Lib Dem nomination was a rather desperate attempt to change career horses - and at the gallop, so as not to lose momentum.'

'That's just the way Mark does things,' Beth agreed. 'I don't; but these days I don't feel it's my function to change him.'

'Did you before?"

'In some ways; not change exactly, but influence - by example and consistent suggestion.'

'By nagging him - you mean?'

Beth smiled. 'Obviously I don't think I've ever been a nagger, and Mark's never accused me of it but I think, perhaps, yes.'

'Why do you think we do it?'

Beth gave speculative shrug. 'A primeval need to control the immediate family environment, perhaps? To ensure that everything within the household – the nest – is being done according to our idea of the best circumstances for child-rearing?'

Boo laughed. 'That all sounds too like Desmond Morris for my taste, though perhaps you're right. But you've considered looking elsewhere, haven't you?'

'I'm not going to tell you, Boo, I'm afraid. It's not the right time.'

'At least there aren't any children to consider.'

'That's just the trouble,' Beth said quietly.

Boo made a guilty face. 'Oh, sorry; though I suppose I should have thought of that. How old are you now?'

'Old enough to fret about it. You must have been quite young when you had yours; they're both in their twenties, aren't they?'

'I wasn't particularly young, but younger than all you career women now.'

'The truth is, you were probably right to start young.'

'Yes, but you're certainly not too old; look at Cherie Blair and little Leo .....'

'You're right, and I think something might happen soon, anyway.'

Boo picked up her coffee cup and took a sip while she looked thoughtfully at Beth. 'Tell me,' she said. 'Did being a Catholic make any difference to the way you approached sex?'

'How could I say? Maybe; I suppose we started later than the High School girls. Of course, the nuns and the Pope had their rigid rules about these things and I felt just a little guilty about it, but then I think all girls do, don't they?'

Boo lifted a shoulder. 'I don't know. For Anglicans, sin isn't about the act itself; it's about getting caught by the outcome; cause and effect rather than moral absolutes. "If you do this, there's a strong chance that that may happen" - rather than, "Don't do that because it's wrong."'

Beth shrugged tolerantly. 'Quite a few moral codes were founded on expediency. Look at the Jews. Mosaic law seems to have been based on practical factors, not absolute goodness. I mean, why should eating pork be inherently any more sinful than eating beef? No reason at all, but it *is* a lot less healthy in a hot climate. Going back to a Catholic girl's guilt, though, I'm sure the nuns' propaganda was always hard to erase; besides, I do still believe that certain acts are intrinsically right or wrong.'

'I can see how that could make certain acts a lot more exciting - Forbidden Fruit and all that. I've often wondered why most Catholics are so much keener to practise their religion than everyone else.'

'Actually, it's not so mysterious for Catholics in England, where we're a minority. Sometimes I think it's a little like being a jazz buff; I mean jazz wouldn't be half so appealing if everyone liked it; I think being part of any cultural minority gives a clearer sense of self.'

'But it seems unfair of your nuns to condemn the girls who had the fun; after all, you're clever and very attractive. You were probably offered a lot more temptation than the average girl.'

'I don't think so; I certainly didn't see it like that. I simply didn't think I had a particular advantage. Now I'd say if anything, it was a positive disadvantage, like it is for men. Look at Mark. He's clever and good-looking; everything came easily to him. He never had to work hard to get his degree or even to launch his business; he was always convincing and plausible, and banks would give him all the money and co-operation he asked for, which he didn't truly deserve. I don't believe even now he's resigned to the truth that success demands more work than he's ever been prepared to offer.'

'And it fooled you too, then?'

Beth grinned ruefully. 'Up to a point, but I'm not saying he got it all wrong; some of his instincts are very well tuned, and I sort of admire him for that. But it means I've come to think of him in a different way than I'd intended - more as a wayward son than as a husband, or a lover...'

'What were you looking for in a man when you met him?'

Beth took a long swig of coffee and shook her head. 'I don't know. It seems to me that a person's physical requirements in a partner often don't match their intellectual needs. I suppose I wanted excitement - and security; mental challenge - and physical beauty. I'm simply ambivalent; almost schizophrenic. I think my mental feet are on the ground but my heart's in the air. But then I find life's full of unavoidable dichotomies. I like the convenient, choiceful life of London. But I also want the romantic, earthy restrictions of life up here in the hills. I'm a realist who craves spirituality.'

Boo looked at her with a faint smile. 'How do you feel about your choice now?'

Beth had trained herself long before to contain her more private emotions; she'd lost the habit of exposing or sharing them at school when she'd discovered that once-trusted friends could turn round and use intimate knowledge as a weapon. Despite the temptation to lighten the load of her guilt by confession, Beth still couldn't bring herself to reveal to Boo that what had started as a simple suggestion – a joke, even – that she should consider the services of a 'surrogate' father, which had whirled around her distraught and increasingly desperate mind while she was going through a period of slight misalignment with Mark, had allowed her to become obsessed with the idea of Owen as that substitute father.

As she was trying to hide these thoughts from Boo, she heard a car come into the yard and looked up. The very cause of her confusion had just driven into Pant-y-Groes.

Thirteen

Owen parked his truck, jumped down and walked towards the house.

The two women watched him through the kitchen window.

'Oh!' Beth pretended to be surprised. 'Here's the man who found our water for us. He must have come round to mark the place.'

Boo had obviously recognised Owen. 'He finds water, does he?'

'Yes.' Beth stood up to let him in. 'And ley lines and energy fields,' she gushed.

'I bet he does.'

Beth walked to the door and opened it.

Owen stood there for a moment. He glanced at Boo's car. 'I see you've got a visitor.'

'Yes, Mrs Llewellyn from The Neuadd,' she said, sounding like a stuffy vicar's wife. 'She just dropped in for a coffee; she's been seeing someone down at Cwmyoy.'

'And I'm off now,' Boo said over Beth's shoulder. 'Hello,' she addressed Owen. 'I think I met you at our party the other week, after Martin Amis?'

Owen nodded. 'I was there.' He stood aside to let her out.

Boo turned to Beth. 'Thanks so much. Lovely chat. We must do it again, soon.' She gave a sweet smile. 'And you can tell me the next instalment.'

She didn't wait for Beth's reaction. She walked briskly to her small car and let herself in. She switched on the engine, backed, waved and shot out of the gate.

The distinctive trumpeting of the Traveller's exhaust echoed through the late afternoon air. Owen and Beth listened without speaking; only when it had faded completely did Beth take Owen's hand and lead him into the house.

'Thanks for coming.'

In the kitchen he faced her and took her elbows in his hands. He stood back a little from her and looked steadily into her eyes. 'Are you all right?'

'Yes.' She nodded quickly. 'Fine. Why?'

'You seem nervous.'

'I am, a bit,' she laughed. 'It's been rather a traumatic week, with what happened to Laura, and Mark not being selected, and the case I've had on in London. And I'm sure Boo – the woman who's just left – has guessed we've...'

Owen opened his eyes a little. 'Does that matter?'

Beth looked away. She shook her head. What anyone else thought had nothing to do with what there was between them. 'No, I suppose it doesn't; but you know, habits, attitudes aren't easy to throw off.' She looked back at him. 'And I really don't want Mark to know - not yet.'

Owen didn't answer and his eyes told her nothing. He raised a brow a few millimetres. 'Did you want me to mark the spring for you?'

'No. You already have, remember?'

He nodded. 'What did you want?'

'Owen, Owen!' she almost groaned. 'What do you think I want? I want you! I want us to make love.' She heard herself with disbelief, and the undercurrent of anxious uncertainty in her voice, and she knew he'd heard it too. She looked again for a reaction in his eyes, but there was no sign in the opaque, dark discs, until a slight parting of his lips and a hint of his white teeth made her thrill with anticipation.

They made love in the sitting room, in the sunlight on the alpaca rug by the fire-place and on the sofa, then later, on the spare bed upstairs with a deep, comfortable, then exquisitely passionate coming together.

Owen was strong, powerful, inexhaustible, it seemed, but always gentle. His smell, his sandpaper cheeks, the wiry hardness of his muscles, the powerful thrust of his hips and, when she saw them, the immobile, immeasurable depths of his dark eyes wrapped her in a cocoon where everything else in the world was excluded, and time had stopped.

But later she listened to the long-case clock ticking at the bottom of the stairs as she lay half draped across him on the big bed.

Beyond Gospel Pass

She was blissfully tired; she had never felt so fulfilled, or so certain that, at last, she had conceived.

She looked with tenderness at his profile, a few inches from her. A dark stubble was beginning to show through the light tan of his cheeks. His eye was closed, covered by a smooth, unwrinkled lid; his lips, slightly apart, trembled in time with the heaving of his thorax.

She wondered how she would tell Mark.

Owen left her bed at six next morning. Sleepily, she watched him dress, easing his narrow hips into his jeans and shrugging a T-shirt over his head. Quietly, he said goodbye with a touch of his lips on hers and she listened to him pad downstairs and the clunk of the heavy iron latch as he let himself out into the dew-bright dawn. And soon the sound of the Daihatsu had faded down the lane and given way to the waking thrushes by the brook.

Ruth came up and let herself into the house in the middle of the morning, while Beth was trying to concentrate on e-mails that had arrived, announcing an unexpected new element in the case of one of her Slovakian gypsies.

'Gosh,' Ruth said, putting her head round the study door, 'are you working?'

Beth nodded without speaking and carried on tapping at her keyboard.

'But you must be exhausted,' Ruth said with a usual dollop of sympathy.

'Just the opposite,' Beth answered. She smiled up at her friend and carried on with what she was doing.

'I heard the car driving off, just after six,' Ruth said, easing herself into the room.

Beth heard. She wanted to spin round and see what Ruth meant. But she tightened her jaw and her fingers hardly faltered at the keyboard. 'Oh? What car?'

'I'm sure it was here.'

Beth couldn't tell Ruth about Owen before she had told Mark. She stopped and turned to her, looking puzzled. 'Nobody left here at six; at least, I didn't see them. I was fast asleep.'

'Then – you haven't been burgled or anything?'

'Not that I've noticed. Maybe it was one of the farmers up early doing something with his sheep.'

'The sheep on the field below here belong to the Rhyses.'

'Then perhaps it was Michael, or Owen. Anyway, there's nothing to worry about; it wasn't a burglar.'

Ruth opened her wide mouth to speak again, to express her certainty, and then changed her mind. She looked at Beth, sitting there, apparently calm and focused.

Inside, Beth was feeling the after-effects of acute pleasure, and was sorry she couldn't share it with Ruth then and there. 'Look, why don't you come over for lunch later?' she proposed. 'I'm afraid I've got rather a lot to do this morning.'

Ruth managed, with only the slightest movement in her face, to look hurt and excluded.

Beth ignored it. 'So I'll see you later?'

'All right,' Ruth said moodily and, with a last soulful gaze at Beth, faded from the room.

As the sun began to drop towards Yr Twmpa at the valley head, Beth became suddenly aware that she had been listening for Owen's vehicle since the middle of the afternoon. Ruth had been back for lunch, eaten Beth's bean and tuna salad, probed a little about Owen and, learning nothing, had left.

The vehicle grinding up the lane towards her wasn't Owen's, though - she could already recognise that. Perhaps it belonged to one of the small farms further up the lane beyond Pant-y-Groes; she hoped so; she didn't feel like any other visitors.

She and Owen had made no specific arrangements, as if tacitly agreed that meetings between them would happen organically, without any manipulation on their part. But she was beginning to wish that she could be sure he was coming again tonight.

She had managed to do some work, but she'd felt all day as if Owen had never left, sensing his presence everywhere; and as she went about the house, a dozen small things triggered vivid recall of the overpowering ecstasy she'd shared with him. Now, she was already aching to have him again.

She was half-conscious of the sound of the car slowing in the lane, then became alert as it turned into the gate. The study was at the back of the house and the only window opened onto the hill behind. She got up from the desk and walked through to the kitchen. With an almost physically painful stab in her chest, she recognised a Hereford taxi. A moment later Mark stepped from the back of the car and pulled his wallet out to pay the driver.

A wave of bitter nausea welled in her gullet at the crushing disappointment and guilt she felt.

She couldn't face him.

She slipped from the kitchen, through the back door, into the vegetable garden, which had progressed no further than panes marked out with pegs and string, and walked briskly away from the house. If ever there had been a true watershed in her life, she thought, this was it; and the slopes on either side seemed beset with obstacles, harsh rocks and hidden gullies.

Half an hour's walking gave her the equilibrium to turn back and deal with immediate circumstances. For the fifteen years they had given each other, she knew that she owed it to Mark at this nadir in his career not to abandon him abruptly, or without warning.

He would have to know soon enough about Owen and the inevitable change to their relationship that meant. But not this week. Not until he had really come to terms with his rejection by the East Brecknock Liberals, and he had achieved some kind of stability at Archimedes.

Resolved, feeling strong and, paradoxically, virtuous in her decision to deceive her husband, she let herself quietly back into the house.

Mark was in the sitting room, on the sofa with a glass of whisky on the table beside him, reading the *Hereford Times*. Beth wondered how on earth he could interest himself in the minutiae of local news when everything around him was crumbling; but she kept the thought to herself.

'Hello, sweetie. How're you doing? I thought you were coming up tomorrow but when I saw a taxi from up the hill, I guessed it was you.'

He had stood up, and was looking at her with a bizarre combination of hubris and self-doubt she knew well. He took a couple of paces towards her and kissed her lightly on the lips. 'Hello, angel,' he murmured. 'I'm afraid things haven't gone well this week and I'd had enough. And frankly, there was nothing else I could usefully do.' He shrugged, as is he weren't responsible for his own commercial failures.

'Poor you; I don't blame you,' Beth made herself say. 'Let's just have a nice quiet weekend while you work out how you're going to deal with it, then you can go back feeling positive and strong.'

Mark nodded, ready to believe, glad to have the load removed from his shoulders for two or three days. 'Oh, by the way, that chap Owen turned up about twenty minutes ago. He said he'd come to mark the spring with a stake. I told him not to bother, I thought the little cairn was enough,' Mark shrugged. 'And we'll get someone up to lay a pipe next week anyway.'

As he spoke, Beth turned and started to walk back towards the kitchen. She couldn't let him see her face.

Owen had come! Owen had come! - she kept repeating to herself, tortured and thrilled at the same time.

'I'll get us something to drink,' she said through a dry throat. 'Why don't we take it outside? It's such a beautiful evening.'

She took a bottle from the fridge and pulled the cork, gritting her teeth, while her eyes stung at the thought that Owen had come back because he wanted her as much as she wanted him.

She inhaled deeply through her nostrils, before letting the spent air out between trembling lips.

'Are you all right, angel?'

'Please don't call me "angel", Mark,' she said quietly, and immediately wished she hadn't.

'I'm sorry; it wasn't meant to be demeaning,' he bridled, then tried to lighten. 'Though I agree - it's rather absurd to call a female an angel. I remember, when I was a kid, I always saw them as sort of Anglo-Saxon chaps - blond, blue-eyed, white-winged.'

Beth had recovered herself enough to face him by now. She emptied a jar of black olives into a small bowl and put them on a tray with the bottle and two glasses.

Mark picked up the tray and carried it out to the courtyard.

With an effort, Beth made herself concentrate on her husband and the trivial domestic matters he was in the mood to discuss despite his indication earlier in the week that the house had become an irrelevance. He still thought he was going to make his raised beds, and Beth talked with him for a while over what vegetables they should grow. She joined in mechanically, while every few minutes, it seemed, her thoughts returned to Owen and how little he would have said, and how much that would have meant.

Beyond Gospel Pass

The rest of the evening dragged purgatorially over supper and when they went to bed later Beth falsely but effectively left an open box of tampons for Mark to find in the bathroom. Mark, anyway, had drunk too much and soon fell noisily asleep.

In the morning, the postman brought final, written confirmation from Henry Llewellyn that, regrettably, Mark had been turned down as prospective candidate for the East Brecknock constituency, and Geraint Pugh was to stand for the Liberals.

Although he'd been prepared for it, Beth admired the fortitude with which Mark absorbed the final blow.

'When Fate decides to hammer you, she's certainly thorough about it,' he said thoughtfully.

'Is fate feminine?' Beth asked, with a grin, because she was expected to.

'She is when she does nice things - Lady Luck, Dame Fortune? So I think she can be when she drops you in the shit, too.'

'What else happened this week, then?' Beth made herself ask, already knowing, and fairly sure that fate, masculine or feminine, had little to do with it.

'Gehring's definitely gone to Orion. Now George Arbuthnott's told me he's doing his next book with Headline.' Mark stood up from the kitchen table where he'd been having a late breakfast after walking up to the ridge and back.

Beth had to accept that Arbuthnott's defection wasn't necessarily a result of any fault of Mark's, beyond his allowing doubts to arise about Archimedes' financial health.

'Between them, they're responsible for about half our sales at the moment. Quite frankly, unless there's a bloody miracle, I can't see anything coming up to replace them. And now they've gone, it won't encourage the others.'

'But surely George must have been pleased with what you did for sales of *The Leys of the Land*?'

'Of course he is, and he's very apologetic, all this coming so soon after the success he's had with us, but frankly, it's just a matter of bucks. I offered him seventy-five grand for the next one, more than I've ever offered for anything, and anyway more money than I've got, unless I can do a back-to-back deal on the paperback.' Mark gestured with a helpless wave of his hand. 'Then these other people come along and offer him a hundred. What can he do? They'll probably try just as hard as us to sell it, and they can afford to give the kind of discounts the big book retailers are demanding now if they're going to promote it in-store. It's hardly a fair contest.'

'What are you going to do, then?'

'I don't know.' Mark shook his head. 'Look for another winnable seat?'

'Mark, you know it's too late for the next election. Anything else worth having will have been fought over and grabbed by now. It seems to me you'd better set up a serious salvaging operation on Archimedes, while you've still got some kind of a list and reputation.'

'Yes, I suppose so, but d'you know,' he seemed to brace himself, 'right now, I've decided I'm going to concentrate on this place,' he said decisively.

'Are you sure?' Beth sighed.

'Don't be so negative,' Mark said tolerantly. 'I'm going to get those raised beds in and planted. At least then, if I go bust, we'll have something to eat.'

'Since when have you been a vegetarian?' Beth asked with a dry smile, though she didn't want to stop Mark absorbing himself in the project for the rest of the weekend. She didn't have any better plans for him.

As it was Sunday, Beth drove to Hereford next morning in time for the early mass at Belmont Abbey and spent an hour arguing with God and her conscience.

She knew that what she most wanted was inexcusable at any non-physical level, however much she felt that there was a deeper bond between Owen and her. But she tried to suppress the thought that despite all the troubles she and Mark may have had in trying to create a family - and they still had several untried options - her moral place was obviously with him.

But how, oh how! - she pleaded - could she disown what she felt for Owen?

She drove away from the serenity of the abbey church, confused and resentful at being offered no choice. But she knew that she must go with Mark to London; that if it was right for her, she would be with Owen in the end, however much the thought of a long separation hurt her in the meantime.

Beyond Gospel Pass

Now she didn't know how she was going to spend a day alone with Mark without letting him see the turmoil she was in. To delay the moment, she drove back the long way but found even the unblemished summer morning scenery of the Golden Valley where it broke through into the valley of the Wye failed to lift her.

Beth was relieved to find an unknown car in the courtyard at Pant-y-Groes, although it turned out to belong to Charles Winter.

He had arrived out of the blue, he explained without apology, because his wife had asked him to drop an unwanted male adolescent relation at the youth hostel. Mark, it turned out, had already asked him to stay to lunch. Beth guessed the author had sensed the tension between her and Mark and was hoping to exploit it, although he asked if his wife would be able to join them later.

Normally, Beth would have been ready to make a stand and concoct a reason why he couldn't stay, but the man was making overt, flattering noises at Mark, even waving the possibility of a book under his nose – solely, Beth was sure, to lead him into a sense of spurious safety. But then, she thought, another day in wonderland before Mark went back to face bleak commercial realities in London would do him good.

Despite this bonus, however, when lunch was over Beth surprised them all by bluntly making an excuse to go over the valley on her own to see Ruth.

When she came back, it was after six and the Winters had gone, but now she found herself uncomfortable about spending a second night with Mark in the place where she'd enjoyed such powerful passion with Owen.

She managed to persuade him that they should both go back to London later that evening. She offered to drive; he agreed, and to her relief, he had fallen asleep by the time they crossed the Severn Bridge. She tried to numb her senses with music from the radio as she struggled with the impossible decision she faced – a decision which could only get harder if her gut instinct turned out to be right, and she really was pregnant.

Beth spent most of Monday in court, and a few hours preparing a fresh appeal for one of her Slovakians.

Jessica Meredith

The *Roma* woman was the only one of her group with enough guile and self-confidence to go back and consult their unwary solicitor on her own. She must have studied a few case histories, Beth thought; certainly the new grounds she had lodged were plausible enough.

Beth stayed in her room until after six, seeing no one, but as she was leaving the building, Jack Devereux called after her. 'Beth, if you're not in a hurry, come and have a drink. I don't seem to have talked to you for months.'

Beth imagined herself back in Hackney, spending the evening in the tall, tidy house, listening to Mark either pretending that nothing was wrong or, if he'd had much to drink, thinking of reasons for his plight which were beyond his control.

'Yes, Jack. Why not? It's been ages, though it'll have to be water.'

They went to an old wine bar, traditionally used by barristers and journalists, though the balance had changed since the national newspapers had moved out of Fleet Street. Nevertheless, the place still had the air of having absorbed into its walls a hundred thousand debates, arguments and downright rows; words chosen and used with skill and abandon by people for whom the use of words was a large part of their livelihood.

Jack was deputy head of her chambers, a well-balanced and uncommonly honest man. He bought a glass of claret for himself and a bottle of San Pellgrino for Beth. She sat opposite him and looked at his amiable face, with a single, heavy black brow above strangely ingenuous but shrewd blue eyes. He was, she knew, a cradle Catholic, bringing up five children in the same way. Although their religion in a predominantly atheistic set of chambers created a tacit bond between him and Beth, they had seldom talked about it. But he'd once said to her that until he was twenty-five, he hadn't seen how it was possible to be a Catholic and not be a socialist; but a few years later he'd come to the view that it wasn't possible intellectually to be a Catholic without also being a conservative in the broadest sense.

Nevertheless, he was still both Catholic and socialist – at least to the extent that he supported most aspects of social democratic legislation, at the same time charging the highest fees he could command – apart from his extensive *pro bono* work – to pay for his sons to be educated by the Benedictines at Ampleforth.

Beyond Gospel Pass

Beth always enjoyed talking with Jack. She'd known him for a dozen years and he'd become like an older brother who held his younger sister in some awe for her precocious talent.

While she talked, she couldn't help floating in front of him her own moral dilemma, though she dressed it up as a client's.

If he thought it odd that she should be concerned about a client's marriage, which was distinctly not her field, he didn't show it.

'Oh, don't ask me about it,' he prevaricated. 'I sometimes wonder if the C of E mightn't have got it right when they more or less abolished sin. It seems almost politically incorrect these days to suggest that someone might have committed an immoral act of their own free choice; after all, psychologically, nearly all our behaviour is attributable either to genes, or to the environment provided by those who reared us.'

Beth enjoyed this. 'But don't you think there is such a thing as innate goodness?'

'That sounds rather like something inherited. Perhaps there's a gene for it, and future generations will all be engineered for goodness!' He smiled.

'God, how boring!' Beth laughed.

'But to answer your question regarding the fundamental morality of this woman's actions, I'd say that as long as she considered everyone else's position, she could be said at least to have behaved with humaneness.'

'Suppose this woman......'

'The one who's gone off to get herself pregnant and fallen in love with the sperm donor?'

Beth tried not to redden at Jack's summary. 'Yes. Suppose this woman, having fallen in love with the man, does become pregnant, but her husband thinks it's by him?'

'I should imagine the husband is going to be seriously hurt if she tells him the child is by a sort of "deputy dad". I dare say he wouldn't want much to do with it.'

'But if he didn't know?'

Jack shrugged. 'It's a risk. Who knows, when something crops up later that convinces him the child isn't his, how much damage it would do to him – and the child?'

'If the woman hasn't already gone off with the "deputy dad".' Beth made a face, using his quip.

'In which case the poor husband has already been harmed; to what extent would depend on various factors – how much he loved her, for instance, or the size of his own ego.'

'You're a blatant cynic, Jack.'

'The privilege of the clean-living.'

She smiled and wondered how often he made wrong moral choices, and if, anyway, he was congenitally incapable of behaving at all differently from the way he did. She was finding these days that the once clear idea that everyone had genuine choices had become muddied for her, but these deterministic ideas offered no real remission, as images of Owen flashed through her head and warmed her inner parts.

Deliberately, she moved the conversation onto her current case, and fresh doubts about her gypsy's *bona fides*.

Jack took the predictable view that as long as there was a chance this woman was truly at risk if she returned to her own country, Beth's job was to invoke Britain's duty to protect her.

Walking along the Strand to the tube at Charing Cross, Beth barely registered the tourists that were a permanent part of the scenery, but the huddled figures of exotic, dark-skinned, high-cheeked women, squatting in doorways with snotty brown babies in their arms and a hand out for money, confused her resentment with her compassion.

Mostly, she found, she envied them their babies.

The sun was shining directly onto the brown brick and white painted lintels of the house. Beth let herself in and stood in the hall for a moment, listening for Mark, as she shuffled through the letters she found on the floor. The absence of sound confirmed the evidence of the post that he wasn't home yet.

With some relief, she went down to the kitchen and switched on a kettle to boil. She made herself a mug of St John's Wort tea with honey and sat at the gleaming white table in a kitchen that was the antitheses of Pant-y-Groes. But simply by closing her eyes, she transported herself back to the hillside above the house where she lay near the spring, looking across the serene valley, basking in the sun's warmth and Owen's magical powers.

The vision was shattered by the sound of Mark unlocking the front door. She heard his steps move along the bare boards of the hall, into the drawing room above her. After a few minutes, the sound of his newest Arvo Paart CD seeped through the ceiling. She didn't move; she knew he would soon come looking for her.

He clattered down the stairs and came into the kitchen with an unconvincing smile on his face. 'Hello, Angel!'

Beth looked pained.

'I'm sorry.' He gave a good-natured laugh. 'How was your day?'

She wondered why he cared, and guessed he was building reserves of reciprocal sympathy, but she told him a little about her asylum seeker, before she forced herself to ask, 'And how was yours?'

'Fucking terrible,' he said with a short, barking laugh, and his face collapsed a little. 'But I made some progress. I've put the lease of the offices up for sale, you'll be glad to hear.'

Beth nodded, and didn't say *about time, too*.

'And I've given a month's notice to all the staff, bar Trish, the book-keeper and two packers.'

'Including all the editorial people?'

'Yes,' Mark nodded with grim pride at his own firmness. 'I can do it myself for the time being, and probably do it better.'

'It won't do any harm for you to be entirely hands-on,' she agreed, 'and picking winners from the slush pile was always your true forte.'

Mark grunted. 'The only trouble is that the slush pile never stops growing. Everyone in England seems to think the world has a need to know all the gory secrets of their adolescence. And this morning we got a manuscript called the *Joys of Urine* from a Ghanaian chieftain – fifty thousand words on the benefits of drinking your own; it's amazing what it can do for you.' Mark had perked up now. 'Apparently it stops baldness, depression, piles and hundreds of other things, as well as increasing your sex drive and potency, and generally extending your life. And the book's stuffed with detailed anecdotes and examples to back up its claims.'

'I take it you're going to pass on that.'

'No, I'm not,' Mark grinned. 'I wrote and told him we'd do it, if he provided an up-front subsidy of fifty grand.'

'My God, Mark, you can't turn into a vanity publisher!'

'Only for Ghanaian chieftains who won't tell anyone. Anyway, he'll probably turn it down; though I have to say, it might fit quite neatly into our New Age and Earth Mysteries list,' he added with a chuckle.

    Beth couldn't help admiring the reckless optimism Mark could conjure from nowhere in the face of disaster, especially as she was beginning to feel sporadic deep stabs of remorse at her own disloyalty. She smiled back. 'Well, you're due a dose of luck, so maybe he'll go for it. Let's open a bottle and drink to the joys of urine.'

    Mark faked a worried frown. 'A bottle of what?'

    They both laughed, and he opened the fridge to see what was there.

    While he was filling two glasses, the telephone rang. Beth picked it up.

    'Hello, Beth? It's Ruth.'

    Beth at once detected a breathlessness in Ruth's voice that must herald some drama. As possible calamities scrolled through her mind, she hoped she wasn't ringing with news of a dead lamb, or to say that Laura's rapist had struck again.

    'You know the police came and took DNA samples last week?'

    'Yes,' Beth said impatiently.

    'They said they were doing it to eliminate everyone and remove any suspicions....'

    'Yes, that always seems a good idea.'

    'But it hasn't.'

    From Ruth's trembling shrillness, Beth guessed she was on the edge of hysteria.

    'Why Ruth? What on earth's happened?' Beth could imagine that if the test had identified one of the men from the valley, whom Ruth would undoubtedly have known, it would be very hard for her to forgive the rape of her famous friend.

    'They've....' Her voice was swallowed in a sob.

    Beth couldn't make out what she was saying. 'They've *what*, Ruth?'

    She heard Ruth sniffing tears away. 'They've arrested Owen!'

It seemed to Beth that an axe had struck the back of her head and cleaved it apart.

    She was numb, couldn't speak, couldn't react to Mark's sudden look of concern. She could still hear Ruth.

    'Beth? Beth? Are you there?'

Beyond Gospel Pass

Slowly, without choosing to, she lowered the hand that held the phone and stared, unfocused, at a point on the wall a few feet above the floor.

Mark was more alarmed now. He put the glasses down and moved to stand in front of Beth. He put his hands gently on her upper arms. 'Beth, angel?' he said and looked her in the eyes, to make her focus on his. But she stared through him, until he shook her lightly, and the phone fell from her hand. Mark stooped and picked it up.

'Hello, Ruth?'

Beth could tell that Ruth hadn't answered Mark, or had gone, or the connection had been broken by the phone hitting the ground.

Mark clicked it off and put it back in its cradle.

'Beth, for God's sake! What did Ruth tell you?'

Beth closed her eyes and felt some control return to her limbs.

'I'll have to go and see her,' she muttered.

'What the hell for? You've only just got back here.'

'I'll have to, Mark.'

'But haven't you got things to do?'

She knew he wanted her near him, to help him deal with his own problems. 'Nothing that won't keep for a few days,' she said. 'I got a lot done today.' She was beginning to see more clearly now. Obviously Owen was the victim of some ridiculous error. She would have to go up and help sort it out; Ruth certainly wasn't in a position to handle it; she wouldn't know how to, on her own.

'Ruth needs help,' she said, lying only by omission.

'What do you mean? What's happened?' Mark asked testily.

'The police think they may have found the rapist, and it's someone Ruth knows.'

'That'll teach her to hang around with all those dodgy travellers.'

Beth boiled with resentment on Owen's behalf, but didn't let Mark see. 'She thinks they've made a mistake. She wants me to go.' Although Ruth hadn't asked, Beth was sure she did want her to go and support her. She spoke decisively, in a way which she knew Mark would recognise, and walked from the kitchen to go upstairs and pack a bag.

When she came down, Mark was standing at the bottom of the stairs, unable to ignore his need for her in London. 'Are you sure it'll help?' he pleaded.

'There could be legal aspects I can help with.'

'Good God!' Mark burst out. 'Rape's hardly your field, and why should you be dishing out your expertise for nothing to a total stranger?'

Beth shook her head to imply that the question didn't merit an answer. She brushed past him and started up the stairs. 'I'll have to take the Saab. Can you look after Grimond, please?'

She didn't wait to hear if he objected. Anyway, he could go to the office by train; he was always going on about the advantages of public transport. She left the house and banged the door behind her.

The car was a few yards up the road. She got in and started it. But before she put it into gear, she opened the window and looked back to see Mark standing at the top of the front steps. 'I'll ring you tonight and tell you what's going on.'

From the moment she turned the car into the traffic streaming along the North Circular, she barely thought of Mark in the two hours it took her to drive along the crowded motorway to the River Severn. Her mind was entirely occupied with denying that Owen was capable of rape.

She told herself a hundred times that he was a gentle, compassionate, thoughtful man, and above all, in control of his passions; that the crime would be utterly anathema to him; but there was about his very self-control something at once attractive, yet disturbingly unhuman which didn't entirely refute the evidence of his DNA. She was appalled at her own disloyalty, though she knew her practised, rational mind would not normally have even attempted to contradict irrefutable evidence.

It was after ten and the sky to the west glowered with the remnants of a sun that had set through the gaps in a curtain of rain-filled clouds already dropping their burden on the soupy waters of the river below.

Beth drove through the blustering wind as the road from Newport swept north past the damply gleaming depressions of Pontypool and Cwmbran, and the hopeless acceptance of a terrible truth enveloped her, until she didn't want to go on - wanted to pass the end of her valley, and carry on, anywhere that led away from confrontation.

Beyond Gospel Pass

But she turned left by the ancient inn at the southern end of the cwm and allowed the sinuous lane to guide her irresistibly, like a tram on rails, to the top of the valley where Ruth was waiting for her.

She saw Ruth – a silhouette framed by the open doorway – as soon as she turned up towards the Hendre. By the time she had climbed stiffly from the car, Ruth was beside her. She flung her arms around Beth and heaved silently for a few moments, and Beth was very glad that she had come.

She gently untwined Ruth's arms and eased her away. 'I thought you'd want me here,' she said.

Ruth nodded. 'Mark told me you were coming; I was so relieved! I just feel as if I'm living in some kind of Kafka world, where truth has been turned inside out. The whole thing must be crazy, mustn't it Beth?'

'Let's get inside,' Beth said. 'We're getting wet.' She pulled her bag from the back seat of the car and squelched up towards the slot of welcoming light in the doorway.

Ruth overtook her and pushed the door open.

It was warm inside the house and smelled of sweet herbs and patchouli oil. 'Do you want tea, or coffee?'

'A large vodka, frankly.'

Ruth gave her a complicit grin and disappeared into her larder for a moment. She came back and poured a drink for Beth and made herself some evening primrose tea. They both sat down at the table where, Beth recalled, they'd had dinner the night Laura had been raped – just ten days ago, she realised.

'What are we going to do?' Ruth asked the question with wide, trusting eyes which revealed her complete confidence that Beth already had an effective course of action to suggest.

Beth looked back. Slowly, feeling almost cruel as she did it, she lifted her shoulders. 'I don't know Ruth. I wish to hell I did, but I just don't know how we can argue with the evidence. Obviously, I can make absolutely certain there hasn't been a technical mix-up with the samples.' Both women screwed up their faces at the thought of what that might involve. 'But that's very unlikely – I mean, the police just don't make mistakes like that; it would cost them too much. But I think, before I do anything, I'll have to see Owen.'

A sheet of flat, grey cloud floated a few feet above the Sugarloaf Mountain as Beth drove down to the police station in Abergavenny. Owen was being held there until he was due to appear in front of the local magistrates later that morning.

Beth had already established that he was being represented by the solicitor who had been on duty when he'd been charged the night before, a partner in a small firm in the town. She went first to the solicitor's office – a drab, grey book-lined cubicle above a chemist's shop in the High Street.

Robert Whittal was a short man with small features and narrow eyes that reflected a sour hostility from the start of his meeting with Beth. At the same time, he was impressed by her legal eminence.

'How are you going to handle this?' she asked, without apologising for her interference.

Whittal shrugged briefly. 'He's not helping himself much.' His voice had a nasal ring with a hint of the Valleys. 'Look, the police have got him sewn up with this DNA profile.' He glanced more keenly at Beth for her reaction. 'But he insists he didn't do it.' He lifted his shoulder again. 'I can't argue with evidence like that. All I can do is go for mitigation; I've already suggested tests for psychological problems and a report from a clinical psychiatrist, but he says he's completely sane – he just wasn't there when it happened.'

Beth stared at the little man who not unreasonably assumed that Owen was clearly guilty of raping Laura. 'Hasn't he given you *any* kind of alibi?'

Whittal shook his head. 'No. It's as if he doesn't even want to try to get off, though he swears he didn't do it and he wants to plead Not Guilty, whatever evidence they produce; but, like I say, he's not giving me anything at all to help him with. And the strange thing is he's not a bit rattled; he's completely calm. I've done a few rapists in my time, and usually they're sitting around in a state of shock and can't really take in they've been caught. But not this chap.'

'Would you mind if I saw him?'

'Just tell me again what your interest is?' The man looked at her more searchingly.

'Owen Rhys is a neighbour of ours. He's done work for us, and everything I've seen or know about him convinces me that he could not be a rapist.' As she spoke, Beth was conscious of how little she really did know about Owen. He had, after all, told her almost nothing about himself.

'Would you consider representing him when it goes to the Crown Court,' Whittal asked, unexpectedly, 'on legal aid terms?'

Beth had already considered and rejected that possibility as soon as she'd heard about Owen's arrest. It would have been fundamentally unprofessional, and she had no direct experience of this kind of law. But she was desperate to see Owen. 'Possibly,' she said. 'I'd have to talk to him first.'

'Okay. I'll let them know.' He glanced at his watch. 'He won't be leaving for court for another hour or so. We've probably just got time if we go to the police station now, if you want?'

'Yes, please.'

Beth wondered if the sergeant who was leading them to the interview room in the police station could see how she was shaking.

She was dreading this meeting with Owen as much as anything she'd ever done. She had no idea what she would feel when she saw him, knowing that such unquestionable evidence of the crime had been produced against him.

Beth and the solicitor were left in a closed room, windowless and soundless apart from the occasional distant ringing of a telephone as the policeman's steps faded down the lino floor of the corridor outside. She sat down on one of two cantilevered iron chairs at a formica-topped table edged with long brown cigarette burns.

Whittal sat opposite her, glancing at her from time to time as he kept up a constant, irritating drumming on the table with his fingers.

A few minutes later, two sets of footsteps approached the room and the door was opened.

Owen stood in the entrance for a moment. He was dressed in jeans and a canvas jacket Beth recognised. There was a flicker of surprise in his eyes when he saw her. She wondered who the policeman had said was waiting to see him.

She stood up. 'Hello, Owen,' she smiled. 'How are you?'

She could hardly believe that she'd been able to say the simple words so calmly, as if nothing in particular had happened since she'd last seen him, in the early hours of the Friday before.

He looked back at her, said nothing, conveyed nothing with his eyes and took a few steps into the room. He nodded at the solicitor without expression.

The policeman behind him looked inquiringly.

'Thank you,' Whittal said. 'We'll be about twenty minutes.'

The policeman left, his noisy footsteps echoing around the inhospitable room.

Beth turned to the solicitor. 'I know I shouldn't ask this, but would you mind if I spent a few minutes alone with Owen.'

'It isn't really...'

'I know it isn't. But I need to talk to Owen alone before I agree to represent him.'

The solicitor's mouth trembled irresolutely. 'All right,' he sighed. 'If anyone comes in, tell 'em I've just gone to make a phone call.'

The door closed behind him, and Beth was alone with Owen. They were standing a few feet apart. Beth wanted to touch him, to reassure him that she was on his side. But his stance, his silence, his eyes – more opaque than ever – discouraged her. She sat down.

'What a mess!' she said, knowing how inadequate it sounded.

Owen raised his brow a few millimetres and tilted his head slightly to one side. He pulled out the other chair to sit opposite her. 'You could say that.' His quiet voice betrayed no fear of his circumstances.

Beth took a deep breath. 'Owen, you must believe me when I say I *know* you didn't do this. I know you're incapable of such a thing.'

He said nothing for a moment. 'There's not much you can do about it, though.' He wasn't offering a challenge, but a statement of simple fact.

'But surely, you can tell us *something* that will prove it wasn't you?'

He shrugged his shoulders. 'I was out in the valley early that morning; I don't deny it, but not till light. I'd heard a lamb caught in a gully above the Hendre and went up to fetch it out. I told them, it was only when I was coming back down the lane I found the woman.'

'You were right to tell them that, of course. If she'd told them and you hadn't, it would have destroyed any chance of proving your innocence.'

'There doesn't seem to be much chance of that anyway.'

Beyond Gospel Pass

'Owen!' She reached a hand across the table towards him and touched him lightly on his left arm, through the canvas of the jacket he was wearing. 'Please, you've got to do something – tell us something to save yourself. Rape's a serious crime, for Christ's sake – you could go to jail for eight or ten years!' Beth almost sobbed.

'Yes, I know.'

'But, please! I couldn't bear it!' Beth tried to stop the tears spilling from her eyes. Lawyers didn't cry when they were visiting clients.

Owen took a long, deep breath and looked at her; she was certain the screen that hid his thoughts lifted for a second. 'I know,' he said softly. 'But there's nothing I can do about it.'

Beth drew away her hand and sat back, trying to be businesslike. 'Owen. There's got to be *something* we can do about it. You didn't do it; someone's made a major error here. I'm going to look into it.'

The screen across Owen's eyes snapped down again, like shutters on a jewellery shop. 'I don't want you to waste your time.'

Beth stood up. She couldn't understand his defeatism. If he didn't do it – she chided herself for even thinking 'if' – then there had to be a way of disproving or discounting the evidence. 'Owen, it's crazy not to fight this. I'm going to have the whole DNA profiling process reviewed.'

Owen sighed and shook his head. 'I promise you; you won't get anywhere. They're certain they've got the right man, and I don't think you should waste your time representing me.'

'No,' Beth shook her head. 'You're right. I couldn't anyway. I'm far too personally involved.'

Fourteen

Two hours after she had left him at the police station, Beth sat at the back of the Victorian courtroom, watching Owen's expressionless face as the chairman of the bench, a cadaverous old man with a reedy voice, ordered that he be remanded in custody to appear in front of them again in seven days' time.

When the hearing was concluded, the magistrate gave the command, 'Now go with the officers.'

Owen didn't show a flicker of emotion as he glanced up at her, and two policemen led him from the dock.

She found Whittal waiting for her outside the court.

'Are you sure you won't take this case?' He sounded genuinely disappointed.

'I'm sure, Mr Whittal. Frankly, it's not an area where I have a lot of expertise. I haven't run a criminal case of any sort for over ten years. Besides, I know the defendant too well.'

Whittal glanced at her, trying to read her face, but she was determined to give nothing away.

'Where will he be taken?' she asked.

'Cardiff, I should think.'

'I suppose it wasn't worth asking for bail?'

'What do you think?' The solicitor pulled a face. 'I only get one crack, and I hadn't a shred of grounds.'

'No,' Beth sighed. 'I suppose not.'

Owen was right; the police weren't in any doubt that they'd got their man, but they couldn't stop Beth making arrangements through the Legal Aid Board for an independent expert to examine the two relevant

Beyond Gospel Pass

DNA samples. But even as she put the process in motion, she was conscious of a horrible certainty that the result would be the same as the Home Office pathologist's.

She drove back to Llanthony utterly confounded by Owen's capitulation. It was totally inexplicable in the light of his innocence, and she was determined that she would never let go of that essential fact. She wouldn't be able to represent him in court, but she'd promised Whittal that her services would be on call, at no charge, any time they might be required.

She took the lane up to Pant-y-Groes; she didn't want to see Ruth yet; she didn't know how to tell her that she'd come back empty-handed. The house was cool to the point of chilliness on such a grey day at eight hundred feet. Beth lit a fire and tried to organise her thoughts. Unless by some miracle the independent tests on the DNA samples did show a different result from the Chepstow laboratory, she would have to support Whittal in his tactic of going for some kind of mitigation. But if Owen refused to abandon his claim of innocence, he would lose any discount in sentence he might have earned from a 'Guilty' plea.

Then, what right had she to expect him to plead guilty to a crime he hadn't committed?

As she contemplated the ghastly conundrum, she lit the Aga and opened some wine. She poured herself a glass and wandered about the house, trying to impose some kind of mental order on herself through physical movement.

With a supreme effort, she recognised that she was going to have to make some painful and far-reaching decisions about her life before it all fell apart. Firmly, she looked at her watch. It was after three; she hadn't eaten anything that day but she didn't want to now. She went out to the car, climbed in and turned up the valley towards Hay.

She parked by the Buttermarket and walked around to the estate agents through whom she and Mark had bought Pant-y-Groes. When she went in, the man sitting at the only desk recognised her and stood up to greet her.

She guessed he already knew about Mark's failure to be selected; these things must have flown around a tiny town like Hay in a matter of hours.

'Good morning, Mrs Powell, what can I do for you?'

'I'd like you to put Pant-y-Groes on the market for us, please.'

'Thinking of moving, then?' Boo Llewellyn was on the other side of the road as Beth walked out of the estate agent's.

Beth nodded. 'Yes.'

'I don't blame you,' Boo said, and Beth knew she understood. 'Shall we have a coffee somewhere?'

'Yes, let's,' Beth said.

They went to the organic café by the clock tower, where once - it seemed like a few years ago, not a few weeks - she had sat and chatted to Owen, enjoying the longest conversation they'd ever had. She found it incredible that so much had happened since then.

'You don't look too good,' Boo said, once they'd sat down.

'No,' Beth agreed, deliberately not expanding.

'This rape business?' Boo asked.

'Yes.'

'I must say I was jolly surprised to hear it was that nice hunk – he didn't look at all the sort who would need to resort to that kind of thing.'

'He didn't do it!'

Boo looked at Beth, with slightly wider eyes. 'But I'd heard there was absolutely conclusive proof.'

'I'm sure there's been a mistake; I know he didn't do it.'

'Of course, I can see why you feel like....'

'Look, Boo, I'd rather we didn't talk about it. Obviously it's hit me very hard – after all, I saw the man quite a lot; he was more or less a neighbour, and I was at dinner with Laura Chichester the night it happened. I've been to see the police.... and Owen. And yes, they've got a hell of a case against him at the moment, but I'm sure new evidence will turn up if they're pushed hard enough.'

Boo looked as if she wanted to say more on the subject but had prudently chosen not to, and waited for Beth to make the next move.

After a short silence, Beth said, 'Do you think it will take long to sell Pant-y-Groes?'

'I shouldn't think so. There are thousands of people coming up here now thinking what an idyll it must be, living up in the hills,' she laughed. 'They never think it is once they've spent a winter there and crossed a few of the locals.'

Beyond Gospel Pass

'It didn't take us all that long to get used to them,' Beth said pointedly.

'Well, you, my dear, are obviously a special case. Anyway, we shall miss you. God knows we need a few lively females in the area. Weekly skirmishes with Belinda Sharp over the bridge table don't present enough of a challenge, I find.'

'I'll make sure I come back.'

'Why should you want to?'

'Believe it or not, despite all the things that have happened here, I've grown rather to love it. But there's no point keeping a house if Mark isn't working up here, and frankly, he's got enough to keep him busy at his office for the next year or two.'

But Boo had seen the misery in her eyes. She reached a sympathetic hand across the table and squeezed Beth's. 'If you ever want to stay with us, just ask.'

The weather changed in the night. Beth woke to a morning so clear and sublime that she thought she couldn't belong to this world – as if she had no share in the beauty all around her. She was still almost sick with the fear she'd felt from the moment Ruth had first whispered over the phone that Owen had been arrested; and as each promise of hope faded, along with any chance of seeing the whole horrible incident dispelled as a crazy mistake, her torment increased.

She tried to calm herself, and took a cup of coffee into the study, determined to treat Owen's case as dispassionately as she would with any client's. She opened a pad and wrote down all the evidence the police had given her and added to it everything else she knew, relying only on the facts, not personal impressions or private emotions. There wasn't a lot to add, but there was one person from whom she was sure she could learn more.

Making up her mind that she had to do something, she went out and drove up to Blaen Fawr.

Beth knocked on the flaking front door of the big stone house, as she had six days earlier, before the world had turned upside down. She had to wait longer than last time for anyone to come, but when they did, the door was opened wider.

Despite the absence of any obvious welcome in Megan Rhys's small brown eyes, Beth sensed at once that she was going to be received more easily.

'Hello, Mrs Rhys; I'm Beth Powell...'

'I know who you are. Are you coming in?'

The old woman spoke with a voice that croaked, perhaps, through lack of use. Beth stepped across the threshold of the house for the first time into a gloomy hall – a long broad corridor containing a few pieces of heavy, age-blackened furniture.

Megan pushed the front door shut and led her into an old-fashioned and evidently seldom used parlour at the front of the house. The oak trees outside and the dirty windows took most of the light. The room was in semi-darkness, even on a bright summer's day.

'Would you like tea?' Megan asked.

'Yes, please,' Beth said, though she didn't care.

Owen's mother disappeared silently. Beth gazed around the room, intrigued. She felt again as if she had been transported back in time; it appeared that this part of the house had never been wired and there was no electric light in the place, only a pair of large brass oil lamps with big, dusty opal globes; a sideboard cluttered with neglected decorative crockery, and candlesticks on a mantelpiece above what had once been a big open fireplace, reduced in Victorian times to a modest little cast-iron orifice.

An unglazed black and white photograph, slightly creased, hung in a frame on an otherwise bare wall. Beth walked over to look at it. It had been taken thirty or forty years before and showed a very handsome man in working clothes, standing beside a woman who must have been Megan. She guessed it was Dai Rhys, Owen's father who, according to Lord Brecon, had taken his own life soon after Owen was born.

Beyond this there wasn't much to look at but Megan still hadn't returned. Beth lowered herself into a large armchair that smelt as if it had lain unused for a few decades. It wasn't surprising, she thought; she couldn't imagine Owen had ever sat around in this mausoleum. She thought of him here in this house – not in police custody, where she'd last seen him – and wondered where he had spent his time.

Probably in the kitchen, she thought, and wanted to see it. She got to her feet, and walked across to let herself out of the room.

Beyond Gospel Pass

In the corridor, she stopped to guess which way to go. She was struck by the stillness of the heavily enclosed house on this quiet afternoon. The silence was broken only by the deep throated *tock* of a long-case clock standing in the gloom somewhere at the end of the passage. She took a few steps towards the end of the hall, with the staircase on her right, but stopped abruptly when a loud thump echoed from up the stairs, just as Megan emerged from the door at the end of the corridor with a tray containing tea things.

Megan stopped and looked at her suspiciously. 'What do you want?' she asked.

'I was only coming to see if I could help,' Beth said.

'I don't need no help.' Megan advanced on her with the tray, almost menacingly.

'I heard something bang upstairs,' Beth said, thinking that Megan hadn't heard it.

Megan looked at her with screwed up eyes for a moment. 'Aye, it was just the gable window blowing shut,' she said dismissively, and carried on to the parlour where she had first left Beth.

Beth followed obediently, and thought how her liaison with Owen had, by extension, given her a relationship with this strange little hermit.

In the front room, Megan pushed away some of the clutter on the sideboard to make room for the tray, and carefully poured dark tea into a cup.

'Sit down,' she said, turning back to Beth and nodding at one of the dusty old chairs.

Beth sank down into it again, enveloped by a musty odour of decay, and took the cup from Megan. The old woman poured one for herself, and sat down slowly in the other upholstered chair opposite.

'So,' she said. 'I heard tell you went to see my Owen in the prison.'

'It's not exactly prison, Mrs Rhys,' Beth said, and felt foolish for being pedantic.

Megan made an impatient gesture. 'It's all the same. Michael says you know about the law.'

'Yes,' Beth nodded, glad that this had been discussed. 'I'm a barrister – that's a kind of lawyer who appears in the courts, not like a solicitor.'

'It's a funny world where women do men's work,' Megan said, and Beth wondered if she ever watched television. 'Any road, you knows about the law. What will happen to my Owen?'

'It's hard to say, exactly...'

'They do say that they knows it's him from his blood or summat.'

Beth noticed that her accent was the local blend of rural West Country English and a strong Welsh cadence. She also recognised some sounds from Owen's speech.

She didn't want to go into the detail of the substances and samples tested by the pathologists. 'They have made what they call a DNA match, which I'm afraid is usually considered pretty conclusive,' she explained as briefly as she could.

'So they're sure he done it?'

Beth tightened her face and nodded. 'Yes, they are.'

Megan looked back at her in silence for a few moments. 'What do you think?' she asked.

'At the moment, I can think of only three things which would mean he hadn't done it; and I want very much for one of them to be true.'

'What's that then?'

Beth went on reluctantly. 'The first is that someone was able to plant some...' she hesitated for the right word, 'fluid on the victim that was Owen's, which he hadn't... er, put there himself.' She felt herself floundering. Out loud, it sounded even more fanciful than it had in her head, as well as being impossible to explain without being brutally blunt.

But she judged from Megan's face that she'd understood, and also found it an unlikely story.

'The second possibility is that Owen and this woman had intercourse by mutual consent, which she then subsequently denied...'

She let the words hang in the air and watched Megan shake her head vigorously and mutter. 'No, no. Not Owen.'

Beth wondered why his mother was so sure.

She wondered why she herself was so certain that this defence was out of the question, until she recalled the grave dignity of Owen's categorical denial that he'd had anything to do with the event. Besides, there was no plausible reason why Laura herself should react in that way.

'Then the final possibility is that the police have rigged the evidence somehow; I don't know how, but if they were anxious to and thought they could get away with it, it wouldn't be hard.'

'Why would they do that?'

'I was hoping you might be able to give me some ideas,' Beth said. 'How did Owen get on with the police locally?'

Megan shrugged. 'We never see 'em, hardly – not this end of the valley. Llanthony people's never got on with the bobbies, though. We're independent folk as likes to look after our own troubles.'

Beth was conscious that the people of the valley were only a generation or two away from isolation. 'But did Owen ever have any dealings with them, over anything?'

Megan shook her head slowly. 'There ain't been a bobby in this house since Dai Rhys died.' Her eyes flickered up to the photograph on the wall above the sideboard.

'Is that Owen's father?'

'Yes,' Megan said with a quick downturn of her mouth.

'He looks very like Owen.'

'Owen's strong like him; same big forearms, but he ain't like him in other ways.'

Beth hoped she might specify, but Megan didn't offer anything more. 'When did he die?' Beth asked innocently.

'Nearly thirty years ago.'

'Why did the police come?'

'They said they had to know why he fell; they tried to say it wasn't an accident.'

Beth nodded slowly, to show she was listening. 'But Owen's never had anything to do with them?'

'Never,' Megan said firmly.

Logically, Beth had not been holding out any serious hope for any of the possible let-outs for Owen , but she had been praying desperately that some explanation would offer itself. She leaned forward in her chair, to get closer to Megan and, perhaps, gain her trust. 'Tell me, Mrs Rhys, did Owen have what you could call enemies in the valley?'

'Not for himself, like, not as I knew about.'

'But has he had any disputes with other farmers?'

'Oh yes. There's a family in this valley that's been feuding with the Rhyses since his grandfather.'

'Who are they?'

'Bebbs, from Lower Cwm.'

'What were they feuding over?'

'I don't know the reason. My husband said it was over a bull as went missing, that they denied, and the families ain't never spoke since.'

'There's still bad feeling after all this time?'

'Oh yes,' Megan nodded. 'You don't forget if someone's done you wrong.'

'But you can't remember what it's about?'

The old woman shook her head. 'I know they done the family wrong, though, and that's it.'

Beth tried to imagine Owen harbouring an absurd, archaic grudge; she realised that she couldn't be sure if he would or would not, although everything she had seen and sensed in him denied such small-mindedness. 'The Bebbs,' she nodded. 'I'll follow that up.'

Megan was looking at her more closely now. There was nervous doubt in her eyes along with desperate expectation. 'Can you do anything to get my Owen back?'

Beth sighed. 'I don't know, Mrs Rhys; but believe me, I've fought all my professional life against injustice, and I can assure you that I'll do everything I can.' She wished she hadn't sounded so pompous, but Megan looked appreciative.

She gazed back at Beth silently, shrewdly appraising her. 'I know you want to see my Owen out of prison, too, but don't mind if he doesn't help you.'

Beth stared at her, bewildered. 'Why on earth shouldn't he help me?'

'I'm just telling you he might not. But please,' Megan was pleading now, 'please help to get him back for me.'

Beth lay awake all night. The torment of losing Owen hadn't eased at all since she'd first heard the news. Frustration and doubt had only increased her despair. In the morning, she looked in the bathroom mirror at the grey-brown semicircles under her eyes and the furrows in her skin, and thought of the ten years between her and Owen.

The sound of a telephone echoed through the gloom. As she went down to answer it, she hoped it might be Mark. She suddenly wanted his voice to give her the reassurance that the world hadn't ended.

'Hello?'

'Can you come?'

Beth took a moment to recognise Megan Rhys's quavering voice. 'What's happened?' she asked.

'The police are come again.'

Beth felt her innards shrink. 'What do they want?'

'They wants to see his things.'

'I'll come up,' Beth said crisply, and put the phone down.

The mist that had draped the mountains since early morning was still dense in the valley. Outside the yard gate at Blaen Fawr stood a single anonymous blue car, immediately cutting down to size the invasion she'd been imagining. She parked beside it and walked briskly across to the house. The front door was opening before she reached it. Megan beckoned her in.

'They're through to Owen's room,' she croaked. She was shaking as she led Beth through a door at the back of the hall, along another corridor to what seemed like a separate apartment on the ground floor, with its own external entrance on the side of the house.

Beth followed Megan into a room furnished with a large, old iron bed with a patchwork cover, a wardrobe, a chest of drawers and a big armchair, all as old as the bed. There was also a compact CD player on top of a well-filled bookcase.

Two plain-clothes policemen were carefully examining the contents of the chest of drawers.

Beth turned to Megan. 'What did you say they were looking for?'

'I don't know. They took a pair of old wellies they found in the cow shed.'

The two men glanced up at Beth. 'We're looking for something to tell us about Owen's hobbies,' one of them said with a smirk. 'Any signs of instability. It's in his own interests really.'

Beth closed her eyes for a second. She wanted to scream at them for their sneaking intrusion into the private places of Owen's life.

'Have you found anything?' she managed to say coolly.

'Nothing in here. And who are you?'

'I'm a lawyer; I saw Mr Rhys at the police station on Tuesday,' she said, lying only by omission.

'But you're a barrister, aren't you? Then you shouldn't be here without Mr Whittal.'

'I'm here because Mrs Rhys asked me, as a neighbour. I'm not acting for Owen, and I won't be asking any more questions either,' she added, as if she were dismissing an unhelpful witness.

The older of the two men looked back at her for a moment, about to make a stand, but shrugged his shoulders and turned back to the job as if neither of the women were in the room.

Beth took the chance to look around and absorb more details of Owen's surroundings.

She moved closer to the bookcase. Without taking any out, she examined the titles of the books. The majority were reference books on birds and plants, but there were also a number of herbal and New Age titles, including George Arbuthnott's *The Leys of the Land*. She wondered if he'd bought it or the author had given it to him.

Beth was slightly surprised. She had an impression of Owen being so self-contained that he didn't need the input of other people's findings; at the same time, she'd realised almost from the start that he was a man who took his knowledge seriously.

She wanted to see his collection of records and CDs, too, but as the police were leafing through them, they heard another vehicle growl up the track and stop outside the house.

Beth followed Megan back to the main part of the house. As they reached the hall, Michael Rhys came in.

'What's going on?'

'The police has come back; they're going through all his things.'

Michael glanced at Beth. 'Can they do that?'

'Of course; they'll have a warrant.'

'What are they looking for?'

'Anything that might help their case.' Beth didn't want to expand.

'To, like show he was....?' Michael's voice faltered.

Beth nodded. 'So far they've only found a pair of boots.'

Michael turned to Megan. 'Have they been up?' he muttered.

The old woman glanced sharply at Beth and nodded. 'No, they only looked in his rooms.'

Beyond Gospel Pass

As she was speaking, the policemen came out into the hall.

'Right then, thank you Mrs Rhys. We've seen all we need to. We'll let you know if we have to come back, all right?'

Megan stared at them without saying anything and stood aside to let them leave the house through the front door.

Beth could tell that Michael resented her presence; she had, anyway, never felt comfortable with him. He had always seemed suspicious of her, and now there was even something accusatory in his manner, as if she were somehow responsible for what had happened to Owen.

Megan, too, seemed to want to be alone with her elder son. Beth couldn't blame her. She said goodbye and offered again to come back if she could help in any way.

Ruth's old Land Rover was standing outside the Hendre. Beth walked through the open front door.

Ruth smiled glumly. 'Hello, Beth. Have you heard anything?'

'I've just come from Blaen Fawr, and I went up there yesterday to see Megan.'

Ruth gaped at her. 'What? Out of the blue?'

'Yes; I thought I might be able to help — you know, legally, having come across Owen recently quite a bit, as a neighbour.'

'What was she like?'

'She asked me in, gave me some tea. It's a most extraordinary old place, like it's been caught in a time warp. The front parlour can't have changed in fifty years.'

Ruth was impressed. 'Not many people get asked in, I can tell you. What did she say?'

'I got the impression that she'd do anything to have Owen back. She'd heard I knew something about the law, so I suppose she was prepared to overcome her xenophobia. Anyway, this morning she rang me and asked me to go there again because the police had turned up to search Owen's things.'

'Oh my God! What did they want?'

'I imagine they were looking for anything that might have suggested he had tendencies to sexual violence.'

'Oh God, how horrible!'

'It's okay. They only took away a pair of boots, but even so, the case is absolutely clear-cut as far as the police are concerned. When I saw Megan yesterday, I told her there were only three possible defences against the DNA evidence, and she told me about some feud that the Rhyses have carried on for generations with a family called Bebb.'

Ruth nodded. 'Yes, that's a standard piece of gossip round here. These feuds start and seem to keep going long after the original reasons for them have been forgotten.'

'But would Owen have let himself get involved?'

'No, not Owen himself, but Michael still won't have anything to do with them, and I think Owen's always felt he must be loyal to Michael.'

'Are he and Michael that close, though? I mean – they're so different.'

'I think Michael's quite jealous of Owen, and Owen's always taken that into account and handled him pretty carefully - always backed down to avoid confrontation. They're much closer than they were when I first came to live here, now Michael's got his own family and everything.'

'Do you think these Bebbs would want to set things up somehow so that Owen got done for this rape?'

'I wouldn't put it past them, especially if one of them actually did it, but I don't see how they could.'

Beth sighed. 'No, nor do I, if I'm honest. That only leaves consent or the police fixing it, but Megan says Owen's never had any problems with the police. And I just don't see that Laura would have called rape if she had consented. Besides, she didn't pinpoint Owen, and she made no sign of accusation against him when he brought her back to the Hendre.'

Ruth didn't answer for a few moments. 'It's hell, isn't it, keeping faith against evidence like that.'

'Yes, it is.'

'You really care about this, don't you?'

Beth looked at Ruth and longed to tell her – to share with someone – the depth of her feelings for Owen. 'I've always cared about justice,' she said, as she had to Megan, 'and from what I know of Owen, it just isn't possible that he's committed this crime, is it?'

Ruth sighed. 'I know him very well, and of course, I agree; but we all know a lot less than we think, even about people close to us.' The words hung in the air between them for a few moments. Ruth turned away awkwardly. 'I'm sorry; perhaps I shouldn't have said that. Look, why not stay and have something to eat? I'm having an early lunch because I've got to be in Hay by one-thirty with one of my ram lambs.'

Beth didn't want to go back to Pant-y-Groes alone. 'Yes, thanks.'

Ruth tossed some jack-in-the-hedge and dandelion leaves together with small tomatoes she'd grown. 'So, do you think there's anything you can do?'

'No, not really. As I know him personally, it would be unprofessional to represent him. Anyway, I don't know much about criminal law. He was taken on by the solicitor who was on duty when he was arrested – a surly little man called Whittal – and he seems content to let him act for him. I didn't ask him if he's got a family lawyer – perhaps I should have done, but anyway, Whittal says he'll be briefing someone from one of the Park Place chambers in Cardiff to handle the Crown Court.'

'When will he appear there?'

'There'll be a few more remand hearings, then a committal hearing in front of the local bench in a week or so and they'll almost certainly get him remanded in custody until the first Pleas and Directions Hearing at the Crown Court, probably six or eight weeks after that.'

'When will the actual trial be?'

'At least a couple of months after that, if he's still pleading 'Not guilty'.'

'My God! Won't they let him out on bail?'

'No. It's hardly worth applying for it with a crime like rape. And you only get one shot anyway.'

'Where will the trial be?'

'Newport, I presume.'

'So, where will he be until then?'

'Cardiff.' Beth took a deep breath and a decision. 'I'm going to go and visit him there next week – to see if he'll tell me anything he hasn't told Whittal.'

'Why should he?' Ruth put a large salad bowl, some bread and goats' cheese on the table and waved Beth towards a chair.

Jessica Meredith

Beth sat down and sighed. She took a gulp of the wine Ruth had just poured. 'I don't suppose he will, but I've got to try.' She stared bleakly at the bowl of leaves and felt she couldn't eat a morsel.

When she rang her chambers from home after lunch, she detected a hint of terseness in Jack Devereux's manner, in so far as he ever allowed himself to be anything other than understanding and accommodating. She promised that she would be back in chambers the following week.

Then she phoned Mark at his office. Guiltily, she did find the reassurance she'd hoped for in his voice, even though he sounded harassed, but was obviously putting a brave face on his problems. 'I've earned a decent weekend,' he said. 'I'm coming up tomorrow morning.'

Early on Sunday, Beth sat outside in bright sunshine, eating a grapefruit. She planned to go to mass at the abbey in Hereford later that morning.

Mark appeared, freshly showered, bright and handsome. 'I'll come with you,' he said, hoping she'd be pleased.

For the past two days, Mark had been attentive, modest, and conscientiously hadn't drunk too much. Beth wanted to feel grateful, but her head was too full of Owen. She tried to make up for it. 'Don't worry, darling; you know you get bored at mass.'

'It's not that it bores me,' he answered. 'It's simply that I don't always see the relevance of it, and that leaves me feeling rather bogus.'

'Then don't come.'

'I want to today; maybe I can relate better to it now and see what it's doing for you.'

Beth didn't even know why she wanted to go, at a time when every feeling she had, every urge conflicted with the standards to which she'd always tried to adhere. And Mark's good-natured, reasonable behaviour, overdue as it was, had confused her. She had to acknowledge that the mess Archimedes was in, while undoubtedly his fault, could not have happened if he hadn't taken the initiative in launching the company in the first place and then nurturing it successfully into existence.

He was fond of using the analogy that any commercial entity, whether it produced books or ball-bearings, was an organic being that underwent birth, growth – to a greater or lesser degree – and, sooner or later, death. While it lived, it offered products to its customers and employed people; and to sustain the energy this required, it fed on profits.

And there was no doubt that Mark had had the courage and conviction to take the risks involved in giving birth to Archimedes – which most people wouldn't or couldn't have done; she'd always given him credit for that.

'What were you praying so hard for?' Mark asked as he drove them back from Hereford, towards mountains that basked mistily in the noon sun.

'I was praying for that poor man sitting in jail for a crime he didn't commit.'

'How can you be so sure he didn't? You certainly weren't with him at the time,' he smiled.

'You can just tell from the way he is that he wouldn't do anything like that.'

'How on earth can you tell?' Mark chuckled. 'Rapists come in all shapes and sizes; you know the straightest-looking people can harbour the most bizarre private lusts.'

'I went to see him, you know,' she said.

'Did you?' He didn't sound surprised. 'I thought you might. I also thought it would be rather unwise. I mean, if he gets convicted after all - and it looks very likely that he will on such solid evidence – you'll carry some of the stigma, just by association, as far as the people round here are concerned.'

'Well that won't matter much, when we've sold the house.'

He turned to her sharply. 'Are you keen to sell it?'

She couldn't tell whether he minded or not. 'I've already put it on the market; in fact I'm surprised we haven't had anyone round to look yet.'

Mark returned his eyes to the road in front. 'You might have told me.'

'I'm sorry Mark,' she said, meaning it. 'I thought you'd just try and talk me out of it, but now you're not going to fight the seat up here, there's no point staying.'

'Except for the fact that it seemed to be doing us some good. I really did feel that you might get pregnant up here. I didn't just say it for the benefit of the selection committee.'

Beth clenched her teeth and fists. She tried to stop tears coming, and turned away to look out of her window.

'I only hope,' Mark went on, 'these troubles of mine and the stress this rape case is giving you won't make us so uptight we still can't have a baby. I *was* thinking that once I'd got Archimedes sorted out and back on its feet, you and I might spend a good long time up here this summer.'

Beth, still staring silently from the car, thought about the life she was certain had already started within her, which she believed owed nothing to Mark.

'D'you know,' he went on, 'I think a child would fill every small chink in our relationship. The other day you thought I was decrying women for the strength of their urge to procreate. But I wasn't; I was admiring a characteristic that's wonderfully and essentially female. Besides, it's not as if men don't have their own dynastic aspirations.'

Beth turned her head to look at him. 'There's a difference between wanting to found a dynasty – which I don't think most men want anyway – and having an individual baby.'

'Agreed,' Mark laughed. 'What I'm saying is that I want this baby, too – very much.' He nodded towards her stomach and gave it a pat. 'And it's time we put one there.'

Halfway through the afternoon Mark announced that he wasn't planning to stay at Pant-y-Groes that night. He had a lot to do next day and wanted to drive back to London with Beth.

'But I've arranged to visit Owen Rhys in prison,' Beth said as lightly as if she were planning to drop in on an old aunt.

If Mark was hurt or annoyed, he didn't show it. 'Since you're so committed, it's a shame you won't appear for him professionally, though of course I understand your reasons for not doing it. I hope you're able to get somewhere by seeing him this time.'

Beth only heard on Monday morning that Owen's committal hearing in front of the Abergavenny magistrates had been set for that day.

She arrived in time to see him led into court, where, in crowded silence, the pale and wrinkled chairman who had presided at his first appearance told him that a Pleas and Directions Hearing at Newport Crown Court had been fixed for Wednesday, 29th July.

Beyond Gospel Pass

When Beth found Mr Whittal twenty minutes later, he confirmed that Owen had been taken straight back to Cardiff jail. She was grimly conscious, that this was a critical stage – that his committal to the slow, hard-grinding process of law was the beginning of an unstoppable journey into oblivion.

Queasy with depression, Beth entered the looming stone building in Cardiff that housed a thousand assorted miscreants. Some had been convicted; others, like Owen, were on remand with the advantage of ready access to visitors and the dignity of their own clothes.

No objection was made to her seeing Owen, but he hadn't arrived back from Abergavenny; prisoners were being picked up from other courts on the way. She went out and sat for half an hour in an anonymous café nearby with her mind in turmoil and a small dry sandwich untouched in front of her. She found herself staring into a place of black and infinite emptiness; but she knew, if she'd been offered the chance to travel back in time, to a point just three weeks earlier when she could still have changed the course of her life, before Owen had come to dowse at Pant-y-Groes and had stayed to sleep with her, she would have changed nothing.

She walked back to the prison and handed her card to the warder on the desk. As she'd hoped, he presumed she was representing the prisoner, Owen Rhys and she was shown into a stale, windowless room to wait.

Ten minutes later, Owen was escorted in by a prison officer who made no secret of his contempt for a rapist, or anyone trying to help him.

Owen didn't seem to have noticed the officer's attitude. There was nothing submissive about him as he stepped free of his restraining hand, into the room.

Beth was standing; she wanted to rush forward and hold him, to show that she had lost none of her faith in him. Instead, she stepped back, away from him, to the far side of the table.

'Hello Owen,' she said, thinking how rarely she'd used his name.

Owen nodded briefly.

Feeling desperate, Beth glanced at the warder, who withdrew and closed the door behind him.

'How are you?' Beth asked, and knew how empty it sounded. 'Is there anything I can do?'

Owen shrugged. 'There's not much you *can* do, is there?'

'Oh God, I wish there were!' Beth blurted. 'But I told you – there's no point my appearing for you; I would if I thought I had any chance of helping, but somehow this evidence – unless someone admits to fixing it – it's irrefutable...' She stared at him. 'Isn't there anything else you can tell us to make a case?'

Owen shook his head. 'No, I'm afraid there isn't. I've told you all there is.'

Beth stared at him. Why was he so resigned – so prepared to accept all the unbearable consequences of conviction when he was so adamant that he hadn't committed the crime?

'Aren't you angry about it?' she asked.

'There's no point in getting angry about it,' he said quietly.

Beth thought of what Megan had said – that she might find he wouldn't help her, and she shouldn't mind. Of course, Megan hadn't meant 'mind', in the sense of 'care', but not to blame herself. That made his attitude no more explicable – if he were innocent.

Beth flinched again at the "if", and pushed it out of her head in the same way she'd tried, as a child, to expel wicked thoughts. 'I'm so sorry Owen. I'll be thinking of you – every minute, and if there's ever anything I can do...' she dipped into the bag that hung from her shoulder '... here's my address in chambers – where I work. Write to me, or ring me there. If you want to see me, just say so, and if I come, it's because I *want* to see you – all right?' She looked at him tenderly 'And I will want to; don't ever forget that.'

He gazed at her through opaque, dark eyes for a few moments, without speaking. He took a deep breath – his first sign of emotion. 'Thanks,' he said.

She stared at him. She was overflowing with love and longing, and as powerless to act on it as if she'd been chained to the wall.

'Right.' She tried to be brisk. 'I'll confirm to Mr Whittal that I can't appear for you.' She arranged herself to go. 'I... I hope it goes all right; I'll be praying for you.'

Owen raised a shoulder philosophically.

She stared at him for a moment.

What was he hiding? Was he being strong – she wanted to scream – or just *totally fucking dumb*?

Beyond Gospel Pass

'Goodbye, Owen.' She took a step towards him and stopped, still a yard away.

'Goodbye, Beth. Thanks for what you've tried to do.'

Beth turned before he could see the tears spilling from her eyes. She let herself out of the door and nodded without looking at the warder waiting outside. Without speaking to anyone, she hurried from the prison building.

As she walked through the crowded pavements outside towards the concrete maze where she'd parked her car, her eyes were narrow with anguish and she repeated in her head, in time with her footsteps, over and over again *–He's innocent; he's innocent!*

Fifteen

Six weeks after Beth had seen Owen in Cardiff jail, she was sitting at the table in the kitchen of her house in Hackney. She listened to Mark's footsteps on the bare boards of the narrow hall above, the clicking and slamming of the front door and his hard-soled shoes clatter down the three stone steps and the path to the front gate. It was only when the footsteps had faded down the road on the way to the station that she got up from her chair and prepared to leave the house herself.

She phoned her chambers and told them she wouldn't be in until midday. Outside she walked straight passed the Saab parked in front of the house and made her way to the parade of small shops in Victoria Park Road.

In the chemist's, feeling clumsy and self-conscious in front of the two gossiping young women behind the counter, she asked for a home pregnancy test.

One of the assistants, a big-breasted West Indian, handed over a small carton with barely a glance at Beth. 'That's four fifty, please.'

Beth handed over a five-pound note.

As the woman passed back the change, her big white teeth flashed in an unexpected smile. 'Best of luck!'

'Oh, thanks,' Beth mumbled, not knowing if the good wishes were for a positive result, or a negative one.

On the way back to her house by the park, she walked slowly, half reluctant to be confronted finally with the truth she had been putting off for the past six weeks, just in case it wasn't what she longed for – although she was sure, as she had been since almost the first occasion she and Owen had made love, that she was pregnant. When her period, usually as punctual as Big Ben, hadn't come, and she'd started to feel unaccountably sick, while harbouring absurd yearnings

Beyond Gospel Pass

for – of all things – avocado pears, she'd had no doubt about the reasons for it.

But again, perhaps, she thought, all the signs that pointed to pregnancy were simply manifestations of some a self-induced fantasy because she so desperately wanted this baby – she clenched her eyes shut – of Owen's.

In the quietness of the house, still in a state of strangely detached reverie, she padded up to the bathroom, opened the box that contained the test and followed the instructions on the folded sheet of paper she found inside.

Even before the telling change of colour, she was as sure as she had ever been that there was a new life inside her, but when the proof of it was clear in front of her eyes, her hand began to shake and her knees wanted to collapse. She put down the plastic cup she was holding and forced herself to walk through into the bedroom. She lowered herself onto the bed and sat with her back propped against the heavy oak head-board Mark had been so keen to buy, and stared through blurred eyes out of the window at the waving heads of the big plane trees in Victoria Park.

She was pregnant, at last, by a man she loved – she was sure of that – who also stood accused of rape; who, after sentencing, would not be free to be with his child until it was five years old at the very least.

For a long time Beth stayed where she was, open-eyed, mostly, staring bleakly at the tees and sky outside, thinking of the spring days in the valley, the bliss of making love with Owen and the jubilation of becoming a mother at last; punctuated by quivering, eye-stinging sobs at the thought of his trial and the imprisonment that must follow.

By the next day – the day before Owen's first Pleas and Directions Hearing at Newport Crown Court – Beth had forced herself to accept the painful truth that she had heard nothing from him for six weeks.

When she'd left him in the visitors' room at Cardiff Prison, she'd had no idea if he would contact her again. She was convinced, though, that what she perceived as his profound sense of honour wouldn't allow him to expect or demand long-term loyalty from her – not as long as the threat that he might be locked up for as long as eight years hung over him.

So she had come back to London and taken on as much work as she could handle. She had advised her *Roma* asylum seeker to abandon her appeal, but the award in the sexual discrimination case had been set at a far higher sum than she'd predicted, at a level where she felt her client was being overcompensated and future expectations would be raised too high. The case and the subsequent judgement had been harshly criticised in *The Times* that morning.

After a day in court, during which it seemed her thoughts had returned every few minutes to the baby inside her, she was about to leave the chambers when Jack Devereux came into to her room. He glanced at the newspaper, still open at the Law Reports.

'Some you win; some you win and lose,' he said with a grunt of laughter. 'You seem to be attacking every case like a gladiator at the moment.'

'Don't I always?'

Jack shook his head. 'Not like this. You're more obsessive – as if you were trying to prove something. What is it?'

He sat down on her desk. Beth detected nothing obviously critical in his manner. He seemed, as always, genuinely concerned.

She leaned back in her chair, relieved to be able to talk about what had been filling her head all day. 'I wonder if you've ever noticed,' she said, 'how most women are inescapably governed by their urge to have babies. You won't have noticed it in Gill, of course; she's produced more than her quota. But I haven't, and as I've got older, it's become more of an issue.'

'Or lack of issue?' Jack grinned.

The pun made Beth think of Mark. 'Listen, it's no joke, and I admit that to a certain extent, I've used my work to compensate. But with a bit of luck, I won't have to any more.'

Jack's face lit up with a spontaneous display of a devoted father's appreciation. 'You mean, you think you're pregnant?'

Beth nodded with a slightly embarrassed smile. 'Yes, I had it confirmed by a doctor on my way to court this morning, but it's only eight weeks in, so please, don't tell anyone yet. I haven't even told Mark.'

Beth went home in a taxi. She justified it with her changed condition. On the way, she rehearsed how she would tell Mark, but when she arrived home, he wasn't there.

Beyond Gospel Pass

Beth was relieved she could put off the moment, and took the opportunity to relax with a little domestic activity. Her cleaner, who came in for three hours most days, was conscientious and tireless, but Beth found herself looking around for jobs she'd done that weren't quite up to her standards. She supposed it was her way of reclaiming her role; she resented it in herself, but she couldn't help it; nor did she deny that there was a real pleasure to be found in washing a floor or pushing a Hoover around one's own home after a day of tough cerebral effort.

So she cleaned the floor again and spent half an hour making what she hoped would turn out to be a perfect moussaka before she was satisfied. She put it in the oven and went upstairs, where she showered and walked around her room until her hair was dry. She forced Owen from her head, thinking of plans for nurseries and of the changes that the new life inside her would make to her own.

When Mark arrived an hour later, she was ready for him.

'I've already made dinner. Let's have a drink in the garden first,' she suggested.

Mark raised his brow at this unexpected suggestion, but agreed happily.

Beth asked him to open a bottle of rosé, and wondered how much she should be drinking, now the test had confirmed her pregnancy.

The sun was still warm among the flowers in the neatly paved courtyard. Beth and Mark sat down there with their glasses.

Mark took a sip and grinned. 'Ideal,' he said in a Herefordshire accent.

Beth nodded. She still wasn't sure how to deliver her news. 'Anything good happen today?' she asked.

He shrugged. 'Not much. We lost another author.'

'Anyone important?'

'No, not really - John Macleod. In fact, I don't suppose we've ever made any money out of him; but he was a good name to have on the list.'

John Macleod, Beth knew, was a high-profile media psychiatrist who had produced a successful series of books for laymen on the subject, which Archimedes didn't publish. He was much more interested in his novels, which Archimedes did publish, though with much less success than his non-fiction titles.

'Good,' Beth said. 'There's not much point being a vanity publisher for authors who don't even make a contribution. How's your Ghanaian, by the way?'

'*The Joys of Urine*?' Mark chortled 'He's talking. At least he's accepted the principle. We're just haggling over how much.'

Beth encouraged Mark to talk for a while about the potential of his various schemes to save Archimedes. There was a slight hint of desperation in them, but she couldn't help admiring his tenacity and was even prepared to believe that he might just manage to revive the business after all.

'And you?' he asked, when he sensed he was losing her attention.

'I've got some good news, actually.'

Mark waited; he hated guessing games.

'If all goes well...' she looked away '...in seven months' time, there'll be a new member in the family.'

Mark gulped and jerked forward in his seat excitedly. 'You mean, we're going to have a baby?!'

Beth dragged her eyes back to meet his. 'Yes,' she smiled weakly.

Mark leaped to his feet and leaned down to kiss her. He put his hands under her arms, lifted her from her seat, high off the ground, as if she were a child, and kissed her again all over her cheeks, and nose and lips. 'That is just wonderful, wonderful news!' he cried. 'At last! And we thought the mountain air would do the trick! Well done, angel!'

'Okay, Mark,' she said, breathless. 'Put me down now before I miscarry.'

He lowered her gingerly into her chair. 'My God! Yes – I'll have to be careful – especially as you're no spring chicken.'

'Thanks a lot!'

'No, I mean it, you'll have to be very careful. Should you be drinking, even?'

'I'm sure the odd glass of wine doesn't hurt.'

'I bet champagne's better, though!' Mark hurried off into the house to find some.

He came out a few minutes later with a bottle in a bucket and put it down beside his chair.

'Beth, angel, how long have you known?'

Beyond Gospel Pass

'I've suspected for a couple of weeks, so I did a test yesterday, which showed up positive, and my gynae confirmed it today.'

'Brilliant! So when was it ... er... started?'

Beth looked away again. She couldn't meet his eye and think of the baby's conception. 'It must have been the weekend of Ruth's dinner party,' she said in a small voice.

'My God! You mean the night Laura had her adventure?'

'I'm not sure "adventure" is the word I'd have chosen - but yes,' Beth said, with a fresh surge of guilt.

Mark was filling two glasses with the champagne. He handed one to Beth, who took it with a show of celebration.

'Here's to us, and young Master Powell!' Mark said with a flourish.

'It may not be a boy,' she said.

Or a Powell, she thought. But she didn't discourage Mark from celebrating; she found she was glad to see him so happy about being a father. She thought perhaps it might have been possible to live with the lie, if only she didn't love the child's real father as she did.

She thought of Owen for most of the night, trying to decide whether or not she should drive to Newport in the morning to see him in court. She'd rung Whittal a few days before. He was still handling the case, but he'd pessimistically confirmed that no new evidence had turned up to help them. The prosecution's case was no stronger than it had been, but then, it was more than strong enough already, he said.

The confirmation that she was pregnant had added a new dimension to her feelings for Owen, without reducing her awareness of the loyalty she owed Mark, and the baby.

She lay awake deep into the night, while Mark snored happily beside her, until she had convinced herself that she should be strong and keep her distance from the proceedings in Newport Crown Court the following day.

In the morning, however, all her resolve had deserted her.

Modern law courts had recently been added to the grandiose nineteen-thirties white stone Civic Centre in Newport, overlooked by a soaring clock tower, which showed the time at a quarter to twelve as Beth arrived. The whole massive complex stood in an area of established trees and Edwardian housing on high ground, well above the rest of the ugly town and its docks. From the leafy carpark, a broad sweep of steps led up to imposing glass doors. Beside the doors was a sign, *Llys y Goron*, which seemed succinctly to amplify to Beth the differences between her and Owen. She wondered for a panicky moment if the hearing would be in Welsh.

The court list indicated that the Pleas and Directions Hearing in the case of Owen Rhys was due to start in Court Two at midday. She went up and found Mr Whittal hurrying through the lobby of the court.

The solicitor appeared more pleased to see her than on their previous meetings. 'Counsel's not here yet,' he said tetchily. Beth guessed he was nervous about dealing with a dilatory barrister.

'But you have briefed him thoroughly?'

'Of course I have. I went specially to Cardiff.'

'Did you get the man you wanted?'

'Not exactly, but from the same chambers. He's not too bad.'

'My God,' Beth snapped without thinking. 'Couldn't you do better than not too bad?'

Whittal bridled. 'I'd say "not too bad" is good enough, Miss Langthorne. Frankly, there isn't a barrister in the world who could do anything with the defence we've got to offer.'

Beth sighed. He was right. 'But a good man might find grounds for mitigation.'

'Like what?' Whittal asked. 'He won't change his plea, and that's all we could hope for.'

'All right. I'm sorry. It's just that I feel bloody terrible about this case.'

'It's not the peachiest one I've ever handled,' the solicitor said unexpectedly. 'And I do see what you mean about your man not being a very likely culprit. But there it is; they've got him bang to rights.'

'Please don't let counsel go into court with that attitude.'

'No,' Whittal sighed. 'I know my duty.' He glanced at his watch. 'His Honour is taking his time sentencing a few guilty pleas. With luck, our case will be held over until after lunch. By the way,' he went on, subtly changing his tone. 'There's another friend of Owen's been here – a young lady.'

For a few seconds Beth felt as if something had grasped her by the throat and was choking her. 'Who...?'

Beyond Gospel Pass

'There she is.' The solicitor nodded across the lobby towards the entrance to the court.

Beth turned. With intense relief she saw that it was Ruth, who smiled and waved. She thanked Mr Whittal, arranged to meet him after the hearing and walked across the lobby.

'Hello, Ruth. I meant to ring you before I came, but I only decided at the very last minute this morning.'

'I'm glad you did. Megan wouldn't come. She asked me to call in and see her this evening. Michael hasn't come either.'

'Shall we go and get a coffee? I couldn't eat anything...'

Ruth nodded and they walked down to a corner of the building where an airy café served the courts. Beth noticed that someone with fresh ideas about making the criminal justice system more user-friendly had named it *Rumpole's*. They sat by a window, and the sunlight outside contrived to make the unprepossessing town look almost pleasing.

'Are you staying up here?' Ruth asked.

'No. I'm going to get back. I really don't feel like staying there, with Pant-y-Groes on the market.'

'I'm surprised you haven't sold it yet.'

'The agents keep saying they're sending people to look at it.'

'I've seen one or two,' Ruth nodded with a grimace.

'We haven't even had an offer yet. I suppose not everyone wants to be that far from anywhere. Still, at least it's saved us having to store everything for the time being.'

'Then please – come back and stay the night with me,' Ruth asked.

Beth thought for a moment. 'Thanks. I will.'

Ruth and Beth went back to court early. They wanted to make sure they would get a seat. There were only fifty public places, which folded like cinema seats, and far too many reporters to fit in the tiny press bench.

The courtroom was already crowded and buzzing with the detached talk of journalists and a few nosy members of the public, glancing around the room, trying to identify the defendant's relations. Beth too swept the rows of public seating, but no other connections of Owen's from the valley appeared to be present.

The courtroom was consciously modern, lined with pale emulsion panels in bland, "designer" colours.

Jessica Meredith

The court quietened as an usher called, 'All rise,' and the judge's door opened. A short man in his fifties, whom Beth remembered having appeared against ten years before, walked towards a plain high-backed leather seat beneath a gilt royal coat of arms. He was wearing a short wig and a junior judge's black gown with purple facings and a scarlet sash.

A few moments later, the Pleas and Directions Hearing in the case of *The Crown* v *Owen Ivor Rhys* was announced, and Owen was escorted by two hatchet-faced prison warders into the dock at the back of the court, facing the judge on his three-foot dais.

Beth felt her innards crawl with indignation at seeing Owen like that, and flushed angrily when she glanced round at the rows of hostile faces directed towards him. Her own eyes were quickly dragged back to him. She hadn't seen him since she'd left him in the visitors' room at Cardiff prison six weeks before. Although she'd hoped and prayed almost daily that he would contact her, as far as she knew, he'd made no attempt.

He looked entirely composed, healthy and alert. He paid no attention to the men either side of him in the dock, and looked straight ahead at the judge.

After the judge had launched the proceedings and the clerk had read out the indictment, Owen spoke only once, when he was asked how he pleaded to the charge that on the morning of Saturday, May 30th, in the county of Powys, he had committed the crime of rape on Laura Chichester.

'Not guilty.'

The judge gazed at him in silence for a few moments, as if he were trying to weigh the accused's guilt on the basis of appearance alone. He cleared his throat and invited submissions from counsel representing the Crown and the defence. He turned first to the prosecuting counsel, a woman who had spared no effort to appear at her best in every way possible.

'Your Honour, ' she said with an unctuous deference Beth couldn't have reproduced. 'We will be calling five expert witnesses...' She went on to detail those who would confirm that rape had occurred and that DNA profiling had identified Owen, and the forensics man who had matched a footprint to a boot found at Owen's place of residence. She would also be calling Miss Laura Chichester.

Beyond Gospel Pass

When she had sat down, Owen's barrister, Mr Humphries, stood up. Beth thought Mr Humphries was probably younger than he looked. He was an obese, balding and slightly soiled journeyman barrister of a type Beth had often seen in her earlier days at the bar. At first sight, he looked no more competent than Whittal had implied.

'Your Honour, the defence will have no witnesses to call, other than the defendant himself.'

There was a loud, cynical murmur from the public galleries, sufficient to draw a sharp glance around the room from the judge, who, after a few more formalities, announced that in his opinion the trial would take two days, that he would like it reserved to himself, and that it should be set for the next suitable date at this court, which was 24th September. And that was it.

'Poor Owen,' Ruth said. 'How do you think he'll get on in the witness box?' She and Beth were back in the warm, reassuring surroundings of the kitchen at the Hendre,

'He'll answer the questions firmly and in a very dignified way, I expect. But the jury will take it as arrogant, bare-faced lying. And of course, they'll dislike him more because he won't be showing any remorse – because he didn't do it. I don't suppose he'll give his counsel much help at all.'

'Oh my God,' Ruth wailed quietly. 'I can't bear it! It seems so crazy – a man like that……'

'And the awful thing is, Ruth, as things stand, there's absolutely *nothing* either of us or anyone else can do.' Beth stood up and walked to the small window that overlooked the valley. The sun had slipped above the roof of Pant-y-Groes but still illuminated the small grove where the stream gushed from the hill... where she had first talked to Owen.

As she looked, she quivered uncontrollably with massive, hopeless sobs, becoming aware of Ruth's arm around her shoulders, gently squeezing.

'There's something else, isn't there?' Ruth asked.

Beth nodded, biting her lip in misery, in a way she couldn't remember doing since she was a small girl. 'Yes. I'm going to have a baby.'

Next morning, walking through the cold rooms of Pant-y-Groes which already smelled of disuse, Beth felt that she was wandering through an old dream, an extended passage of déjà vu.

It seemed that her connections with the place, short as they'd been, were already severed and had become part of her past. All the things that had happened there with Mark, and with Owen, belonged to an earlier chapter, now closed, and the fresh life stirring in her womb was defining a new phase in her personal history.

She packed two cases of small personal things and gathered up some workbooks she had left in the study. She thought about the furniture; she would rather sell it with the house if a serious buyer ever appeared.

Outside, the stack of timber Mark had bought for his unrealised raised beds huddled redundantly in the back of the open barn. When Ishy Price had phoned them in London and threatened to come and take it all away, Mark had sent him a cheque, rather than admit his local defeat. Perhaps the next owners would like to do what Mark had planned, Beth thought.

She conceded now that the romantic, rustic idyll was a short-lived bloom unless you had time and care to lavish on it.

She loaded the car and drove away, perhaps for the last time, and tears stung her eyes. She remembered her first flat in London, in a pretty house on Primrose Hill, where she'd learned so much and which she'd loved but had left without a murmur of regret as the next phase in her life had beckoned.

It was half past six when Beth parked her car outside the house in Hackney. She prayed that Mark hadn't come back yet, so that she could shower and repair her tear-ravaged make-up before he did.

Inside the house, her heart sank when she glanced through the door of the dining-room, which was seldom used, and saw the table laid for six. At the same time, she heard Mark clattering about down in the kitchen.

She went to the top of the narrow, open-slatted stairs. 'Hi, Mark. I'm just going up to have a shower.' She ran up to the first floor before he could hold her back with his explanations.

Under the shower, she understood the psychological benefits of sluicing the body with water; she'd always seen the significance of ablution and its association with spiritual cleanliness – the washing away of what the nuns had called original sin, and which she called the acknowledgement of human consciousness and the essential difference between animals and mankind.

Resigned to whatever Mark had arranged for that evening, she made an effort to repair her appearance. As she inspected herself in the mirror of her dressing table, she wondered if the baby had given her the special radiance she'd seen in other pregnant women.

Mark was enjoying himself in the kitchen. The Roux Brothers' cook book he had given Beth stood on a stand, spattered with flour and sauce as, with spectacles on his head, he pounced on it and swooped around the kitchen amidst clusters of exotic ingredients required for the *foie d'agneau provencale* he was preparing.

Beth gazed at him, perplexed by his cheerful mood. 'Is this some kind of replacement therapy, or what?'

'What should it be replacing?'

'The severe angst of the last few months, maybe? Or concern for the critical condition of the business you say you've nurtured like a baby for the last ten years?'

'There's nothing like good news to elbow out angst,' Mark grinned and came over to give Beth a quick kiss on the lips – a certain sign of revitalised spirits.

'Good news? Real, bankable good news?' Beth tried not to sound doubtful.

'No,' Mark said frankly, with his clever way of making the word sound positive. 'But there's a lot of reasons why the deal I'm after should come off; and very few why it shouldn't.'

The first of Mark's guests to arrive was Adam Yorke, a tall, bonily handsome Englishman in his mid-fifties who looked and talked like the faded anti-hero of an early Evelyn Waugh novel. With him was a wife from Argentina, who did nothing to disguise her wealth and powerful libido.

Adam took Beth's hand and held it for a few seconds while he nodded his head of thinning, sandy hair and inspected her with a secretive grin that hinted at shared pleasures to come. She loathed him on sight and instinctively felt she should protect Mark from a man so transparently dishonest.

Jessica Meredith

His business partner – with an Armenian name, middle-eastern skin and a precise public school accent – was more sinister. Unlike Adam Yorke, Oliver Matoubian didn't smile at all; his face lost its stoniness only with sporadic grimaces – as if he'd just driven a canine tooth through his tongue – when anything was said with which he strongly disagreed. He had brought with him a wife he introduced as Anna, who, Beth thought, could have been born in almost any Mediterranean land, but offered no clue as to which one.

Mark hadn't told her, though it soon became clear, that he had invited these two men to invest substantially in part of his business. Beth gathered that they already owned, among many diverse businesses, a profitable vanity publishing house, unusually unsullied by law suits or defamatory outcries from dissatisfied authors.

She listened and tried to say nothing that might be taken by Mark to be unhelpful or even faintly negative while she marvelled at his appalling lack of judgement.

It was astonishing to her that he could even remotely consider going into business with these two reptilian predators. They could have swallowed him whole, belched and gone looking for more before breakfast, but she knew Mark had just finalised, verbally, a deal with the Ghanaian chief – the proponent of urine-drinking - and felt that he'd pulled off a vanity publishing coup so spectacular that these men would feel they needed him more than he needed them.

Over dinner he was expansive about his newly adopted commercial frugality. He boasted of the cheapness of his premises and low payroll in a way that was in complete contrast to his attitude only a few months before.

Beth did her best with the wives, but the European woman could barely speak English and had no obvious wish to improve it, and the Argentinian only wanted to talk about shopping, although she already had such an intimate knowledge of the layout of Harvey Nichols and Harrods that Beth didn't feel she could contribute much.

For a while, she stayed silent. In her head, she strayed away to the Welsh hills until she was harshly dragged back to the present and the pantomime going on around her table when Mark referred to Owen.

He was talking about the sustained and frankly unexpected great success of George Arbuthnott's *The Leys of the Land*, which had lingered in the non-fiction best-seller lists since the time of the Hay

Festival. 'Of course, living where we do in the Welsh Marches,' he chuckled, 'the land of Merlin and Celtic legend, we see a lot of this at first hand. There's one local – sadly soon to be convicted of the rape of Laura Chichester – who can read the earth's energy through an ancient gold ring dangling on a piece of grimy chain.'

Beth caught the brief glance of guilt he gave her over his flippant treatment of Owen's tragedy. He would probably excuse himself for the sake of a story that would appeal to the sophisticated cynicism of Adam Yorke, although Matoubian's face remained as expressionless as a lump of wholemeal dough.

'So it's a field we really understand, and Joe Public's fascination for all this stuff is growing the whole time.' Mark glanced again at Beth. 'If my Catholic wife is to be believed, the thirst for spiritual nourishment, in whatever misguided form, is unquenchable, but people want new flavours in their religion, in much the same way as they do in yoghurt or ice cream.'

'I didn't quite say that,' Beth said indulgently.

But she noticed Adam Yorke nodding with an appreciative grin, and Mark congratulating himself.

'Quite honestly, although we're talking about an entirely different imprint for our subsidy publishing, the loose association with Archimedes won't do any harm.'

Matoubian opened his lizard eyes into slightly wider slits. 'I assumed when you came to us that you were talking in terms of using Archimedes as the imprint; isn't that the basis of our discussions?' He gave Adam Yorke a warning glance.

Yorke nodded. 'Yes, it was the reputation of Archimedes we wanted. I certainly didn't understand that you wanted us to help you establish an entirely new imprint from scratch. After all, we could do that ourselves.' He gave a broad, cold grin. 'Indeed, we have done it ourselves. Your proposal was only interesting as long as we are able to operate Archimedes along the lines we have already established – which has made us a *great deal of money*, may I say.'

Beth saw Mark's jaw tremble slightly, as he realised he'd allowed his own obfuscation to get in the way of what he'd actually wanted to sell. 'Well, n...no,' he stammered. 'I felt what I could offer was a particular skill in selling very top-of-the-range subsidy publishing, with which your existing operation isn't... as it were….equipped…' His voice faded as he looked for a way of extracting himself.

The Armenian wasn't going to let him. 'What do you feel we are not equipped to do?' he asked quietly, for once allowing a chilly smile to play across his fleshy lips.

'Well, obviously, you are equipped to do whatever's needed in your field, but what I'm talking about is the external perception, you know – to counter all the bad publicity some of the vanity press has had.'

'What bad publicity have we had?'

'Not you, I realise.'

'Let's not go into that now, Ed,' Adam Yorke broke in with a cold grin. Although he had no obvious natural charm, he was sophisticated enough to know that any kind of row over the dining table could only be unproductive. 'I can't see that there's anything to be achieved. We can deal with it tomorrow.'

Beth saw the colour fade from Mark's face, showing that he knew the deal was almost certainly off. 'But anyway,' he managed to say with an unconvincing shrug, 'there's no real reason why we shouldn't use the Archimedes imprint, I suppose, given the plan is to publish only books that would be a commercial success in their own right, with or without the subsidy we'll be demanding.'

'You feel,' Adam Yorke said with an eyebrow at an acute angle, ' that *The Joys of Urine* would be a likely candidate for commercial success?'

'As a matter of fact,' Mark came back, more sure of himself. 'I'm bloody certain it will be; Chief Bekwe will see a healthy return on his investment which will help sell the idea for plenty of similar projects.'

'I wish you the very best of luck,' Oliver Matoubian growled as he folded his napkin in a gesture of departure and glanced at his wife, who quailed compliantly like a dark, timid mouse.

A little over a week later, towards the end of July, Beth sat alone at a small round table in a busy seafood restaurant in Holland Park Avenue. Outside, the sun warmed the wide pavements of the street and the mottled boles of the tall plane trees that lined it.

Beth wondered what was keeping her mother. Moira Langthorne had chosen the restaurant. She was on a flying visit to

Beyond Gospel Pass

London – a diversion on her way to Rome with one of her brothers. She'd asked Beth to meet her there at one o'clock; it was nearly twenty past. Beth guessed her mother was late as a result of her normal optimism over journey times, but she still found herself nervous with apprehension at their meeting.

She was sure that if she didn't say anything about the baby – now in its eleventh week – her mother would guess from the evidence of a dozen small signs. But it wasn't her pregnancy that Beth wanted to hide when her mother walked serenely into the restaurant a few minutes later.

The French head waiter instinctively assumed, despite her old-fashioned clothes and minimally styled grey hair, that Moira Langthorne was important in some way. With conspicuous deference he brought her to the table where Beth waited, asking her if she was happy with its position, or would prefer a larger one.

When her mother received this sort of treatment it amused Beth, who knew that she never noticed; and Moira, of course, had no objection to the position or size of the table. She placed a small bag of shopping on the tiled floor before she met Beth's greeting kiss with a gentle hug and sat down.

'I'm so glad you could take time off, darling,' Moira said. 'I hope it wasn't too disruptive for you.'

'It was fine,' Beth lied a little. 'I rearranged my meetings; I see you so rarely...'

'Yes, I know sweetie, and you sounded a little distraught, at least, sort of preoccupied last time we talked on the phone – it must have been two or three weeks ago – and I've been worried.'

Beth put on a puzzled, sturdy smile. 'No,' she said. 'I've been fine.'

Her mother didn't press her. 'So, what's your best news?' It was typically her first question when they met, and Beth was grateful for it.

'Guess.'

Moira's already smiling lips broke into a broad, happy grin. 'You really are pregnant?'

Beth saw that her mother had wanted to add, 'at last', but had resisted. She nodded with a smile. 'Yes, at last,' she said for her.

'Oh, darling!' Moira stretched her hand across the table and squeezed Beth's. 'That is wonderful news!'

Beth laughed. 'Is becoming a grandmother for the third time so important to you?'

Moira nodded. 'Especially to yours. For some reason a daughter's child feels that much closer than a son's.' She smiled. 'And your father always used to say that until a woman was twenty, the only thing she thought about was getting married, and then for the next twenty years, having babies, and after that, having grandchildren.'

Beth looked shocked. 'I had no idea he was such an old chauvinist.'

'The truth is, although he may have exaggerated a little, he was more or less right.'

'Oh no!' Beth expostulated. 'My priority has always been my career, and what I could do for the people I represented,' she said self-righteously, while she thought of the agonies of longing she'd been through which had almost displaced all her professional ambition.

'Whatever,' Moira said, unchallenging. 'I'm truly delighted at the prospect, so you must be very, very careful.'

'At my age,' Beth added for her.

The head waiter came back with menus and to see if they wanted drinks. Moira ordered some Chablis, while Beth asked for a bottle of Welsh spring water.

'You must be so thrilled about the baby, too, darling,' Moira said when the waiter had gone. 'And so must Mark.'

Beth didn't miss a quick sharpening of Moira's focus.

'He is,' she said. 'He's been having rather a bad time with Archimedes recently, but knowing we're having a baby at last seems to have made it easier for him to cope.'

'He's always been rather impractical, hasn't he – like your father. When most men hear there's a baby on the way, the first thing they ask themselves is how are they going to pay for it. Presumably, your own earnings will drop when you start taking time off?'

'I suppose so, but frankly, we've both made enough money over the last fifteen years to weather a bad patch. I absolutely refuse to allow financial considerations to affect my attitude.'

'That's very commendable but a little romantic. Babies are very expensive things, and go on getting more expensive. Your father never had any idea how much help I had from my own family to keep you and Edward in clothes and holidays, not to mention schools.'

'Oh well, our child won't be going to private schools.'

'This is what you say now,' Moira said mildly.

Beth ignored the challenge. The waiter arrived with the wine and the Welsh spring water.

'So, when do you think the baby was conceived?' Moira asked, as if she'd read Beth's mind.

Beth glanced away guiltily before she could stop herself, thinking of Owen and the water gushing from the mountainside above Pant-y-Groes.

'I'm sorry, darling. That was much too personal.'

Beth nodded with an attempt at coyness. 'It was rather. There are some things I couldn't tell even you.'

'But not much?'

Beth looked straight back at her. 'What do you mean?'

'I don't mean anything more than a mother knows her daughter perhaps a lot better than the daughter may think.'

It wasn't until they had shared a tender fresh lobster that Moira raised any more challenges. She had drunk half the Chablis on her own, an unusually large quantity for her, which had made her bold. She lowered her head and looked at Beth from below a puckered forehead. 'I presume the baby is Mark's?'

Beth looked down at her plate, picked up a fork and dug fruitlessly at the empty case of lobster shell, aware that her face was red and her hands were shaking.

Her mother didn't press her. Beth tried to arrive at some judgement over whether or not her mother - the baby's grandmother - had a natural right to know the child's true paternity.

Wasn't it enough for her to know that the child was her daughter's?

She raised her head and looked her mother straight in the eye. 'Mama! Of course it is.'

After that, thinking of her mother's practical advice, Beth took on several more cases, one of which was strictly commercial, with a large fee attached. Animated by her doctor's opinion that she was as fit as any late mother he'd seen, she had decided to work right up to the thirty-ninth week, if she could, and started to arrange her diary accordingly. It would stop her thinking about Owen; and she'd concluded that, realistically, the only way she could deal with it was to block him, and everything to do with him, from her mind.

She arrived home one Tuesday, a week after her mother had gone on to Italy, and found Mark waiting excitedly to tell her the estate agents in Hay had rung with an offer for Pant-y-Groes.

'It's ten grand under the asking price he said, but it's a firm offer.'

'So after the cost of the mortgage, all the work we've had done, and the furniture, the whole adventure will have cost us around twenty thousand?'

'Well, yes,' Mark nodded, 'but I suppose we always knew there was something of a gamble in buying the house before I was selected.'

'I suppose you're right and we'd better cut our losses, especially if you're going to concentrate on Archimedes and I'm busy having a baby. Besides, I'm planning to work as much as I can right up to the last minute so you don't have to draw on the business.'

Mark swallowed his response. 'Well, there it is. I've told them to take it.'

'We'd better go up and organise packing up the rest of the furniture, then.'

'I said we'd chuck in most of it,' Mark said quickly. 'And I haven't got time to get up there just at the moment.'

Beth sighed. She didn't blame him for not wanting to face the evidence of his failed venture into politics. 'Any news at Archimedes?' she asked.

'Yorke and Matoubian aren't returning my calls,' Mark said, as matter of fact as he could. 'And the people who were going to take the old office have backed down.' He paused, with his incorrigible taste for effect. 'And George Arbuthnott's come back and said he'd like us to do his next book after all.'

'For seventy-five thousand?'

'No,' Mark grinned. 'I tickled his vanity and offered to double the royalty for a token advance. And there's a contract on its way to Chief Bekwe.'

'Good,' she said, genuinely pleased for him. 'Though I suppose that means I'll have to go up and sort out Pant-y-Groes.'

'Have you got time?'

Beth was already feeling almost physically sick at the prospect of returning to the valley, and at thoughts of Owen which she'd kept at bay for the last three weeks.

Beyond Gospel Pass

'I can make time,' she tried to say lightly. 'I'll see if I can go next week.'

A small lorry left Pant-y-Groes with the last of the possessions which Beth and Mark had decided not to sell to the new owners. It crawled down the narrow lane towards the mouth of the valley. Beth watched until it was out of sight before she turned back to look at the house with regret, relief, sadness and resentment at the events and changes it had witnessed in her recent life. She wanted to thank it and blame it at the same time. Overwhelmingly, though, she was grateful for the world it had shown her.

She went back in and walked around the half empty rooms for the last time, and wondered what the retired engineer and his faded wife from the Wirral who had bought the place would make of it with all its history and the awkward questions the valley would ask.

Beth was inclined to resent their intrusion and absence of understanding, but reproached herself for her intolerance. She walked out, locked the door for the last time, and drove up towards Gospel Pass to take the key to the estate agents in Hay.

She felt that she was leaving the valley, too, for the last time; as if there were something symbolic in her present passing between the great green shoulders that guarded its head.

In contrast to the gloom of the valley, on the other side of the pass the sun beat down unhindered on groups of energetic youths clambering up the Bluff with paragliders. And along the eastern face of the ridge, where the currents took them, were scattered bright yellow and pink bulging blimps, like bright bees hovering about a giant nest.

As she dropped down towards the vale of green pasture, she felt herself discard the weight of her past; whatever had happened wouldn't happen again; the baby would come, and coming, would make her happy, and make Mark happy too. But as she steered her way through the sunken lanes towards Hay, tears flowed freely from her eyes from the fear that nothing could ever make her truly happy again.

Sixteen

The trial of Owen Rhys opened at Newport Crown Court on the last Thursday of September at ten o'clock.

Beth didn't look for Whittal this time; there was nothing to say to him that would help. But Ruth was waiting for her outside the court when she arrived at nine. They went in together, to be sure of a place. Half an hour before the case was due to start, the court was full. Once again, none of Owen's family had come.

Beth was glad of Ruth's company but she didn't want to talk. She sat and stared unfocused at the pale blandness of the walls, trying to prepare herself for the inevitable decision that the court would come to.

The judge was announced. He entered and, despite his lack of height, progressed importantly to his seat of office.

Owen was brought in, as at the last hearing, between two prison officers. He looked calm and self-possessed. There was a quiet dignity about him, which no one in the room could have missed. It was the first time Beth had seen him in the two months since his previous appearance in this court. She couldn't take her eyes from him.

All the time he had been in jail she had longed to go and see him, but she'd been determined not to go unless he asked; and he had not.

Once or twice, he turned slightly to look at her across the rows of lawyers in the middle of the court, but no muscle moved in his face. Beth felt Ruth's hand take hers and squeeze. She squeezed back, with a quick, grateful smile.

She felt no impatience during the opening procedure of the trial. She watched calmly, as if from a distant place, while the jury was sworn in. The five men and seven women were dressed in an array of dull garments, which, Beth assumed, reflected their various attitudes to the law and a jury's status. She didn't even resent their power over Owen's future as they stumbled their way through their pledge to listen and judge from the evidence they would hear. It wasn't their fault that they would never see the real evidence, hidden beneath the surface, in the defendant's soul.

By the time the judge adjourned for lunch, Miss Hywel-Jones, for the Crown, had presented most of her case without calling Laura Chichester, much to Beth's astonishment and the frustration of the journalists and paparazzi who had traipsed out to South Wales with the sole purpose of covering her appearance.

In a silent, sympathetic court, prosecuting counsel had relied on the forensic evidence of the DNA-matched semen, corroborated by Owen's counsel's inability to challenge the evidence with any conviction.

After lunch Bronwen Hywel-Jones at last announced the star witness.

The court rippled with curiosity as Britain's most famous celebrity hiker appeared through the main doors of the court and walked to the witness box. She was plainly dressed in a fawn fleece and blue jeans, with her hair simply styled and her make-up basic and natural but ineluctably eye-catching.

As Laura answered the questions put to her, Beth began to appreciate why the prosecuting counsel hadn't relied on her to launch the case. With a faint tingle of hope, Beth sensed that there was a tension between Laura and the barrister, which was not simply the wariness of two ambitious women confronting one another.

Laura confirmed, with unembellished answers, the circumstances of the rape as they had been outlined before lunch.

Beth was still wondering why Laura had not been called before when her next answer suggested a reason.

'Could you identify the man who attacked you?'

Laura looked straight at the jury. 'No.'

'Have you ever seen the defendant before?'

'Yes.'

'When?'

'After I was attacked, I felt shocked and weak; I pulled my clothes back on and sat down with my back to a tree, meaning to stay there for a few minutes while I got myself together before walking back to the cottage. I don't know what happened after that – my mind's a complete blank. Maybe I was hit; I don't know; there was no bruise when I came to, but I must have lain there unconscious or asleep for a while because when I woke, it was light, and the defendant,' she glanced at Owen, 'was leaning over me. He asked me if I was all right.'

'Had you ever seen him before that?'

'No. I'd only arrived in the valley that evening.'

'What was his manner?'

'I would say,' she paused and looked at the jury while she found the right word, 'solicitous. He seemed genuinely concerned that I had been out all night.'

'*Seemed* genuinely concerned?'

Laura shrugged. 'I can only say what I saw. And of course, at that time I had no idea of the evidence that subsequently came to light through the DNA profiling, and it simply didn't occur to me that he could be the man who had attacked and raped me.'

The journalists in the press box all scribbled eagerly, anxious not to miss one word of the TV personality's evidence, but Miss Hywel-Jones looked irritated by Laura's unhelpful answers. Abruptly, announcing that she had no further questions, she sat down. It was a few moments before Mr Humphries realised she'd finished with her witness, and got to his feet, red in the face from the sudden effort.

Ruth leaned forward in expectation.

Beth looked across at the jury, thrilled to see doubt in their faces where before there had been only certainty. But as soon as Owen's counsel began to examine Laura, it was clear that he was determined to make the most of his day in the limelight, even if he didn't think the witness could do anything substantive for his client's case.

Beth prayed that he wouldn't pursue the only plausible defence open to him – that intercourse had taken place between Owen and Laura by mutual consent.

'Was or was not the accused the man who attacked and sexually assaulted you in the early hours of Saturday, 30th May?'

Laura shook her head. 'I didn't see the man who did it. I heard him, and I smelled him.'

'I think it would be inappropriate to invite you to smell my client,' Mr Humphries said, provoking a ripple of laughter. 'Besides he has probably bathed several times since then. But is there anything about his voice and delivery that you recognise from your attacker?'

'Nothing whatsoever,' Laura said.

Beth sighed. Pleasing though it was to hear, this testimony was valueless against the Crown's evidence, and yet somehow it was making Laura look heroic and compassionate. Beth studied the jury and saw that their demeanour had already reverted to wary scepticism.

She guessed bitterly that Laura's motive for taking this line was no more than a cynical wish to demonstrate to her devoted public how fair and unvindictive she could be.

Humphries asked a few more questions before he sat down, looking pleased that at least no one could say he hadn't tried to defend his client in what was generally perceived to be a hopeless case.

Laura left the court to murmurs of approval. As the prosecution had now concluded their case, it was Mr Humphries' turn to call his own witness.

Owen was brought from the dock to the witness box, where one of the security officers stood behind him. He passed so close to Beth that she could almost smell him. But he let his eyes meet hers for only a particle of a second.

He took the oath in the quiet, deep voice that Beth still vividly remembered. In the same low voice, in answer to his counsel's questions, he told the court that he had risen early on the morning of May 30th, shortly after dawn, because he had a lot of lambs on the hillside. He heard a ewe in trouble in a gully above the farm known as the Hendre, from where Laura Chichester had set out the night before.

He had gone up to investigate the plight of the lamb, dealt with it, and carried on down the track, past the Hendre towards the priory.

On this track he had found Laura Chichester, lying apparently asleep. What had happened after that, the court had already been told by prosecuting counsel and the victim herself.

And no, he had never seen Miss Chichester before, either in real life or on the television, and he had no idea who she was until Ruth Calloway at the Hendre told him.

Owen gave his evidence calmly, with a lack of self-justification that wasn't lost on the jury. His counsel thanked him, and sat down, feeling that even if his client had said nothing to undo the Crown's case, he had at least managed to arouse some sympathy in the jury.

Bronwen Hywel-Jones rose to her feet and tucked a long, stray lock of black hair beneath her pale gray wig. There was a look of iron determination on her face; she knew she'd won, but she wanted to finish off the job as cleanly as possible.

'Mr Rhys, you have told the court that you were out early on Saturday morning; that you found the victim of this heinous crime lying asleep beside the track?'

Owen nodded with his dark eyes fixed on the lawyer's.

'Can you speak your answers, please.'

'That's correct,' Owen said in a low, clear voice.

'Let's look at that answer a little more closely. At what time, precisely did you find the victim?'

Owen shrugged. 'It's in the statement I gave the police when they arrested me that you read out this morning.'

'But not recorded in any previous interviews you'd had with them.'

'There weren't any previous interviews.'

'But you didn't volunteer the fact that it was you who had found and carried Miss Chichester back to Ruth Calloway's house.'

'No,' Owen agreed. 'Miss Chichester's a very famous woman, and she thought I might be bothered by journalists and such if I told the police that; she said she wanted to tell them she'd come back on her own.'

'She nevertheless subsequently told them that you had found her and helped her back to the house.'

Owen nodded again, and slightly raised one shoulder. 'I didn't know that, but once they brought me in, I thought they should know the whole story.'

'The whole story?' Miss Hywel-Jones raised an eyebrow. 'You say she was asleep when you found her? Do you think that's very likely in someone who had just been subjected to a violent sexual assault?'

'I don't know. But I should have thought when something like that happens, it must take a lot out of a woman. If she was lying on the ground already, it wouldn't be so surprising if she fell asleep; it had been a hot day and it was very mild night.'

'Are you seriously expecting this jury to believe that after a savage rape, a victim is in the frame of mind to just fall asleep?'

Beyond Gospel Pass

Owen shrugged a shoulder. 'I can only tell you what I saw.'

The barrister glanced at the jury smugly, as if to say – there you have it.

Turning back to Owen she asked, 'Can you tell us again why you were on the track at four thirty in the morning?'

'I'd gone out early...'

'Why had you gone out early?'

Owen looked at the lawyer as if she were a child asking a stupid question. 'In summertime it's the best time to be out. It's not too hot to work, there's no one around to disturb you, and it's the most beautiful time if the sun's coming up.'

'So you'd like us to believe you're a bit of a romantic, eh? Someone who loves the beauties of nature?'

Owen gazed back at her disdainfully. He didn't answer; she hurried on. 'But the Hendre where Miss Chichester was staying is a mile from your house; why did you go there that morning?'

'Me and my brother farm a lot of the ground round there too, and we just sent two hundred ewes back onto the hill with some late lambs. Sometimes they can get a bit careless when they first go up, and I wanted to check them.'

'How did you get there?'

'I took the ATV and left it below the Hendre.'

'Why?'

'I preferred to walk.'

'And that makes no noise.'

'That's right. It's the sounds of a summer dawn I like best.'

The barrister raised her eyebrows at this unlikely justification. 'And what did you find when you got to the Hendre?'

'I didn't go to the Hendre. When I turned off the quad, I heard a lamb in distress, and I went to look for it.'

'And did you find it?'

'Yes; it was caught in a gully, must have fallen over the edge; it couldn't get out and its mother couldn't get down, and it was hungry.'

'So you got it out?'

Owen nodded. 'Yes.'

'And after that you carried on walking down the track in the direction of the Priory, where you happened on Miss Chichester, fast asleep?'

'That's right.'

Miss Hywel-Jones tilted her head. She gazed at Owen down her short nose and said nothing for a few moments before she turned to the jury. 'A touching version of events, I'm sure we're all agreed, but obviously, totally without foundation.' She turned to the judge who still presided over his court with an inscrutable face. 'I have no further questions, Your Honour.'

Owen left the stand and returned to the dock.

Mr Humphries rose to his feet and summed up his defence, based entirely on the story as Owen had just given it, and Laura's assertion that she had not recognised Owen's voice.

When Humphries had finished, Bronwen Hywel-Jones stood to wrap up her case wearing a cynical grin. She turned to face the jury. 'Ladies and gentlemen, this is a case where the hard, scientific evidence speaks so loudly that no further proof of guilt is needed. You've heard from two expert witnesses who have confirmed that the body fluids left by the attacker must have come from the accused – *and no one else!* At least, the odds against it being anyone else are around thirty million to one, so we can be entirely satisfied that it could only have been the accused.' The barrister stared silently at Owen for a few moments before turning back to the jury. 'Owen Rhys is accused of the harsh, cold-blooded violation of a woman, who, despite her own strength and fitness, was no match for a man of his age and powerful build. Nothing he or his counsel have told you has altered one iota the weight of the evidence against him. It is your duty to ensure that this dangerous man is convicted and removed to a place where society will be safe from him.'

Miss Hywel-Jones sat down.

The judge leaned back in his chair, evidently pleased to have got the evidence presented so neatly, which meant that, provided the jury didn't mess about, he would be able to sentence the following morning, leaving the afternoon free, perhaps, for a round of golf.

He tidily summarised the evidence, and instructed the jury on the precise meaning of the law as it related to the crime of rape. Beth listened with closed eyes and growing dread of Owen's conviction. She knew that however reasonable and unaggressive Owen might have been in the witness box, the jury could reach only one conclusion.

When he had finished, the judge turned to them. 'I would like you to leave now to consider your verdict.' He looked at his watch. 'As I do not want to press you into unseemly haste, and this court is now due to rise, I will ask you to stay together until the court sits again tomorrow morning. If you have reached a verdict on which you are all agreed, I will hear it then.'

He stood up. The usher intoned, 'All rise', and Owen was led away between the two prison officers. Beth looked at the jury, whose accusing eyes, already discounting the good impression Owen had made in the stand, followed him from the court. From the set of their jaws she could see they resented being asked to take eighteen hours to reach a decision that was already patently clear to all of them.

Beth followed Ruth back to the Hendre.
'Coffee?' Ruth asked when she arrived.
'Yes, a quick one. Then I must go.'
'Go? Where?'
'Back to London.'
'But aren't you going to stay and hear the verdict?'
'No. I don't think I can bear it.'
'You're so certain he'll be found guilty?'

Beth bit her lip and nodded. 'I just don't understand it. It seems to me so obvious it wasn't him... and yet..' her shoulders dropped in resignation, 'there was nothing he could do against that evidence. Something happened, somehow, to interfere after the event. God knows how or who or why anyone should do it... The only thing I can think....' her face creased painfully at the idea, '..is that Owen and Laura did meet up by chance, and he did make love to her.... But for some reason, Laura decided to cry rape..'

Ruth stared at her. 'But that's crazy! Why should she do that? And if she did, why didn't Owen tell the court that's what happened?'

At last, the only possible interpretation of the powerful forensic evidence overwhelmed Beth. Her breath started to come in great, long sobs. 'I just can't bear it... I don't know anything, I don't understand how it's happened.... It's all so horrible...'

Ruth, sitting opposite her at the table, stood up and came round to lay an arm across her shoulder. 'Beth, of course it is, but why are you so very upset about it?'

'I feel I should have been able to do much more for him,' she mumbled, still unable to admit to her love for Owen. 'I feel his mother was expecting more – even if he wasn't... and I just couldn't deliver.

It's not my field, but even if it were, I don't see how I could have produced a better result.'

'Laura didn't help, one way or the other, did she?' Ruth said thoughtfully. 'I don't know why she bothered, really.'

'Oh, that was all to do with column inches.'

Ruth straightened, a little shocked. 'Do you think she's that hard-nosed?'

'Yes, for God's sake. People in her business have to be. I know she's a friend of yours Ruth but you've got to face the fact that she's a professional celebrity first, and an old friend a long way second.'

'But she couldn't have just set Owen up, could she?'

'I don't suppose so. God knows!' Beth wailed. 'The whole thing's a bloody nightmare!'

'What are you going to do now?'

'I told you, I'm driving back to London.'

'Don't go tonight; you're too upset. Please stay, and leave early in the morning if you have to. I need a little company too, you know.'

Beth switched on the radio for the midday news as she drove over the Chiswick flyover into London. The verdict in the rape trial was the third item.

'At the Crown Court in Newport, South Wales, this morning, Owen Rhys, a twenty-nine year old farmer from Abergavenny, was found guilty of raping television personality Laura Chichester. The jury's decision was unanimous. Miss Chichester was attacked while walking......'

Beth let the words fade from her consciousness while her whole body seemed to grow numb.

Although the verdict had been inevitable, it was almost more than she could bear to hear it reported so dispassionately, or to conceive what millions of people all over Britain would think of the twenty nine year old farmer from Abergavenny – the father of the child inside her.

Two weeks after the judge in Newport had sentenced Owen to ten years imprisonment, Beth swallowed her resolution and revisited the Llanthony Valley.

An oblique shaft of autumn sun emphasised the deep clefts in the green shoulders on either side of Gospel Pass. The face of Yr

Beyond Gospel Pass

Twmpa looked smoothly carved, as if by giants, where streams trickled down their gullies in fine silver streaks on the face of the mountain. A small herd of piebald ponies and half a dozen growing foals grazed shoulder high among the bracken while a stallion with angry pink eyes and a long white mane stood guard with nostrils wide.

Over the pass, the road dropped slowly, until it sank between banks of clustered birch and alder, still in leaf, and the light reached the road in dappled splashes, offering glimpses of abandoned homes on the high, ungenerous hillside.

When Beth passed the youth hostel, she thought of the walker who had seen her with Owen in the Wergin pool, and wove a fantasy in which he had somehow planted the blame for his crime on Owen.

She reached the point where the valley joined the branch from the north-west. She stopped and turned off the engine of the car. She listened to the wind rustling the alders and hissing gently through the ring of dark yews that circled the small church at Capel-y-ffin. In the distance she heard a clank of metal on metal, where someone was mending a tractor, perhaps, and a splash in the river that raced along the valley floor.

Taking a deep breath, she started the car, turned it and headed up the west branch of the valley towards Blaen Fawr.

She knocked on the big faded door, and heard the sound echo through the long corridor beyond. It was the first time she'd been up to the house since the day the police had come, when Megan had rung her in early June.

The place seemed somehow even quieter, now the old woman was living here alone. Beth stood for a few minutes, but nothing happened. She knocked again, louder this time, and the sharp sound ricocheted around the old buildings , and roused the crows in the oaks.

After several minutes when there was still no response, Beth walked to the window of the front room where Megan had given her tea the first time she'd visited. She peered through the dirty glass into the gloom, where everything looked just as it had last time. She waited a little longer before she walked through the gap between the barn and the house, towards where she guessed she would find the back door.

She recognised it as the part of the house where Owen's room had been, with the half-glass door ajar, as if someone had just slipped out for a while, and knew anyway, that they wouldn't be disturbed up here.

Jessica Meredith

Beth knocked on the glass, which rattled in its frame. She stretched her head through the door and listened. She called, 'Mrs Rhys? Mrs Rhys?'

When she heard nothing, she walked with a twinge of guilt through the door into a dark, stone-flagged corridor, past the door to Owen's room, towards the kitchen. She called out a few more times as she went, and pushed the door at the end of the passage that opened into the kitchen.

The kitchen was in semidarkness. The window gave onto the steep hillside behind, and with curtains still half drawn across it. An old iron range, a deep china sink and a small electric cooker all dated from before the war. On a table, whose top had been covered in lino at some point in the past fifty years, was a tray with a couple of unwashed plates and some cutlery. Beth judged that it must have been for two and guessed that Megan had had a visitor up for a meal, but had gone out afterwards.

She felt bad about intruding any more, and half backed out of the room. She retraced her steps along the passage to the back door and stood outside the house, irresolute. Megan couldn't have gone far, unless her guest had come and taken her off in a car. But Ruth had said that Owen's mother left the farm only a few times a year, for particular events in the valley.

She walked back through the gap between the stone walls of the house and barn, into the courtyard, where her car was parked beyond the gate. Feeling like a trespasser for having intruded as far as she had, she decided to drive on to Ruth's and ring from there later.

Beth was opening the car door when Megan appeared, walking slowly up the steep meadow that bordered the brook. She reached Beth, breathing heavily from her climb, and put down a large plastic bag she was carrying.

Beth saw protruding from the bag a big wooden hive rack, oozing light golden honey. She thought of Owen and the sun setting by the pool, and glanced away sharply, not wanting Megan to see.

When she looked back, though, Owen's mother was staring at her waist, as if the four month old person inside her was already obvious.

Beth started. How could she have guessed?

Beyond Gospel Pass

But when Megan raised her head and looked her in the eye, she showed no special insight, and Beth was conscious how prone to paranoia she'd become lately.

She tried a smile. 'Hello, Mrs Rhys.'

'Why have you come back?'

'I wondered how Owen was. Have you heard from him?'

'He's wrote me some letters. He don't say much.' She shrugged. 'He was always a strong boy – never needed no help.'

'I'm going to see him. I managed to get a PVO for tomorrow.'

'Did he want that?'

'If he'd objected, it wouldn't have been issued.'

Megan started to walk towards the house in silence. She reached the front steps and climbed them slowly. When she reached the top, she turned and spoke. 'Is there anything else you can do for him?' The words came out stiffly, as if they'd taken all her strength.

'Not unless some new evidence comes to light...' Beth shook her head.

The old woman looked at her steadily for a few moments. 'It's not right; he shouldn't be there.'

Beth felt that Megan wanted to tell her more, but was afraid to. She didn't speak, waiting to see if she offered anything, but without another word, Megan shook her head a few times, walked through the door and closed it behind her.

Owen entered a noisy hall that echoed with the sound of metal chairs and tables being restlessly, ceaselessly scraped across the hard floor by prisoners and their visitors.

Beth spotted him at once. Not just because she was waiting for him; nothing had altered in his self-possession to diminish the attention he commanded. She'd sat waiting for ten minutes for him to arrive, and for the last five had become convinced he wouldn't appear at all; that something – shame, pride or, *God help me,* Beth prayed, guilt – had changed his mind about seeing her.

But now, as soon as she'd seen him, she realised that nothing had quelled his spirit.

There was exactly the same calm self-containment she'd seen and admired - rare in any twenty-nine year old; almost unique among time-serving convicts.

Beth had managed to get an interview with the governor when she arrived; he knew her name and admired her reputation, he said.

He also said that Owen had been a spectacularly successful prisoner, in as much as he caused no trouble, and had been a very able student since he'd arrived. 'He has a wonderful instinctive understanding of literature, especially the metaphysical poets – most unexpected in someone with his background and offender profile.'

'You mean, unusual for a rapist?'

'Unprecedented, in my experience. He shows signs already of total rejection of what he did, though, of course, he still won't admit his guilt.'

Owen sat down opposite her at the table. He looked at her through deep coffee eyes, silent for a few moments, before lowering his chin with a faint nod.

'Hello,' he said quietly.

Beth yearned to stand up, walk round and hug him, but prison rules and her own inhibitions prevented her.

'Hello, Owen,' she answered, knowing how inadequately the words conveyed her feelings.

In reply, his eyes seemed to search her soul, but showed nothing of himself, as if he couldn't let himself register his own emotions.

'You look... very well,' he said as if he were visiting her, not vice versa, and allowed a faint smile to raise his lips.

'I'm fine,' Beth said, feeling exposed and naked in the strength of his gaze. 'But you... how are you coping?'

'All right.' He tilted his head and lifted a brow. 'I'd rather be on the hills.' He allowed a faint smile on his lips.

'You must feel so bitter...'

'The jury had to come to their verdict, with what they'd been told,' he said. 'And I won't die in here.'

She stared at him to find the faintest signs of recognition of the passionate forces that had pulled them together so strongly for those few lyrical days in May. 'I hope you don't mind my coming to see you,' she said.

'Of course I don't. But I shouldn't think you like it much.' He waved an arm towards the small huddles of glum people around each table. 'It's not a happy place.'

Beyond Gospel Pass

'Oh, Owen, how can you stand it?' Beth asked in exactly the way she'd been determined not to, but still holding back her tears.

He held up one hand, palm down, in a placating gesture, like a priest about to give a blessing, Beth thought. 'It's all right,' he said. 'You don't have to worry about me. I'm not part of this.' His eyes indicated the other people in the room. 'And as long as I'm not part of it, I'll survive.'

Beth believed him, but she couldn't come to terms with his conviction, any more now than when Ruth had first told her he'd been arrested.

She couldn't stay. She wanted to touch him, to kiss him, to squeeze him, to wrap her arms around him, to let him know, to remind him of everything they'd shared.

She stood up. She didn't even shake his hand. 'Goodbye, Owen. I have to go; if there's ever anything I can do, I'll always be there for you. But I won't come again unless you ask.'

He said nothing. His dark eyes were motionless as he gazed up at her before rising slowly to his feet.

It was only as she turned towards the guarded double doors to leave, that he spoke again. 'Goodbye. Thanks for coming. It was very good to see you. Say hello to Ruth...' he paused and smiled '...and the Wergin stone.'

Beth turned back. 'I will, I will,' she murmured and with a last farewell look, she walked away.

'Why did you go and see him?' Ruth asked that evening, cooking pasta for them in her warm kitchen.

'Haven't you been to visit him?'

'God, no! I simply couldn't take seeing him cooped up.'

Beth agreed. 'It wasn't easy, but you know, he's bigger than the system. He looked totally in control and unaffected by it all.'

'But what made you go?'

'I still don't think he could have done it,' she said carefully. 'I know all the evidence, the facts, everything – the lack of alibi, the DNA – everything says he did, but I still don't believe it.'

Ruth carried on slicing cloves of fresh wild garlic.

'Well?' Beth asked insistently. 'You don't believe it either, do you?'

'No,' Ruth said slowly. 'I don't, but....' She heaved her shoulders in a helpless gesture. 'I can't claim to really *know* Owen, I mean, even though I've known him for ten years or more, since he was a teenager, I suppose, and he's been kind, and done things for me over the years, he's never, ever opened the window of his soul to me.'

Beth listened and nodded. Despite the intensity of their physical contact, she knew that Owen had not allowed her in, either. It was agony to admit, but perhaps she didn't know him any better than Ruth. After all, they'd exchanged no more than a few dozen sentences throughout their brief liaisons.

And yet... She sighed.

'Was there something more to you and Owen?' Ruth asked suddenly.

Beth looked up quickly. 'More? How do you mean?'

'I mean, you seem to have been to a lot of trouble for a man you've only known a few weeks when all he's done for you is dowse for water.'

'I don't mind admitting that I found him an exceptional person and I sensed a sort of extraordinary strength in him which you can't just overlook. Besides, I'm a professional lawyer with a specific commitment to fight injustice within the legal system and I know somehow, something's gone wrong here.'

'Beth, I know exactly what you're feeling, but don't you think Owen would prove his innocence if he really could, and wanted to?'

'What on earth do you mean?'

'I don't know what I mean – but it's as if he's somehow just decided to take it lying down.'

'And get the sentence over with as fast as possible, with as little fuss?'

Ruth nodded.

'But doesn't he realise, it's about public perception as well.'

'No,' Ruth shook her head. 'Owen isn't one to worry about what people think.' She stood up and carried the food she'd been preparing to the oven. Beth watched her, light-headed, confused by trying to extract the truth from the irrefutable facts behind Owen's position.

'How are Michael and his mother taking it?' she asked, not wanting to own up to the snooping she'd done at Blaen Fawr the day before.

'I think Megan's more distraught than she'd ever let on. I went up to see her yesterday, but she wouldn't talk about it to me.'

That explained the plates, Beth thought, and felt pleased that Megan had chosen to ask her help. 'And Michael?'

'He won't talk about it either. But Susie's found it very embarrassing. No one in the valley will openly condemn him, but no one can see what else could have happened. If they excuse it at all, they probably think he had some kind of freak mental aberration. The papers round here just stuck to the facts and hoped that Laura wouldn't hold it against the local people.'

'Have you spoken to Laura since the trial?'

'Just once. She sounded okay; to tell you the truth – not that upset. In fact, I think she's got some plan to go public on it all.'

'I should have thought it was all public enough already.'

'She means about the emotions and everything – a sort of first hand analysis of the trauma.'

'No one could accuse her of not making the most of her chances.'

'I just wish it didn't involve Owen,' Ruth said. 'I feel sort of responsible as it is. If I hadn't invited her, she wouldn't have been anywhere near the valley that night.'

'That's a very peripheral responsibility, for God's sake – I could blame myself for telling her about the ley that leads down the track to the Priory.'

'No, you're right, of course,' Ruth nodded. 'Only the man who did it was to blame.'

Seventeen

When Moira Langthorne had suggested that Beth and Mark should spend Christmas week with her, Edward, Jemma and the boys at the family house in Vermont, Beth's first reaction was that she shouldn't fly; she would be nearly twenty-eight weeks into her pregnancy.

But her doctor told her it wasn't a risk; that she was showing all the signs of a straightforward and healthy pregnancy, despite her comparative maturity, and Mark settled down in front of his Applemac to find the cheapest tickets.

Because she was already large enough to feel uncomfortable behind the wheel of a car, Mark drove them from Boston out to Middlebury in the Green Mountains, two days before Christmas.

He didn't complain about the slow traffic or the snow that was beginning to fall; Beth had always been impressed at his lack of irritation by things he knew he could do nothing to alter.

'Are Edward and Jemma staying with the kids tomorrow night?' he asked.

'I doubt it,' Beth said. 'Jemma thinks the cottage is too small.'

'Poor Edward.'

Mark had always liked Beth's brother. In some ways they were similar, although Edward was more practical and worked harder, but he didn't have any of Mark's enthusiastic charm or the generous laughter that was often helpful at a family party. Nevertheless, there was a well-informed gravitas to him; he never discussed anything he didn't know about, and only made statements on subjects of which he was certain. Beth was fond of Edward, too, but comparing him to Mark, she was reminded of the qualities in her husband that had first attracted her.

Beyond Gospel Pass

Beth was thinking about these qualities later, when she was alone with her mother, taking the dogs for a gentle walk along a trail through the leafless maple woods behind the cosy clapboard house.

'Mark seems pretty happy,' Moira said, 'considering the terrible time you say he's been having.'

Beth smiled. 'He never lets anything get him down for long. That's the trouble in a way; he always thinks something will turn up to let him off the hook; and often it does, so he never worries enough to make the radical decisions he sometimes should.'

'I call buying a house in the Welsh mountains on the strength of a seat in Parliament he hadn't even been invited to fight quite radical – if not totally crazy,' Moira said, and gave Beth a long look before she spoke again. 'How does he feel about the baby?'

Beth tried not to redden. Although she had already strenuously assured her that the baby was Mark's, she sensed that, perhaps intuitively, her mother was still doubtful. She had no idea what telltale sign in her own manner might have given away the truth, but she hadn't mentioned Owen by name to Moira since she'd known she was pregnant. 'He's very chuffed about it,' she smiled. 'I think he'll be a rather good father.'

'Then he isn't worried about money?'

'We'll cope, and things are looking a little better for him. He seems to have got over being rejected by the Liberals in Hay, and the ghastly George Arbuthnott has delivered his next book. Oh, and an obscure, mega-rich Ghanaian has come up with a load of money to subsidise his own book. I expect Mark'll pull through. What I do know is he'd never respond to my nagging or suggesting he did something else.'

'I see you've had your hair changed,' Moira said, in an apparent non-sequitur.

Beth flicked the looser, wavier auburn curls that she had allowed to grow since the summer. 'What do you think?'

'The benefits of a new hairstyle don't last long,' her mother said.

'Mum, I'm okay. There wasn't anything therapeutic about it. I just felt like a softer cut, I suppose, knowing I'm going to be a mother.'

'Are you over all the traumas of the Welsh house yet?'

Beth was walking a little ahead of her mother. She looked back over her shoulder. 'What makes you think it was so traumatic?'

'At the time, you seemed kind of nervous about it, really quite agitated, though I always guessed you weren't really interested in that whole Welsh foray.'

'I wasn't to begin with, but Mark was so enthusiastic about the seat and everything,' she said facing ahead now. 'And in the end, I was glad of the experience – even if it did all go wrong.'

'Do you think you should let Mark push you into these major upheavals, especially when you've got your own busy career to think about, and now a baby?'

'I won't,' Beth sighed. 'Anyway, his latest business crisis has made him a little more careful - at least, more prepared to listen to me.'

'Were you and he going through a sticky patch, then, last summer?'

'Nothing serious,' Beth said, and hoped her mother couldn't hear the quaver in her voice. 'You know there's always a bit of adjusting to do during the course of a marriage, and I suppose you just have to bend with it if you want it to survive. I mean, I don't regard Mark with quite the same awe as I did when I first knew him, but I still love him... more like a wayward son, maybe, than a lover, but I don't have any doubt about my feelings of loyalty towards him.'

As she spoke, she walked a little faster and let herself think of Owen as she'd seen him in the visiting hall in prison – what he had said and how he had stood as she was leaving. And she wondered if he had restrained himself from contacting her out of generosity to her, to destroy any hope in her that they might come together again, to release her from any commitment to wait for him for another five years or more.

Moira caught up with her. 'I'm glad, sweetie,' she said, believing her daughter. 'You wouldn't be the first woman to have doubts, or to have to make readjustments, because people alter in themselves and in relation to each other – maybe sometimes only by perception. But then it's your shared history that can become important and truly valuable much later in your lives.'

Beth took Moira's hand and swung it like she had when she was five years old, and wondered if her mother had ever had an affair.

Edward and Jemma, with Edward Junior and Charlie had driven up from friends near Holyoke and arrived at noon on Christmas Day.

Beyond Gospel Pass

Edward and the boys carried in armfuls of beautifully wrapped presents, stacking them with neat precision under the small pine tree in the big open living room where Moira contrived to keep a log fire permanently blazing.

Jemma, already showing a hint of resentment that she was no longer the sole reproducer in the family, complimented Beth on how well she was looking. 'And you're already *humungous*!' she added.

'Can't help that, I'm afraid. How are you and the boys?'

Beth hadn't seen much of Edward Junior and Charlie in the last few years, although Moira had said that when they'd been told about their future cousin, they had shown unexpected enthusiasm.

Jemma glanced at them now with possessive fondness. 'They're fine, thanks. Edward just passed First Grade on the piano, and Charlie's already going for his Initial.'

'That's great! They're obviously going to be musical like their papa.' Beth knew that having launched this conversation, she would have to listen to a short litany of the boy's skills and achievements, but she minded less than she might have done, knowing she'd be competing with her own entry in a few months' time.

The boys themselves seemed to have developed a little more self-assurance lately, and were showing encouraging signs of independence, defying their mother in a way which, Beth observed, seemed to amuse Mark.

Seeing Mark with them, it occurred to her for the first time that Mark had many of the qualities that produced a good, inspiring father. And she thought her baby was going to need a good father, in case she turned out to be as bad a mother as she had proved to be a wife.

Inevitably, between bouts of banter with the boys, a lot of the conversation over Christmas dinner centred on Beth's baby – where and how she was having it and what she was going to do about cribs and childcare. And Beth was relieved to find that focussing on these practical issues did a lot to calm some of the invisible though powerful emotions still churning inside her.

Towards the end of lunch, after several bottles of good French wine had circulated and the boys were allowed down from the table to tear at a pile of carefully wrapped presents, Edward mentioned that he had seen *The Leys of the Land* on sale in Border Books in Cambridge. 'Sorry I didn't buy it,' he said. 'I can't see much merit in most of this

New Age stuff; it seems like, "think of a theory and bend the facts to fit".'

'You can't knock the technique,' Mark said, fairly drunk by now. 'Desmond Morris used it for years and made a fortune from it. Dawkins still does – and he's meant to be a bona fide scientist.'

'Anyway,' Edward went on, 'I had a flick through George Arbuthnott's book and I see he's written about a large standing stone near that house of yours in Wales which has very exciting fertility properties, like the King Stone in the Rollrights.'

'I suppose you'd have made me go over to England to look at it, if I hadn't produced on cue? ' Jemma said.

'You'd have to do more than look at it,' Mark said with a grin. 'Traditionally the barren womenfolk of the valley used to go up to the Wergin stone and rub their naked breasts against it to achieve fertility.'

'Surely, more than just their naked breasts?' Edward asked.

Beth laughed. 'No, Edward, but I've been there, and I can tell you, there really is something amazingly numinous about the place; some ambient force in the ground around it.'

'Why?' Jemma asked sharply. 'Is that how you got pregnant? Did you rub your breasts on it?'

Beth grinned awkwardly, not wanting to respond. She was aware how strongly Jemma felt her status within the family had been diminished now she was no longer the only child-bearing female in it.

Mark ignored the edge in Jemma's voice. 'There's a middle-aged hippy called Ruth Calloway who lives in the next farm up the valley,' he observed lightly, 'who says it's what the Australian aborigines refer to as a "site of the dream time", where they call up *Kurunba,* to promote fertility.'

'It's not surprising that there should be common myths among primitive folk,' Edward remarked. 'The native Americans have a whole mass of special sacred sites which they want returned to them – mostly with minerals underground.'

'Who are you calling primitive?' Beth said sharply, thinking of Owen's perceptive compassion.

'Those Welsh mountain men can't be exactly sophisticated, any more than the people from the Southern Appalachians, say.'

'That would depend on what you meant by "sophisticated".'

Beyond Gospel Pass

'Now, children,' Moira said in a bossy voice, and they all laughed, anxious to avoid overt dissent.

'One of our local farmers used a pendulum to dowse for our water,' Mark said, 'which I considered fairly sophisticated.'

Beth glanced at him to see if he was relating it to her in any way, but he seemed only to be addressing Edward and Jemma.

'Beth told me a bit about him,' Moira said, interested.

'Did she tell you he also dowses for muscular trauma in people?' Mark went on. 'He cured that old sleaze-ball Martin Evans-Finch of some major back problem.'

'A politican, now Lord Brecon,' Beth explained.

'That's right. Anyway, this chap Owen was going to do my elbow but we never got round to it.' Now he glanced at Beth. 'Unfortunately, we left it a bit late because he'll be banged up for at least the next five years for rape.'

Beth saw her knuckles whiten where her hand clutched a glass. She knew Mark was just employing a favourite tactic in putting up targets for opponents to shoot down, and then shooting them down himself first. To react too strongly now would arouse suspicions.

'So it was probably all nonsense,' Jemma said.

'I don't know.' Beth tried to sound reasonable. 'For a start, there's some doubt about the conviction.'

'Not much....' Mark started to protest.

'All right,' Beth held up her hand, and reined in her own responses. 'But I did talk to Martin Brecon about his back, and he said he'd been all over the place to have it cured and Owen Rhys was the only man who actually did anything. I looked up the art of using a pendulum to locate an object or a physical trauma and it's a recognised phenomenon called radiesthesia – a kind of sensitivity to radiation. Apparently ancient stresses leave a trauma in the ground which can still be detected this way hundreds of years later. These days the Japanese use the same thing for telling the sex of chicks still in their eggs.'

'You mean like old ladies dangling rings over pregnant women's stomachs and checking the rotation to find the sex of a baby and stuff like that?' Jemma asked.

'Yes, I suppose I do.'

'Maybe we should try it on Beth,' Mark laughed, 'so Jemma can decide what to send him or her, when he or she emerges.'

'I'm sure it would work,' Beth said. 'But I just don't want to know.'

Edward had been silent for a while, though Beth saw he'd been following the conversation closely. 'I do believe there must be some truth in this thing about people's magnetic fields. A research scientist at Yale has established that there's a measurable change in a woman's personal electrical field during ovulation. I suppose that could be divined in the same way, or even detected through the hands of a healer?'

Beth remembered Owen, before they had made love for the last time, passing his hands over her and saying, 'You feel very ready...'

'He must be a fascinating character, this Owen,' her mother said, as if she'd read Beth's thoughts.

'Well, obviously the rape, whether he did it or not, has rather blighted the valley. We were there, at dinner with Laura Chichester the night it happened,' Beth tried to explain her interest and involvement.

'It sounds ghastly. Why did they convict him?'

'They matched the DNA, and that was that,' Mark said with bald conclusiveness.

Up until now, Beth had not dared to risk discussing in depth the question of Owen's guilt with Mark.

She realised now with a rude shock that Mark, like ninety-nine per cent of the population, had absolutely no doubt that Owen had raped Laura.

Eighteen

The week spent below the snowy slopes of the Green Mountains seemed to melt into a warm memory and two grey, damp months in London had passed quickly since Christmas. Beth's baby was almost due and she had reached the point where she was beginning almost to resent the bulky, restless presence inside her.

She woke feeling bloated, crippled with cramp and desperate to get to the bathroom to relieve the pressure on her bladder. She managed to roll over and for a moment looked at Mark on the far side of their six-foot bed. He was sound asleep with a look of contentment on his face.

Lucky guy, Beth thought with teeth clenched in irony and discomfort.

She heaved herself out of bed and lurched painfully to the bathroom. She sat on the lavatory for a while, listening to the early morning winter noise of hot water clicking and thumping its way through the central heating. It was a noise she'd always disliked, especially now, when she wanted to hear the summer dawn sounds of Pant-y-Groes.

Before she went back into the bedroom, she paused in front of the large mirror over the basin and gazed at herself. She thought that considering her permanent discomfort, she didn't look bad, if she ignored the oversize of her breasts and the massive bulge beneath them.

She wondered, for the thousandth time, what her child would look like. She was convinced that Owen's Celtic genes, diluted only, perhaps, by an Irish variant, would run true and she had decided that if there were a visible Welshness about the child, she would attribute it to Mark's own supposed Welsh ancestry.

It was still half an hour before the time Mark usually got up. Thoughtfully, she took herself quietly downstairs. She was on her second cup of St John's Wort tea when he appeared.

'Angel!' he said, concerned. 'Have you been up for hours?'

She nodded.

'How do you feel?'

'Horrible. About to explode. I think this person must be coming any minute.'

'Contractions?'

'Not that I know of, but then I've never had them before; maybe my pain threshold is higher than normal.'

When Mark came home after a frustrating day in his new, cost-efficient offices, Beth made it clear that her pain threshold was no higher than anyone's.

'Thank God you're back,' she gasped. 'I was just about to phone for an ambulance.'

'Oh my God! Is it beginning to hurt?'

'Yes, it fucking well is!' Beth grunted.

Mark grinned happily while he dialled Queen Charlotte's hospital, as if he'd prepared himself for the abuse; he'd been told about some women's propensity to blame their partners for the pain of childbirth and took it as a positive sign that parenthood was imminent, after all the years of anxious trying and waiting.

Half an hour later, Beth was wallowing in mild anaesthetic and yards of rustling white bed-linen.

She was too preoccupied with the present to care about post-natal problems; she could think of nothing but getting the birth over and done. She hadn't worked on any case for the last two weeks, and for at least a part of every waking minute of that time, she'd been conscious of what was soon to happen.

Mark was sitting on the other side of the room, jumping up every few minutes to see if he could do anything for her. She had told him a dozen times that all he had to do was keep out of the way, but now, when the big push came, she really did want him to hold her hand.

Even if it wasn't his child, she thought, as far as he was concerned, it was. And she owed both – her husband and her child - the opportunity to believe it.

At two in the morning, the corridors of the hospital were empty and half-lit. The silence was interrupted sporadically by the agonised cries of a birthing mother, calm murmuring between nurses and the occasional clunk of a trolley bed being wheeled from ward to ward.

For some blissful minutes, Beth enjoyed a respite from the violent surges of pain in her stomach. A nurse and midwife had just left, assuring her that everything looked normal and, with luck, she would be a mother before dawn.

She looked across the room at Mark. He was sitting upright, but asleep in a big armchair with *The Guardian* on his lap, folded at the half-completed crossword.

Abruptly, a massive spasm seared through the muscles of Beth's womb. She didn't have time to stop herself from yelling at the unexpected severity of the pain.

A moment later, a nurse was leaning over, with Mark hovering behind, following her inspection of Beth's cervix. 'It's further on than we thought it would be,' she said calmly. 'Not long now.'

Beth grimaced fiercely as another pain burned through her.

It was extraordinary, she managed to think, how pain could exclude every other thought – how nothing mattered but finding a way to make it end. 'I can't stand this....' she whispered hoarsely through clenched teeth. 'Can you give me something... please?' she begged.

'All right, dear,' the nurse said in a voice that Beth recognised as taking into account that she was thirty-nine years old and having her first baby. 'We'll get some gas and air for you.'

The easing of pain brought, by contrast, a sense almost of well-being for a while, until the hard, muscular work began in earnest, and all Beth's instincts became focused on pushing this new life from her womb into the world.

Blindly, she reached out for Mark's hand, which she knew would be there, and squeezed it as hard as she could to reassure herself of his nearness; to let him share in the birth-pains of his child.

Besides, the baby needed a father, and Mark's hand was there.

Only later, watching Mark smile ecstatically as he held the tiny, squashed, pink boy, was Beth properly conscious of her dishonesty.

There was nothing obvious in the emerging features of the newly born William Powell to suggest that Mark Powell was his father.

Beth gazed at him in his cot in the nursery that had been prepared in the house in Hackney and searched for signs of Owen Rhys. But the boy's eyes were pale green-blue and his hair a light, sandy red, as hers had been.

She picked him up and held him with fierce joy. Tears of pride still leaked from her eyes each time she held him, and she knew that whatever she'd had to do to achieve this child's birth had been validated.

But from time to time in the first month, between moments of happiness and supreme fulfilment, there were periods of deep despair, when Owen's face would drift into her head; the strong, secret eyes that had surveyed her so calmly as she'd left him in prison at the beginning of October. When these bouts of misery overwhelmed her, she sometimes, in her mind, began to compose a letter to him, to tell him, to thank him and praise him for what he had done for her.

But always she thought of her baby, and stopped.

She knew that the moment she told Owen, she would create the possibility that one day, even at some future, sensitive point in the child's young life, William would hear, or be told, or have reason to guess that Owen Rhys – a convicted rapist – was his father.

A month after William was born, Moira Langthorne came to London to see her third grandchild.

They were in the little sitting room at the back of the house in Hackney, halfway between the basement and the ground floor. Beth fed William while her mother admired him, as she had vigorously from the moment she'd arrived. 'And I'm not just a besotted, doting grandmother, either,' she added. 'That is certainly a good-looking, well-built baby.'

Beth laughed; she agreed.

'He looks just like you did,' Moira went on. 'It's a pity he's not a girl.'

'Oh, Mum!' Beth said with an indignant laugh. 'Now look – can't you see a little of Mark in him?'

She waited, trying not to let it show how much it mattered.

Moira lifted the child from the floor mat where he'd been gurgling over a squeaking rubber lorry. She held him at arm's length and looked him in the face. She turned to Beth. 'Do you know, I think I can. Just a hint from the shape of his face - those slightly high Celtic bones – I presume with a name like his, there's a bit of Welsh in Mark?'

'Yes, of course. He's always going on about it. That's why he tried for a Welsh seat last year.'

Moira handed the baby to Beth. 'It's funny,' she said, 'that crazy episode seems like it never existed, now it's over.'

'If you'd ever come to visit us in the valley, you might have seen the point of it.'

'Maybe, but to be honest, I never really thought it would last.'

'It was important for me, in the end,' Beth said quietly.

'Well, it produced the baby, after all.'

Beth looked at her mother for a moment, and wondered what she meant. 'There's no doubt we were both miles more relaxed up there, and perhaps that did the trick,' Beth said, suddenly feeling defensive of her dozen years of marriage to Mark. 'Though neither of us ever said so openly, I'm sure we both always thought the baby would make our lives complete; now he's come into it and, frankly, made the difference between marriage and co-existence.'

'Was it getting that bad?'

'It wasn't bad, just a little stale, and the frustration wore us both down; though, now I look back on it, Mark's been bloody good, in spite of all the hassles he's been having.'

'And how's the practical side of your love life?'

Beth was astonished. Her mother had never asked her that sort of thing before. 'He understands,' she mumbled, 'that it's more or less out of the question for a while, at least until my body gets over all the traumas of child birth.'

'I hope it does soon,' Moira said. 'He won't understand for ever.'

Nineteen

At the beginning of April, Penny Lewis moved into one of the small rooms on the top floor of the Powell's house. She had come to be William's nanny, well recommended by one of Beth's colleagues in chambers.

Penny was twenty-three; she'd left her comprehensive school in the rural Marches at sixteen to concentrate on a course in child-care. Despite her self-confessed academic short-comings, her obvious practicality had prevailed; she'd passed her exams and come to London to find her first job.

Broad-beamed and big breasted, she reminded Beth of the women she used to see in the supermarkets in Hereford and, having lost none of her ingenuousness, she laughed all the time and seemed to love every child she met. Beth gave her a room at the top of the house and took her off to Camden Lock to find things to help make it her own. Penny hung the walls with Indian fabrics and burned joss sticks, like her parents still did in their Herefordshire cottage, which she said helped to soothe her while she sat on a bean bag and listened to Dido.

After just two weeks, Beth felt that she had never known a more reliable and consistently warm-hearted individual, and she was already in the habit of telling the girl things she wouldn't have shared with her mother. She felt she could trust her utterly and would soon be able to go back to work, at least part time, with confidence that from a practical point of view, William would be at least as well cared for by Penny as by her.

But while she'd managed to quell most of her guilt feelings over leaving her young son with a nanny, she was nowhere near dealing with her guilt over his paternity.

And of course, though she had a shared a lot of private thoughts with her new aid and ally, she'd given no hint that the baby's father was anyone other than Mark.

She had contained this secret now for nearly a year, and she was aware that she was almost bursting with the need to unload it.

Really, she thought, she should go and see Father Aidan, but she knew Aidan's views, founded on the principle that any seriously committed Catholic should be able to subjugate their physical instincts, would not allow him to say she'd done anything other than commit adultery.

The only lay person she knew with the spiritual gravitas to understand her state of mind was Jack Devereux, now head of her chambers.

On her second day back at work, she saw the door of his room open, and took the opportunity to put her head round it.

'Any chance of a drink later?'

'About seven?' he suggested.

'Great. See you then.'

Beth felt strangely nervous for the rest of the afternoon as she primed herself for her confession.

She saw, as soon as they had sat down in the bar where they'd talked hypothetically the previous June, that Jack's sensitive antennae had already warned him she wanted to discuss something personal, not professional.

'So, what can I do for you?'

'Bless me father, for I have sinned,' Beth intoned with a quick tilt of her mouth.

'I can't give you absolution, you know,' Jack smiled back. 'Anyway, how are you finding motherhood?'

'Wonderful, actually, once the pain was over. I had no idea how complete it would make me feel.'

'And Mark?'

'Oh, he's thrilled.' Beth made a guilty noise with her lips.

Jack raised one side of his single brow. 'Isn't that good?'

'Yes, of course it is.'

Jack swallowed a mouthful of Fuller's bitter while he waited for her to go on.

'The trouble is....' She stopped. She thought, now she faced the choice, it might be even harder to share this secret than to retain it.

Jack saw her difficulty. 'The trouble is what?'

'Ahh,' Beth sighed. 'I was going to confide in you, ask your opinion, but now it's come to it, I just can't.'

'May I guess what it's about?'

Beth said nothing. She didn't know whether or not she wanted him to guess.

'I remember a conversation we had, early last summer, about a "deputy" dad. Is that what you wanted to talk about?'

Beth nodded slowly.

'Your son isn't Mark's?'

Beth shook her head. 'No,' she said almost inaudibly. 'He isn't.'

'Are you sure?'

'Oh yes.'

'Have you had it checked?'

'No, but I don't need to. Mark and I had been trying for years without getting anywhere. The whole idea of this other man started as a sort of joke – well not a joke exactly, more as a light-hearted suggestion about surrogate fathers.'

'But it happened, and it worked?'

'The living proof is back at home in Hackney.'

'Why did you want to tell me?' Jack asked.

'I wanted to tell someone. I couldn't go to Father Aidan; he would have made me feel too guilty.'

'Maybe that's right. After all, you'd only feel guilty if you thought you *were* guilty... of something.'

Beth sighed and lowered her eyes. 'I know, and of course I feel bad about the way it happened. But then consider, a healthy child has come into the world to parents who love him. Mark is thrilled; I'm as happy as I can be – most of the time – and frankly, our marriage is the better for it.'

Jack looked at her with an understanding that didn't compromise his own moral perspective. 'I can't tell you what to do, Beth. I'm not a priest. It's obvious to me that if Mark or your son ever found out what you've told me, there'd be a lot of unhappiness. At the same time if they don't, you're going to have to live the lie all your life. Of course, I'll never tell a living soul about it, but you've got two choices, and I can't begin to tell you which to take. Either you must keep it to yourself and make the very most you can of your marriage and your child. Or you must be true to yourself – to God, if you like – and take the moral consequences.'

Beth looked back at him bleakly. She'd always known that this was her choice. 'Jack,' she said with earnest pleading. 'Which would you do?'

Jack Devereux sucked deeply through muscular nostrils and his face wrinkled as he considered his answer. 'There maybe a case for approaching this from a Utilitarian point of view... Did you ever read Jeremy Bentham and John Stuart Mill?'

Beth shook her head. 'Never did much philosophy – not enough anyway.'

'They developed a morality called Utilitarianism, of which the guiding principles were the maximisation of pleasure and the minimisation of pain to those affected by an individual's decisions. It seems to me, Beth, on that basis, that fewer people would be hurt if you decided to make the most of what you now have and kept the truth to yourself. So, best of luck to you.'

Beth stared at the phone next morning, summoning up the courage to make a call she knew she shouldn't .

Penny was upstairs playing with William.

Mark had already left for the Archimedes offices. He had been buoyant the evening before when she'd come home after seeing Jack. He'd just heard that the two men he had courted so zealously but ineffectually the previous autumn – the Armenian and Adam Yorke – had put their business into receivership and were facing tax evasion charges that would keep them out of Great Britain for a long time.

'Thank God,' Mark had said, 'you talked me out of letting them into Archimedes.'

'I didn't talk you out of it,' Beth had replied evenly. 'They had no intention of coming in with you anyway, except to take over the name and the back list for nothing.'

But, she thought next morning, it was generous of him to credit her with the advice.

It was obvious to her now that the events of the past twelve months, culminating in the apparent miracle of William's birth, had brought about a major beneficial change in Mark's outlook on life.

So why, she asked herself, was she going to pick up the phone, and request a PVO to see Owen the following week?

Ruth said she would be happy to look after William while Beth went to the prison.

'He looks quite a Celt,' she said provocatively when Beth showed her the baby boy for the first time.

'What's Celtic about him?'

'His cheekbones.' Ruth squeezed the boy's chubby face between her thumb and skinny forefinger. 'His dark hair, and those pale blue eyes.'

'His hair's dark red, like mine, and all babies have pale blue eyes. And besides, it's perfectly normal that he should have inherited some of Mark's Welsh genes.'

'But I never really thought there were many of those left in Mark.'

Beth didn't pursue it. If Ruth was suggesting that Owen might be the boy's father, she almost wished she would come out and confront her with it – to test the strength of her loyalty to him.

The faint but pervasive smell of disinfectant increased Beth's nervous nausea as she sat and waited for Owen in the prison visiting hall.

It was worse than last time; she hadn't seen him for so long – over six months. Their whole affair – if it could be called that – had only lasted two weeks.

When she saw him, she thought he hadn't changed at all. She was struck by how much healthier than the other prisoners he looked as he walked across the hall with his usual presence and dignified self-containment.

She stood up, not knowing what she wanted to do; no gesture seemed remotely adequate to convey the chaos in her head. She had never in her life been balanced so precariously between two such diverse, possible courses of action.

'Hello,' he said, when she hadn't spoken.

She stood and faced him. The muscles of his conker-brown forearms reminded her of the rest of his body as she'd seen it in the setting sun by the Wergin pool. 'You... you look really well,' she blurted, 'quite tanned.'

'I do a lot in the garden,' he shrugged.

'That's good.'
'Do you want to sit down?' he asked, seeing her indecision.
'Yes, let's.'
They both drew up plastic chairs either side of the small square table allocated for their meeting.
'So, what do you do in the garden?' Beth asked. She thought she sounded like an aunt talking to a child.
Owen didn't seem to object. 'I've got them planting a lot more good stuff; anything I tell them I want to grow, they get the seeds for me.'
'It must be good to be outside at least some of the time.'
'That's why I said I'd do it.'
'Are you doing anything else interesting?'
'I've been doing a course in English Literature – the metaphysical poets, Shakespeare.'
'How are you getting on?' Beth thought she sounded even more like an old aunt.
'Pretty good.'
Beth thought she couldn't sit there and talk about seventeenth-century poets when all she wanted to tell Owen was that he was a father; that part of him was alive and well, and not in prison – to give him that lifeline.
And yet, it seemed to her that he didn't need a lifeline.
'How else are they treating you?' she asked.
'Not bad. They say they'd treat me better if I admitted I'd committed the crime.'
'You haven't admitted it though, have you?'
'No, I haven't.'
'But you'd get earlier parole if you did.'
'I won't tell them I've done something I didn't do. If they have to keep me in for the full sentence, that's too bad.'
'But Owen, it could mean five years off...' She didn't go on. There was no point.
When she left, she'd made no mention of the baby or its parentage.

When Beth arrived back at the Hendre, Ruth looked doubtful about her motives for going to see Owen.
'What did you talk about?' Ruth asked.

'We discussed the fact that he'd stand a much better chance of early parole if he was prepared to admit to the crime, and he agreed.'

'So why doesn't he just admit to it?'

'Because he didn't do it, of course,' Beth said.

Ruth didn't answer at once. She appeared to concentrate on the small Peruvian rug she was repairing from the ravages of the six sheepdog puppies that had appeared in the kitchen since Beth had last been there.

When she looked up, Beth tried to see what she was thinking.

'But Beth, he must have done.'

Ruth's loss of faith shook Beth. But then, she was familiar with the notion of belief without palpable evidence; her own religious faith depended on it; whereas Ruth maintained that her spiritual beliefs were confirmed by direct physical experiences – a hot flush while contemplating the power of Gaia was tangible evidence to her.

Beth shook her head. She knew that on Ruth's terms she had no case to argue. 'I'm certain that somehow the truth will come out,' she said.

'You know Laura's doing a programme about it?'

'Oh, no!' Beth gasped. 'What the hell for?'

'She didn't tell me,' Ruth said, exonerating herself. 'I read a blurb about it in the paper. She says it's a kind of therapy for her and other victims.'

'Will she bring Owen into it?'

'I've no idea.'

Twenty

It was early May and in the first heat of summer, stale discoloured air lay over London like a stuffy old duvet, Beth thought as she walked out into the narrow garden at the back of the house in Hackney. She was wearing only one of Mark's long, striped cotton shirts and a pair of flip-flops. She leaned under the canopy of William's pram and lifted him from it. Carrying the baby over her left shoulder, she took him from the sunlight, through a French window into the cool gloom of the small sitting room.

She walked across the room and switched on the television in the corner. Still holding William, she sat down on a large pale yellow sofa. She tried to fight off the anxiety threatening to overwhelm her at the thought of what she was going to see on the screen; but she knew that she had to watch, however painful the memories it stirred.

She leaned back on the feather cushions, unbuttoned the shirt and jiggled her son into a position where he could comfortably reach the breast that she'd exposed. As his twitching lips found her nipple and he began to suck, Laura Chichester appeared on the screen.

Since Beth had met her the previous year, Laura had become *the* television walker – wholesome, caring and correct – a quirky broadcasting success that had defied prevailing fashion. On screen, she spoke in a fluting, convent-girl voice, which Beth didn't recognise and which didn't go with her healthy cheeks and Doris Day hair. In the same way, Beth thought, her breathy, apologetic delivery didn't match the long, tanned legs which stretched from her denim cut-offs to short white socks in hiking boots.

As she spoke, the camera pulled back to show her standing on the ridge of a hill, a small mountain which at first sight could have been on any of the moorland margins of Britain. With a harsh jolt,

Beth recognised the place; of course, she'd known she would, and she wondered again what masochistic urge was making her watch.

Laura began by describing the hills and the tracks etched across them – '*Earth's Ancient Ways,*' she called them – and then Hay-on-Wye, two thousand feet below by the ribbon loop of river, and the night she had walked in the moonlight through a valley hidden between the ridges to the west, to visit the picturesque ruins of the Augustinian Priory at Llanthony.

'A year ago, almost to the day, after a wonderful dinner with old and trusted friends in an ancient homestead towards the head of this valley....' She swept an arm, which a zooming camera obediently followed to a small, whitewashed farmhouse clinging to the hillside in the valley below Gospel Pass.

Beth vividly remembered the dinner in Ruth's house, and the casual media talk which seemed naturally to have centred around Laura, although it was the first time Beth and Mark had met her.

'If I'm honest,' Laura confided to her millions of watching friends, *'I'm going to talk about the events of that fateful night as a sort of catharsis for myself; but at the same time, if I talk about it, maybe, just maybe, the thousands of women who have suffered and will suffer similar attacks and degradation every year will find it in themselves to exorcise the horror by talking about it to people close to them. Or maybe, at the very least, they'll find some small comfort in the knowledge that they aren't alone.'*

With a skill that was barely perceptible, Laura described how, at the suggestion of her friends – she didn't mention Beth or Ruth – she'd decided after dinner to walk two miles down the valley by the drovers' old straight track – a ley line from a cairn by the pass at the head of the valley, through a derelict chapel on the farm where they were gathered – to the ancient priory.

She had arrived there under a moon which floated high above the deep valley. The graceful ruins, she said breathlessly, seemed almost to quiver, dissolve and reassemble before her eyes. She wandered among the broken arches and empty gothic lancets, and absorbed the tranquil energy of the martyred stones for half an hour before she started on her way back to her friend's house up the valley.

The path was clear in the bright silver light, she said, though flanked by tall, waving hedgerows and sometimes cast in deep shadow by the sprawling limbs of an oak.

She was in one of these darker places, where she couldn't even see the sides of the track, when the oldest of man-made sounds – the snapping of a twig – alerted her to the possible presence of another human being.

The next moment, a hand over her mouth confirmed it. Another strong hand fumbled savagely with the buttons of her shirt as she struggled for breath. She remembered vividly – as if it were just a few hours ago, she said – the incongruous scent of plain soap and mothballs in the air which she sucked desperately through her tightened nostrils.

She longed to scream as she grappled hopelessly with the strong invisible limbs. She heard a grunt of triumph as fleshy fingers forced up her bra and found her breasts and nipples.

After that, her attacker hadn't needed to threaten her with his knife to keep her from screaming; but he did, until she was paralysed with fear, in the absolute certainty of what was about to happen. It seemed to her a miracle that her lungs had still been able to deliver oxygen to her arteries.

Laura was telling the story in the same breathy tones of her introduction, with the help of retrospective camera shots of the place, a soundtrack from Stravinsky's *Rite of Spring* and a shadowy reconstruction of the attack.

With powerful, shocking candour, she described the mental and physical horror of the rape. Her delivery became slower, as each dreadful word seemed to free her from the evil of an atrocity that still lingered in her.

Beth found that just listening to Laura was a draining experience and she glanced at the burnt sienna down on her son's head, as it moved with each deliberate tug at her breast, and wondered if her baby should even *hear* these things; like hearing music from within the womb, maybe the words would enter his consciousness and stay to haunt him.

Jessica Meredith

She kissed William's head, breathed in his sweet, warm smell and murmured soothingly, her own disquiet eased by the joy of having him at her breast.

When Laura had finished telling her story and pleaded with humble sincerity that no one should think the worse of her for sharing her pain and shame, the credits rolled over a view of untroubled sheep grazing among the heather that covered the hilltop.

Beth sank further back into the cushions of the sofa and groped numbly with the remote control to turn off the television, almost unaware of the baby still sucking at her breast. For a few moments, she stared straight ahead at the empty screen, until Owen's face seemed to emerge like a ghost from the blank greyness.

Laura hadn't mentioned Owen's name during her broadcast; nor had his image appeared on the screen. Beth couldn't think why he'd been granted this anonymity, but she was limp with relief that he had.

It occurred to her briefly that Laura might be unconvinced of his guilt, too, but she rejected the idea as an optimistic fantasy. Laura had never met Owen before that day; she had no reason to doubt the absolute proof provided by the DNA match.

With a sudden lurch of logic, she was conscious that the boy, full of her own milk and breathing deeply on her lap, shared some of the genetic material in that DNA, and she was conscious of the harsh unfairness that the man he shared it with should be denied that knowledge, however much misery and frustration it would cost.

When she had put William down for a post-feed rest, she phoned Mark at his office and told him she wanted to take the baby up to visit Hay and the valley beyond Gospel Pass.

'But you only went there a few weeks ago.'

'To tell you the truth, in spite of everything I said when we first moved there, I really miss the place. I feel sort of grateful to it – for giving us William; it's become part of our own personal history.'

She heard Mark's soft, understanding laugh down the phone. 'All right then, go. I suppose there's no point in hanging around London in this heat if you don't have to.'

'Exactly, and I've told Jack I'll start working full time next month. And the other thing is, you know Paul Ricardo's asked me to talk in this "Women and the Law" debate he's chairing at the Hay Festival? I thought I'd go and see him about it – maybe get an idea of what way he's going to treat it.'

Beth had tacked on this supplementary justification for her trip, as it occurred to her at the last minute, although she doubted that Paul had the time or any desire to plan what was meant to be a spontaneous debate.

'I should think that's the last thing he wants to do,' Mark echoed her thoughts with a laugh. 'But why not. Where can I contact you if I need to?'

'I'll have my mobile.'

'You know you can't get a signal in those valleys.'

'I'll be staying at Ruth's,' Beth admitted reluctantly.

'You haven't forgotten that your boss has asked us for dinner on Friday?'

'I hadn't forgotten. I'll be back.'

'But Paul's not in Hay,' Ruth said when Beth offered her specious reason for the surprise visit. 'He's in London for a few days, finalising things there. Didn't you check with him first?'

'Well, no,' Beth said, waving it aside. 'I just told Mark that because I wanted to get away from London for a bit. I hope you don't mind?'

'No, of course I don't. It's lovely to see you and William!'

Beth looked proudly at her son. 'We were wondering if you might be godmother to him,' she said, wondering how Mark would feel if Ruth said 'yes'.

'I don't think I can, but I'm honoured to be asked. I know how important it is to you.'

'But why can't you?'

'I just can't – I can't tell you why.' Ruth shut her mouth coyly.

Beth tried to read Ruth's thoughts; she wondered if Owen was the reason for turning her down and made up her mind not to tell her about her plans to see him, uncertain as they were; though she was determined that this time she wouldn't leave without telling him about his son.

She had tried to get a visiting order at short notice, but had been told that Owen had used up his quota. She hadn't persuaded the prison that she had grounds for an exceptional visit in a quasi-legal capacity. However, she was confident that once she'd got hold of the governor, she'd be allowed to see him.

William woke Beth with his hungry bleating. It was a fine early morning – just as she liked to remember those of the previous summer. She carried the baby downstairs and sat outside on a wooden bench in front of Ruth's white house to feed him.

The smells and sounds that floated through the quiet air drew her mind back to the joy-filled days she'd spent on the other side of the valley a year before. She found herself trembling at her minutely detailed recollection of it, and for a while the memory banished everything else from her head.

When the baby had stopped drinking and began to doze, she carried him into the house and laid him in a down-padded basket which Ruth had produced the evening before. While she tidied the kitchen and prepared breakfast for them, she thought about Ruth's denial of any strong reproductive drive and wondered what lay behind it.

When Ruth still hadn't come down half an hour later, Beth started to become restless. She decided to go out and walk down towards the brook, where she could look up at Pant-y-Groes; she was curious to see what emotions the place would evoke in her.

Despite the dread and exhilaration she felt at the thought of seeing Owen later, she walked lightly through the warming air, down the stony track, past her car. Her eye caught the flutter of white paper under the windscreen wiper for a few moments before she registered that it might be meant for her; she'd gone a few paces beyond the car when she stopped and turned to see what it was.

A page from a school exercise book had been neatly folded in a way that reflected the tidiness of the short message written in a laborious old-fashioned copperplate.

Go and see Mary Prosser in Crickhowell.

As she drove from the Hendre, Beth gripped the wheel white-knuckle tight to keep her hands from shaking.

Ruth had moaned a little at being asked to look after William for the morning; she'd been hurt that Beth wouldn't say where she was going.

'I can't tell you what I think it's about, in case I'm wrong,' Beth had said, as softly as she could.

Beth pushed the car as fast as she could through the narrow lanes that skirted the southern end of the Black Mountains towards Crickhowell. As she swerved and juddered between high hazel hedges and blind corners, a parade of roles for Mary Prosser flickered through her head. But she arrived at the pretty, ancient crossing of the Usk, without any firm idea of what she was looking for.

She parked in the middle of Crickhowell and found a small public library. It was open and a helpful librarian quickly produced the electoral role for her. Beth found only one Mary Prosser, aged eighty-seven, who lived half a mile out of town on the far side of the river. She scribbled the address and the librarian marked a map to show her exactly where she would find the place.

Outside the coolness of the library, the sun seemed hotter than earlier. Beth reluctantly got back into her baking car and drove across the long stone bridge that spanned the sparkling ripples of the shallow river.

She followed the map to a small humpback bridge over a canal that traced the contour on the southern slope of the river valley.

The register had listed Mary Prosser living in a house called Wharf Cottage, a hundred yards west of the bridge, where the canal widened to allow a few barges to be moored without affecting through traffic. Now only a few over-decorated domestic narrow boats and a river cruiser were tethered there, in front of a small, neglected stone building.

Beth tucked the Saab into a gateway above the bridge and walked down a curved incline to the towpath. The water in the canal was dark and oily calm beneath a canopy of alders, and amplified the quietness of the hot morning. Only the sound of an occasional car on the road in the valley below floated up the hillside.

A flaking wooden sign beside the front door of the stone house confirmed that it was Wharf Cottage.

There was no knocker or bell, as if Mary Prosser expected no callers. Beth rapped her knuckles on the flaking green door and listened for sounds of movement inside. The silence was broken for a few minutes by three laughing children, chasing each other up the towpath on bicycles. When they'd gone on under the bridge where the great barge horses had plodded a century before, there was still no sign of movement from inside the cottage.

Beth suddenly felt bilious with frustration. In her rush from the Hendre, it hadn't occurred to her that Mary Prosser might not be at home. Angry at herself for being hasty and unprepared, Beth wanted to see if she could at least find out more about the old woman by looking through the windows. There were only two at the front; one was heavily curtained; the other looked into a spotless front-room, too neat for regular use, like Megan Rhys's. A clutter of inexpensive china ornaments and pre-war chain-store furniture suggested only that an old person of regular habits had occupied the house for a long time.

Feeling thwarted, Beth brazenly pushed her way past a barrage of uncontrolled rambling roses to get around to the rear of the house where she discovered a much more regularly used path up to the back door.

She stopped at the first window she came to, and found herself peering into a dingy kitchen. As her pupils adjusted, she saw a large white face staring back at her. She stepped away quickly, embarrassed at being caught prying, and knocked over a metal watering can. She picked it up and was still hesitating in front of the bare planks of the back door, when it was opened.

The woman who stood in the doorway, despite her pallor, showed signs of having once been a stout, robust person. Her doughy features were arranged in soft wrinkles, with a large furry mole on her right cheek. She was dressed in a clean grey skirt and an old, neatly darned maroon cardigan with horn buttons. Below a shapeless mop of white hair, her misty grey eyes showed no suspicion; only the curiosity of someone accustomed to living alone.

'What do you want?'

Beth was still holding the watering can. She put it down beside the doorstep. 'I wanted to talk to Mary Prosser.'

The old woman nodded. 'That's me.'

Beth held out a hand, feeling slightly foolish as Mary took it. 'My name's Beth Langthorne; I'm a lawyer.'

'Oh yes?'

'Can I come in?'

Mary Prosser nodded as her lips twitched an inaudible answer. She turned and shuffled towards the front of the house. Beth followed, and Mary opened the door to the room Beth had seen through the window. The old woman looked at Beth before showing her in. 'Will it take long?' Her voice was more Herefordshire than Welsh.

'Perhaps,' Beth nodded.

'Would you like a cup of tea and some cake?'

'Yes, please.'

Mary stepped back and Beth carried on into the room. She walked to the window and stood between two armchairs upholstered in dark red moquette with wooden arms and white lace antimacassars.

On the mantle-shelf a shiny, wooden-cased clock ticked ostentatiously. She looked around for anything that might tell her why she had been sent to see Mary. There were no pictures or signs of any connection with the Llanthony valley in the room, but a small, framed certificate hung above the clock. It expressed the appreciation of Brecon and District Health authority on the occasion of Mary Prosser's retirement in 1975 after thirty years as a district nurse and midwife.

Beth's hands began to shake like they had when she'd found the note that morning.

Mary came back into the room with a tray containing cups, a teapot and a Dundee cake; Beth could hardly hold the cup she handed her. She put it on a tiny occasional table and tried to get a grip on her thoughts.

Whatever she did, she couldn't let her own desperate hopes lead this woman to offer her anything beyond the absolute facts.

The old woman wanted her to sit down; Beth lowered herself into one of the chairs and Mary did the same.

'The reason I've come to see you,' Beth started, 'is that I found this note on my car this morning.' She had taken the paper from a pocket of her cotton jacket. She passed it to Mary, who read it without any obvious reaction.

'Where were you?' she asked.

'I've been staying at a farm called the Hendre, above Llanthony Priory, just down from Blaen Fawr .'

This time, Mary did react. She glanced at Beth, though with little more than mild curiosity, and said nothing.

'Do you know Blaen Fawr?' Beth asked.

'Rhyses? Yes,' Mary nodded.

'Do you know them?'

'I delivered there once, but I come from Longtown, on the other side of the hill in England, so I never knew them, like, as a family.'

'What made you settle in Wales, then?' Beth asked, using small talk to delay the impact of whatever she was going to hear.

'I'd always worked here, and one of my mothers from years ago left me the house; she always said she would after I delivered her only son, though I never believed her, until she'd died.'

Beth nodded slowly at the arbitrariness of events that moved people around and made decisions for them.

She took a deep breath. 'You've heard what happened to Owen Rhys?'

'He's gone to prison.' Mary shook her head regretfully.

'I've been involved in his case,' Beth said, and sensed that the old woman immediately recognised the false implication.

'Are you his solicitor, then?'

'No,' Beth said quickly. 'I'm a barrister. I was living in the valley last year, and I got to know Owen – he came and found water for us – for my husband and me.' She paused for a moment. 'When he was accused of.... that crime... I found I just couldn't believe it; it didn't seem one bit like the sort of thing he would do.'

'But they proved he did, it said in the *Hereford Times*.'

'Do you understand that proof?'

'Yes.' Mary nodded slowly and took a sip from the cup she held in her podgy, wrinkled hand

Beth waited.

The clock ticked louder; the children on their bicycles came back along the tow-path outside the window, still shouting and laughing with each other. But Mary said nothing more.

'Do you think the person who left this note thought you could tell me something?'

'Tell you something about what?'

'About what happened? About Owen Rhys?'

'I don't know anything about Owen Rhys, except I delivered him.' Mary glanced at Beth, 'and his twin,' she added quietly.

Beth didn't breathe.

'It was a difficult birth.' Mary wasn't looking at Beth now; her eyes were fixed on the wall opposite, at a framed print of a Landseer stag on a misty Scottish mountain. 'The first one was easy – out in no time. It was the other caused the problems. He wouldn't come and wouldn't come for hours, but it was too late to take her to hospital then; anyway, she'd never have gone. Some of those families in the hills, they won't come down to the towns for nothing. But Megan was almost drained of all her strength when she said I could help her inside, and I found the baby's head. He was stuck, with the cord twisted round his neck. I turned him, and he came quickly then.' Mary paused and took a deep breath. 'I felt it was my fault at the time, but it wasn't really. It just sometimes happens. There was nothing else I could do. The baby looked terrible white, but I slapped him and he coughed and cried like hell.'

Mary paused and looked at Beth, who was sitting forward on the hard front edge of the chair, with an image in her head of Megan, lying, bathed in sweat, with the baby Owen beside her, while she strained to produce the second twin.

'Dai Rhys knew that baby was wrong,' Mary said. 'I think he would have had it taken away and destroyed. Megan knew too, but she was beside herself – you could see she already loved the child more, for all the sweat it had taken to produce him, and she begged me never, ever to say a word about that second child. I only saw the family once more after that, but when I heard what happened to Dai, when he fell in the quarry, I knew it wasn't no accident. He wasn't a man to handle a problem son.'

'But you never saw them again? How did you know the child was badly damaged?'

'I'd seen it happen before, and when I went back there a week later, it was obvious when you saw him beside the other, even though they were same-egg twins and you shouldn't have been able to tell them apart. It was something in the eyes.'

As the two women contemplated the thirty years of grief and frustration those moments of confusion in the womb had caused, and Beth thought of the robust, smiling health of the baby she had so recently produced, the room became silent except for the clock, and a sunbeam highlighted the dust stirred up by their presence in the seldom used room.

Beth took a deep breath that seemed to hiss noisily through her nostrils. 'Did you ever tell anyone else about the second boy?'

Mary shook her head emphatically. 'No. I gave my word.'

'Then why are you telling me now?'

Mary looked at the note that she still clutched in her hand. 'Megan Rhys wrote to me, about a month after the babies were born, begging me to keep my promise. I've still got the letter, and this is her writing. Besides, there's no one in the world, besides her and me, that ever knew what happened that day.'

'You, her, and presumably Owen and Michael, the elder brother,' Beth corrected.

'But you can see – this is an old person's writing.'

Beth took the note, looked at it again and knew that Mary was right.

The governor at Owen's prison, whom Beth had met and liked, had been replaced by a small, silver-haired man, with the voice and manner of an Anglican vicar in a smart London parish.

'I'm sorry, Miss Langthorne,' he said, pointedly refusing to be impressed by Beth's legal status. 'You're not officially acting for Rhys – we've checked. And he's used up all his regular visits.'

'Why?' Beth blurted. 'Who's been to see him?'

'I don't have to tell you, but his mother has started coming as often as she can.' The governor, evidently feeling he'd made his point, became conciliatory. ' If you want, I'll issue you with an order for Wednesday next week,'

Beth could tell the man had no intention of being persuaded by her. She did her best to control her frustration and had to accept this almost unbearable delay in confronting Owen with what Mary Prosser had told her.

Twenty-One

Michael Rhys's pickup was outside Ruth's house. Beth groaned to herself as she parked her car beside it.

In the kitchen, Owen's brother and Ruth were sitting at the table, talking without any apparent urgency about sheep and a show being held in the valley the following month.

Beth joined in, and asked about Abby and Dai, the children she'd tried to make friends with the summer before; but under a cloak of politeness, she was dying for him to go.

After ten minutes or so, Michael pushed back his chair. He stood up with a ritual rubbing of oil-stained hands and said an awkward goodbye. As he left the house, Beth thought again what an utterly different little creature he was to his princely younger brother, whose name had not even been mentioned.

As soon as she heard his truck rumble off down the track, she took Ruth in her arms, and hugged her in a way she never had before. Ruth didn't know how to react to this unexpectedly physical display of affection.

'Beth? What's the matter? What's happened?'

'Oh Ruth, I'm so relieved, but so frustrated. I've got to tell you everything. You should know, and there's no one else for me to tell anyway.'

'What?' Ruth asked with her eyes glowing.

Beth straightened her elbows and faced Ruth, holding her at arm's length. 'First, I can tell you with absolute certainty that Owen did not rape Laura.'

'My God!' Ruth shrieked hoarsely and wriggled herself from Beth's grasp. She sat down at the kitchen table, staring at Beth. 'But how? Everyone said it had to be him. I didn't want to believe it, but there was no choice.'

Beth sat down opposite her, still unsure if Ruth had guessed about her and Owen. 'I never doubted him; I knew a man like that would never have raped anyone.'

'I know, I know,' Ruth said hurriedly, ashamed of her disloyalty, 'but I suppose I thought it must have been some crazy male aberration – I mean, I always guessed he had a powerful sex drive, but I never heard of him involved with any of the girls from the valley, so I thought...'

'Oh yes. He's got a powerful sex drive all right,' Beth said quietly.

Ruth looked across at her with big brown eyes open wide. 'You know, don't you! You slept with him! I was sure you had for a while, then..... ' Ruth sighed. '...then I sort of got the impression that perhaps you just weren't interested in sex; I thought that was why you weren't conceiving.'

Beth shook her head. 'It wasn't that. Do you remember at dinner that time someone – you, I think – suggested a surrogate father? I was getting so desperate by then it sort of sowed a seed in my mind and I couldn't get rid of it. When I saw Owen a few times and he came round about the water.... I hadn't got any choice.'

Ruth was looking at her, vicariously excited, Beth thought, not in any way censorious. 'How often...?'

'Ruth, it wasn't a sort of statistical thing; several times over those two weeks; I wasn't counting. I'd fallen in love with him, for God's sake!'

Ruth's eyes opened wider in disbelief. 'You? Fell in love with Owen?' she gasped.

'Why shouldn't I? He's a totally exceptional person...'

'Yes, yes, of course he is, but you're so self-possessed; it just seems out of character.'

'Thanks, but that's the way it happens.'

'And this was last summer?'

'Obviously – between the time I met him, when he came up and helped you deliver that lamb, and when he was arrested.'

'But...' Ruth put her hand to her mouth like a character in an old-fashioned storybook and looked at the baby still asleep in the basket. '...that must have been about the time William was conceived!'

Beth didn't answer. She stood up, and walked over to gather up the boy protectively. He woke with a grizzling murmur. She put his small head on her shoulder and paced the flag-stoned floor.

Ruth gazed at them in silence, adjusting her perspective to the revelation of something she had only reluctantly suspected. Abruptly, she stood up and clattered a kettle onto the range before setting cups and a teapot on the table. 'And now you say Owen didn't rape Laura. How can you be so sure?'

Still holding the baby, Beth pulled the note from her pocket with her spare hand. She put it on the table. 'Here's the note I found this morning.'

Ruth picked it up. '"Go and see Mary Prosser in Crickhowell"?' she read. 'Is that where you went?'

'Yes, and I found Mary Prosser, in a cottage by the canal. She's in her eighties now, but still totally together. She was the midwife who delivered Owen...' Beth paused '...and his twin brother – from the same egg.'

The note fluttered from Ruth's hands and dropped to the floor. 'My God!' she whispered. '*Twin brother?* But, no one's *ever* said anything about another brother, ever since I've lived up here,' Ruth went on, indignant at being excluded by people she thought trusted her.

'Only the family ever knew – and Mary Prosser. And Megan made her promise never to say a word about him to anyone.'

'But why?'

'Because he was badly brain damaged at birth – at least that's what I think must have happened. He was partially strangled inside the womb as he was being born.' Beth instinctively hugged her own boy tighter to he chest. 'Megan was terrified he'd be taken away from her and persuaded Mary to leave him off the birth certificate. Their farm's half a mile from any other house and I suppose they thought they could keep him up there without anyone knowing. But Mary thinks Dai Rhys, Owen's father, killed himself from the strain of it.'

'I can hardly believe all this has been going on, just at the top of the valley. But are you saying the brother's still alive, and he sort of escaped from Blaen Fawr and did this rape?'

'Yes. I'm certain, and now I know, I realise there were a few signs someone else was up at the house. And of course, that's why

Megan hardly ever left the place, and when she did, Owen was never with her. They did everything to discourage visitors.'

'And Owen's this man's identical twin! He must have an extraordinary relationship with him.'

Beth nodded, already conscious of the powerful influence this relationship must have had on Owen. 'All along he said he hadn't committed this crime, but he wouldn't offer the one piece of evidence that would get him off.'

'His brother's DNA – identical to his own?'

'Right!' Beth nodded emphatically. She lifted William from her shoulder and checked that he'd fallen asleep again. With heightened tenderness, she put him back in the basket. 'I'm afraid to say I think Owen would do anything to protect his brother.'

'But Megan told you to go to the midwife – the one person who knew about the twin.'

Beth nodded. 'She wants to see Owen out of prison, and she's prepared to lose her other son to whatever secure hospital they put him in.'

'Wouldn't you – given the choice? But she must realise how angry Owen will be with whoever does it, so she's passed the buck to you.'

'Unless she simply felt she wasn't up to the job of going to the police herself?'

Ruth stared at Beth, not envying her. 'What on earth are you going to do about it?'

'Owen shouldn't be where he is – it's against all natural justice.'

'But you simply don't know how strongly he feels about his brother. I mean, all his life he must have had to look after him. I bet he was out looking for him when he found Laura – or maybe he'd seen him come back home and suspected trouble.'

'Whatever he thinks; however he reacts, I'm certain it's my moral duty to tell the police about the brother.'

'Moral duty? Are you sure it's not just because you want to see Owen out? Or do you think if Owen knows he's got a son waiting for him, he'll change his mind?'

'Good God – I'm not going to bribe him out by telling him about William. It'd probably backfire anyway; and he'd end up resenting William for coming between him and his twin.'

'But he won't come voluntarily, will he? After all, he could have told the police about his brother any time, and he's deliberately chosen not to; I think Megan's right; he'll be furious if anyone else does.'

'I'll have to take that risk, now that I know the truth.'

'You'd lose whatever there is between you and Owen for the sake of his freedom?'

Beth took a few deep breaths and looked at William, serene in his basket. 'I have William. A year ago, I'd have given almost anything for this son, and now I have him. At the time I wasn't looking for love, or another man. I mean, Mark's got his flaws – God knows, everyone has – but I fell in love with him and I married him. In a lot of ways, he's a good husband; he's totally loyal and he's made an amazing effort to come to terms with reality in the last year.'

'He was very upset about not getting selected, wasn't he?' Ruth said.

Beth nodded. 'More than you think.'

'Oh no; I know how he felt,' Ruth cooed.

Beth looked up at Ruth's habitually solicitous face. She wondered how much Mark had confided in her, and felt a faint stirring of jealousy.

'The fact is, he was relying on becoming an MP to counteract the collapse of his business; but once he knew he had no options and William appeared, he started trying to sort out a lot of the problems. He's so chuffed about William.'

'But if you left him for Owen and took William with you, Mark would know the baby wasn't his.'

'Yes,' Beth said slowly. 'That too.'

'Whatever you do,' Ruth said. 'Don't do it at once. Think it through first.'

'I went to see Owen today, as soon as I left Mary Prosser.'

'My God...!' Ruth gasped.

'Don't worry; I didn't see him. The governor wouldn't give me a visiting order because I'm not his representative, and Megan's been using all his visits. I've got a visiting order for *next* Wednesday.'

'You should ask him then what he wants. It's a week away but you'll just have to wait till then. It must be his choice, if you ever want him to respect you.'

Beth stared at Ruth. 'Respect? I don't want his respect. I just want him free.'

Mark seemed very pleased to see William again when he got back from Archimedes that evening. Beth watched him play with the baby.

'How's everything at the office?' she asked.

'Fine, fine. Really looking good. Gehring's new book's been a flop for his new publisher.'

'Is that good for Archimedes?'

'Not directly, but it makes me feel better. Anyway, how was Hay? What did Paul Ricardo have to say?'

Beth hesitated, but she didn't want to lie. 'As a matter of fact, he wasn't there. I'd assumed he would be and I never checked. But I spent a nice couple of days with Ruth. I went and had a look at Pant-y-Hose.' Mark glanced up, surprised at her use of his name for the place. 'It all looks rather twee, but apparently the new people are hardly ever there, and nobody's met them.'

She knew that would please Mark.

'Has Ruth got a new lover or anything?'

Beth thought about Ruth "understanding" Mark. 'No. I think she's reached the stage where she's so wrapped up in her own thing, she doesn't want the hassle of accommodating anyone else's needs.'

'That's a bit harsh.'

Beth laughed. 'All right, and she's asked us to stay when we go up for the debate in Hay, if we want to. I said we might just stay that night.'

Mark nodded absently. He was absorbed again by William. 'He's beginning to have a real Powell face, isn't he?' he grinned.

'I hear your chambers are going to specialise in human rights, in line with Europe?'

Beth's mind went blank. *Human rights*? What the hell were *human rights*? An absurd political catch-all whose original meaning had been diluted and abused out of existence.

She'd spent all day thinking about the individual rights of one man and faced with the terrifying prospect that if she used what she knew to deliver his rightful freedom, he would end up hating her for it. And she couldn't decide if it was better to be loved by an incarcerated man, than to be resented for freeing him.

She turned to the man sitting beside her at the dining table in Jack Devereux's big white house in Notting Hill. Hugh Jenkins was a serious political journalist on one of the Sunday broadsheets, and Jack had evidently felt that he and Beth would have something to say to each other.

Knowing the political stance of the paper Hugh worked for, when Beth could focus on the question, she was instinctively defensive. 'We can't just ignore European law and hope it'll go away,' she said. 'And human rights legislation is a growing part of it. It would be irresponsible for the whole profession to pretend it didn't exist.'

'I entirely agree. Some intelligent, constructive challenges from London lawyers might do something to neutralise the absurd anomalies that keep on appearing.'

Beth sighed. 'D'you know, I've hardly been into chambers since I had our baby in February, and frankly, my mind's rather flabby and out of tune with the whole thing.'

'But I also hear Jack's thinking of standing for the European Parliament himself.'

It was the first Beth had heard of it. She hid her surprise, but felt as if she'd been away for a year. She glanced at Jack, too far away to hear her at the other end of the table. 'No. He's far too nice to indulge himself in that sort of thing,' she said, hoping that she was right.

There were ten people at the dinner table – four couples and a pair of ostensibly well-matched singles, of whom Hugh Jenkins was one. On his far side was an American art historian who had used her looks, her social skills and her father's money to become a strong influence in the London art world. She evidently saw Hugh as another possible source of influence and used a lull in his conversation with Beth to jump in.

For a while, Beth was left with no one to talk to. She didn't mind; it gave her a chance to make some order of the thoughts that had been spinning chaotically through her head all day.

She looked around the table – at her husband, smiling attentively at the woman beside him while he talked about fatherhood; at Jack, thoughtful and resilient; and at his wife's serene face; and she knew how lucky she was, even to hold just the memory of those two sublime weeks last summer.

And, of course, she had William, too.

Jessica Meredith

As soon as she heard the letter drop inside the pillar box at the end of the street on the Saturday morning after Jack's dinner party, Beth was plagued with misgivings about what she'd done.

She hadn't even known how to begin the letter, especially as she'd known it would be read by a prison officer before it reached Owen.

Now, the irrevocable words made her cringe....

> Dear Owen,
> I know what I am going to do is not what you want. If it were, you would have done it yourself a year ago. I think I understand your reasons, but it seems to me that it's not possible for a man in your place to make an objective judgement of what might be best for the other people in his life (and I'm not including myself).
>
> Last week, the day I tried to visit you, I went to see Mary Prosser in Crickhowell. She told me what happened when you were born. So, at last, I understood how you were innocent – which I'd always believed – and yet were found so irrefutably guilty.
>
> On Monday, probably before you've seen this letter, I'm going to see DI Price-Watkins and your solicitor and tell them what I know. After that, you should be released within a few hours.
>
> I'm longing to see you, but I won't wait outside the prison; I'll be at Ruth's.
>
> With all my love,

On Monday morning Beth expressed some of her own milk to leave for William, and Penny was thrilled that she was going to have the baby to herself for a couple of days.

Mark looked puzzled and a little anxious when she announced that she was going to Wales yet again, although they were going there anyway the following week for the debate, but he didn't try to dissuade her.

In her car outside the police station in Abergavenny, Beth picked up her mobile phone and thumbed Mark's number.

'Hello. It's me. Just to say sorry I ran out this morning. I don't really know why; I suddenly felt sort of hemmed in by everything... Yes, maybe it's part of changing from a maiden into a mother and it should have happened twenty years ago.' She laughed, now she had William.

Mark said he understood and he would enjoy being a single father for a night.

He sounded reassured when he rang off.

Beth closed her eyes and leaned back in her seat; there was a part of her that hated herself for deceiving him. But, she pleaded in her defence, she just couldn't help it – not after those few brief hours last summer.

She took a deep breath, collected herself and rang Ruth.

'Do you mind if I come and stay again?' she asked.

'Of course not. Have you decided what to do – about Owen?'

'Yes. I'll tell you when I see you. I'm in Abergavenny now.'

Detective Inspector Price-Watkins leaned back in his chair and stretched his small mouth to express his resentment of an unwanted interview. Beth guessed he didn't want a case which had been quickly and neatly resolved a year ago to be resurrected and re-examined. It could well lead to some procedural shortcomings being exposed.

'Mrs Powell,' he said, 'we searched Blaen Fawr very thoroughly when we were looking for evidence. I can assure you there was no sign of any other inhabitant besides Rhys and his mother.'

'Inspector, I don't know where they keep him, but I've heard sounds and seen indications that he's there. Go and see Mary Prosser first, if you don't believe me. You'll see for yourself she isn't making it up.'

'Maybe a second brother was born, but he must have died since then. No one could hide a living person for that long – over thirty years – with never any record of his existence.'

'Up there they could. You know how isolated some of those families still are – never seeing anyone for days on end sometimes, keeping themselves to themselves, never talking to outsiders. And Blaen Fawr's a big house, half a mile from any other. I'm sure there are attic rooms you never found. Besides, Megan Rhys will probably take you to him. She told me to go to Mary Prosser in the first place.'

'So you said, but do you know it was her? Have you asked her?'

'No,' Beth admitted. 'I haven't seen her since. I don't want to press her on it. She won't admit it anyway, because she knows Owen doesn't want to be released.'

'So you say, but he'd be a very unusual bloke to want to stay banged up for someone else's crime – even his brother's.'

'Inspector, Owen Rhys is a very unusual man.'

The policeman heard the ardour in her voice, and watched her, at first with contempt for being in love with a convicted sex-offender, then with a glimmering of respect.

Beth walked from the police station out into the rain-soaked streets of the small grey town. She'd arrived there just after midday. It was now one. She'd spent an hour trying to convince DI Price-Watkins that he'd got the wrong man. She didn't know if she'd succeeded, but if he didn't react within twenty-four hours, she was ready to go to the Chief Constable, although she already dreaded the consequences of what she had started.

After the prolonged heat of the previous week, Beth shivered in the clinging grey air outside The Hendre. She felt as if the world was closing in on her. Pant-y-Groes was barely visible across the valley. Collected moisture glistened and dripped from the fresh leaves of the alders on the brook below. But Ruth came out with a big smile on her thin pale face.

'Hi! I *knew* you'd come back soon. Isn't it miserable for the middle of May? I lit the Rayburn to make the house nice and warm for you.'

Inside, they huddled in front of the glowing range and Beth passed on to Ruth what she'd told the policeman, and how he hadn't believed her.

'He'll have to check it out, though, and act on it, whatever he thinks,' she said. 'I told him I'd go to the Chief Constable if he didn't.'

'But why shouldn't he believe you?'

'I'm not sure. Maybe he thinks I'm obsessed with Owen and clutching at straws to get him out. After all, it's a pretty fantastic story.'

'When do you think they'll come out to Blaen Fawr?'

'I don't know. He'll probably do what I suggested and go to see Mary Prosser first. I should think she'll convince him that the second twin was born, at least. Then,' Beth shrugged, 'I don't think he'll have any option but to follow it up.'

The kettle which Ruth had put on when Beth arrived was hissing on a hot plate. She took it off and poured the boiling water into a pot over her own blend of dried herbs. When she'd filled two large cups, they sat down at the table.

'I went to see Megan yesterday,' Ruth said, glancing anxiously at Beth, afraid that she would object.

'You didn't say anything, did you? About my going to Mary?'

'No, but she asked me if you'd been staying last week, and what you'd done. I said you had, but I didn't know where you'd been.'

For the rest of the afternoon, as they talked, Beth helped Ruth with jobs around the farm. For Beth, it was a period of calm before the events which were going to erupt over the next few days.

'What worries me,' she said, standing in the kitchen shelling beans, 'is that it's not just Owen's life, or Megan's, or yours and mine that are going to be affected by the discovery of this twin. The media are going to love it. I mean – they gave the rape maximum coverage at the time because of who Laura is. But with a bizarre twist like this, they'll go totally over the top. I don't suppose Megan's got any idea of the hordes of people who'll come traipsing up the valley to interview her and Owen, and photograph them and the house. It will be the most horrendous invasion, and these are people who happily go for weeks without seeing anybody.'

Ruth was looking at her. 'My God! I hadn't even thought about that side of things. And Laura only did that programme on TV last week!'

'Exactly, but thank God, she didn't mention Owen's name. Not that it will matter now if she had, and everyone knew last year that he'd been convicted for it.'

'He's going to *hate* a mass of reporters turning up,' Ruth gasped.

Later, when the cloud had been lifted a little by a breeze that presaged a return of the warm early summer, Beth walked briskly up the steep hillside behind The Hendre, towards the Y Fan ridge. As she neared the top, she was startled when her feeling of transcendence was abruptly dissolved by the trilling of her mobile phone.

Reluctantly, she aswered it. 'Hello?'

'This is Owen Rhys.'

Beth froze. She had heard Owen speak only a few words over the phone, when he had phoned once from Michael's. This disembodied voice sounded utterly unfamiliar. And why had he said "Owen Rhys" – as if they were strangers?

'H... hello,' she mumbled.

'I got your letter.'

Beth remained transfixed, with the phone clamped to her ear. She wasn't breathing. She couldn't speak.

'You don't have the right to interfere in my life like this. If you know why I didn't defend myself, then you must also know it was my choice. I knew what I was doing; I could handle the consequences.' Without his face, she couldn't connect this voice to him. It sounded more foreign than she remembered. 'There's no reason you should understand why I'm doing it,' he went on, with barely a hint of the gentleness she'd known. 'Nobody could, unless they'd been in the same position. But I'll never forgive you if you tell the police that you know.'

Beth's eyes misted over, and the corners began to sting. She had never felt so humiliated and desolate.

Never forgive.

Her shoulders began to shake; she tried to speak, but all that emerged was an agonised whimper. She sank to the gound, blindly feeling for as tussock on which to sit.

'Have you done it already?' the alien voice asked.

Beth gasped, and begged God to turn the clock back twelve hours. But, with an effort, she managed to squeeze a whisper between the silent sobs. 'Yes.'

With a sharp bleep, the mobile connection was cut.

****

The police didn't come to Blaen Fawr that afternoon, or that night.

Beth listened for any sound in the valley, and tried to spot every car that drove up the winding lane. And she couldn't stop trembling with nauseous fear at what she'd done.

Owen had been completely right.

She had no right to interfere. She had betrayed whatever trust he might have had in her; she had overturned his own selfless intentions without any consultation.

Of course, at the time, after the dinner party in London when she'd lain in bed all night thinking about it, having decided, knowing she was doing the right thing, that pure justice demanded the man should be freed, it hadn't occurred to her that she should consult him or listen to his reasons for his decision.

Now she felt small, foolish and arrogant. She didn't blame Owen for despising her.

Then in the midst of her agony of self-condemnation, she stopped, and thought of William.

Owen is William's father! she told herself. The child has a right to a father. Owen doesn't know, so he couldn't have taken that into account. Surely, otherwise, he would agree?

But she already knew that if she'd told him before she'd gone to the police, or told him now, either way he would have reason to resent the child for influencing his determination to accept the penalty for his deranged twin brother's horrible crime.

In a pine sleigh bed in Ruth's spare room, Beth thought over the sublime experience she'd shared with Owen on the other side of the valley, while she listened to a new breeze hissing through the small round leaves of the hornbeams close by the house, hearing the night sounds of a vixen yowling for her cubs and a tawny owl uttering a hollow call to his mate until the earliest moments of a new day were heralded in by the lengthy trilling of a lark a little way up the hillside.

She didn't fall asleep until the sun glinted over the top of the ridge, unobscured by the clouds, which the night's wind had plucked up and carried away, across England.

Beth woke sharply at the sound of several cars being driven fast up the valley. She knew at once where they were headed. She leapt out of bed, and blinked at the bright sun as she pulled back the curtains.

One police car, two plain cars flashed past the gateways on the lane. Beth looked at her watch. It was nine o'clock. Not a dawn raid, but a serious one, and unstoppable now.

Sporadically during the night, she had imagined herself ringing DI Price-Watkins and telling him that she'd made the whole thing up, that there was no Mary Prosser, nor any note.

But she knew, even if the policeman did think she was simply the hysterical lover of a hopeless case, he would have to follow up what she'd told him – perhaps more so if she suddenly phoned him to deny it all.

The die had been cast irretrievably, she realised, the moment she'd walked from the musty, stale tobacco air of his office. Now, she was desperate to see what was going on up the valley.

She scrambled across to Pant-y-Groes and stood outside the five-bar gate Mark had bought the year before. She could see Blaen Fawr from there, but she couldn't see the police vehicles outside the cold grey house until, after a few minutes, the three cars appeared from behind the trees on the track she'd run up the morning she'd first met Megan.

The cars started to crawl in convoy back down the narrow valley lane. Beth ran down the field by the road to watch them go by, to get a glimpse of Owen's unhappy defective twin, who, perhaps without knowing, had caused so much anxiety and grief to the people who cared for him. She hid behind the tall hedgerow and stretched her neck, but she couldn't tell which of the men sitting in the dark rear of each car was the new culprit.

As soon as they were out of sight, she crossed back over the road and the brook below it. Ruth was waiting for her outside the Hendre.

'Have they got him?'

Beth lifted her shoulders in uncertainty. 'I think so, but I couldn't see for sure.'

'Let's go up and see Megan.' Ruth's eyes were shining with excitement.

Michael's red pickup was parked outside Blaen Fawr. He came out of the house as Beth turned her car into the courtyard.

His thick brows stretched in a knotted black cord across his forehead. 'You know what's happened, don't you.' It wasn't a question.

Beth brushed aside the accusation in his eyes. 'How's your mother?'

'How the hell do you think?'

'I must see her.'

Beth tried to side-step Michael to go into the house.

He firmly moved across to block her way. 'She don't want to see you.'

Beth took an angry pace back. 'Why not? This has happened because she wanted it to.'

'You think she wanted to lose Bryn?' Michael's blue-black eyes flared at her. 'After all the years she's hidden him, protected him? The copper said it was you came to the station and told them about him.'

'Michael,' Beth tried to sound reasonable. 'Who do you think told me? How do you think I knew – if your mother hadn't wanted me to. You, and Owen and she – you were the only ones who ever knew about Bryn.' She gasped out the new name for the first time.

'Us, and that meddling midwife. We paid her enough to keep quiet, too.'

'She didn't come to *me* for God's sake!'

'Oh no?'

'No. Your mother left a note.'

'Who said it was my mother left a note?'

'Mary Pross....' Beth swallowed to clear her dry throat as Michael's implication sank in. She thought back, as clearly, as professionally as she could, to her conversation in Mary Prosser's little stone house.

Nothing about the old woman's manner had suggested that she was expecting Beth. All her reactions had seemed genuine.

And yet...

Beth became cold, but she wouldn't let Michael see.

She shook her head. 'My visit to her was a total surprise; I'm certain of it. Besides, what possible reason could Mary have for wanting this to happen?'

Michael looked at her as if she were a silly child. 'Who cares why she done it? She's an old woman, and they can make you think whatever they want. What I want to know is why you done it.'

'I've told you: because your mother wanted it, and because I knew all along Owen was innocent; he didn't deserve to lose so much of his life for his brother's actions.'

'It was *his* choice, *his* decision,' Michael growled the same words Owen had used. 'He's always loved Bryn and protected him. He won't thank you for what you've done, I can tell you that for certain.'

He flashed his angry eyes at her, ignoring Ruth, as he had all along. He turned to stamp up the stone steps and slam the front door behind him.

Beth stared at the door, then at Ruth, who had stood silent behind her since they had arrived.

She wanted to run up and hammer on the flaking boards and demand a fair hearing, the chance to put her case, to explain her misinterpretation of events, to convince herself that Owen would understand her motives.

Instead, she started to cry. Avoiding Ruth's gaze, she turned and ran on shaking legs to her car.

When Mark walked into the sitting room in Hackney, where Beth was feeding William, she glanced down at her son's sandy-red hair.

Mark leaned over and kissed the top of her head. 'How was the valley? Action-packed, I should think.' He sat down beside her on the small sofa.

Beth nodded. The story of Bryn's arrest for the rape of Laura Chichester and Owen's release had appeared in the later editions of the *Evening Standard* and all the evening TV news bulletins. 'Ruth and I saw the police cars going past; we went up to Blaen Fawr after they'd gone. Michael told us what had happened,' she dissembled.

'What an extraordinary thing for Owen to have done,' Mark said. 'You wouldn't have thought he had it in him to make a sacrifice like that for a brother who presumably didn't really know what he'd done anyway.'

Beth glanced at Mark. She wondered if he could see how much she'd been crying. For a few seconds, she wanted to tell him. 'Sometimes one has to make sacrifices, whether people know it or not.'

Mark looked back at her.

'Extraordinary to think that brother was living there, under everyone's nose, and no one ever knew,' he said, shaking his head. 'Right,' he went on, dismissing the subject, 'I suppose I'd better feed Grimond.' He stood up and walked from the room.

Twenty-Two

On Thursday, 22nd May the General Election called by the Prime Minister six weeks earlier took place. The Labour Government was returned to power, despite a marked swing to the right.

East Brecknock constituency bucked the trend by replacing its Conservative member with a Liberal Democrat. Beth, sitting up with Mark at home in Hackney to watch the results as they came in, looked at his face as the result of the East Brecknock count was flashed on the screen.

Mark took it well. 'The boring old duffer did it! Well done him; though maybe he'd have done even better if he hadn't worn that terrible old cord jacket for the whole campaign.'

'How do you know he did?'

'Henry Llewellyn told me,' Mark laughed. 'I phoned him a few times to hear how it was going – just thinking ahead. He hinted that if Pugh lost, he might be able to get me selected next time round.'

'For heaven's sake, Mark,' Beth groaned more than she meant, unable to bear even the thought of living close to Owen but not being with him. 'You've just got stuck into sorting out Archimedes; do you really think you'd want that kind of hassle now?'

'Pugh may not stand next time but it won't be for another three or four years, angel,' he protested mildly, 'and if I'm ever going to get the business running smoothly, I should have done it by then, don't you think?'

Beth closed her eyes and prayed that the idea would be dispersed on the winds of time.

By two in the morning she felt the result of the current election was beyond doubt. She left Mark still on the edge of his seat in front of the television and went upstairs sleepily, right to the top floor of the house.

Jessica Meredith

When she had first become pregnant, Mark had insisted despite any financial constraints, that they should have a mansard roof inserted to provide space for their new son and the nanny.

In a small room, decorated with boyish wallpaper and tractor mobiles, William was contentedly asleep in his cot. Beth and Penny had been giving him small helpings of solid food recently, which seemed to have the useful side-effect of sending him off soundly to sleep at night. In the muted glow of the night light, Beth watched his tiny lips bubble and flutter with each breath. After a while, resisting the urge to pick him up and cuddle him, she left the room and gently closed the door.

On the small landing outside, she smiled at the incense smell of a smouldering joss stick whose smoke was seeping under Penny's door and she thought about the haphazard ways in which some habits of previous generations seemed to have been passed on, while others, like the musk that Ruth still wore, had not.

Before she went down, she glanced at the painting of Hay Bluff she had bought in her euphoria the day after she and Owen had made love by the Wergin Stone. She'd hung it in the top landing above a small chest of drawers, on which she'd placed deliberately, unobtrusively among a collection of miscellaneous Welsh *objets trouvées*, the hazel whistle Owen had made for her. She gazed at the precious twig for a moment until she felt tears begin to rise. Before she let them, she called up all the strength it took to block out the ache of longing.

She turned away and walked slowly downstairs. In the bedroom, tired but relieved that Mark seemed to have accepted Geraint Pugh's victory philosophically, Beth climbed into the empty bed, where she lay thinking of the valley and Owen, and, allowing the tears now, quietly cried herself to sleep.

It was the unfamiliar noises that roused her first – the crackle and wheeze of burning timber that didn't belong in the bedroom or the hours of sleep. Almost as soon as she became half conscious and was beginning to think about identifying the sounds and their source, she heard Mark's feet thumping fast and noisily up the stairs. The bedroom door burst open.

'Beth, get out! Get downstairs, quick! There's a fire at the top of the house.'

In the next fraction of a second, she was totally awake.

'Billy!' she screamed. 'My God! Billy!'

'I'll get him. For God's sake, get down and get out, please – right now!'

Through the open door, the sound of the fire was harsher; the smoke and smells billowed in. Beth leaped out of bed and staggered towards the door.

Mark shouted over his shoulder, 'Take something to keep warm and get outside quick! Take your phone – call 999!'

'But Billy?'

Mark was already on the stairs up to the next floor. 'It's okay – I'll get him. Please get down so you're not in the way,' he yelled as Beth emerged. 'And for God's sake call the fire brigade!'

All Beth's maternal instincts urged her to follow, but she saw Mark almost swallowed up in the smoke now pouring relentlessly down the narrow top flight.

She gasped at the sight of it, rigid with fear for a moment before she gave in to simple panic. She knew she shouldn't want to turn and run but without waiting to fight her shame she plunged down the stairs. Besides, she told herself, since Bill had been born, she could rely on Mark in a way she never had before.

At the first floor landing, she found all the lights still on and the door open into the small sitting-room where Mark had been watching the television. She heard the even tones of a tired election commentator assess the implications of some recent poll result.

She rushed on down until she reached the narrow hall, and she remembered the telephone call she had to make. Although she wanted desperately to get out of the burning house, she made herself stop and think where she'd left her mobile phone.

Gritting her teeth against her terror of the fire rampaging through the upper part of her home where her baby had been sleeping so soundly when she'd last seen him, she forced herself down the last flight of stairs to the basement kitchen.

The lights were on; she saw the phone on the table. Almost faint with relief that she could leave the house now, she grabbed it and ran wildly back to the ground floor. She pulled open the front door and let herself out, rushing down the short path to the small gate that opened onto to the tree-lined pavement of the quiet street.

Jessica Meredith

She ran on a few more yards from the house before she could bring herself to stop and look back.

For a moment she saw no sign of the fire and thought she had imagined it, maybe it was all some horrible dream. But as she looked a flame seared up the curtains in the window of the front room on the top floor – Penny's room. As the glass cracked and smoke billowed out for the first time she thought guiltily of the nanny.

'My God,' she muttered, trying to rally her thoughts. 'I've got to phone.'

She looked down at the small instrument clenched in her left hand and took three attempts to stab '999' on the key pad with a quivering finger.

A man answered. Beth took a deep breath and spoke in a level voice. 'Fire service, please,'

She managed calmly to give her address, hearing herself as if she were another person.

'Are there people in danger?'

Abruptly, Beth lost her composure. 'Yes, yes! My baby! Please help me!' she wailed.

'It's all right, madam. A unit will be there as soon as possible.'

As she ended the call, in a moment of surreal detachment, Beth wondered why the anonymous man had called her 'madam', as if she were in some old-fashioned dress shop.

But her eyes and thoughts were drawn straight back to the spreading incandescence at the top of the house, and her panic grew.

Where was Billy? Where was Mark?!

From there, her thoughts leaped abruptly to the hazel twig that Owen had crafted for her and the painting she had bought of Gospel Pass – the two remaining physical reminders of her time with Owen, besides William.

At the edge of her vision, she saw people gathered, staring from the other side of the street, as if they were in a TV report of an event somewhere else. She felt suddenly powerless – useless. She was a mother; she should be doing something – anything to save her baby!

'Billy!' she screamed, and Mark appeared in the doorway of the house, carrying the cat's basket.

'Oh, no,' Beth muttered breathlessly to herself. 'He's got Grimond! Where's Billy?'

She couldn't understand. Was he mad? Did he think she cared more about the cat than her baby? Did he really think she was so bad a mother?

'Billy! Where's Billy?!' she screamed, dimly conscious of her voice echoing off the fronts of the other houses in the street, clear above the mounting roar and crackle of the fire up above.

Mark was walking quickly towards her, his face anxious but triumphant, streaked with sweat and soot.

Beth stared at him, unable to speak. Why, why hadn't he brought Billy down?

'I've got him,' Mark said.

Beth tried to understand what he was saying; she felt something at her legs, rubbing her calves. She looked down; it was Grimond, pleased to see her at this unexpected hour.

Beth lifted her eyes and gazed, bemused, not allowing hope to burst in her chest too soon, and watched as Mark came and put his arm around her, still holding Grimond's bed.

She stared into the small open basket. Her twelve-week-old son lay in it, wrapped in a blanket from his cot.

Beth felt as if she would evaporate with relief. 'Oh God! Thank God!' she blubbered, reaching down to grasp the baby – to pick him up and hold him to her as tears soaked her cheeks. The baby coughed and bleated faintly in protest. His night had been disrupted enough already.

'Did you call the fire brigade?' Mark was asking urgently, in control of the priorities.

'Yes, yes,' Beth nodded, biting her lip, feeling unaccountably guilty, not stopping to question the emotion. 'Why did you carry him in the basket?'

Mark looked at her as if she were mad. 'I don't know. It was there, in the landing. I thought he would be more comfortable. Does it matter; he's safe!'

'No, no, of course it doesn't matter. Thank you love! Thank you so much for saving my baby!'

He looked at her with a quick, puzzled frown. 'I've got to get Penny. The fire's in her room.'

He turned and ran back to the house And Beth tried to imagine him making his way up into the smoke. Suddenly she was desperately worried for him.

'Marco, darling! Be careful,' she called, but he had already disappeared into the house – brisk and without any apparent fear.

After the fire, Mark, Beth, William and Penny moved into Jack Devereux's house in Notting Hill. Jack's wife was eager and tireless in her attempts to help them deal with the trauma and physical inconvenience it had caused. Their children were fascinated, demanding detailed descriptions and drawing dozens of pictures of the event.

The fire brigade had arrived quickly and had dampened the last vestiges of the blaze within half an hour. In the morning light, it emerged that the new top floor was gutted, along with everything in it – the painting of the Bluff, Owen's whistle – and Beth couldn't rid herself of the superstition that the loss of these objects which sustained her connection with Owen, signified the final destruction of the relationship.

The damage to the rest of the house below, however, was superficial – smoke and a little soot. Carpets, curtains and furniture would have to be cleaned or replaced, and the top floor rebuilt.

Mark was determined that they would move back in as soon as the lower floors were habitable again. After a few days in Jack's house, Beth felt the same; in any case, she found it easier to agree with Mark, since he had carried William to her from the burning house.

At the end of the following week, the principal debate – 'Women and the Law' – was being held on the first Saturday of the ten-day festival in Hay.

When she had received an invitation from Boo Llewellyn to stay for the event, it was the first time Beth had heard from her for several months. She knew that Paul Ricardo always liked to billet contributors to his festival on the willing owners of large houses around Hay, and she hoped Boo wasn't simply responding to his request.

Anyway, she and Mark had decided before the fire that they'd like to spend the weekend there with William. When she had phoned her, Ruth said she didn't blame them, as long as they promised to come and see her too when they could. Now she felt the whole weekend might help her come to terms with the confusing emotions the disaster had brought on.

Nevertheless, on Friday morning she woke early, still in the Devereux's house, feeling sick at the thought of being in Hay, so close to Owen. She hadn't heard anything of him since his release; she still dreaded what he would say if she saw him; yet she longed to see him.

As she lay in bed beside Mark in the expansive spare room in her boss's house, waiting for William to wake, she thought of ringing Paul Ricardo to tell him she had to cancel. It was only as she fed William that she considered rationally that Owen was unlikely to come near the Festival when she was due to appear. And she and Mark wouldn't need to go near the valley beyond Gospel Pass if they arranged to meet Ruth in Hay.

Beth was distracted from her misgivings about being back near Hay, and Owen, by the pleasure of introducing William to Boo, although Boo turned out not to be as impressed as Beth had hoped.

'I know they're jolly sweet at that age,' Boo said, 'but frankly, I'm bloody glad I haven't got one now. I can tell you, if my children start procreating, they won't catch me changing soggy nappies for them.'

But from the windows of their bedroom, the warm, soft view of the mountains, the oaks in the park, a glimpse of shimmering river between the alders were all as serene as Beth remembered – better, even – and the birds were singing their evening chorus as she changed for the dinner party Boo had arranged for them.

Mark and Beth had met most of the people at dinner – Paul Ricardo and his new wife, Lord and Lady Brecon, and Eleanor, the artist whose show Beth had been at with Boo. There was also an author from London, due to appear at the festival next day and basking in the unaccustomed glory of a novel, which had recently – and unexpectedly – hit the top of the best-seller lists.

Beth managed to keep her thoughts of Owen under control, even when Boo, opposite her, leaned across the table, and said in what seemed an overloud voice, 'I see Laura Chichester isn't appearing this year, after she promised she would. Paul was saying she has to film in Bosnia or something, but I bet it's just that she couldn't face bumping into the man who spent a year in jail for not raping her. By the way, Beth, isn't that the same chap you brought to the party we had here last year?'

Mark glanced up; Beth saw and kept cool. 'You know perfectly well we didn't bring him, Boo. I think he brought Ruth.'

'Yes, yes, but it was the same chap, wasn't it?'

'Yes – Owen Rhys.'

'Have you seen him?'

'Since he was released? No, of course not. He must have only come out last week, and we haven't been up here for ages.'

'No, I meant had you seen him in prison? I'd heard that you had – since he was convicted.'

Beth tried not to let the colour of her face change. She didn't dare look at Mark. She nodded. 'Yes, I did once. I was sure even then he couldn't have committed that rape – he just didn't seem the type, and I thought I might be able to do something to help.'

'Nice to be proved right,' Boo said.

Mark turned to his wife. 'You never told me that.'

Beth shrugged. 'There was nothing I could do. He said he hadn't done it, but he wouldn't offer any defence against the DNA evidence. Of course, now we know why.'

'Quite the noble savage, eh?' Boo laughed.

Beth winced; she couldn't stop herself asking sharply, 'Savage? Why savage?'

Boo pretended to look surprised by Beth's reaction. 'Well, you must admit there is something of the wild animal about him – something pagan and sort of other-worldly with all that dowsing, and great wafts of earth energy coursing through his veins.'

Beth took a deep breath. 'I found him a deep, spiritual man – from what I saw of him. Of course, he's not educated in the conventional way, but I thought he had amazing sensitivity – look at his healing powers,' Beth appealed to Lord Brecon. 'You were cured by him weren't you?'

Lord Brecon nodded. 'Yes, God knows how. It was rather like going to a witch doctor.'

'That's what I meant,' said Boo, 'when I said savage.'

Lord Brecon turned to Mark, looking mischievous. 'By the way, what do you think about your Liberal getting in? You must be very fed up it wasn't you – after all that expense you went to.'

Four lawyers – two men and two women – were taking part in the Festival Debate. As soon as she'd heard who the others were, Beth concluded that the women would win. The teams were, quite simply, not an even match.

She had prepared herself well and once she was on the platform, managed to contain her churning emotions over Owen. She knew she was speaking well and was picking up on the opposition's weaknesses as soon as they revealed themselves.

The audience liked her, too – more, she felt, than the high-flying feminist lawyer beside her. Like any barrister, she always enjoyed the effective articulation of a difficult argument, and doing it in front of an audibly appreciative crowd instead of a judge or jury was a stimulating new experience for her.

In the morning, Beth told Mark that she was going to Mass in Hay.

'Are you taking William?' he asked.

'Yes.'

'Why?'

'I just want to. Maybe to get him used to it.' Beth prayed that Mark wouldn't decide to come with her.

But Mark laughed. 'Babies in church are my idea of hell,' he said. 'But if you think the suffering will cleanse your guilty soul....'

As she drove away from The Neuadd with William, Beth smiled dolefully at the irony in what Mark had said, conscious that she was creating a further cause for guilt in what she was intending to do – even if Ruth had failed to convey her message to Owen.

She steered her car through the cluttered streets of Hay, barely glancing at the small Victorian Catholic church on her way to the turning up to Capel-y-ffin and Gospel Pass.

It was another bright morning. A few wispy clouds trailed high over the top of the ridges. When Beth reached the valley it looked just as it had at that time the year before. She drove slowly down the unfenced lane, through the dappled light of the lower woodland, until she passed the opening of a track that spanned the young brook and snaked southwards up the hillside to the Wergin Stone. There was a place where she could park at the side of the road, under a pair of squat oak trees.

Beth stopped the car and lifted William from his seat in the back. She harnessed him into a papoose, which she hefted onto her back, tightening the straps until the baby felt secure.

Half an hour of steady, uphill walking brought Beth to the tall, russet stone that seemed to have become an icon in her life. She crouched down beside it, grateful to be there and pleased that she wasn't puffing after the long climb. She loosened the straps of the papoose and eased one shoulder from it to let it swing round, so she could lift William out. She sat and leaned her back against the softly sculpted south face of the stone in the full brightness of the mid-morning sun. Trying to ignore premonitions of all that could go wrong with her plan, dismissing the loss of the whistle and the painting of the Bluff in the house fire, she gently rocked the baby in her arms.

The calls of the wheatears in the gorse mingled with the bleating of lambs and the deep grunts of their mothers. Beth gazed across the valley, where a squadron of crows relentlessly attacked an intruding buzzard over the chimney tops of Blaen Fawr, just visible above the trees, and she thought of everything that had happened since she'd come to meet Owen here a year ago. The crows retired from their onslaught and the raptor soared away over the ridge. After a while, drowsy with the heat, Beth closed her eyes; her rocking became sporadic and lost its rhythm.

The quiet panting of the dog woke her only a moment before its wet nose touched her hand. Her eyes snapped open and she recognised the collie's blue green eyes.

'Mack?' she whispered, not daring to look up. 'What are you doing?'

A shadow fell across her. She closed her eyes tight as if to deny its existence and hugged William more closely to her.

'I got your message.' His voice seemed to resonate in the rock behind her. 'Why did you come here?'

Slowly, Beth raised her head, determined to meet his eyes straight on. But his face was in shadow. It seemed thinner and darker. His hair, like glistening black coffee, was longer than she'd seen it and curling as if it had not been combed for days. 'I wanted to show William this place.' She lowered her chin towards the baby without moving her eyes from Owen's.

Owen looked down briefly at the sleeping child, before his gaze followed Mack across the small horseshoe plateau, where the dog was sniffing at a crack in the rocky hillside.

Beth watched every movement he made, every flicker of his eyes, trying to read his thoughts. She longed for him to lean down and take her and the baby in his arms. But he came no nearer.

She cleared her throat. 'I also wanted to tell you I'm sorry.'

The words came out cracked and dry, like an old woman's.

Owen – reluctantly, it seemed – dragged his eyes back to her. 'You should be saying sorry to Bryn. He'll spend the rest of his life in a mental prison – forty or fifty years – thanks to you.'

'Was it worth losing ten years of your own life to save him?'

'I wouldn't have done it if I didn't think so.'

She didn't expect him to say more. She closed her eyes tight to hold back the tears. She shook her head and spoke very slowly. 'I am truly sorry for having presumed to know what you should do.' She hugged her baby tighter. 'I realise now it was crass, and vain and selfish of me. Please believe me when I tell you I only meant good to come from it.'

He sighed, and her heart rose like one of the larks trilling in the sky above them.

'I do believe you,' he said.

Bolder now, she opened her eyes and looked directly at him again. 'I had another reason for coming,' she almost whispered. She held her breath, overwhelmed for a moment by the memory of lying in this very place, when she had tasted the honey on him, and they had made love.

It seemed to her for a few seconds that he was looking around for a place to sit and her hopes soared; until it was clear that he was going to stay standing and his implacable face offered her no more grounds for optimism.

He raised an eyebrow, prompting her to go on.

'I wanted you to see William,' she said.

Owen narrowed his eyes until tiny creases appeared on the brown skin at his temples. Slowly, still unwilling, he lowered his gaze to the face of the baby whose eyelids fluttered with imminent sleep.

'Why?'

Beth gazed at him; she didn't try any more to stop the tears she could feel slithering over her cheeks. 'Owen,' she gasped through a pain that gripped her whole body. 'You know why!'

There was not a flicker of warmth or recognition in Owen's eyes as he shook his head. 'If the child was mine, you would be mine too, and you can't be... ever.'

'Owen!' Beth heard her shrill cry like a frightened animal's echo from the rock walls of the clearing. 'How can you be so cruel?'

Jessica Meredith

'How cruel is it to lock up a gentle, simple man? To surround him with concrete walls, like some rat in a trap, pushed around by people who can never know him or love him?'

Beth gazed through tear soaked eyes at the stones and the sheep droppings between the tufts of grass in the clearing. She thought if she could sweep them away, as he had once done for her, perhaps he would sit down beside her like he should. Through a delirium of desperate unhappiness and mental pain, she heard him talking again.

'That's what I call cruel. And to take the trust of another person, to abuse it, and destroy what they were hoping for. I told you once – up here in the hills there is *truth*; we don't just *talk* about love.'

With an effort she raised her head again to look at him, not caring that her face was streaked with tears, her nose running, her eyes wild with pain. Now, she knew at last, for certain, that she had earned this much punishment.

'Please Owen; don't hurt me any more. I know you're right; I know I deserve to be despised by you; I despise myself. But please, please believe I loved you truly and deeply; I hated losing you. I know what I did was wrong. But please, one day, try to forgive me.'

He looked down at her in silence. His eyes seemed to have retreated deeper into their sockets. 'You might think you can undo harm with words, but some harm can never be undone, however much you talk.' He looked away, beyond the stone, towards the blunt crest of Yr Twmpa, and took a deep breath. Slowly he lowered his gaze and his eyes met hers once more. When he spoke, his voice was still distant, but softer. 'Look after the child... and teach him to love the truth.'

The next moment he was whistling for his dog, a few seconds later, striding down the track away from Beth, until he soon disappeared from view in the deep bracken.

Twenty-Three

Some time – it might have been twenty minutes, Beth couldn't tell – after Owen had left her by the Wergin stone, she walked back down the hill to her car with William on her back and tears streaming down her face while she prayed.

She begged God, and any other omnipotent spiritual being who might listen, as well as the ancient mountains themselves, to persuade Owen to forgive her, and recognise his son. As she prayed, though, she knew deep within her that she had lost him forever.

Uncertain that God was listening, or was even there at all; sure that she didn't deserve to be heard, she drove on down the valley to the Hendre, hoping that Ruth, at least, would listen.

Ruth came out and saw her face as she climbed out of the car.

'My God, Beth! Are you all right?'

Beth shook her head mutely as she looked at the slumbering baby in the back of the car.

'Leave him there for now,' Ruth urged. 'We'll keep an ear open. Come in, for God's sake, and tell me what's happened.'

Inside, she made a mug of tea and put it in front of Beth, sitting at the kitchen table once more.

For the first time, Beth told her everything; the truth in almost every detail of the dozen life-changing days her affair with Owen had lasted; of her meetings with him in prison, her decision to take the evidence of his innocence to the police, her letter, his phone call to her on the Y Fan ridge the week before, and his complete and final rejection of her less than an hour before.

Slowly, as Beth spoke, the tears ebbed, and she opened the way to reconcile herself to this brutal truth.

She sniffed and gulped the last mouthful of soothing tea. 'I've lost Owen, but I had two such beautiful weeks I could never have dreamed of. And as they get further away, they seem to grow, and I'll always be able to bring them back to mind in the smallest detail. And of course I've got William – after I'd been *aching* for a baby for the last ten years. I didn't realise it before but that's how long ago I started wanting him. It's only now that I can see how much it's affected almost everything I've done. It's as if all I've been doing – in my marriage, in my career – was preparing me for this. Yes, I know,' she went on, as Ruth gaped at this apparent reversal of all Beth's priorities, 'I couldn't believe it either, but I promise you that's how it feels. The sense of achievement is extraordinary.'

Beth abruptly remembered Ruth's childlessness, and stopped.

Ruth understood why. 'Oh, don't worry; you're not hurting me. Of course I know what you mean; I've heard it before. But like I said, I just don't seem to have this urge like most women.'

'But there's more,' Beth said. 'I also accept that though I don't love Mark quite as much as I did, and now in a different way, I have a good, loyal husband who'll be a brilliant, creative and stimulating father. Even with all his weaknesses and vanities, he's thoughtful, he's original and he's good company, when I let him be. Besides, he seems finally to have admitted his shortcomings as a businessman and he's dealing with them. He even seems to be making some money at last, which might mean I can spend more time with William before I have to go back to work.' Beth looked down at her hands, and felt the tears return. 'But I don't deserve it Ruth. I just don't deserve it.'

On Monday morning, Mark insisted that they should keep their word and go over Gospel Pass to the Hendre. He said he had phoned Ruth from the Llewellyn's while Beth was still having breakfast.

'Don't you have to get back to London?' she asked.

'Nope. I've checked. There's nothing I can't deal with tomorrow. I thought as it was so lovely up here, we should take our time; anyway, I quite want to see Paxman doing his live *Start the Week* at the Lit Fest and talk to him afterwards. I thought I might get him to do a book for us.'

Beth wanted to go back to London. But she said, 'Fine,' as if it didn't matter, although Mark's proposal – *fait accompli*, it seemed – would upset the equilibrium she was desperately trying to achieve. Going back to the valley now would be like pulling the dressing from a wound that hadn't yet formed its own scab, and scratching at it. But there was no way of stopping it without telling Mark at least some of what had happened.

The Llewellyns said an affectionate goodbye. Mark and Beth drove to Hay where Boo had arranged for them to pick up tickets to the live broadcast of the radio programme.

A group of assorted writers and a political journalist who happened to be in Hay for the Festival had been gathered on the stage, and talked glibly at one another and their unexpectedly benign chairman.

Mark managed a brief chat with the infamous news presenter afterwards, and came away with a realistic view – Beth thought – of his chances of signing him up for a book on Irish salmon rivers.

Ruth greeted them with no hint that she had spent an hour talking and commiserating with Beth the day before.

She had made lunch for them entirely from meat and vegetables grown on her farm. It was impressive enough to provoke Mark into ideas for a cookery book – *Living off the Land*, which occupied most of their conversation during the meal.

As if by tacit agreement, neither Ruth nor Mark referred to Owen, or to Laura's rape, or to the extraordinary events of the past fortnight.

After lunch, Beth brought William in and fed him in an armchair in the tiny sitting-room, looking out across the valley at Pant-y-Groes, while Ruth and Mark walked up the hill to see Ruth's llama kids.

When they came back, Beth got into the back of the car to hold her wakeful, grizzling baby. Ruth kissed them all and waved vigorously as Mark drove them away from The Hendre, down the lane towards the Priory.

Beth sank back in her seat hugging William and sighed with relief that Owen hadn't appeared while they'd been at Ruth's.

'What an excellent weekend,' Mark was saying. 'The Llewellyn's were much friendlier than I thought they'd be after I was trounced in the selection last year; Paxman was very affable; that was a wonderful lunch, and I've just been told that we're Number One in the *Bookwatch* non-fiction list.' He turned to Beth with a smile free of irony and full of affection. 'Maybe you won't have to go back to work quite so soon now.'

Beth tried to smile back, before turning her head casually to look up the hill on their right, above The Hendre.

Even half a mile away, she recognised the silhouettes on the ridge – a dog, and a man.

When the taller figure stopped and raised one arm, she knew it was Owen. And, as if his hand had reached down inside her and torn her heart out, her face contorted with pain and she clutched the little boy closer to her breast.

Mark glanced in the driving mirror, which was set so he could see his wife and child. He saw her face. 'Are you all right, angel?' he asked anxiously. 'You look quite ill.'

Beth swallowed to keep the quaver from her voice. 'I'll be fine, Marco. I think it was just something I ate.'

Mark's eyes were back on the winding lane again. 'I'd better cancel that book I asked Ruth to do.' He laughed. 'I've never heard of a court finding a publisher liable for illness caused by one of their cookery books, but I'm sure it'll happen sooner or later.'

He turned to look at Beth again. 'Are you positive you're all right? You look exhausted.'

'It's okay, Mark. Please don't worry about me. I... don't deserve it.'

****

Two weeks after the visit to Hay, Beth unlocked the door and let herself into the house in Hackney, glad to escape the sticky urban heat of a June day. She walked downstairs and found Mark sitting at the kitchen table with an almost empty bottle of champagne in front of him.

'Hi, how was Jack?' he greeted her.

She hadn't expected him to be at home. After a long lunch with Jack Devereux, she had walked back from Inner Temple, but it was still only half past three.

'Fine,' she said lightly. 'He's flatteringly anxious to have me back full time. Are you just having a drink, or are you celebrating something?'

He smiled. 'You could say I'm celebrating. I don't mean to seem uncaring, but Geraint Pugh's dodgy ticker has already let him down. I turned on the One o'clock news and they were just announcing that he'd died of a heart attack.'

'Good God!' Beth gasped, still amazed at the way events could reverse themselves so completely. 'Poor man, and with all those kids!'

'Well, yes. Perhaps the job was too much for him. Anyway, Henry's already rung to ask if I'll put myself up again. He says if I do, the selection's almost a formality, and the feeling is we'll walk straight back in at the by-election. I said 'yes', and he's delighted.' Mark uttered a short laugh. 'Pity we sold Pant-y-Hose in such a hurry.'

Beth closed her eyes and turned her head away. 'Oh, Mark,' she said quietly. 'Do you really want to move back there?'

It seemed he hadn't heard the tremble in her voice. 'Yes, of course.' he chuckled. 'I can't wait – it'll feel like going home again, don't you think?' Beth clenched her eyes and turned away so he couldn't see.

'I've been celebrating something else, too,' he went on. A different note in his voice made Beth look up again sharply. 'My own pathetic insecurity, I suppose.'

'Why?' Beth asked, suddenly alarmed, and she tried to guess what he'd done to revert to this after months of self-control and reborn self-esteem.

'Maybe I've got pissed because I want to tell you the truth, and it's not going to be easy.'

Beth wondered for a fascinated moment if he was about to admit to an affair. From time to time she'd imagined dealing with it, faintly curious to know how she would react to the news, if he ever were to divulge it.

'The truth is,' he said lurching from foot to foot, 'someone… who shall be nameless … Here, have a glass, it might soften the blow.' He clumsily filled a tall thin glass until froth dribbled over onto the table. He passed it to her. 'Someone who, as I say, shall be nameless suggested to me that our lovely boy child, Bill the Conqueror, might not in fact be mine.'

Beth's heart seized up as the words came from his mouth.

She took a swig from her glass; coughed and spluttered as the bubbles went up her nose. She tried to laugh. 'What? Who told you that? Who would his father be besides you?'

'If anyone else were, I imagine you'd know better than me…' Mark snorted and took a quick gulp. He looked at her with slightly bemused, drunken eyes. 'But, as it happens, that's not the question. *I'm* his dad.' He grinned, proudly, triumphantly. 'I've had a DNA test done.' He waved a hand at an envelope on the table. 'At least, the chances of my not being his father are about one to six million.'

Beth slowly, without speaking, picked up the envelope, which had no stamp; she guessed Mark must have collected it by hand. She pulled out the letter it contained to read it, and the computer printout attached to it, which confirmed beyond question that Mark Powell was the natural father of William Arthur Powell.

She put the papers down and took another drink. 'Well,' she said mildly, 'I'm sorry someone was malicious enough to put the idea that you're not Bill's father into your head, but if it's cleared up any doubts in your mind, thank the Lord.'

'Thanks, angel; I hoped you'd see it like that. Of course, I didn't think it was anyone else. I know when he was conceived, for God's sake! There's a rather grisly irony to it, really. It had to be the night we were in Pant-y-Hose, after dinner at Ruth's – the night Laura was there, before she....'

'It's all right.' Beth lifted a hand to protest. 'Don't talk about that; it doesn't matter when it happened.' She reached out to squeeze his arm. 'I'm just so happy at last we have the child we wanted, haven't we?'

THE END